Jump Off

by

Rebecca Kodritsch

The Conrad Press

Jump Off

Published by The Conrad Press in the United Kingdom 2024

Tel: +44(0)1227 472 874
www.theconradpress.com
info@theconradpress.com

ISBN 978-1-916966-15-4

Typesetting and Cover Design by:
Levellers

The Conrad Press logo was designed by Maria Priestley.

Printed and bound in Great Britain by Clays Ltd, Elcograf S.p.A.

Dedication

To Kevin, Alice and Taggart

Prologue

'And last to jump in the Riders Championship for Great Britain is the former Junior European Gold Medallist, Maxim Tarasov riding his father's stallion Zhivago.'

Feeling sick with nerves, Max rode down the tunnel and into the bright lights of the arena where he was met with cheers and applause. Trying to reassure himself, he gave his horse a gentle pat, 'come on then boy, we can do this,' he whispered. As he rode passed the judges box, giving a courteous nod, the commentator continued, 'Maxim and Zhivago jumped clear in the first round, and with only two other riders having jumped double clears this evening this pair have nothing to lose.'

What the commentator didn't say of course was that the double clears came from two of the best riders in the world; Germany's Frederick Seipp the reigning world champion, and Britain's highest ranking rider Marcus Wallis. Looking up at the VIP area Max could see his father watching intently. Max gave him a weak smile before turning towards the first jump.

As he counted down the strides to the huge upright fence he became oblivious to the noise of the crowds. With jumps as tall as a man it was vital that he placed Zhivago in exactly the right spot for take-off. Fortunately, Zhivago didn't seem to be affected by Max's nerves. Focusing on the jump, he pricked his ears, and after one last bouncy stride, lifted off the ground and sailed over the fence. Encouraged by the power of his horse on top form, Max focused on the next jump that was a large, wide square oxer. Again, Zhivago jumped like a stag, clearing the massive fence with ease, and for the first time in months Max realised he was in with a chance of winning.

Having jumped safely over the next two fences Max knew he had to take a gamble. The only way to beat Seipp's time was to cut the corner between the fifth and sixth fence. He'd paced it out when he'd walked the course, but had then dismissed it as being too tricky, but suddenly the fifth fence approached, and he had to take the challenge. He took Zhivago right into the corner so he jumped at an angle. As soon as they landed Max pushed with his legs, lengthening the canter so they reached the next fence off three strides. He reached the sixth a little early, forcing Zhivago to stand back off the fence and launch himself over. As they landed, Max heard the sickening rattle of a pole, followed by a collective gasp from the crowd. For once, luck was on his side, for rather than falling, the pole landed back in its cup.

Within seconds Max was onto the final line, a three-jump combination. Sensing the tension and excitement in the crowd, Zhivago tried to rush but Max just managed to hold him in check, and they got to the first part of the combination in the right place. Max gasped for breath; concentrating so hard, he'd forgotten to breathe. Suddenly the audience roared with applause as the commentator announced Max as the winner by one tenth of a second.

Max stood up in his stirrups and waved to the cheering crowd as he circled, trying to slow his horse down. As he left the arena, Lee his groom was waiting to take the reins. Max quickly slipped off and flung his arms around Zhivago's neck. Immediately the gleaming black stallion flattened back his ears, swung his head around to bite. 'I'm just trying to say thank you, you miserable bugger,' Max said laughing. 'Where's his treat?' he asked Lee, as a large juicy apple was produced. Max bit into it and fed a chunk to his beloved horse.

'Look, behind you!' Lee hissed.

Max turned to see the BBC's sports presenter Clara Barker standing there, microphone at the ready. Hurriedly, Max wiped sticky apple juice from his chin before giving Clara a huge grin.

'Congratulations on winning the Leading Show jumper of the Year. It was a superb bit of riding and will certainly silence the critics.'

'Thanks. When Zhivago is on top form he's one of the best in the world.'

Not satisfied with playing it safe, Clara continued. 'It's good to see you winning again, after a less than successful summer.'

Undeterred, Max answered, 'We let Zhivago service a few mares earlier on in the season, and I'm afraid it went to his head a bit; couldn't concentrate for months after that. Now he's got his mind back on his job, he's on top form.'

'From what I read in the tabloids, it's not just Zhivago that's distracted,' Clara teased.

'Let me assure you Clara that I've never failed to perform,' Max replied. 'And as you well know, any rider is only as good as his mount.'

Satisfied, Clara closed the interview, allowing Max to remount as the prize giving was about to begin.

Both Frederick Seipp and Marcus, who'd been 2nd and 3rd respectively, shook hands with Max as they waited in the line up to receive their prizes. As Max accepted his award, he glanced up towards the VIP area where he saw his father standing to clap. He grinned, delighted at receiving a cheque for £10,500. Until now it had been a dismal few months, and he was determined to make the most of his win. The jumps had been removed in preparation for the finale, so the arena was empty as Max cantered around on his lap of honour, the spotlights directly on him as he gave a final wave to the adoring public.

Once he was back out into the blackness of the night, Max brought Zhivago back to a walk, and they quietly made their way back to the stabling area. In the background, Max could still hear the music for the finale. It was the closing night, and he had intended to watch the performance, but winning the top show jumping event of the week was certainly a fair exchange.

As he reached the stable, Lee stripped off Zhivago's tack, and quickly threw on his rug before the horse cooled off too quickly. Once his horse was settled, Max went off in search of his father, whilst Lee hurried to catch up with the rest of the grooms who were having a last night party of their own. Max wished he could join them, but duty prevented him. His father bank-rolled Max's show jumping career, never complaining when Max failed to win, but supporting him without question. The fact that Max was effectively the guest of honour at the party Ivan Tarasov was hosting, meant that he needed to at least show his face.

Ivan Tarasov had hired an entire floor of the NEC Hilton for a post-show party, which incorporated several of the best suites. Normally Max and Lee slept in the horse lorry when at shows, but this time his father had provided him with the luxury of a bedroom. Although he was conscious of the smell of horse and saddle soap, Max remained in his riding gear. It made him look sexier, and more dashing. It was what people expected.

After a few minutes' walk, Max reached the hotel lobby where the duty concierge warmly congratulated him. He then took the lift to the party, which was already in full swing. As he made his entrance he was greeted by cheers, and a glass of champagne was thrust into his hand. Max quickly looked around, hoping to see someone he recognised amongst the sea of faces. Apart from his father, and wife number four, he couldn't make out anyone he knew. Ivan stood up and embraced his son enthusiastically. 'Well done, Maxim, that was excellent,' he said, speaking with only a hint of his Russian accent. 'Now let me introduce you to some of my guests.'

Most of Ivan's associates were other multi-millionaire businessmen, but recently his choice of guests had extended to anyone with political influence. Determined to gain acceptance as an adopted Englishman, Ivan had decided to run for parliament. He had it all planned. A few years in a safe Tory seat before being elevated to the House of Lords. Consequently, Max was introduced to his father's new best friend, Sir Malcolm Ward, the party chairman of a soon to be vacant decent Tory seat, accompanied by his very attractive wife. Sir Malcolm was clearly far more interested in wealthy Russian backers than show jumpers, but Lady Ward held Max's gaze a little longer than was strictly necessary.

Max hadn't eaten anything for hours and he could feel the champagne starting to affect him. All the other guests had been fed earlier with a buffet during the show, so having spent a few minutes being polite, he slipped off to his accommodation to order room service. Having requested a sandwich, he did a line of coke to help keep his spirits up. He desperately wanted to get back, join his fellow competitors, and talk horses. He also wanted sex. Winning always made him incredibly horny, but with Cindy still in London, and only his father's associates to mix with, he guessed that the chances of satisfying his desires were slim.

The coke was making him restless, so whilst he waited for the food to arrive, he went out into the corridor to see who was around. Seconds later he spotted Lady Ward coming out of a nearby bedroom. Shutting the door carefully behind her, she waved in acknowledgement.

'Just waiting for room service,' he called out, having felt strangely compelled to speak.

'Would you like some company?' she offered.

'Please.' He opened wide his door, and held it back inviting her in. As she glided past him, it occurred to him that he had absolutely no idea what he was going to do with her now. She headed straight for his bed and sat down with one leg tucked up under her like a young child.

'Would you like a drink?' he asked.

She flicked her hair back with her hand and leant back and stretched so her breasts could be seen to their best advantage. 'Gin and tonic if you have one,' she replied.

Max opened the drinks cabinet and retrieved a small bottle of gin and a mixer, before deciding on a vodka for himself.

Having taken a sip, she said, 'you can call me Janie. You're Maxim of course,' she added.

'You know my name? But of course, you were at the show tonight.'

'Darling, I knew who you were long before tonight. In fact, I doubt there's a female under sixty in the country who doesn't know who you are.'

'You flatter me,' he said, grinning. 'Look, will you excuse me whilst I have a quick shower?'

'Go ahead, don't mind me. I'm quite able to look after myself. And if you want your back

11

scrubbed just give me a shout.'

Max dived into the shower, practically ripping his clothes off in his haste. His body tingled with anticipation. Part lust, part cocaine, but he didn't care. It was a long time since he'd had a much older woman, and the thought thrilled him. The fact that this one was a Lady with an obviously expensive boob job would be a new experience. The shower cooled his hot, sticky torso, but did nothing to lessen his ardour, and as he wrapped a towel around his wet body, he felt his excitement rise.

'My God, you should come with a health warning you're so gorgeous,' Janie exclaimed as he walked back into the room, his muscular chest on full display. Max was secretly delighted at her outburst but tried to remain cool. He then noticed that his sandwiches had arrived. 'Do you mind?' he asked as he picked one up. 'I'm starving.'

'Sure darling. You need to keep your strength up,' she replied. He sat on the bed beside her and began eating. Janie pulled away the towel and gently began to rub his body dry. As she got close to him, he could smell her scent, which reminded him of his stepmother. Promptly putting that rather disconcerting image to the back of his mind he closed his eyes and let her hands caress him.

Janie proved to be a thoughtful, and energetic lover, thinking about his pleasure as much as her own, and he had to withdraw more than once to stop himself coming too early. When she eventually came, her shrieks of ecstasy were enough to wake the whole hotel, and the shock nearly made Max lose his erection. 'Let's hope your husband didn't hear you,' he hissed nervously.

'Darling, he's half deaf, and besides I've never been able to come like that with him before.' No longer put off his stroke, Max continued until he too had been satisfied.

Whilst Max walked around the room looking for something to wear, Janie continued to lie on the bed, admiring the view. She had remained almost entirely clothed throughout and only needed a quick tidy to avoid arousing suspicion.'Do you know; you've made me feel desirable for the first time in years. Thank you.'

'It's been a pleasure,' Max answered as he hopped around on one foot trying to get a sock on.

'I thought I'd read somewhere that you have a stunning girlfriend. Doesn't she mind you pleasuring the elderly?'

'Cindy and I have a very open relationship. No exclusivity. Her decision I hasten to add, but it suits me as well.'

'Is she very beautiful?'

'Yes. She's a former model who now has her own fashion label. That's where she is tonight – at a fashion show.'

'You must miss her.'

'I was, but then you came along.' He smiled at her, 'So really it should be me thanking you.'

They both managed to slip back into the party, although it was noticeable that it was on the verge of breaking up. Whilst Max hunted down a drink,

Janie found her husband.

'Oh, there you are. Early start in the morning. Time we were getting to bed.'

Max made his way over towards them, determined to say goodbye. As his father shook Sir Malcolm's hand, Max gently touched Janie on her arm. 'Thank you for coming' he said loudly, smiling at the corniness of the line.

'It was a pleasure,' she smiled graciously.

Once most guests had retired, Ivan strode over to his son who was quietly getting drunk in the corner of the room. 'It's been a very successful evening all round,' Ivan announced. 'The sitting MP in Sir Malcolm's constituency has said that he's retiring at the next election, and Sir Malcolm is intending to nominate me as his successor.'

'That's great news,' Max replied, trying to show interest. 'I had a quick chat with his wife. She seems nice.'

'Glad to hear that you were circulating.' Ivan answered, not suspecting a thing. Satisfied he walked off back to his few remaining guests.

Finally, Max felt able to leave. Grabbing a couple of unopened bottles of champagne, he slipped off back to the NEC in search of his friends and a decent party.

Chapter 1

As the taxi drew up outside the London Excel conference centre, Lottie nearly vomited with nerves. The next couple of hours could be potentially life changing as far as her career was concerned, but with the dice already cast there was nothing she could do now that could possibly make a difference. Her marketing proposal that she'd submitted two weeks earlier was the best bit of work she'd ever produced. She'd written with both passion and careful consideration for all the facts and could do no more. She was however up against other regional marketing managers with way more experience. Always priding herself on being a realist, she knew that her chances of success were limited.

The conference centre had been completely taken over by The Yangtze Motor Corporation, as they intended to use this as their opportunity to launch their latest new vehicle in the UK. Walking into the foyer Lottie saw a massive poster of the Intrepid towing a small boat. Resigning herself to her obvious failure, she headed to the registration desk to pick up her badge, before making her way into the main hall. There, directly in front of her were two more posters of the Intrepid. One showed the big, heavy beast of a car halfway up a mountain track, and the other was of it towing a horse trailer. Lottie's hopes lifted slightly – perhaps they had taken some notice of her proposal after all.

She headed directly to the table occupied by the other West of England managers including her colleague who covered Somerset and Dorset. Being neighbours, they'd helped each other out on many occasions when major promotions were required. Upon seeing her he stood up and gave her a kiss on her cheek.

'I was beginning to wonder where you'd got to?' he said before offering to fetch her a coffee.

Before long the main players took to the stage, including Florian the German head of marketing for Europe together with one of the Chinese owners. Florian spoke first, explaining that the Intrepid was Yangtze Motor's direct answer to the Mitsubishi Shogun and Toyota Landcruiser, and that it had been decided that its initial launch should be in the UK. In broken English, the Chinese director talked about the car's spec and capabilities. The essential bits of information were then summarised. Essentially the 2.8 turbo diesel Intrepid was to retail at 2/3rds of the price of its main rivals and had been designed to be 1/3rd more fuel efficient, and a semi electric hybrid model was also available. There were claps of approval from the sale force and Lottie noticed that her work mates looked almost excited at the prospect.

Then came the bit that Lottie and many others had been waiting for – the decision on the marketing campaign. The European Marketing Manager again took centre stage, alongside a peculiar looking man from the company's PR company.

16

'Thank you, those of you who submitted ideas for a major impact campaign to get Intrepid up there alongside its main rivals. There have been some excellent suggestions, and some interesting ones. Intrepid may be an excellent vehicle for deer stalking in Scotland, but a major advertising campaign showing a stag carcass strapped to the bonnet isn't going to win us any friends.' The audience laughed politely.

'Although the target market is perfect, we decided to stay away from hunting, shooting, and fishing in all its forms, because it simply isn't worth upsetting the animal rights activists. Overall, there were two potential suggestions that really caught our eye, sailing being one, and equestrian sports the other.

Lottie held her breath, the next few seconds would be make or break.

'Both sailing and equestrian sports are an excellent match for Intrepid, but as equestrian sports have a more natural link to our larger target market. I have pleasure in congratulating the Devon and Cornwall area manager Charlotte Wilkins. Lottie, please come up on stage and explain your ideas further.

'Well done,' Lottie's colleagues said, slapping her on the back. Flustered with embarrassment and excitement, Lottie scrambled to her feet, nearly tripping over her handbag, the strap of which had wrapped itself around the leg of the chair. As she made her way to the front, people around her clapped. While she could feel her face burning, her hands were cold and clammy. Lottie

17

made her way over to the podium where Florian shook her hand before directing her to the microphone. Trying to steady her voice, Lottie took a deep breath then began.

'My target market is pony club mum. She is in social-economic group A/B and has at least one horse mad daughter, so she needs a vehicle that can tow a horse trailer. She wants her car to be safe but stylish, enough room for the dogs and saddles, but comfortable enough for driving up the motorway to visit her mother and for trips to Waitrose.

Of course, Mitsubishi Shogun and Land Rover Discovery also want pony club mum. Mitsubishi were synonymous with Badminton Horse Trials for many years whilst Land Rover remain the main sponsor of Burghley Horse Trials. Unfortunately, these are the only major televised 3-day events in the UK, so I looked at other equestrian activities. Racing is currently upsetting animal rights activists, whilst polo and dressage are too elitist, but even non-horsey people know a bit about show jumping, and I doubt there's a pony club mum, or teenage girl in the country who hasn't fantasised about top show jumper Maxim Tarasov, and this is my recommendation for our sponsorship campaign.'

Lottie's throat had gone dry, and as she carried on with a few supportive statistics she began to struggle, but as she finished there was loud applause from the floor.

'Thank you, Lottie, for such a clear analysis,' Florian said. 'If you'd like to return to your seat now, I will bring on the next guest.'

Lottie almost floated back to her table. They must select Maxim, she thought to herself. She could hardly believe that she may actually get to meet him. With her head swimming with ideas, she barely heard the next introduction. As she sat back at her table she looked up at the stage and saw a smart middle-aged man who looked vaguely familiar. Florian shook his hand and said, 'Please give a big Yangtze welcome to the Chef de Equip and head of selection for the British Show Jumping Team, Simon Palmer.'

'Oh my God,' Lottie exclaimed rather too loudly. 'He is practically God in horsey circles,' she added in a whisper, trying to justify her outburst. A few people around her chuckled politely.

After the usual pleasantries, Simon explained to the audience that following discussions with the Yangtze board, it had been agreed to sponsor riders, rather than a specific competition. This would provide a longer-term impact, and the sponsorship would continue through the following year's World Equestrian Games and on to the next Olympics. Simon was to draw up a shortlist of riders, all of whom were potential future Olympic prospects from which the Yangtze directors would choose two or three.

'Please let Maxim be one of them,' Lottie prayed. Not only did she have a bit of a crush on him, but he was perfect for the campaign. A superbly talented horseman and devastatingly handsome, and known for being kind to his horses, posters of him graced the walls of thousands of bedrooms. Although his father was a Russian billionaire, Max's mother had been English and he'd been born in London, so was eligible to ride for Great Britain.

After seemingly endless updates, the meeting finally finished, and everyone moved through to a separate room for drinks and nibbles. Lottie was feeling extremely hungry and made a beeline for the food table. She'd just taken a rather large bite from a vol-au-vent when Simon Palmer approached her.

'It's Charlotte isn't it?'

Frantically switching her food plate to her left hand, Lottie accepted his handshake, but was only able to nod helplessly rather than risk showering the God of British Equestrian teams with bits of pastry case.

Having retrieved her hand, she covered her mouth, 'Sorry. Yes, I am. Most people call me Lottie'.

'Thank you for your great suggestion Lottie. Show Jumping is such an expensive sport we are always desperate for decent sponsors, and I know that this will make a huge difference to the riders we select.'

As Lottie swallowed the rest of her vol-au-vent he asked, 'Do you compete yourself?' 'Yes, but only low key stuff – local grade C classes. I'm neither sufficiently brave nor rich enough to do anything more.'

'Don't be so dismissive of yourself. You must be a decent rider to do what you do, especially as you hold down a high-powered job like yours.'

Lottie blushed, 'I'm just delighted to be part of this.'

Getting down to business, Simon explained that over the following few weeks he would be visiting the six top riders to sound them out about possible selection. 'I would like you to join me. You can explain the whole sponsorship deal in more detail than me.'

Lottie nodded. 'That would be lovely. It will be a great excuse to get out the office,' she said as calmly as possible, and trying to quell the childlike impulse to scream with excitement.

They had just swapped contact details when Simon was set-upon by Florian so Lottie slipped away in search of her colleagues.

'Are you going out partying to celebrate? her Somerset colleague asked.

'No, I'm being taken out for a meal by my little brother,' Lottie answered. 'He has a flat in Kensington,' she added.

'What does he do?

'Since he left Oxford he's been writing obscure biographies that only a few intellectuals read. He supports himself by doing free-lance journalism.'

'What papers does he sell to?'

'Mainly the broadsheets, but he isn't fussy. He does a lot of society gossip stuff which he claims to hate – reckons he needs to purge his soul with the dry academic stuff.'

'Does that mean he gets invited to loads of glamorous parties? I mean – what a lifestyle. Just imagine all that free booze.'

'Tom doesn't actually drink, so he probably finds it a bit tedious.'

'What a waste. If he ever needs someone to stand in for him, I'm ready and willing.'

'Thanks, I'll tell him.'

'So why doesn't he drink?'

'It's a family thing.' Lottie didn't want to expand. 'Tom reckons he does a better job when he remains sober and everyone else is drunkenly indiscrete – that's when the newsworthy snippets tend to get out.'

Tom was already waiting for Lottie as she left the Excel centre. Spotting her, he jumped out of his sports car, and came around to open the passenger door. Delighted to see his big sister, he smiled broadly, 'How did it go?' he asked, having noticed the huge grin on her face.

'I did it. They chose my idea,' she announced triumphantly. 'I'm now head of sponsorship for the UK.'

'Oh, that's great. I'm so pleased for you,' he said hugging her. He grabbed her bag and squeezed it into the boot of the car. 'Well, I've managed to get a table at a fabulous restaurant. It will be perfect for a celebration.'

Within moments of them setting off, Tom was bombarded with phone calls, his Bluetooth connection enabling him to chat whilst negotiating the busy roads. Lottie took the opportunity to call home and let them know the good news, knowing that her uber horsey mother would truly appreciate the significance of her achievement.

Stuck in heavy rush-hour traffic, it took ages to get to Kensington, giving them only a short time to get ready for the evening ahead. Tom lived rent free in a wing of his uncle's house. The Mansion House, Kensington had been the home of the Dukes of Chiswick for over three hundred years, and being Crispin, the current Duke's favourite nephew had its advantages.

Crispin had always been a serious man, now well into his sixties, his only passion was politics. Having served for a few years as a Conservative member of parliament, he had rapidly risen through the ranks to become a government minister. Once he'd gone to the upper house, he continued to serve the party and had recently become party chairman.

Happily married for over forty years to the beautiful and devoted Felicity, they had two grown-up sons, Will who was in the Army, and Rufus who worked for the Foreign Office and was currently based in Brussels. Even with live in staff, the huge house felt quite empty, so Crispin was glad to be able to help studious, sensible Tom who was the polar opposite of his rebellious father.

Having rapidly showered and changed, Lottie was ready for a night out in London. Having not seen her half-brother dressed up for quite a while she'd forgotten how gorgeous he looked in his dinner jacket. He was naturally handsome, tall, and athletic with almost perfect features. His dark brown hair flopped forward over his sparkling hazel eyes. Both funny and charming he was a delight to be with.

Caring more about his academic research than finding a girlfriend however, unless he was working, Tom normally slobbed around in clothes barely fit for a tramp, unshaven and with manic unkempt hair. Under such a scruffy guise he generally passed under the radar of most predatory women.

'I thought I ought to make an effort,' he said with a wry smile, 'I was thinking we could go on to Lizzies after the meal if you're not too tired. I don't expect you've been clubbing for months.'

When the taxi drew up outside The Ivy, Lottie was shocked for the third time that day. Tom was totally oblivious to the extent of his privileged existence where seemingly all doors were open to him. The fact that the Ivy staff all treated him like an old friend he accepted with an air of almost childlike innocence. Once they were seated Tom whispered, 'Order what you want. I get a huge discount in return for regular mentions in my celebrity columns.'

As Lottie tried to nibble delicately on a caviar hors-d'oerve, she started to explain to Tom about the sponsorship deal. 'It's so strange. I mean last night I was cuddled up on the sofa with Shadow watching the show jumping and dreaming that I was part of it. And now, it's actually going to happen.'

She always watched international show jumping with mixed emotions. For as long as she could remember, she'd dreamt of being a famous show jumper, and hated herself for her cowardice. Had she been braver she could have possibly had a chance of making it. Her horse Taggart certainly had enough ability, and although her immediate family weren't exactly cash rich, they would have supported her. Now, albeit vicariously, she was joining that exclusive world of international show jumping, and ultimately her ticket to the Olympics.

'How's Dad?' Tom asked. 'I spoke to him on the phone last week and he seemed cheerful.'

'Yes fine. He's got another appointment with the liver specialist next month, but he's in good spirits.'

'So not on the spirits then?'

'Not as far as Mum knows. He's been very restrained recently. I just hope that Rupert and Marina's New Year's Eve bash doesn't set him off.'

'Why doesn't he just make his excuses and stay away. Its public knowledge that Dad and Rupert detest each other, so why pretend any different.'

Lottie shrugged. 'I guess its dad's old-fashioned belief in duty. Anyway, are you coming down for it?'

'Wouldn't miss it for the world?'

'What! Seriously! – Like forgo the best night of the year in London?'

Tom smiled, 'Don't forget I inherit the Dewerstone estate in just over a year's time, so I really ought to make the effort to go down there when I'm invited. Besides, Verity is a nice girl. If

25

I didn't go it would look like I was snubbing her.'

They stopped talking for a few moments to eat, but they'd seen too little of each other recently to be silent for long. 'Will you be bringing anyone?' Tom asked his older sister.

'No just myself as usual,' Lottie said with a sigh.

'So, there's no current boyfriend for me to vet?'

Lottie took a sip of water, 'I've given up on men. Because of whom I am, guys assume that I'm sitting on a huge trust fund, and that I'm a sure bet as a fun-loving party animal. Without fail, they all do a runner when they realise how boring and ordinary I am.'

'If it's any consolation, I have the same problem. People find it hard to comprehend that I drink mineral water, and don't keep a gram of coke in my back pocket. People are more shocked that I'm a dull academic. I know I'll be rich soon, but sometimes funds are so tight I can barely afford to eat, which is a bit of a turn-off to fortune hunting debutants.'

'Well,' Lottie announced, 'I've decided that the next time I meet someone I fancy, I'm going to avoid all mention of our family. At least that way, if they like me, it will be for myself.'

'My New Year's resolution is to spend more time in the country and find a nice wholesome country girl.' Tom said.

'What, like Alice Tinker?' Lottie giggled, thinking about *The Vicar of Dibley*.

'Close - Someone like you sis.'

'And if our plan doesn't work?'

'You can come and live with me in Dewerstone, and we'll grow old and eccentric together.'

Chapter 2

A week later Lottie received a call from Simon inviting her to accompany him on his visits around the various show jumping yards. 'We'll start in the Midlands at Marcus Wallis' yard, then head north up to Yorkshire to Paul Denton and Karen Allen, then down the east coast to Mary and Giles Downing-Dunn. We'll finish our tour of England in Surrey at Maxim Tarasov's yard if that's OK?'

'Yes fine,' Lottie said enthusiastically as she practically bounced with joy on the other end of the phone line.

Having made arrangements with her mum and Nick to look after her dog Shadow and her horse Taggart she called Simon back and they confirmed their plan.

The following Monday, instead of driving into work, Lottie set off on the train to Gloucestershire to meet Simon. As Simon was packing her case in the boot of his Range Rover Lottie asked, 'Does your wife mind you travelling off around the countryside for days on end with a strange woman?'

'No, she's fine about it. After all, you are probably a similar age to my daughter. Neither would I describe you as strange,' he said smiling warmly.

As they set off up the M5 towards Marcus's house, Lottie quizzed Simon about himself. The basics such as his glorious military career she had gleaned from Wikipedia, but she still didn't know how an ex RAF officer came to be in charge of the British Equestrian team. He explained that after he'd left the RAF, he got the job of running Olympia, which was perfect as it tied in with his first love which was show jumping. He told Lottie that he'd competed himself for a few years, until a bad fall caused permanent damage to his spine and he was forced to retire. As compensation, he had one of the most prestigious jobs in the equestrian world.

Marcus Wallis's yard was just as Lottie had imagined it would be. A neat courtyard surrounded by well-tended paddocks and a large sand and shredded rubber arena that was packed with massive show jumps. As Britain's top show jumper, who consistently retained a top 5 place in the FEI rankings, Lottie was tempted to ask for his autograph, but felt that it would be too unprofessional to enquire. Despite his status, Marcus proved to be delightfully normal and down-to-earth as he proudly introduced Lottie to his top show jumper Speedy Sid.

In his late forties, Marcus was one of the most experienced riders of the selection. A devoted family man, he was calm and sensible and the reliable stalwart of many a team. Marcus' wife Tracey had prepared a lunch for them, so Lottie enjoyed the luxury of a pleasant meal as she got down to the business of explaining the sponsorship deal. Sat at the large oak kitchen table she felt relaxed and at ease as she did her bit.

'Yangtze will be having a get together in January when they will meet all the riders.

'It's not all about performance you see. They need to have a strong working relationship with the two or three riders they select.'

'What does that entail – It's just that I have an obligation to my current sponsors and can't afford to upset them?' Marcus questioned.

'No that's fine,' Lottie replied reassuringly. 'Your long-term sponsors are your bread and butter. It's not going to be hard. - you'll be given a logo covered Intrepid 4 by 4 to drive around in, and there will be a TV ad campaign, and if you get to the World Equestrian Games or the Olympics there will be a couple of corporate drinks parties to attend. That's it really.'

'At the risk of sounding mercenary, how much is the deal worth in financial terms?'

'It depends on whether they go for 2 or 3 riders, but the pot is about £5 million.'

Lottie glanced at Marcus who looked rather taken aback. 'Yangtze want to be seen to make a difference,' she added.

Lottie watched as Marcus looked thoughtfully through the paperwork she'd given him. His greying hair suited him. He wasn't conventionally good looking. His features were craggy and weather-beaten, but he had a kind, open face which softened his masculinity. Looking around the room the walls were covered with horse pictures. Some were of Marcus at international events, and others of his children on hairy ponies at local horse shows and pony club rallies.

'It all seems very exciting,' he concluded agreeably.

By mid-afternoon Simon and Lottie were back on the road travelling north. The plan was to stay overnight in a hotel just outside York, and to fit in Paul and Karen the following day. Having completed her first visit, Lottie had gained in confidence. Marcus had been so lovely and put her at her ease and now she felt ready to tackle the rest. Her only reservation was Maxim, knowing that the mere sight of him would have her weak at the knees.

Paul Denton came from a show jumping dynasty which had started over fifty years before with his grandfather. A dour, no-nonsense Yorkshire man, Paul seemed outwardly unimpressed by the sponsorship opportunity, but agreed to attend the meeting in January. Still in his mid-twenties, he was one of the most eligible bachelors on the circuit. He had a round, reddish face and dark, slightly wavy hair. A powerful, stocky man of 5ft 8, he would have been a farmer but for his prowess as a rider. Paul was regularly featured in Pony Magazine and as a result had almost as large a teenage following as Maxim. He was easily recognised, partly because he always went around dressed in a black padded blouson jacket.

Karen Allen came from a similar background to Paul; her mother having previously been one of the top lady show jumpers. Being one of only a handful of ladies competing at the highest level,

31

Karen was feisty and determined, and greeted Lottie with slight suspicion. Close up, she wasn't as attractive as Lottie had imagined, although with her fit twenty-four-year-old toned body Lottie suspected that Karen would be tough competition. Karen certainly made Lottie seem inadequate, however unintentional being that as she was younger and ten times the horse woman. Karen too showed little emotion at the sponsorship deal but seemed keen on spending a few days away at a top hotel.

That evening Lottie and Simon spent the evening together having a meal in the hotel restaurant. Having spent a great deal of time together, Lottie felt very comfortable in Simon's presence. They worked well together and their mutual love of horses and jumping made conversation easy. The previous evening, Lottie had been the one quizzing Simon, but now it was her turn to entertain with tales of her own unconventional family.

The next morning was the penultimate visit to the yard of Mary and Giles, a successful husband and wife team based in the East Midlands. Mary had started off as an eventer but having married Giles she gradually switched allegiance. She had been Britain's leading lady rider for the previous 4 years, whilst Giles was one of Simon's automatic choices when selecting for Nations Cup teams. Giles wasn't the fastest, flashiest rider, but consistently produced steady clears, making him an ideal team player.

Now in their fifties they had a successful

business both as sports horse breeders and trainers but were delighted to be offered the chance of additional sponsorship and insisted that they really needed a new four-wheel drive.

As they made their way south, Simon said. 'I've left Max until last deliberately. He can be quite intimidating, especially for young ladies, so I thought it best that you get some practice with the others first.'

Lottie groaned inwardly. Already nervous, Simon had simply compounded her fears. She pondered whether she could feign illness and leave Simon to do it on his own. The only problem was she couldn't act her way out of a paper bag, let alone give a convincing at death's door impression. They only thing for it was to man up and if necessary, to play Max at his own game.

As Simon drove up the lane into Max's yard, Lottie was surprised at how twee and old-fashioned Lark Rise Stables were. The stables had been around for a few hundred years and set in a square around a cobbled yard. Everything was tidy and well organised however to the side was a scruffy, unkempt looking farmhouse. It certainly wasn't the glamorous set-up that she'd imagined. The yard was silent, all the boxes were empty and there seemed to be no-one around. Suddenly, tearing around the side of the house came the welcoming party in the form of a very excited short legged Jack Russell who barked enthusiastically before running around their legs.

'Max is probably in the school,' Simon said.

Obediently Lottie followed as he strode off up the yard and around the back of the oldest looking stables. Immediately in front of them was a large sand arena. Lottie almost pinched herself to make sure she wasn't dreaming. There, in front of her, doing a rather decent half pass diagonally across the arena towards them were Max and Zhivago.

Suddenly aware of their arrival, Max brought his stallion to a halt, clocking the hot looking female that was accompanying Simon. He guessed she must be Simon's personal assistant. Whoever she was she'd purposely dressed to fit in, with her tweed Dubarry coat, tight trousers and Fairfax and Favour boots, a fact that slightly irritated him. He disliked hangers-on, but still, she was definitely a future shag target. She had a very pretty, heart shaped face, with soft, warm eyes, perfect teeth, and flawless skin. Her light brown hair was elegantly swept back off her face. She had small, but neat round breasts and a curvy bottom. Dropping the contact on Zhivago's mouth, the stallion stretched his neck before rubbing his sweaty, itchy head against his leg.

Max slid to the ground, gave him a pat before taking the reins over Zhivago's head. At that moment his mobile phone started buzzing in his pocket. Retrieving it, his father's name came up on the display. 'I'd better take this call,' he announced whilst leading Zhivago over to where his visitors were standing. 'Put him back in his stable,' he ordered, handing Lottie the reins.

'Which stable is...' Lottie tried to ask as he turned away, ignoring her. 'Come on then,' she

34

said to Zhivago, 'you lead the way.'

Immediately the huge black stallion swung his head around, intending to take a chunk out of her. Instinctively she flicked the buckle end of the reins, smacking him right across the nose. 'You can stop that you arrogant sod,' she muttered, then grinned as she decided that the statement applied equally to the owner. Zhivago gave her an evil look out of the corner of his eye but decided against an immediate repeat attack.

As Lottie led him back into the yard, the horse instinctively turned right. In front of him was a stable with his name on. 'No wonder you're so special – you can read,' Lottie joked. Having taken him in, she decided not to risk another attempted savaging, so taking his head collar and lead rope, she whipped off his bridle and tied him up. She was then able to bend over safely to remove his tendon boots without having the seat of her trousers ripped apart by a set of massive teeth.

Once he'd been untacked, she sponged down his sweaty patches before putting on his cooler rug. It felt strange handling one of the most valuable horses in the world - one she'd watched on her TV screen countless times. Taking her life in her hands, she slipped off the head collar. She tensed, anticipating an attack, but Zhivago could smell the herbal horse treats in her pocket. Deciding that he deserved some, he nudged her with his nose before licking the pocket flap.

'Oh, you can have some.' Lottie retrieved a handful which he gently took from her hand.

'Is that girl your PA?' Max asked Simon.

'No, she's the head of sponsorship for Yangtze Motors,' Simon answered, trying to hide a sly smirk.

'Guess I'd better check that she's OK.' Max said. *Shit, shit, shit. I could have just blown a major sponsorship deal,* he thought to himself as he hurriedly headed off towards the stables. Cautiously peering over the stable door, he was half relieved, but also slightly miffed to see the cantankerous stallion nuzzling softly into the coat of a stranger.

'I've given him a quick wipe down and put on his cooler. Is that OK?' Lottie asked.

'Er yes, thanks,' Max muttered, lowering his gaze to the floor, hoping he didn't look as awkward as he felt. He was certain that he simply had to have her. As well as having a great body, she was obviously a total natural with horses, probably extremely smart given that she had a high-powered job, yet she gave off an air of delicious indifference.

'I'll show you around the rest of the yard if you like?' he said casually.

'Thank you, that will be nice,' Lottie replied, hoping that she sounded businesslike and polite rather than fan girl desperate.

Max then escorted them down to the paddocks behind the house. 'The large bay mare is Tilly. She used to be quite a good jumper, but now she's a brood mare. Has had a couple of Zhivago's foals, but she's having a year off. Will probably put her back to Zhivago in the next few weeks.'

He walked up to her, giving her an affectionate rub on her neck. 'The antisocial black filly standing under the tree is Roxy, 2-year-old daughter of Zhivago.' They crossed the field, then having gone through a second gate they were introduced to a large bright chestnut horse.

'This is Harvey my 7-year-old grade B warmblood. Has loads of talent but is still a novice. Give him a couple more years and he'll be a great Nations Cup Horse.' He looked straight at Simon and grinned mischievously.

'OK, mental note made,' Simon replied.

'My speed horse Lenny is out on a hack at the moment,' Max continued, referring to his bay thoroughbred gelding.

'Oh yes, Leningrad,' Lottie said, recognising the name.

'You're one of my fans are you?' Max asked, with an arrogant smirk.

'It's my job to know,' Lottie quickly answered in as professional a voice as she could muster.

It was starting to rain, so Max took them back through the yard, and into the warmth of the house. As he opened the kitchen door, Max cursed himself for not tidying up. The place was a tip, with every surface covered in a mixture of dirty dishes, empty bottles and papers. 'Our cleaner's off sick,' he said as way of apology, hurriedly sweeping debris off the chairs so they could sit down.

Having hunted around for some cleanish

looking cups, he offered them a coffee. Lottie then started to explain about the sponsorship deal. In an attempt to re-assert himself, Max interrupted her. 'It's all very well you saying that Yangtze are going to probably sponsor two or three riders, but what if it's just one. That will mean that Marcus Wallis gets all the money, and it's going to waste our valuable time. I don't suppose you're intending to compensate us.' He stared, challenging her to respond.

Irritated by his arrogance, Lottie turned on him. 'I'd have thought it was blatantly obvious that Yangtze aren't going to just sponsor one person. Their whole strategy revolves around having a presence at the next Olympics. Putting millions of pounds on just one horse/rider combination could be potential marketing suicide.' Lottie glared at Max, 'And why would you expect compensation for failure? Now may I continue?'

Max glanced at the floor, 'Thank you for clearing that up. Carry on.' His voice still sounded arrogant, but privately he was cursing himself.

As Lottie finished speaking there was a clatter of hooves in the yard. Both Lottie and Simon stood up to have a look through the window. 'Is that Lee?' Simon asked hesitantly. 'Yep, that's him. My right-hand man – great guy.'

Whilst his visitors were still watching Lenin, Max started rummaging in the welsh dresser drawers. Tucked right at the back was a half empty packet of cigarettes. Grabbing them, he reached above the Aga for the matches, before lighting one. He only inhaled gently, but immediately started to cough. 'Sorry, something stuck in my throat,' he mumbled.

'Is it just you and Lee living here?' Lottie asked, trying not to sound too interested.

'I thought it was your job to know everything?'

'I only care about your performance in the saddle, not in the sack.'

Max set his jaw and he paused before replying.'Yes, Lee lives here too. My other groom Fran lives in the village with her boyfriend.' Max hesitated again before adding, 'I also share a flat in Canary Wharf with my girlfriend.'

'So Max, if you were to be given a substantial sum of money from sponsorship what would you do with it?' she asked, deliberately not reacting to the news of the girlfriend.

'Put it towards a second Grand Prix horse. Harvey won't be ready for a while, so it would be good to have more than just Zhivago to rely on.'

Lottie simply nodded, determined not to give anything away. Simon then asked Max how many horses he was intending to take to Mannheim the following week.

'Just Zhivago and Lenny. The tracks will be too much for Harvey. Why?'

'There's an up-and-coming rider, Ed Carter whose transport has just fallen through. He's only taking the one horse, and I wondered whether you had room?'

'The lorry takes four, but I can only take it if it's a gelding, otherwise my £180k lorry will only be good for firewood by the time Zhivago has got over his sexual frustration.'

Quietly watching Max, a wry smile appeared on Lottie's face. Standing there in his tight jodhpurs and expensive leather riding boots, Max was quite the sexiest man she'd ever met. His slightly dishevelled blonde hair flopped onto his beautiful, clever, arrogant face. His eyes were piercing blue, and they shone with the confidence of privilege. In the flesh, without his riding hat obscuring his amazing bone structure, he looked even more handsome than he appeared on television. As he spoke, he kept flicking his hair out of his eyes, but it looked more like an act of preening than as a resuult of annoying hat-flattened hair. Although Lottie could match him in any verbal showdown, sexually she could see that he would eat her for breakfast. She decided then that her desire for him would remain her own little secret, and promised herself that he would never find out how she truly felt.

Once they were back in the safety of the car, Simon started chuckling to himself. 'Oh, that was great sport.'

'What d'you mean?' Lottie couldn't help but smile.

'Much as I really like Max, he can be such an arrogant little shit – but you terrorised him.'

'Oh come on – I wasn't that bad..... Anyway, what makes you think that?'

'Because Max doesn't smoke,' Simon answered.

Chapter 3

The morning they were due to leave for Mannheim, Ed Harvey turned up with a battered Land Rover, towing a borrowed trailer into which he's squeezed his 17-hand showjumper Trooper. Lee, who'd been in the stable with Zhivago putting on the horse's travelling boots, came out to greet him.

'Take him will you?' Ed ordered, handing Lee the lead rope. Oblivious to Lee's raised eyebrows, Ed headed off towards the house. Lee put the horse in an empty stable, made sure it had hay and water, before going back to finish off preparing Zhivago.

The next time Lee ventured onto the yard Ed collared him to unpack the Land Rover and load Ed's belongings into the lorry. By the time Lee had finished he was hot and flustered as well has having formed a firm opinion on their new travelling companion.

Half an hour later they had hit the road. Lee was driving whilst Max sat beside him playing with the sat nav. Back in the living area Ed helped himself to a cold beer from the fridge. Having finished working out the route Max decided to try some conversation.

'Tell me about your horse,' Max called back to Ed.

'Trooper's an 8-year-old Dutch Warmblood,

who I bought off the Whitakers as a novice. This is his first year jumping Grand Prix courses – he's had a couple of good placings which have brought me up the rankings. I've got a classy mare too – of course I'd have liked to bring her but couldn't.' He trailed off sounding resentful.

Max bit his tongue, whilst Lee raised his eyebrows skyward. Max's first impression of his strapping, good looking travelling companion had been that of a potential partner in crime. He was now rapidly going off the idea.

Once they reached France Max took over the driving whilst Lee dosed. Max decided to quiz Ed some more, on the basis that it was good to know the competition. Although Max had no memory of previous meetings, Ed claimed to have competed against him on the junior circuit when they'd been children. Whereas Max had then simply moved on to horses and the senior circuit bankrolled by his father, Ed's parents stopped supporting him.

Ed explained that his parents only ever saw horses as a hobby, and wanted him to go to university and into a profession. Going against his parents' wishes, and with no money, Ed managed to get a job as a groom. Because he was good, people started paying him to jump their horses. After a couple of years, he was talent spotted and this led to him getting a position as a working pupil under Paul Denton's father Roger.

'Eventually my parents came around to accepting my career choice, and 2 years ago paid out for Trooper and Dolly. What I really need now is a decent sponsor so I can take on my own yard and get some proper transport so I can get over to Europe.'

Max felt a small pang of guilt. His own father gave him everything he asked for and expected little in return. He suspected that Ed harboured a certain amount of resentment as a result.

Once they were close to the German border they stopped for a rest, both for themselves and the horses. Whilst Max was topping up the haynets, Ed asked him how much he'd paid for Zhivago. 'Peanuts compared to how much he's worth now.'

'What's he valued at now?' Ed pressed.

'I was offered 3 ½ million a couple of weeks ago, but it's academic as I'd never sell him.'

'I bet you've got a whole yard of top horses,' Ed said sulkily and sounding more like a petulant child than a 6ft 2inches man.

'No, just these two and a young grade B. I am currently looking for another Grand Prix horse,' Max added knowing that his string of horses was woefully inadequate for a top international show jumper.

By early evening they had arrived at Mannheim. The priority was to settle the horses into their stables, then it was off to the club house for refreshments and a gossip. Ed felt out of his depth and stuck with Max and Lee as they grabbed a table. Before long they were joined by Marcus Wallis and Mary and Giles. Much to Max's annoyance Paul Denton pulled up a chair next to Ed, and finally Karen sauntered across, having dragged herself away from her French boyfriend.

The main topic of conversation was the Yangtze sponsorship deal, with everyone trying to find out as much information as possible.

'That Lottie is a nice girl.' Mary announced, 'I do prefer it when sponsors at least know one end of a horse from another. It does make things easier for everyone.'

'Well, I find that people with a little knowledge are often the biggest pains in the arse,' Paul said.

Lee, who was just sneaking off to meet up with a few of his stable lad mates then piped up, 'No, she's good- She knows how to handle Zhivago.' Realising that he'd just dropped his boss in it, he suddenly went bright red.

'What do you mean by that?' Karen demanded to know. Lee tried to make a dash for it, but she persisted. 'Come on, you can't just come out with statements like that, and think you can disappear.'

Lee had the look of a startled deer, cornered by hunters. 'Max made her take Zhivago back to the stables for him.'

'But Zhivago could have ripped her to pieces,' Marcus exclaimed, horrified.

'When you've all quite finished,' Max exclaimed. 'I thought she was some bimbo PA of Simon's. I reckoned she was quite hot but trying too hard to fit into the horsey scene, so I thought she needed teaching a lesson.'

44

'By nearly being torn apart by a stallion? I'm obviously missing something here.' Marcus replied.

Lee decided to jump in and reply in defence of his boss. 'Max has the idea that if he manages to intimidate a girl on their first meeting, it's more effective when he turns on the charm later.'

'And you thought it would be a good idea to try it on with the head of sponsorship for Yangtze. You're more of a bell-end than I'd thought,' Paul sneered.

'I can't believe you've risked losing the opportunity of a major sponsorship deal for the chance of a shag,' Karen added.

'Spoilt rich bastard,' Paul muttered.

Max looked like he was about to explode, so Marcus tactfully changed the subject before Paul and Max came to blows.

The next day the show jumping started in earnest. The classes were dominated by the Germans who were on home territory, however Max managed a 5th place with Lenny in the speed class and Ed came 10th in the afternoon competition. Max then schooled Zhivago over a few fences having decided to give the highly-strung stallion a day to settle.

Day two of the competition saw the first of the big money Grand Prix courses, and predictably Ed and Trooper crashed out in the first round, however Zhivago was on good form and he and Max managed a financially lucrative 4th place. The following couple of days proved equally successful for Max as he continued to reap the financial rewards of more good placings.

Most evenings were spent socialising in the bar, and Ed found that he made some useful contacts, however the evening prior to the world cup qualifier was traditionally the highlight of the German social calendar. Every year it coincided with Frederick Seipp's birthday party held in his uncle's castle on the bank of the Rhine. At 6pm that evening a fleet of coaches rolled up ready to transport everyone to the party.

Whilst in his late teens, Max had spent two years training under Frederick and consequently had visited the castle on numerous occasions, yet he still got pangs of excitement as the coaches drove towards the austere Norman style castle, surrounded as it was on three sides by thick dark forest. As they approached the large wooden drawbridge which marked the entrance to the castle, those guests that hadn't visited before looked rather aghast.

"God it's like something out of Grimm's fairy tales', Ed exclaimed.'Is this some sort of Gestapo hideout? I'd put money on it having a torture chamber.'

In front of them the large front door opened and a stream of light welcomed them inside as they disembarked from the coaches. The riders entered the great hall which was reminiscent of a hunting lodge. The walls were filled with stuffed heads of deer and wild boar, alongside mediaeval swords and armoury.

'What did I say?', Ed whispered to Lee.

Once everyone was inside, staff led them through into a modernised part of the castle. Having gone down a corridor with elderly looking radiators and signs showing the way to toilets, they finally arrived at the massive ballroom. It was lit by thousands of flickering candles, creating an eerie appearance.

'OK, now we've walked onto the set of the Addams family,' Ed remarked.

Along the near side were tables laden with food and drink. At the far end of the room a string quartet were playing. As everyone streamed into the room, the smokers headed for the huge French windows which opened up onto the battlements. Following out of shear curiosity, Ed went outside and peered over the thick stone walls into the blackness.

'Don't lean over too far. It's a hundred feet shear drop down to the river,' Giles announced casually, whilst offering Ed a cigarette.

Ed grinned before refusing graciously. He almost felt the need to pinch himself to make sure he wasn't dreaming. He could hardly believe that after years of being on the fringes of elite show jumping, he was here amongst them, being treated as an equal.

Inside the others were huddled around the buffet table, trying to soak up the alcohol. Max had just popped to the loo and done a line of coke. He was now feeling restless and ready for some action. Scanning the room for a suitable female target his eyes fell on Corinna, the young German rider. She wasn't stunning like Cindy, but she was

47

pretty, only in her early twenties, fit and a superbly natural horsewoman. Max decided to chat her up but having taken a detour to pick up a drink he saw that Paul Denton had beaten him to it. Angrily knocking back his vodka, Max headed back to the bar for a refill.

It soon became apparent to Max that Corinna needed rescuing. Like most international riders, her grasp of English was good, but it was obvious that she was struggling to understand Paul's thick Yorkshire accent. As Paul moved in closer to her, Max saw her shrink away.

Strolling casually up to them, Max looked straight at her and, in near perfect German, asked, 'Dieser schwanz ist sie langweilig? Sie sehen, wie sie rettling brauchen.' Which translated to - Is this prick boring you? You look like you need rescuing?

She smiled gratefully. Paul barely spoke the language, but guessed that it was something derogatory, and that he was about to receive a brush off.

'Fuck off Denton?' Max snapped rudely.

Paul was about to argue, but it was clear that the girl had lost interest in him now that his greatest rival had appeared on the scene. Angrily he stormed off, heading back to join the other British riders.

'You speak very good German,' she complimented Max.

'I spent a couple of years being bellowed at by our host, the birthday boy, anyway you're good at speaking English,' Max answered.

48

'Thank you,' she replied, 'but I had problems understanding that Paul chap,'

'So do I,' Max smiled.

Before long Max had Corinna under his spell, and within an hour, he led her away from the party to the guest bedrooms where they enjoyed the most exhilarating sex. Whilst he was in the bathroom having a post coital wash, Max did a couple more lines of coke to get him back into the party mood. With his head buzzing, he escorted Corinna back to the party where he continued to flirt with her whilst drinking vodka shots, trying to look cool and worldly-wise.

When Max eventually made his way back to the British corner, he was taken aback by their hostility towards him. Even in his drunken state it was obvious that he was in the doghouse.

'How could you do that to Paul you bastard?' Karen demanded.

'The girl needed saving. She was in danger of being bored to unconsciousness,' Max replied defensively.

'Paul's fancied her for ages. He's been planning how to ask her out, then you just come along and ruin it.'

Max shrugged dismissively. 'She wasn't interested in him.'

'He never stood a chance,' she paused, glaring at him in disgust, 'What gives you the right to interfere?'

'I'm not, but I can't help it if beautiful women just fall at my feet.'

Karen looked at him with pure loathing. 'Well

count me out.'

'I said beautiful women.' Max replied more cruelly than warranted, but the heady mix of cocaine and indignation made him vicious. Not that she was his type anyway. He much preferred females with a bit of breeding.

Before long their bickering had attracted the attention of the rest of the British riders, who also took sides with Karen. Feeling increasingly anxious and upset, Max stormed off to the lavatory for another fix. Before long he felt totally wired, but thinking it was best to avoid the other Brits, less he punch somebody, he headed to the bar.

The next half hour passed in a blur. He had a vague recollection of a conversation with a couple of Swiss riders, but otherwise the heavy mix of vodka and coke was having a very strange effect on him. Without any real plan he wandered outside, whereupon the sharp chill of the night air hit him like a sledgehammer. The feelings of anger came rushing back and he could feel adrenaline surging through his body. At that moment Paul, Karen, Ed and Giles all appeared in the entrance. Max wanted to bolt, but they blocked his exit. Like a cornered, wild animal, he snapped.

'Why don't you all sod off and leave me alone?'

'Can't you handle it?' Paul sneered. 'All the more reason to stay. You haven't got your Russian mafia Daddy to hide behind now have you?'

'What the hell are you talking about, loser?'

Paul realised that he had the upper hand. 'Without your father you are nothing – just a snivelling coward. The only thing you're capable of is screwing.'

Max's brain was in overload. 'I'll show you who's a coward you little shit.' Turning, he vaulted up onto the wall of the castle. Pulling himself up, he stood on the top overlooking the black of nothingness below.

'For Christ's sake Max, get down before you fall and kill yourself,' Giles called, the panic rising in his voice.

Max looked at Paul. 'Have you got the balls to join me? Come on,' he challenged.

'Stop showing off you idiot,' Karen shouted. In disgust, Paul laughed and walked away.

The commotion had attracted quite an audience including Marcus and Lee.

'Come on down mate, please,' Lee pleaded with his boss, who was swaying precariously on top of the narrow ledge.

'You'll kill yourself. Look you've proved your point. Come back down.' Marcus added.

Max just laughed. He wasn't afraid of falling and was simply enjoying the attention. He certainly wasn't in a rush to climb back down. He was getting a buzz from watching the horror on their faces.

Thinking quickly, Lee went to fetch Frederick. He was the one person whom Max really respected, and thus most likely to talk him down. Max saw Lee leave, and guessed he must be bored, so to liven things up he started hopping around on one foot and doing some small jumps. On his third jump his foot slipped and he nearly overbalanced. Encouraged, and amused by the collective gasp, he carried on.

Suddenly Lee returned with Frederick. In German, Frederick yelled at Max to get off the wall immediately. He said that Max's behaviour was an insult to his family and their hospitality. Feeling deflated by his ticking off, Max decided that he'd had enough. It was no longer fun, so sulkily he climbed back down to the relief of those around him.

The next morning Max woke with the most dreadful hangover and almost no memory of the previous evening. As he changed into his riding clothes, he felt sick and dizzy. In less than two hours he had to jump in the world cup qualifier but even standing was proving difficult. Having thrown up three times he staggered outside and over to the stables. As he got to Zhivago's stable he had to hold on to the door for support.

'You look terrible,' Lee said, 'But I'm not surprised.'

'What du mean?... Actually I'm too ill to care.' Max rested his throbbing head against the wall of the stable.

Max just managed to walk the course without vomiting but had to get Lee to warm up his horse. Lee gave him a leg up on to Zhivago moments before he was due in the ring.

As his name was called, Max rode into the arena, but he was no more than a passenger. He strained to remember the location of the first jump. Zhivago broke into his lolloping canter. Max tried to pull himself together, but the dizziness was getting worse. The bell rang for the start of his round. In the absence of any proper leadership Zhivago took charge and headed for a jump. Max saw a fence looming closer, but a second later it was the ground rushing towards him. Then he blacked out.

A few days later Max was back sitting in his kitchen at home reading about himself in the latest edition of *Horse and Hound*. His father's publicity agent had made sure that his collapse was put down to an unidentified bug, rather than alcohol poisoning. His memories of that evening at the castle were still hazy, although Lee had taken great pleasure in telling him about the most embarrassing bits. Ultimately Max knew he'd got away with it. If he'd been blood tested, FEI officials would have found cocaine in his system, and that would have meant a lifetime ban. As it was, he'd lived to fight another day.

The weekend following Mannheim, Max took Harvey his young grade B horse to a low-key event at an equestrian centre in Kent. Harvey jumped well and Max was having a good day, but he was just having a well-earned coffee in the café when his privacy was disturbed by a pushy and rather butch female journalist from the local paper.

'I have it on good authority that your collapse at the World Cup Qualifier last weekend was due to a cocaine overdose. Would you care to comment?'

Max nearly choked on his coffee.'Where on earth did you hear nonsense like that?'

Although he was shocked, he suddenly realised who was behind the story; Paul Denton's lorry was on the other side of the parking area.

'I can't reveal my sources,' the hard-faced woman replied.

'Well I'm no expert on drugs, but from what I remember from the school drugs talks, cocaine is a stimulant, so how would that make me pass out?'

The journalist glared at him, but she didn't have an immediate answer, so Max quickly continued. 'I suggest that you do your homework before you believe malicious gossip in future. I know your precious source and he's just pissed off because I shagged a girl he fancied. Perhaps you'd like to write about that instead.'

Chapter 4

Ben did some breathing exercises to steady his nerves. Here he was, eighteen months out of stage school, and yet he was having an audition for a major role in one of the biggest BBC TV remakes in years. When the original series of Brideshead Revisited had been shown back in the early 1980's it had made instant stars of the main actors, Jeremy Irons and Anthony Andrews. It had been a massive financial gamble, but the production team had been rewarded a hundred times over as it became one of Granada Television's great exports. Now the BBC were attempting to reproduce the magic with a multi-million pound re-make, and Ben was up for the part of Sebastian Flyte.

Both his friends and his agent had convinced him that he was perfect for the part. Certainly he had the right background, and had even been to Eton – The same school as the fictional Sebastian. Ben wasn't a big drinker, but he'd seen his father drunk so often, that he reckoned he could play a convincing alcoholic. He was also the right age to play Sebastian, whereas Antony Andrews had been in his mid-thirties.

His biggest concern was that deep down he knew that the BBC wouldn't risk license fee payers' money on an inexperienced, virtual unknown. Granada TV hadn't taken a chance – they'd used older, seasoned actors and that had paid off. Being realistic, he knew he was wasting his time, but by turning up at least he had the chance of being offered a minor part.

After what seemed like an age, his name was called, and he walked into the room and stood in front of the director who happened to be one of the most famous in the country.

'Thank you for coming Mr Marchbank, said a smartly dressed lady. 'From your CV I see you've recently graduated from RADA and have had a few small roles. What makes you think you can take on the role of Sebastian?'

Ben reddened slightly as he disliked blowing his own trumpet. He cleared his throat with a small nervous cough, 'I've been told that I have the looks and the background to be naturally convincing, plus I know it's a part I could play. What I lack in experience, I make up for in sheer natural suitability.' It wasn't the best reply, but he was too star struck to think of anything clever.

'Well I agree - you do look the part Mr Marchbank, but I shall reserve judgement until I've seen your acting skills. I want you to act out the Easter scene at Brideshead when Sebastian enters the drawing room and is rude to his family.'

He was handed a script, whilst a member of the production team stood up to take the place of the other characters. Ben quickly glanced at the sheet of paper, but he didn't really need to use it. He'd studied the book for A-level English and had fallen in love with the beauty of the language. He knew practically every sentence off by heart.

As the words of Charles Ryder broke the silence, Ben jumped into character. He could feel Sebastian's anguish – after all his own father was a living embodiment of a character on the road to self-destruction. Barely looking at the script, Sebastian's words poured out his mouth. He felt a sense of empowerment as he spoke, together with a heady adrenalin rush, the like of which he'd never experienced before.

As he finished, the room felt silent. Ben could hardly breathe. He knew he'd done well, but whether it was good enough to impress the director, he was unsure. He dared to glance across to where the production team were sitting. The director was leaning forward talking quietly to the scary woman next to him.

'Not bad Mr Marchbank. Thank you. You should be pleased with that performance. We will definitely be in touch soon.'

A couple of hours later, Ben was on the bus making his way home when he received a call from the PA telling him he'd been shortlisted for the part of Lord Sebastian Flyte.

Meanwhile, three hundred miles away, Ben's sister Lottie was dancing around her parent's drawing room, ecstatic with joy, having received through the post, four VIP tickets for the World Cup Qualifier at London International courtesy of Simon. Quickly reading through the letter, the passes extended to a post-show party which would enable her to get re-acquainted with riders she'd met a few weeks earlier. Still holding the letter in her hand, she tore around the house like an excited child as she searched for her mother and Nick, Shadow running cheerfully beside her. She found them in the kitchen, her mother was in her yard clothes, about to put on her boots, whilst Nick was leant against the Aga drinking from a mug.

Lottie blurted out her news, bouncing around the kitchen as she spoke. 'You will both come won't you?' she pleaded.

'Just try and stop me,' Beth answered, having only been to London International a couple of times in her life, and delighted to have an excuse to go again.

'Dad?'

Nick hesitated. 'Which Saturday is it?'

'The last one before Christmas.'

'In that case, sorry I can't. It's the Conservative Party Christmas bash and I've already promised that I'll attend. Under normal circumstances I'd have got out of it, but they've commissioned a portrait of my Grandfather which is being unveiled that night. Sorry sweetheart.'

'Why don't you ask the boys?' Beth suggested.

'I was going to ask Tom anyway, but Ben will probably be too busy.'

Grabbing her coat and wellies Lottie added, 'We can start planning the trip whilst we do the horses.' She sighed, 'I can't wait for Christmas. It's going to be so amazing.'

Having got one of Lottie's riding club friends to horse and dog sit, Lottie, Nick and Beth made their way up to London early on the Friday before Christmas. Since Nick had sold his London flat, they were expected to accept the hospitality of Crispin at the Mansion House. After a short taxi ride to the house, servants took their bags and showed them to their rooms. They were then obliged to join Crispin and Felicity for lunch.

As expected, it proved to be rather an ordeal, especially for Nick. He hadn't seen his brother for a few months, and subsequently it wasn't just the fish that was grilled. Crispin insisted on knowing every little detail regarding Nick's health, and by the end Nick was not only exhausted, but craving a proper drink. Alas for Nick the opportunity wouldn't arise as Crispin was fastidious about keeping alcoholic drinks hidden away behind locked doors when his brother was in residence.

Beth and Lottie then went off Christmas shopping, whilst Nick had a rest. By 7.30 that evening, they'd been joined by Tom, and were sat in Nick's favourite private members dining club in Belgravia waiting for Ben to arrive. Lottie hadn't seen her youngest brother for months and was desperate to catch up with him. He arrived, fifteen minutes late, rushing through the door of the club looking flustered. He hurriedly apologised, before bending over to hug his mother. Ben sat down, with a heavy thud, and impatiently yanked his chair in closer to the table.'Before I burst with the pressure of pent-up excitement, I've got to share my news with you all.'

'Hang on, will you,' his father stopped him. 'This sounds like a celebration.' With that he summoned the sommelier to bring them something special.

'Just as I was walking to the tube on my way here, I received a call from the film director. You know I was up for a major role in a new BBC adaption of Brideshead.'

'Yes darling it's wonderful,' Beth interrupted him. 'Which part have you gone for?'

'Actually Mum, he's just rung to tell me that I've got the part.'

'Which part?' Tom half shrieked, finding the suspense unbearable.

'Lord Sebastian Flyte.'

'Oh my God! Lottie nearly screamed in delight. 'You're gonna end up as famous as Anthony Andrews and Ben Whishaw. That's awesome.'

Ben sat there beaming. 'I can hardly take it in myself. The director is taking a huge risk – after all I'm barely out of drama school, but he reckons that I'm perfect for the part.'

'Of course you are,' Nick said, warmly patting his son on the shoulder. 'Good breeding will always show through. Saying that, it's a wonderful achievement. We're all very proud of you.'

Discretely, a bottle of low alcohol champagne and five glasses were brought to the table. In a manner reminiscent of wilder times, Nick slightly shook the bottle, before popping the cork and allowing the contents to gush into the delicate fluted glasses beneath it. Then raising his glass, he toasted the success of his youngest child.

Chapter 5

The next morning Beth and Lottie went to the shopping village inside the show for some last-minute Christmas presents. Lottie bought horsey stockings filled with treats for Taggart and her old pony Aragon, whilst Beth bought a new bridle for her horse Grace. Later they met up with the boys before making their way to the VIP area for the main show jumping event – the British round of the world cup qualifier.

For both Beth and Lottie the next couple of hours proved to be a 'money can't buy' horse lovers dream as they brushed shoulders with the great and the good of the British Equestrian world. Simon made a point of introducing them to everyone he came across including Beth's childhood heroes David Groom and Malcolm Payne. Once the show jumping started however, most people in the room became transfixed on the competition and the room slowly fell quiet.

Up close the jumps looked massive, and a huge test for both horse and rider. Max's pretty German friend Corinna was one of the first to go, but her lack of experience showed through and she ended on sixteen faults. Poles continues to fall before finally Paul Denton got the first clear round of the day, much to the delight of the mainly British audience. He was shortly followed by Karen on her pretty bay mare who also went clear. Both Mary and Giles Downing Dunn each had an unlucky pole down, then Marcus' Speedy Sid, uncharacteristically brought down the planks having slipped in an extra stride.

Lottie was momentarily distracted by a waiter offering her a drink, but her attention was hurriedly brought back to the main arena by the screams of adulation from teenage girls as Max and Zhivago entered the arena. Lottie noticed the extreme concentration on his face, whilst underneath him his horse quivered with excitement. As the starting bell rang the commentator asked for quiet, but Max looked as though he'd barely noticed as he fixed his gaze on the first fence.

Max's riding was so subtle, and Zhivago so in tune with his rider, that to the untrained eye, they seemed to simply glide effortlessly over every fence. Certainly it had been the best round of the day, with only a handful of riders still to jump, the odds of a British win shortened dramatically. It wasn't only Lottie who had been impressed by Max's riding. There were murmurs of approval from all those around her, including from both the head of the British Show Jumping Association and the President of the FEI.   Following Max, a Dutch rider got 8 faults and then a rather handsome French man went clear. Last to go was Frederick Seipp. He too jumped a copybook round on his priceless Holstein stallion named Wolfgang.

The second round produced another top-class performance from both Max and Frederick, whilst both Paul and Karen scraped through despite some serious pole rattling. In total eight riders were through to the nail-biting jump-off with Max being drawn second to last before Paul. Karen was unlucky to have been drawn first, but as she rode into the arena there were huge cheers from the partisan crowd.

There were only two opportunities to take short cuts within the eight fence jump off, the second of which, coming after jump six meant an awkward three and a half strides to the next fence, a square oxer, which was so large a small car could easily be parked between the wings. Upon landing there was an eight-stride gallop to the wall, which was the final fence.

Karen set off quickly, determined to set a fast time, and thus hoping the others would make errors in trying to beat it. Her mare, a light thoroughbred, was naturally fast and long striding, and flew around the course until they reached jump six. Here Karen took a chance. Rather than shorten her mare up to fit in four strides, she gambled on pushing for three. The mare responded, and stretched, reaching the oxer a little early. As her horse left the ground Karen knew she had made a mistake. The jump was simply too wide, and half a second later there came the inevitable thud as the back rail came down. Unsettled, the mare then hit the final fence too, giving her eight faults. Karen's only consolation was that she'd set an almost impossible time of 34 seconds.

The next two riders both went for safe, but slower clears, with the hope that everyone else would have fences down. Following them came Karen's now ex -boyfriend the handsome French rider Jacq Le Cock. He also tried to ride off three strides into fence seven and had it down. Then Frederick Seipp and his stallion entered the arena. As the reigning World and Olympic champion, the smart money was on him to win, and the crowd fell silent in anticipation of yet another German domination.

Wolfgang was in fantastic form and jumped superbly, however Frederick had decided not to take a huge risk and rode four strides into the oxer before jumping the last in identical time to Karen. Then it was Max's turn to jump. The commentator explained to the audience that Max's only chance of beating the German was to take a chance on the three-stride shortcut. Max had never won a world cup qualifier before; luck had been against him.

The tension in the arena was almost unbearable as the starting buzzer sounded. Zhivago sensed the electric charge in the arena, and practically jumped out of his skin as he leapt over the first fence. As Max was sailing in the air over the 5th fence his time was identical to Frederick's. With adrenalin fuelled determination, Max pushed Zhivago faster. The huge black stallion soared over the next fence before Max gave him a pony-club style kick, driving him on towards the massive oxer. A lesser horse would have bailed out, but Zhivago was both bold and powerful. Giving his rider everything he had, he launched himself over the fence, clearing it easily.

Lottie had stopped breathing as she watched the gallop towards the last. She thought Max was going too fast, and Zhivago would be too flat to jump cleanly. Zhivago had other ideas. Egged on by the crowd, he ignored Max's pleas to slow down, but charged towards the last. Having lengthened his stride, he got practically underneath the wall. Using all his natural ability and talent, the stallion propelled himself upwards, as if jumping a puissance fence. As he came over the top, he kicked his hind legs upwards, determined the keep them out of harm's way.

As they landed, the crowd started screaming with delight. Zhivago was feeling empowered and did a series of bucks as he cavorted around the arena, and oblivious to his rider, who unable to stop, had tears of joy streaming down his face. Lottie gasped for air as she suddenly remembered to breathe. She was still recovering when Paul rode into the arena on his mare Cara. Wrapped up in the excitement of Max's performance, the audience seemed to have forgotten that the competition wasn't yet over.

'This is a lovely mare, but she hasn't quite got the scope to beat Max's round,' Lottie heard Simon announce to those around him. In all fairness to Paul, he looked extremely calm and professional, despite the pressure. Cara was jumping well, and went clear, but the time was slower, putting them third behind Ludwig.

The prize giving was very emotional, especially as Britain had two riders in the top three. Lottie began to get the now familiar feeling of regret at her own lack of ability as she watched the riders on their lap of honour. Despite Max's arrogance towards her at their last meeting, she secretly hoped that he would be coming to the post competition party, and wondered whether he would remember her.

Once the horse events were over, the audience started to leave the arena, however the hospitality suite sprung to life as waiters began their preparations. Before long the riders themselves started to arrive and soon the room was filled with the lively buzz of conversation. Marcus had recognised Lottie and came over for a chat, meanwhile Corinna made a point of striking up a conversation with Ben and Tom who, in the absence of Max, were by far the best-looking men in the room.

Max, with Cindy in tow, was the last to arrive. Immediately bottles of champagne were opened and rivalries temporarily suspended as the other riders shared in his success. Lottie looked on in envy at the beauty of Max's girlfriend, knowing that she didn't stand a chance of winning over Max in the face of such competition. She really wanted to congratulate him, but doubted that he would even remember her, and she didn't want to come across as some sort of crazed fan who'd gate crashed the party.

Having soaked up the praise, however insincerely given, Max was feeling invincible. He and Cindy had already had post winning sex, but he didn't feel satisfied. Across the other side of the room he suddenly spotted the girl from Yangtze. She was looking very sexy, and he realised how much he still wanted her. He was just about to make a move, when he noticed that two extremely handsome men accompanied her. He wasn't sure which of them was her boyfriend, but either could have walked straight out of the pages of *Hello Magazine*, in fact he was sure he recognised one of them from somewhere.

Max made his way over to where Lottie had just finished a conversation with Giles. They both turned and acknowledged him, 'Congratulations on your win,' she said, and Max detected the slightest hint of nervousness in her voice.

Feeling that he had the upper hand, Max replied 'Thank you.' He then paused before adding in his smoothest private school drawl, 'have we met before?'

'Yes, in your kitchen a few weeks ago.'

'Did we. Oh, do you work for Yangtze?' Max asked, pretending that he'd just remembered.

'I'm surprised you've forgotten Lottie, after your stunt with Zhivago,' Giles intervened.

'Yes, I do work for Yangtze.' She paused. 'I take it that's Cindy who's with you?' Lottie added just for something to say.

'I thought it was your job to know everything about me,' Max challenged, attempting to add to the pressure, but to his surprise Lottie laughed.

'How strange that you claim not to remember who I am, but you do remember what

68

I said.' She grinned as she noticed the slightest flicker of embarrassment.

Knowing he'd been caught out; Max hurriedly manoeuvred the conversation away from his suspect memory.'Are you going to introduced me to the rest of your party?'

Lottie was taken aback. 'Yes, of course. I'm here with my mum Beth,' she said as she gestured towards her mother. I have also brought along my two younger brothers, Tom, and Ben.'

Upon hearing their names mentioned, they came across to meet Max. Beth just said hello in a quiet voice, but both brothers shook Max's hand and congratulated him.

'Do you all ride?' Max asked.

'Not as often as we'd like,' Tom answered. 'Ben and I both live in London so other than when we go home at Christmas and get out hunting, it's pretty limited.'

'We do play polo down at Windsor when we get the chance, but I haven't sat on a horse for months,' Ben added.

'You're not professional players then?' Max asked, trying to assess Lottie's background.

'I'm an actor and Tom's a writer and journalist.'

'Are you famous? Sorry, but I don't watch TV or anything, so I have no idea who people are.'

Ben grinned, 'Not famous yet, but I am about to play one of the lead rolls in a major new TV adaption, so watch this space.'

Max looked across at Tom. His face did seem familiar. He wondered where he'd seen him before. 'Who do you work for?' he asked.

'I'm a freelance society correspondent,' Tom answered, as it suddenly dawned on him that he'd seen Max at a rather raunchy party in Soho a few months earlier. He thought he noticed a slight flicker of concern come across Max's face, before the arrogant, confident look returned. *Yes, you remember me don't you,* Tom thought to himself.

Nearby, Cindy was feeling increasingly agitated. It wasn't like Max to willingly make small talk, and she hated not knowing what had caused his sudden change in behaviour. She wasn't normally paranoid when it came to her relationship with Max. She knew he slept around when she wasn't available, and she too had had numerous one-night stands whilst Max had been abroad on tour. There was however an unwritten agreement between them, that when together at a function, they stuck together.

Although she was five years older than Max, it had never been an issue for Cindy. Although now in her early thirties, she knew she was fitter and sexier than many girls ten years younger. Also, financially, in spite not being in Ivan Tarasov's league, by most people's standards she was rich, and there was no need for her to feel inferior. In fact, she was financially more secure than Max, as her money was her own, whereas he was solely reliant on the generosity of his father.

Despite being brought up in a lower middle-class area of Essex, Cindy had used her success wisely. She had found fame and fortune as a model, and then before she got too old, had established herself as a fashion consultant. Through the pages of the glossies, she influenced styles, often modelling the latest wardrobes herself. She'd all but eliminated her Essex accent and had rapidly ascended the social ladder.

Like all extremely wealthy people, Max had always been wary of relationships, less he fall victim to gold diggers or those after celebrity status. With Cindy he had no such worries. In the fame stakes she was his equal, and she didn't need his money. Knowing that Max not only found her irresistible but was everything else he looked for in a partner, Cindy felt confident that he wouldn't simply ditch her for someone younger.

Although Cindy didn't take a great deal of interest in Max's career, she was aware of the huge Yangtze sponsorship deal. Max didn't need the sponsorship, but she knew that he desperately wanted it. It wasn't the money itself he required – he simply could bear the thought of being overlooked. It was unsettling for Cindy that the face of the multi- million-pound sponsorship deal happened to be an attractive younger female. She tried to re-assure herself that Max's interest in the Lottie girl was purely motivated by the deal, but she still had a niggling doubt that simply would not go away. Therefore, before Max got too cosy, she decided to get his attention back on her.

Close by stood Max's arch rival Paul. Cindy considered him to be a revolting little man, but it was worth making a play for him as it would make Max insanely jealous. She quickly grabbed two glasses of champagne from the bar, before sauntering over to the unsuspecting Yorkshireman.

'Here Paul, have a glass of champers,' she said, giving him her best winning smile as she slipped between him and the old lady he'd been conversing with.

'but...' Paul looked stunned.

'It was such bad luck that you were so narrowly beaten. I know I should be loyal to Max, but I just felt you deserved it so much more than he did.'

She purposely placed her hand on his arm and looked directly into his eyes. 'Ivan can just buy Max any horse in the world, but you are here due to pure talent.' Leaning into him, whilst her hand moved across his chest, she whispered in his ear, 'I admire that in a man.'

Once she was certain she wasn't going to be rejected, Cindy kissed Paul on the mouth. Instinctively he reacted, and they began a full embrace. Cindy continued to play along, just to the point where Paul's ardour was reaching a peak, then, with a shriek, she jumped backwards, pushing him away. Max spun around. 'What's wrong?' Seeing his girlfriend in tears, and Paul backing away, panic struck, there was only one thing to do. Rushing forward, he punched Paul, knocking him to the ground. 'Leave my girlfriend alone you bastard,' he growled.

Dizzy and confused, Paul struggled to his feet, 'I didn't start it, it was her,' he spluttered.

'Yeah, well I'm finishing it. Don't you ever touch my girlfriend again, or you'll end up in hospital next time. Why would she want you? You ugly, talentless little shit.' Max sneered.

Now furious, Paul took a swing at Max, and both men fell to the ground kicking and grabbing at each other.

'That's enough,' Simon shouted, red-faced with fury as he shot forward, dragging them apart. He then told them that they would both face disciplinary action and suggested that they leave.

'Come on Max, let's get you cleared up', Cindy slipped her arm through his before escorting him out of the room. Delighted that her plan had worked, she tried not to look too triumphant.

Beth grabbed some paper napkins and went over to Paul who had blood streaming down his face, from where it dripped onto his faithful black jacket.'I saw it all. You were totally set up by Max's girlfriend.' She started to clean him up whilst Lottie commiserated. 'I will have a word with Simon,' she promised.

'Thanks,' Paul muttered.'Max can be a total bastard when he's coked up.' He'd never planned to mention the drug habit of his rival to the woman behind the Yangtze sponsorship, but with the probability that he now had a broken nose, he was determined to get pay-back somehow.

Lottie suddenly felt hot as a sick panic rose inside her. She'd idolised Max as the perfect face of Yangtze, but if he took drugs then that changed everything. Were there to be any sort of drugs scandal and Yangtze discovered that she had known, then she would lose her job. But surely she needed more proof, than just an angry throw-away comment from Paul before she acted.

Tom whispered to his sister, 'the last time I saw Max he was snorting a line of coke. I hadn't liked to say anything, but there seems to be a pattern emerging.' Lottie groaned with the pain of the knowledge. The evidence was rapidly becoming too great for her to ignore.

Chapter 6

Dewerstone House looked amazing. Twinkling lights hung from the ceiling, and on the long table, beautifully laid for dinner, the glassware sparkled. Not only was it New Year's Eve, but it was also Verity Horton –Thomas' 21st birthday, and a winter ball was being held in her honour.

She'd been planning it for months and could barely contain her excitement now the day had finally arrived. It was such a novelty for her to be the centre of attention. Being that she was rather plain, studious, and quiet, she was naturally overlooked, and particularly so at parties. To make things even better, her best friend Indira was bringing her gorgeous older brother to be her date for the evening. The fact that Verity had met him before meant at least he wouldn't be disappointed – he knew what to expect.

Verity made her way back up to her bedroom, and for the hundredth time that day, checked that her beautiful black silk dress was still there. It was the most expensive thing she'd ever worn, and together with her grandmother's pearls, she knew she would look her best. Her wild mop of ginger hair had already been brought into line by a professional hairdresser, and her mother had arranged for a local beautician to come and do her makeup. With all the treatments completed she was too scared to scratch, eat or drink less she make a mess.

To kill time, she sat on her bed and re-read for the thousandth time the first ball scene from *Pride and Prejudice,* imagining herself in the place of Elizabeth Bennett, and the handsome but unobtainable Tom Marchbank as Mr Darcy. She'd had a secret crush on him ever since she'd developed an interest in the opposite sex, and although he was kind, he treated her more like a younger sister than a potential lover. She knew that because he was so clever, sexy, and sophisticated, he probably had hundreds of women throwing themselves at his feet, and certainly would never be interested in her. Even if, by some miracle, or blindness, he had fallen in love with her, her father would never allow them to be together. Her father's bitter hatred of Nick Marchbank, formed when they were teenagers, had never relented. Rupert's aunt had married Nick's uncle, so they were only tenuously related by marriage, but the fate of the Dewerstone estate trapped them into a lifetime of path-crossing.

On the death of Silas Marchbank twenty years earlier, Rupert had inherited Dewerstone, but only as a glorified caretaker. After all, he wasn't a Marchbank. The estate was supposed to have gone straight to Nick, but although Silas adored his nephew, he couldn't trust him not to blow the whole inheritance on drugs and booze. As a compromise the Dewerstone estate had been entailed to Tom upon reaching his 25th birthday.

Unfortunately, Rupert's hatred was so strong,

that it blinded his views on clever, hard-working, and sensible Tom. Rupert's opinion was simple. Tom was the offspring of Nick, and ultimately, given time and opportunity, would resort to type. Rupert refused to hear anything positive about the boy. If Rupert had had his way, neither Tom, his siblings or parents would be allowed anywhere near the house until the time came for Tom to take over. Although Tom did his utmost to stay out of the way, his uncle, the Duke of Chiswick, had other ideas and Nick's older brother was one person who Rupert was too scared to disagree with. The consequence of Crispin's demands meant that Rupert was afraid to exclude Nick and his family from any of the larger family social gatherings, and in the past, had led to disastrous results.

Verity placed her book down on the bed. She didn't know whether it was excitement or pre-date nerves, but she couldn't concentrate. She got up and started wandering aimlessly around the room, unsure of what to do to kill time. She had just got to the point where the wait was getting unbearable when she heard car tyres on the gravel driveway. Looking out the window she spotted Indira's mini pulling up outside. With a mixture of joy and relief, she tore downstairs in readiness to greet her friend.

The two girls embraced before Verity's attention was drawn to Ed, who was extracting the luggage from the boot. 'Happy birthday Verity, and may I say how lovely you are looking.' Ed smiled warmly as he dropped the bags and kissed her on the cheek.

'Its... err. lovely to see you. Um .. thanks for coming,' Verity stuttered in embarrassment.

'We've been looking forward to it. I can't think of anything nicer than to start the new year with great company and in a wonderful country house,' Ed replied.

Verity smiled, 'let me show you to your rooms so you can freshen up. Tea will be served in the drawing room at 4.30.'

'Thank you,' Ed replied. 'I have some emails to catch up on, so I'll see you both at tea. Until then I'm sure you two have loads of catching up to do.'

He is lovely, it's going to be so perfect, Verity thought to herself as she led the way towards the guest wing.

At Stapletor Beth was making the most of having her family all under one roof. Both Ben and Tom had come down for Christmas, and were staying for the New Year's Day hunt, before setting off back to London. Beth loved having everyone around to be made a fuss over and tried to make the most of every precious moment. She was however dreading Verity's party. No event where her husband and Rupert crossed paths ever went well.

Now Nick was older and calmer, off drugs and on the wagon, there was a chance that he would just blend into the background. Beth hoped he would behave himself but having been the centre of attention for most of his life, he was never going to stop being an extrovert. It would soon be time to get changed, so she hurried around finishing the dirty jobs before she cleaned herself up.

When she eventually made it upstairs, she opened the door of her bedroom to be greeted by the site of her husband, lounging on her bed, dressed only in his underpants, and smoking an enormous spliff.

'Is that a Camberwell Carrot?' she asked, as she glanced downwards and spotted his enormous erection.

'I made it especially for you darling,' Nick drawled.

'But I don't smoke.'

'I wasn't talking about that. Now come and comfort me before I have to meet my ghastly relations.'

Beth started to giggle as she started to feel the side-effects of the smoke. Climbing onto the bed, she slid behind him and started to massage his bare shoulders. She still found him so beautiful, that despite only having half an hour to get ready, she knew she had to have him right away.

The first guests to arrive at Dewerstone were Nick's older brother Crispin, the Duke of Chiswick, accompanied by his wife Felicity who turned up in an immaculate Range Rover, having driven down from London. Verity found Crispin even more intimidating than her father did, and secretly wished that they hadn't been invited. She was just relieved that his sons were still abroad as it saved the humiliation of them snubbing her. Fortunately, she didn't need to make small talk for long as the other guests began appearing in quick succession.

By the time dinner was announced most of those invited had turned up. With a little cajoling, Rupert and his wife Marina managed to shepherd everyone through to the dining room where the staff were able to direct people to their seats. Verity had purposely put herself on a table with her friends and younger family members, and well away from her parents.

There weren't even numbers of male and female, so Verity had placed Ed on her left and Indira on her right. Then were a couple more unattached girlfriends. Across the other side of the table she had seated Lottie, between her two brothers. For Verity it had been a strategic placing, as the gorgeous Tom was directly in her line of sight, but too far away for Verity to have to worry about making conversation.

As a result of previous misdemeanours, Nick and Beth were kept away from the top table which consisted of Rupert and Marina, their direct relatives, and Crispin and Felicity. This suited them well. Nick was so stoned he didn't know whether it was Christmas or Easter, and Beth was simply grateful that they were nowhere near Crispin who would have taken a dim view on the state of his younger sibling. It did mean that they were on the same table as her ex-husband Peter, but Lottie's recent success at least provided a mutually safe topic of conversation.

Verity didn't know Ed very well, just that he was into horses in a big way. She rode a little, but had never been particularly brave, but reckoned she could just about get away with making small talk. She was worried that he looked bored.

'Are you still competing with your horses?' she asked shyly.

'Oh yes, very much so. Managed to get over to Germany to complete at Mannheim in November, and then won a bit of money at London just before Christmas.'

Lottie, who'd been trying to listen in from across the table from the moment the word horse was mentioned, suddenly exclaimed aloud. 'Oh, are you Ed Carter?'

Rather taken aback, but pleasantly surprised that the attractive female sat opposite him was obviously a fan, replied smugly. 'Yes, but how did you guess?'

Lottie smiled mischievously, 'I was sat at Max Tarasov's kitchen table when Simon Palmer fixed up your lift.'

'Oh my God! So you're *the* Lottie, from Yangtze.' Ed could barely believe his luck. 'You've been the main topic of conversation on the British team circuit for the last two months. Well, it's lovely to meet you in person.'

Ed's mind started to work overtime. He just had to get to know her better. She would make a wonderful girlfriend. He knew he didn't stand a chance of being in the running for the major sponsorship deal, but with her knowledge and connections she could really help him. She was also stunningly attractive and evidently from an extremely well-off background. He decided to make a play for her.

With only the slightest hint of guilt at the fact he was completely failing in his duty as Verity's supposed date, Ed started the charm offensive. Beside him, Verity sat ignored whilst Indira, thinking her best friend was being looked after by Ed, had been concentrating on flirting with Ben. Verity had always been slightly envious of Lottie, who was older, far more confident, successful, and pretty. Noticing her distress, Tom interrupted the conversation between his sister and Ed.

'As you two have so much to chat about, why don't Ed and I swap places. Then you won't have to talk across the table, and I can spend some time with the birthday girl.'

As Tom came and sat by her, Verity could have cried with gratitude. Although Ed was good looking and well mannered, his conversation was limited, and was no loss in comparison to her beloved Tom. Within a few minutes Verity had totally overcome her nerves as they discussed their mutual love of literature.

It was only once dinner had finished and everyone began to make their way through to the ball room that Ed remembered he was supposed to be chaperoning Verity. He started explaining to Lottie about his obligation to their host but was relieved when she pointed out that her brother had taken over the role, and at that moment was leading Verity onto the floor for the first dance.

Nick had wandered out into the garden to smoke, but Beth couldn't help but notice the look of disapproval on Rupert's face as he watched her eldest son dance with their precious only daughter. She instantly felt a flash of irritation. Her own opinion was that Rupert should think himself lucky, bearing in mind that Tom was such a good catch. Beth liked Verity and could see that they would be well suited. Verity's quiet, studious nature suited Tom, although Beth wished that Verity had been a little prettier.

After a couple of dances, Ed and Lottie stopped and chatted. Ed was determined to make the most of Lottie's free advice and quizzed her on the best way to get sponsorship. She advised him to get several smaller sponsors at first and recommended a couple of horse box manufacturers to approach. Lottie was so passionate when talking about marketing, she forgot where she was as she spent the next half hour lecturing Ed on the best way to approach potential sponsors, what to offer them, and what they would look for as part of a deal.

Lottie was still talking when the band stopped for a break, and staff brought in plates in readiness for the birthday cake. Flutes of champagne cup were handed out for the toast. Nick, who hadn't touched alcohol all evening, gratefully accepted a glass, but was irritated to find a slice of fruit in the drink. Crossly, he pulled it out before flicking it out onto the floor.

The caterers then brought in the cake, aglow with 21 lit candles. As it was placed on the table, some indoor fireworks were set off to add to the theatre. Thrilled, Verity went up to the display and blew out the candles to the cheers of those around her. Rupert then joined her, and decided to make a short speech, extolling the virtues of his wonderful daughter. As he went to announce the toast, he realised that his wife Marina was still at the back of the room, so he summoned her to join them.

Marina was a well-built woman who shunned attention, but reluctantly she agreed to join them. Conscious that everyone was waiting for her, she hurried across the dance floor. Almost reaching the table, she suddenly slipped on the discarded fruit slice and landed with a thud on the floor. Falling heavily on her ankle, she cried out in pain. The room fell silent as everyone looked on in horror. The hushed silence was broken by the unexpected sound of laughter. Everyone looked across at Nick, who was bent double in an uncontrollable fit of giggles.

'Shit. I've brought down the elephant in the room.' Nick said loudly.

Immediately the room was filled with the sound of disapproving mutterings, as well as those expressing concern over Marina, still on the floor and in considerable discomfort. Nick, still laughing, was being ushered outside by Beth who was mortified by her husband's behaviour. It wasn't that he was unfeeling, it was just that he was too stoned to act appropriately, and she could hardly call out, *sorry, my husband's off his face on skunk.*

One of the guests was a trained nurse and concluded that Marina's ankle was fractured and therefore she needed treatment. Marina hated making a fuss and refused to allow Rupert to call an ambulance for something so minor. To make up for her stepfather's black mark, Lottie offered to take Marina to casualty on the basis that she hadn't been drinking, and both Rupert and Verity still had their guests to see too. Ed offered to accompany them, and reluctantly Marina agreed to go. Lottie suddenly realised that her car was still at home, so plucking up the courage, she asked Nick's brother if she could borrow the Range Rover on the basis that they were staying at Dewerstone.

Having been handed the keys, Lottie went to bring the Range Rover closer to the house, whilst Ed waited by the door, ready to help Marina to the car. Moments later Marina hobbled to the door, leaning on a pair of ancient crutches. She was in a great deal of pain, but desperate not to be a nuisance and embarrassed by her heaviness, insisted that she could manage.

Ed jumped into the front passenger seat, and they set off carefully down the driveway. Poor Marina kept apologising for ruining Lottie's evening despite her protest that she really didn't mind, and that it was a great excuse to drive a posh car.

'Anyway, 'Lottie added, 'I should be the one apologising after yet another spectacularly inappropriate performance by my step-father. I'm quite sure he didn't mean to be offensive, but

Mum says he's totally wasted on skunk I'm afraid.'

'What really!' Ed was shocked. His own parents were so straight laced, he couldn't imagine charming Lottie having such a reprobate father.

'It's quite all right,' Marina said. 'I understand. It's not as if Nick's behaviour is anything new. To be honest, if he were to behave himself at a family event it would be almost a disappointment.' She gave a small laugh, before once more wincing with pain.

Before long they had reached the hospital. Lottie drove up to the entrance of A&E, and Ed jumped out before running inside and commandeering a wheelchair. Marina wriggled off the back seat, to stand on the pavement on her good leg. When the wheelchair arrived, she managed to get herself into it, before Ed wheeled her inside, and Lottie found somewhere to park.

Being a typical New Year's Eve, half the casualty department was made up of drunks. It was noisy and unpleasant, and they were stuck there for well over an hour before Marina was called for. After that Marina was quickly taken to x-ray, and Lottie and Ed were able to go to a quieter area to chat.

'Is your stepfather some sort of elderly party animal?' Ed was desperate to find out more.

'It started when he was sixteen. One summer his family were away, and instead of coming to Dewerstone, he stayed in London where he started going to a dubious local night club. There he fell in with a bad crowd who got him using heroin. By the time he went back to Eton he was injecting.'

'Bloody Hell,' Ed exclaimed, 'Do carry on.'

'He went into rehab where my grandmother worked – that's how he met mum – they bumped into each other in the reception area. For a long time he was just a heavy drinker who partied a lot, but being an addict he succumbed to alcoholism. It was at that time that he opened the night club Lizzies.'

'That's your stepfather. I had no idea.'

'Lizzies is named after my mum.'

'But that's one of the coolest clubs in London. That's awesome.' Ed was impressed.

'Anyway, over the years Nick has been in an out of rehab, having nearly killed himself on cocaine and vodka. He's got so much liver damage now that he must be good, but there are occasions...' Lottie tailed off.'Well you get the picture.'

Ed was now certain that he'd done the right thing in targeting Lottie. Having heard enough he switched the conversation back to himself.

'My aim this year is to rent my own yard and get more rides. It's what I need to make myself look like a serious contender.'

'Most of the top riders do seem to have huge numbers of horses,' Lottie agreed.

'The plan is to follow Marcus Wallis' business strategy. I need to attract a couple of generous owners, then the decent sponsors should follow. Marcus reckons he needs about four grand a week to hold everything together. He gets a fair amount of income from bringing on youngsters then selling them at a premium once they've won a bit of money.'

'Marcus certainly seems very hard working and dedicated,' Lottie agreed.

'Unlike Maxim Tarasov who seems to treat show jumping like a glorified hobby of course,' Ed said with a small amount of bitterness in his voice.'

'Don't you like him?' Lottie asked, sounding surprised.

'He's OK in small doses, but everyone else finds it a bit frustrating that he gets everything handed to him on a plate.'

'He is genuinely talented. He is wonderful with Zhivago,' Lottie suddenly felt the urge to defend him.

'Oh, I'd never knock his ability,' Ed hurriedly backtracked. 'But in all fairness, he has plenty of time to get the best from his horses. He doesn't spend three quarters of his life flying around Europe trying to please sponsors and owners by appearing at every senior show jumping event in existence. Maxim is bankrolled by his father. We've all wondered whether Maxim would carry on as a professional show jumper if he had to put in the hours of graft that everyone else does. He only has his few select horses, so he has time for socialising.'

Lottie gave a conciliatory smile and was about to agree that he had a valid point when she was distracted by the TV in the corner of the room. It was the New Year countdown. As Big Ben struck midnight Ed and Lottie kissed for the first time. It started off tentatively, but gradually became stronger and passionate. 'It's probably just as well we are stuck here, otherwise I'm not sure I could be accountable for my actions,' Ed whispered.

Lottie giggled. She was still rather inexperienced with men, and relationships with fit, sexy men simply didn't happen to her. Lottie glanced up at the TV screen, the fireworks on the screen were a physical manifestation of her own emotions. She was suddenly brought back to reality by a nurse approaching them.

'Just thought I'd let you know; your mother will be ready to go home soon,' the nurse said kindly.

'Thank you,' Lottie replied gratefully, not bothering to correct the misunderstanding.

She sat back down and Ed copied her. Feeling that Ed was now on her side, and therefore likely to be truthful, she decided to risk asking him the burning question about Max. 'Ed, will you answer me truthfully. There is something I need to ask you?' He looked puzzled, 'Yes of course.'

'I've heard rumours about Maxim having a cocaine habit. I wondered how much truth there is in it. I know it's not directly any of my business, but with the sponsorship...' she trailed off.

Ed hesitated, quickly weighing up the options. There would be no direct benefit to be gained from Maxim losing out on the sponsorship. Ed decided to answer in a way that showed himself in the best possible light – as fair and non-judgemental. Lottie mistook his hesitation for a thorough recall of events.

'Well,' Ed said cautiously, 'there was one occasion – it was Frederick Seipp's birthday party. Maxim was off his head that night. I'm no expert, but I reckon his behaviour wasn't just down to alcohol. As to what he'd taken – I don't know.... But who's to say his drink hadn't been spiked.' He stopped to check Lottie's reaction. He thought she looked tense.

'Other than that, there was no evidence of drug taking. I spent a week with him in his lorry, and if there had been a stash of white powder anywhere, I'm sure I'd have found it.'

'Thank you,' Lottie sounded relieved. 'It's not that I wish to be judgemental, especially given whom my stepfather is, but I simply couldn't put Yangtze in a position where they put their name to a rider that was involved in any sort of drugs scandal.'

At that moment Marina appeared, being pushed in a wheelchair by one of the nurses. Her ankle was heavily bandaged, and she had been issued with some modern crutches. She looked cheerful, glad to be going home.

Chapter 7

Three weeks later Lottie arrived at the luxury five-star hotel in the Cotswolds for the weekend where the Yangtze directors were to meet the shortlisted group of show jumpers. She was exhausted, having found the organisation and preparation to be far harder than she could ever have imagined.

Lottie's relationship with Ed had been limited to long distance communication, and much to his irritation, she hadn't had any time to help him with his search for sponsors. She suspected that his friendship was almost entirely self-serving, but her life was so full-on and exciting, she wasn't particularly concerned.

Having checked in to her room, Lottie changed into her office clothes before making her way back down to the reception foyer. As per her instructions, a desk and chair had been set up for her to use for meeting and greeting her guests. She retrieved the Yangtze sponsorship banner from the back of her car, and the welcome packs with the itinerary for each guest.

Having set everything up, she didn't have to wait long before Simon arrived, dressed very smartly in blazer and flannel trousers. He was followed by Marcus and Tracey, who lived the closest to the hotel. Lottie had just sorted them out when the Yangtze helicopter landed. For the next half an hour Lottie was kept busy with two Chinese VIPs, their translator, and Florian, the head of marketing for Europe.

Karen Allen arrived with Paul Denton, having shared a lift, quickly followed by husband-and-wife team Mary and Giles Downing-Dunn, who were in excellent spirits and clearly looking forward to an all-expenses paid weekend away.

Lottie waited a further hour, but there was no sign of Max. She couldn't decide between anger and disappointment at his rudeness. With an air of resignation, she tidied away, leaving his information pack with the reception desk, should he arrive late. She made her way back up to her room to get ready for dinner.

Having showered and changed, Lottie was about to make her way back down, when the phone rang. It was the duty manager to say that Mr Tarasov had called to say he was caught in a tail back on the M4 due to an accident but was on his way. Lottie was so relieved she almost cried. Stunningly handsome Max was the face of her entire campaign, and the thought that he couldn't be bothered to even attend the weekend had been almost unbearable.

Lottie managed to get dinner service delayed for half an hour, which gave Max time to arrive. Lottie's previous feelings of loathing were hurriedly replaced by adoration as Max apologised profusely for the delay and charmed his way into everyone's' good books. She also noticed that he'd gone to the effort of dressing in a beautifully tailored Saville Row suit.

To make things fair, Lottie had divided the showjumpers into two groups. Max, Giles, and Karen were to sit with the Yangtze directors the first evening, whilst Paul, Mary and Marcus sat with Lottie, Simon and Tracey. The plan was to switch the groups the following evening. Lottie had planned it very carefully. Her priority had been to keep apart Paul and Max, although her second thought was to put those riders most likely to drink too much with the directors on the first night, where there was less time to get inebriated.

As the first course was being served, Lottie was pleased to hear Giles laughing loudly from across the room. 'Sorry about my husband,' Mary said. 'He'll be chuckling at his own jokes. Unfortunately, once a friend of ours was foolish enough to tell Giles that he found him hilarious. Alas Giles has been dining out on it ever since. Those poor Chinese gentlemen look quite scared.'

Lottie and Simon immediately turned around, but the Yangtze directors looked fine. Max was chatting to Florian and appeared happy and relaxed. Karen, however looked miserable, and out of place.'She looks like a bulldog chewing a wasp,' Paul offered. 'I've owned horses with shorter faces.'

'Do you think it's her time of the month?' Marcus asked.

'What are you implying?' Tracey snapped at her husband.

'Forgot you were here my sweet,' Marcus cringed. 'Not that you ever change when you're due on,' he added hastily.

After three amazing courses, coffee, and mints, both groups made their way back to the bar, but as most people had had their usual early starts, the party broke up early.

The next morning after a sumptuous breakfast the six riders were taken to a local 4*4 off road adventure track where they were given a chance to put the Intrepid through its paces. To create more of a challenge, they were put into two teams with Marcus heading up Paul and Mary, whilst Giles was team leader over Max and Karen.

The course involved driving up and down steep inclines, woodland tracks and a very muddy river crossing. The competition was intense; for horsey people, four-wheel drive vehicles and mud went hand in hand. After the first four drivers had been Paul was in the lead, with Giles a few seconds behind him. Karen had a respectable time in third place whilst Mary was rather slower back in forth position.

Marcus was the next to go and complained that he was being handicapped as Tracey was insisting on accompanying him.'I should get at least five seconds off my time,' he moaned, 'I've got to put up with a back seat driver, plus all the additional weight.'

'You pig – just you wait.' Tracey hissed.

'There's no time allowance,' ruled Simon, 'but there will be a time penalty if you fail to start in the next sixty seconds,' he added to prevent a domestic.

Marcus clocked up a very respectable time despite his handicap and ended up in second place, one second behind Paul. Last to go was Max. His team were trailing and needed him to get a good time. Knowing how ruthlessly competitive Max was, his team were confident of victory.

Simon lowered the starting flag but instead of the Intrepid roaring away in a cloud of dust, Max stalled the engine. Cursing, he hurriedly restarted before pulling away cautiously. The trouble was that unlike the others who effectively managed farms, Max had never had to do anything remotely agricultural. The only vehicles he'd ever driven were sports cars or horse lorries. Having no real idea about off road driving, he went too slowly and twice got the vehicle stuck in mud.

'Christ, Max drives like he's a bloody hairdresser,' Giles said in despair and disbelief.

When Max eventually reached the finish line he was greeted by mock cheers from the opposing team, and irritation by Giles who hated losing.

Over lunch Max became the butt of jokes by Paul and Marcus. 'Who taught you to drive, Saga Motoring?' asked Giles. Paul followed with, 'Did you imagine you were doing a remake of the film 'Driving Miss Daisy'?

Once everyone had finished eating, they got changed into their riding gear before filing back into the minibus which took them to a large equestrian centre for a game of indoor polo. To make up team numbers Simon and Lottie got the chance to join in. As their team was behind, Giles had first choice and making it obvious what little value he put on Lottie, gloated at the opportunity to secure Simon.

Marcus was more gracious in accepting Lottie on his team. Lottie gave away nothing but was secretly confident. Although her first love was show jumping, and big, powerful Taggart was no polo pony, her brothers both adored the sport and over the years she had developed into a half decent player, partly from countless demands to help make up numbers, but also having played at university.

When they arrived at the location, 8 polo ponies were already tacked up and waiting for them, their grooms finding the whole experience highly amusing. Max and Marcus pushed themselves forward and insisted on riding the fieriest looking ponies, whilst Karen insisted that she wanted something steady due to her terrible hand eye coordination. The first twenty minutes were spent with the showjumpers learning how to handle a polo stick and everyone practised hitting the ball. They were all hopeless, although Giles was the one who performed best. Simon was rusty, but soon got back into the swing of things. Lottie could have hit the ball from a gallop, so found approaching in trot quite strange. She didn't want to give herself away however and pretended that her skill was simply beginners' luck.

Once everyone had just about grasped the essentials of the game, an attempt was made to play a chukka. Simon, as the only experienced player took charge of his team, then Marcus offered Lottie the opportunity to lead, suspecting that she was far more experienced than she'd let on. Although the arena was large, it was nowhere near big enough for a proper game of high-speed polo, so Lottie had to limit her speed to that of a steady canter. Luckily her pony was sensible, and didn't seem to mind, however Marcus and Max's more fiery mounts were getting frustrated at the lack of action and kept spinning around and napping sideways which wasn't very conducive to hitting a ball. With Paul and Karen in defence, this left Mary and Giles up front with their team captains.

Lottie was used to far tougher competition and quickly pushed through to score the first goal. A couple of minutes later she got another, but after that things got harder as Simon and Giles switched from trying to score, to simply blocking her. Although they weren't great at hitting the ball, as top riders they were very good at getting in her way. After a few minutes Simon summoned Max to take over as blocker whilst he attempted to even the score. Paul initially did a good job in defence, although he looked hot and sweaty as he'd refused to remove his beloved padded jacket, but eventually Simon found a way through to the goal.

Whilst their team celebrated, Lottie managed to snatch the ball. Tearing up the arena, she scored her third. Crossly, Simon came back up to the middle, practically knocking over Mary's horse. In the confusion, the ball ended up in front of Simon's goal. Max rushed down to hit it in but missed completely. As he turned his horse back on itself, the ball got caught under its legs. It kicked out in annoyance, knocking the ball into the mouth of the goal. Max started to celebrate, but Paul remarked that his horse was better at playing polo than its rider.

After more shoving and pushing the game finished. Lottie, Marcus, Paul, and Mary were declared winners, both of the polo and the day's activities. Having now gained respect from the professional riders, Lottie began to feel more confident around them. Back at the hotel, whilst the riders were having their complimentary de-stress massages, Lottie went for a swim in the pool as she wanted to make the most of the luxurious hotel facilities.

Having spent far longer in the pool than she had initially intended, Lottie had to rush to change before meeting everyone for pre-dinner drinks. The Chinese directors had spent the morning watching the off-road driving, but as horses didn't feature in their direct agenda, had flown off for a factory visit in the afternoon. The polo had been recorded on video, and the directors did enjoy watching the highlights on a large screen. Lottie was summoned over whilst their translator explained that they had been impressed with her riding, and that reflected well on the company.

Amongst the pre-dinner drinks a special rice-wine was being served. Known for being somewhat hallucinogenic, it was popular amongst the Chinese business community. Florian, having had a previous bad experience, warned Lottie away from it, but reckoned that everyone else could take their chance. Lottie was concerned about Karen who'd been very quiet the whole weekend. Suspecting that Karen was unwell, she decided to pass on the information about the lethal drink, which to the uninitiated looked harmless. Karen seemed grateful but barely responded.'I know it's none of my business, but are you OK? Do you feel unwell?' Lottie asked.

'I'm fine,' Karen replied, however, she didn't look it. She sighed, and looked as if she wanted to say something, but stopped herself.'Would it help to talk?' Lottie asked. Karen nodded.

Being as discrete as possible, they slipped out into the foyer and found a quiet alcove.'Just before I left to come here this weekend, I found out that I'm pregnant,' Karen said.

'I did wonder when I saw you sticking to soft drinks,' Lottie replied. 'How do you feel about it?'

'Bloody gutted to be honest. It wasn't exactly part of my career plan, and Jacq and I split up a few weeks ago. The baby is his, but he's hardly going to come rushing back to me wanting to play happy families.

'Are you going to keep it?'

'My parents will expect me to. They will be angry that I've got pregnant but would never forgive me if I had an abortion.'

'Could you just not tell them?'

'I guess so. I haven't really got my head around it yet. I'm just not very good a lying, and it's not as if I don't ever want a kid – I just wasn't planning on having one yet.'

'Just make sure that the decision is right for you. Forget what anyone else thinks. It's your life after all. At least you are in a sport that doesn't have a limited time span. You could have ten children and still have a good show jumping career afterwards.'

Karen smiled for the first time in days. 'Thanks. I'm glad I told you. I think I would have exploded if I hadn't told someone soon.'

'Any time you want an unbiased opinion, just let me know. I've always admired you as a rider, so it would be an honour to be a sounding board.'

'Of course, it means I'm out of the running regarding the sponsorship deal,' Karen added ruefully.

'The final decision isn't being made until May, by which time you will have made your mind up about what you are doing. Until then I won't say anything.'

'I appreciate it. Cheers,' Karen replied.

Back in the function room, everyone was having a good time, the rice wine having had its desired effect. Lottie grabbed herself a mineral water before scanning the room for someone to talk to. She was immediately approached by Max, who had barely spoken a word to her since his arrival the evening before.

''I had no idea you were a good polo player?' he said.

'I'm not very – everything is relative. It was good fun though.'

'Would you like to come back to my room later for a night cap? We can take turns at playing horse and jockey?'

Lottie, so shocked by his directness, nearly

choked on her water.'Christ, you don't mess around do you? Hasn't anyone told you about the subtle art of gentle seduction?'

'Can't say I've ever needed to,' Max replied. 'Are you up for it then?'

'No, definitely not,' Lottie said, failing to hide the indignation from her voice.

Max clearly wasn't used to being rejected and seemed momentarily lost for words.

'Am I not your type or something?'

'That's got nothing to do with it. It would be unprofessional. If you get selected it would be argued that you had an unfair advantage, and that I was biased.'

'So will you sleep with me once the selection process is over?'

'It's still no. Whilst I'm in charge of this 3-year project I will never sleep with you,' Lottie insisted. Without bothering to reply, Max shrugged indifferently then turned and headed off back towards the bar, where he immediately started flirting with a pretty waitress.

The meal went without any major incident. As expected, Marcus seemed to make a good impression on the directors. Paul looked to be out of his comfort zone, but behaved himself, and Mary appeared relaxed. Meanwhile on Lottie's table, Giles announced that he regretted his team selection procedure, and in future would do his homework first.

Max continued to flirt with the female waiting staff. A couple of times he caught her looking at him, but each time his response was a barely perceptible ice-cold glare. The more Max drank, the more he began to goad her; making loaded comments about frigid bloody bitches destined to end up as sad, lonely, dried-up old hags. By this point he was noticeably very drunk, but as he kept rubbing his unfocused eyes in the hope of clearing his blurred vision, it was evident that his spiteful comments were aimed at Lottie. Having gone from pinning her hopes on him as the poster boy for Yangtze, she now wanted to stick pins in every picture of his smug arrogant face. As she sat there, she mused to herself that if she merely suggested that there may be an association between him with drug taking, his chances of selection would be blown out the water. Whether he realised it or not, he'd picked a fight with the wrong person.

The next morning as everyone met for breakfast, most people looked worse for wear. Giles looked particularly hung-over. Max too looked tired, but with his bloodshot eyes hidden behind dark glasses, he boasted that it was due entirely to his long night love making session with a particularly hot waitress. Lottie noted that he'd taken care to ensure that she had been in earshot as he made his announcement. Lottie began to visualise a Max doll with pins penetrating certain parts of his anatomy.

Chapter 8

The following weekend Lottie was back focusing on her own, less glamorous show jumping ambitions. Along with three of her friends from the local riding club, they attended the regional team show jumping event at a nearby equestrian centre. For once luck was on their side and they won the open class. This meant the team would now have to travel up to Buckinghamshire in April for the National championships. For Lottie this was going to be her first time properly away with Taggart, and really was the icing on the cake for what had already started as an amazing year.

Two weeks later Lottie was back competing in the British Show jumping Foxhunter championship class. It was her second year of competing at that height, and although she often got lower places, had never been fast enough to win through to the ultimate final at horse of the year show.

Unbeknown to Lottie, Max had also decided to attend the same show, albeit without a horse. He had been hunting for a decent Grand Prix level horse for several weeks now, and earlier that day had driven down to Cornwall to view a potential top jumping stallion. Unfortunately, when he'd arrived the horse was found to be lame in a hind leg, nothing too serious, but it meant he couldn't ride it. Rather than waste the entire day, he googled the nearest British Show jumping event, and found one in Devon, close to the A30 which was the route home. Although he wasn't particularly interested in buying another novice horse, he hoped the Foxhunter class may offer up some untapped potential.

Max didn't want to draw attention to himself, so when he arrived at the equestrian centre he put on a Toggi baseball cap and an old waxed jacket he kept in the boot of his Aston Martin. He'd deliberately parked away from the horse boxes and managed to walk through into the public viewing area without being spotted.

Max watched with interest, but the calibre of horses in the class didn't excite him sufficiently for him to warrant making an offer. He was about to give up and continue his journey when he heard Lottie's name being announced over the tanoy. Highly amused at the thought of seeing her riding, he decided to wait.

He'd expected to see Lottie on a little dainty thoroughbred type, so was surprised when she entered the arena on a large, powerful dapple-grey gelding. Horse and rider began with a steady canter around the arena, before effortlessly sailing over the first fence. Max watched intently as Lottie and Taggart jumped a good solid clear round. The fences weren't small, but the horse clearly had massive scope, and obviously loved to jump. Max thought it was ironic that the one horse he'd seen all day that was worthy of buying belonged to the one woman who drove him mad with frustration.

Wondering how to approach her, Max made his way to the café for a coffee and something to eat whilst he devised a plan of attack. As he gave his order the show jumping enthusiast who owned the equestrian centre recognised him. Max was explaining that he was horse hunting as Lottie entered the café, unnoticed, looking for a chocolate fix and some polos for Taggart.

'The only ride I've seen today that interests me is unavailable,' he complained to the centre owner.

'Oh the big grey. Yes, he's a nice sort. Wouldn't mind him myself. There have been plenty of offers made for him but he isn't for sale. May be for the right price...'he stopped mid-sentence as Lottie approached.

'Hi Lottie. Didn't expect to bump into you so soon. You jumped well,' Max decided on a less direct approach, having failed with her before. Alarmed, she spun around to look at him. 'Thanks. That's praise indeed from you,' Lottie replied reddening slightly with embarrassment.

'Max wants to know if you'd sell him your horse?' the centre owner asked.

Lottie was taken aback, 'oh, er... well that's very flattering, but no I'd never sell him. Besides, he isn't exactly in Zhivago's league.'

'Maybe not, but he has power and loves his job which is half the battle,' Max answered. 'I could soon make him up to a grade A, and he'd be a useful addition to my team.'

'I am pleased that you like Taggart, but I've had him since a foal, and he is the only man in my life, so I could never get rid of him,' jokingly she added, 'but if by some freak of misfortune your father suddenly disowned you and you didn't have a horse to ride, I may lend him to you.'

Max smiled warmly, 'Well thank you for that at least. I no longer feel that I've completely wasted my time. Now would you like me to give you some advice on how to ride the jump off course?'

'Yes, OK. Thank you,' Lottie responded.

'Please don't think I'm being presumptuous in assuming I know more than you,' he added hastily, hoping she didn't think he was patronising her.

'No, I'm glad for help. After all, if I was an expert, I wouldn't be stuck never proceeding beyond the first round of the Foxhunter championship.' Lottie smiled warmly, her desire to stick pins in his effigy having temporarily evaporated.

Max grabbed his coffee and accompanied Lottie back to her small, scruffy horse box, where Taggart stood dozing. To keep the conversation on neutral territory Lottie told Max about the riding club championships. ` It's my first time away with Taggart and I'm really looking forward to it,' she exclaimed, her voice animated with excitement.

'When is it?' Max asked.

'Second weekend in April.'

'How are you all getting there?'

'Not sure yet – probably each make our own way there.'

'Bear with me a moment,' Max smiled. He grabbed his iPhone from his inside pocket and started thumbing through it. With his attention focused on his phone, Lottie took the opportunity to have a proper look at him without feeling embarrassed. His normal, arrogant features appeared softer, and the usual haughty expression had mellowed. Lottie suddenly found herself fighting an overwhelming desire to kiss him.

'You know I floored Denton at Christmas?'

'It was one of the highlights of the evening.'

'Unfortunately the British Show jumping board didn't view it in the same generous light, and I've been given a two-week ban – as it happens it's the first two weeks in April. So, I come back from the Spanish sunshine tour, and then it's a fortnight's forced shut down before a Nations Cup in Düsseldorf. It means my lorry will be sat around doing nothing if you'd like to all travel together in style.'

'Wow that's very generous of you,' Lottie exclaimed, 'but I can't imagine any of the team having a HGV license.'

'I was intending to throw in Lee as part of the package. I won't be around, but Lee is all anyone needs. And before you refuse because it would be seen as bribery, it isn't. It's my way of apologising for being a dickhead.'

As the jump off started Max sat with Lottie and they watched the first couple of competitors.

Max talked her through how to ride the course. She then left him sitting in the viewing gallery whilst she fetched Taggart and started to warm him up in the practice arena. She usually had butterflies in her stomach prior to jumping, but now, knowing that Max would be watching, the butterflies had turned into giant toads. Her heart was pounding, and she felt clammy and sweaty.

As she entered the arena, Lottie thought she may pass out with fear, but Taggart ignored his rider's sudden nerves, his ears pricked forward expectantly as he saw the jumps in front of him. As they waited for the starting bell to ring, Lottie's mind suddenly went blank. She could barely remember the course, let alone Max's instructions. Almost on autopilot Lottie steered Taggart towards the start. As he broke into canter she managed to snap out of her dazed state just in time to jump the first fence. Heading Max's instructions, she turned tightly between the 3rd and 4th fence, but losing impulsion, Taggart clipped the fence and brought down a pole. They finished in a fast time, much better than they'd ever done before, but of course the 4 faults meant they were out of the placings.

As they left the arena, Max was there to meet them. 'You need to get Taggart lighter in front. If he'd been less on his forehand he'd have cleared that fence. Still, a good try.'

Lottie dismounted, and Taggart immediately rubbed his head on her back, leaving white hairs on her jacket. She gave him some polos, then flicking the reins over his head she led him back to the lorry.

'I do appreciate the advice,' she said to Max. 'Sorry I messed up.'

'Look, I've had years of practice, and I've been taught by some of the top riders in the world. Maybe once the Yangtze selection process is over and things aren't so political, you could bring Taggart up to my yard for a week, and I'll give you both some one-on-one tuition...and with no hidden agenda.'

Lottie grinned, 'It's a tempting offer, thank you.'

'So long as your boyfriend doesn't mind – I'd have thought he'd have offered to give you some lessons.'

Lottie looked confused. Then it suddenly dawned on her, 'Sorry, do you mean Ed Carter?'

'I'd heard on the grapevine that you were his latest mount.'

Feeling herself going bright red Lottie hurriedly replied, 'God. No. Nothing like that. We happened to meet up at a New Year's Eve party. We did get on, but he just wanted my help to get him a sponsor.'

'Surely not even Ed can have imagined that he could have shagged his way to the Yangtze deal?'

'Shagging was never on offer,' Lottie replied hotly. 'He just wanted to pick my brains. Unfortunately, I've been so busy with Yangtze I haven't been much help, and the distinct lack of recent communication would imply that I've outlived my usefulness.'

'Well, I'm glad. He's a sponger and you

deserve better. And before you tell me to mind my own business, I'd better get going. I've a long drive.' He headed off towards the top end of the car park, but before he'd got out of earshot he called back, 'I won't forget my promises. I just want you to forgive me.'

'You're already forgiven,' Lottie shouted back cheerfully.

Max was as good as his word and the day before the competition, Lee turned up with the lorry ready to take the four women and their horses to the riding club championships. The group were so excited to be travelling in the glorious, plush lorry, which really enhanced the fun of the road trip. Lee was friendly and helpful, and showed no sign of resentment at having been volunteered by his boss into ferrying a bunch of over excited females and their horses.

Once they were on the motorway, the team members took it in turns to make Lee snacks and hot drinks. They were only allowed one quick rest break as Lee was concerned about the tachograph time limits. When they stopped for fuel, Lee was under strict instructions not to accept any payment from Lottie or her friends. Instead, they saved the money to give to Lee as a tip.

Once they were back in the cab, and heading back onto the motorway, Lottie was sat beside Lee, giving her a chance to study him. Of indeterminate age, Lottie could only guess that he was in his early to mid-thirties. Wiry, fit and with a weather worn face, he looked like he didn't have

110

an ounce of spare flesh on him. Although Lee's skin had never seen moisturiser, he had an open, kind face and Lottie quickly warmed to him. He drove the lorry with as much care for the girls' horses as he would a cargo load of international show jumpers, and for that Lottie was grateful.

When they arrived at the show-ground, they created a huge stir amongst fellow competitors. With the Tarasov name, and international show jumping logos emblazoned on the side of the huge Scania, it was never going to make a subtle entrance. Lottie noticed the look of disappointment from onlookers when four young women with bog standard horses unloaded.

Once they had settled their horses in the temporary stables, Max's other groom Fran appeared in her car ready to pick Lee up and take him back to Surrey. That evening, laden with chocolates, pizza, and wine, the four teammates sat in the lorry, watching satellite TV, whilst many of their fellow competitors shivered in tents, or in the back of their small transit vans.

When Lottie headed off to check on Taggart later that evening, one group of women from a neighbouring lorry appeared at the same moment. One of them turned to Lottie and said, 'So how come your staying in Max Tarasov's lorry?'

'He's a good friend of mine.' Lottie replied politely.

'Oh, come off it,' the woman muttered rather aggressively. 'You expect us to believe that?'

Lottie grinned in amusement at the stupidity. 'So, you'd rather believe that we've just taken the

111

lorry without him noticing?'

The woman glared but didn't reply. Shrugging, Lottie headed off to the stables.

Lottie managed a double clear the next day, much to her delight, and the others got eight faults between them. Overall their team came 3rd, which was amazing given the standard of the competition. Once the prize giving was finished, they cleaned out their stables and brought the horses back to the lorry in preparation to load. They'd just finished getting ready when they heard the roar of a sports car engine. Seconds later, driving towards them was a fabulous Aston Martin car driven by Max himself, having offered to bring Lee back.

He jumped out of the car and headed straight for Lottie. Having kissed her on both cheeks he asked how they'd got on. All the women excitedly waved their rosettes at him.

'Well done,' he said kindly.

Having loaded the horses, the team individually thanked Max for his generosity, both in terms of the lorry and the fuel.

'I'm just glad I could help. I've been giving Lottie a hard time over the sponsorship, so I owed her a favour.' He then produced a bottle of sparkling wine from the boot of his car and insisted that they all have a celebratory drink. Sadly, for Lottie, who was so thrilled to see him, Max then had to shoot back to see to his horses. Having said goodbye, they too headed off back to Devon.

Chapter 9

After his third place at the World Cup final, Max's prize-winning fund bank balance was the healthiest ever, and for the first time in his career he had reached the top 10 in the FEI world rankings.

With a couple of days off before travelling to Dublin, Max had popped up to London to visit Cindy. Lying in bed with his beautiful girlfriend curled up beside him, he couldn't help but think that life didn't get much better than this.

'I'm thinking of having a party,' he drawled lazily.

'When?' Cindy answered with enthusiasm.

'End of May. Everyone's going to be in London for the British leg of the Longines World Series. We could have it at Dad's house. I'm sure he won't mind.'

'Why does everything always have to revolve around show jumping?' Cindy asked sulkily.

'Because it's my career, and the other competitors are my friends.'

'But they are all so boorish and dull.'

'Well, I don't much like your friends either,' Max retorted irritably.

'At least they are interesting.'

'They're freaks.'

'They are intelligent and artistic with a conversation range that extends beyond four hooves.'

Max could see her point. 'I'm sure you'll be

inviting plenty of them to the party, so they can entertain you. Then I won't feel guilty, will I?'

'We must have a theme?' Cindy announced, having regained her enthusiasm.

'Really?'

Cindy decided to test the water, 'What about making it an engagement party?'

'I don't know anyone who's getting engaged?'

Cindy looked at him in despair. 'I meant us.'

Max swallowed hard. 'I'm not sure I'm ready for all the marriage stuff yet.'

'You are about to spend 2 weeks away on Charlie's stag bash. He's your age. And I'm not prepared to hang around too much longer. If I want to have children, I need to get on with it. I'm sure your Dad would be delighted.'

Max laughed, 'Come off it Cindy, you're hardly an earth mother type. In fact, let's face it, we'd make terrible parents.'

'I'm sure I could change,' Cindy replied quietly, trying to hide the hurt.

'But I love you for exactly the reason that you are always the same.' Max slapped her arse playfully as he got out of bed.

As Max showered, Cindy's suggestion played on his mind. He adored her, but she wasn't marriage material. A show jumper's wife needed to be sensible and uncomplaining. Also, genetically they would be a disaster. Any offspring would be beautiful but would probably die of a drug overdose before they reached twenty. He also had unfinished business with Lottie Wilkins. In fact, although he didn't like to admit

114

it, she was becoming a bit of an obsession, and rarely far from his mind. If he didn't have her soon, he felt he would go quite mad.

Whilst Max was away in Ireland jumping, Cindy started the preparations for the party. She decided against pushing for an engagement, feeling that Max needed time for the concept to sink in. Instead, she worked on his father. She charmed Ivan into allowing them the use of his house for the party. As it happened, the weekend they'd chosen, Ivan had planned to be in Scotland. Cindy hinted at the possibility of an engagement, but much to her frustration, Ivan seemed to deliberately overlook the suggestion.

Max and his speed horse Lenny had a successful week at the Dublin show, and his young horse Harvey gave a good performance, getting himself a respectable lower placing. Meanwhile Cindy went on a spending spree with Max's Amex card, having hired London's most prestigious party organisers. Using her contacts, pulling several strings, and then parting with a great deal of cash she managed to secure the services of chart-topping DJ Ian Masters. Once Max returned home having managed to secure a list of competitors for the London show jumping, he and Cindy sent out invitations, although Cindy insisted that for every show jumper invited, she could have her own guest. Max stipulated that they also invited a few of his old-school friends and made sure that he slipped in an invitation to

Lottie.

Three weeks later came the long-awaited London leg of the World Series, with the Olympic Park as the spectacular venue. There was a great atmosphere, helped by the massive prize fund. The competition had even sparked interest amongst the normally indifferent media, and the BBC had film crews capturing the main competition. For riders such as Max and Paul, who'd been too young and in-experienced to be selected for London 2012, this was the closest thing to it.

Zhivago had been rested since the world cup and was literally boiling over with excitement in the first round. When too fresh, Zhivago generally over jumped even the largest fences, but being head strong he would try to rush as he locked on to the jumps and could easily mess up his striding. Max had a hard time in the first round as the stallion tried to take charge. Their round was nerve racking and nail biting for the many fans watching. It was more by luck than skill that they achieved a clear.

Paul, Giles, and Marcus all had excellent first rounds, as did Frederick Seipp for Germany. Along with a number of other riders from the USA, France, Netherlands, Spain, and the Arab Emirates, there were twenty-one riders through to the second round. By the time it came from Max to jump again, and after half an hour's intensive working –in in the warm-up area, Zhivago jumped a calmer round. There were a couple of pole rattling moments, but far less stressful for the watching fans. Again, the other three British riders jumped clear, although Paul's horse had a few hairy moments.

By the time the competition reached the jump off there were ten riders still left in the competition. The competitor with the slowest time in the previous rounds went first- a pretty, young American girl on a large European Warm Blood. Knowing she didn't have the experience, she went for a safe, slow clear, which would at least guarantee her a slice of the prize money. Next to go was a rider from the Arab Emirate. He had an amazing horse, but he was out of his league as a rider, and they finished on sixteen faults. France's top rider Jacq Le Cock went next and set a good fast time, although this was promptly beaten by Paul. A Dutch rider went next but had 4 faults. He was followed by a teammate who knocked the pole on the exact same fence as his fellow countryman.

Max followed, but as Zhivago was not in the best of moods, he did a couple of tight turns, but didn't push him too hard. They put in a good, sound performance, but Max was realistic enough to know that it was beatable. Marcus and Speedy Sid followed him, and narrowly beat Max's time. Marcus wasn't on top for long, as he too was beaten by Frederick Seipp on his great horse.

Last to go was Giles on a home bred stallion. Giles was a game rider, but not normally the fastest. Giles and Mary were however always short of cash, and with the first prize being half a million euros, it was a tempting proposition to go

117

for broke. Giles' stallion Gilmar Gold Star was really on form, so he decided to take a risk. From the moment he re-entered the arena he was determined to get the fastest time. Seipp had done an amazing job, but Giles knew if he pushed just that little bit more, he may just do it. Putting his horse into a fast canter, he pushed towards the first fence.

Star responded well to the pressure and upped his game. They flew around the course, and as they thundered towards the final jump combination the crowd fell silent with tense anticipation of a home win. Star took off a little too far away from the first fence, and as he landed the pole rattled ominously. There was a collective gasp from the crowd. Giles then kicked like mad to get the distance to the last fence. Star felt the urgency and lengthened into gallop towards the massive oxer. Giles felt his heart thumping as the fence loomed threateningly ahead of them. Forgetting the principles of collection, in the heat of the moment, Giles resorted to prayer. Again, Star took off too early and a little flat, but with a huge effort, somehow managed to twist his body cleanly over the fence and safely over the finish line. Overjoyed, Giles galloped around the arena. As he went, he undid his hat and flung it into the crowd.

Lottie had been watching the competition with Simon in the VIP area. Having a vague awareness of Giles and Mary's finances, she was delighted by the win. Since Max's kindness to her, he was always her favourite, but she knew that the

118

prize fund meant far less to him. As Lottie was making her way out of the stands, she got a phone call from Ed.

'Are you going to Max's party tonight?'

'Yes, I've been invited.'

'Shall we go together – moral support and all that?' he asked.

Lottie hated arriving at social occasions alone so accepted gratefully. 'My brother Tom is giving me a lift there. Would you like us to pick you up on the way?'

'If you don't mind?' he replied, barely able to believe his luck. He had suspected for a long time that Max fancied her, so it was a great opportunity to make a point.

Chapter 10

Two hours later Tom and Lottie headed back to the Olympic Park to collect Ed. Tom was dressed in black tie as he was heading off to report on a film premiere, meanwhile, Lottie had on her favourite little black cocktail dress which was both slimming and sexy without looking sluttish. Ed was stood waiting for them in the entrance to the park, and Lottie had to admit that he too looked extremely handsome standing there in his evening wear.

As he squeezed into the back of the car, Ed said in a slightly strained voice, 'Thanks for the lift Tom. Are you joining us?'

'No unfortunately, I'm working tonight. I'm reporting on the film premiere of the new Di Caprio movie.'

'Tom has such a hard life,' Lottie retorted sarcastically.

After a seemingly endless battle with the traffic, they reached the magnificent frontage of Ivan Tarasov's Green Park mansion. Tom quickly hopped out the car and ran around to open the door for his sister. 'Make sure you behave yourself,' he lectured, smiling at her. 'If you need rescuing later, give me a ring. I should be finished by midnight.'

'Thanks little bro,' Lottie smiled. 'I may well hold you to that offer.'

Lottie and Ed climbed up the imposing steps to the entrance. Immediately the vast doors opened and there stood two of the hugest security men that Lottie had ever seen. Shaved heads, and solid to the point that even their neck muscles looked pumped.

'Name,' they demanded in heavy Russian accents.

'Lottie Wilkins and Edward Carter.'

The more menacing of the two men scanned down through a list of names. Once satisfied, he gave a grunt and allowed them through. As they headed off down a spectacularly ornate corridor following the general noise Ed whispered, 'Christ, you wouldn't want to knock over their beer.'

Lottie couldn't help but wonder what sort of person Ivan Tarasov was that he needed thugs like that on his payroll. Officially the family's money came from a media empire, but popular wisdom also suggested a mafia involvement. Whatever it was, there was something dodgy. After all her Uncle Crispin was rich and powerful, and yet when she knocked on his front door a liveried footman opened it.

The first room Lottie and Ed came across was the dining room. A long table was filled with exotic buffet food. There were huge joints of meats, bread, fish, bowls of caviar, lobster, cheeses, fruit, salad and delicate canapés. At the far end of the room was a bar lined with what looked like fire extinguishers and stacks of shot glasses. Beside the bar was an open doorway leading through into a room where loud music was playing.

Cautiously Lottie followed Ed as he made his

way over to the bar. On closer inspection, what she'd mistaken for a health and safety obsession were in fact rows of Firestarter Vodka. Ed picked up a shot glass and tentatively squeezed the pump on the top of the bottle. Having filled his glass, he took a sip. 'Wow,' that's awesome stuff. Hell of a strong, but really smooth. Why don't you try some?' he offered Lottie.

'No that's fine,' Lottie said. She scanned the bar and spotted a bottle of tonic water. Taking a glass, she poured herself a drink so at least she had something to hold. There was some raucous laughter coming from the other room. Suddenly a group of people Lottie didn't know practically fell through the doorway, almost knocking Ed off his feet. Lottie and Ed headed through the gap and into a huge ballroom which had been set up with a stage at the far end, ready for a DJ, with turntables, large screens and rigged up lights. The music was thumping, although there were very few people.

Lottie and Ed walked across the room and through another door. This led to a light airy room with lots of comfortable seating. Immediately Lottie spotted some of the show jumpers sitting around, drinking, and laughing. Among them, holding a huge bottle of champagne, and grinning inanely sat Giles.

'Congratulations,' Lottie called across to him, to break the ice.

'Come over and join us,' he called, much to Lottie's relief.

There was a frantic shuffling of chairs as

riders squeezed up to make room. Lottie found herself perched on the end of a sofa beside Paul Denton, dressed in a suit, his black jacket having been surgically removed.

'A profitable day for you too Paul,' she said.

'Yep. Not bad,' he replied, almost with a smile.

For the next hour, Lottie sat contentedly listening to the rider gossip, delighted that they were treating her as one of them, although she still hadn't set eyes on Max. Various groups of Cindy's arty and fashion friends came wandering passed, and at one point Lottie thought she saw Cindy herself, but still no sign of the host. Eventually she plucked up the courage to ask Paul if Max was around.

'He's down the corridor at the casino if you want him,' Paul muttered.

'I suppose I ought to say hello. It seems rude not too. Plus, I'm starving.'

'Bring us back some food will you,' Mary called. 'I'm far too comfortable to want to move.'

'Sure. I'll bring back a few plates,' Lottie agreed.

Although she was hungry, Lottie set off first to see Max. She decided that she would just have a quick peak. If he was busy, she'd pop back later. As she entered the room with the casino, it wasn't easy to even locate Max amongst the bustling crowd, but after standing on tip toe she caught a glance of him over by the roulette table. Slipping through the crowds, she headed in his direction. He was stood laughing with a man his own age, whilst betting large amounts of real cash on what Lottie had assumed was the fun casino one normally had at office parties.

Max suddenly spotted her, 'Lottie. Great to see you. Glad you could make it.' He flung his arms out, before giving her a huge hug, then kissed her on the cheek.

'Thanks for inviting me. It's an amazing party,' Lottie replied sweetly. She held his gaze and smiled, his eyes betraying recent drug use.

'Let me introduce you to Charlie. My best mate from school whose getting married next month.'

The tall dark headed man standing next to Max smiled and shook Lottie's hand. 'So I finally get to meet the infamous face of Yangtze.'

Almost, as if an invisible radar distress beam had been activated, Cindy appeared and staked her claim to Max. Slipping in front of Lottie, she kissed Max seductively, before rubbing her beautiful, scantily clothed body against his. Then, as if by magic, she produced a wrap of cocaine which she tipped down her breast. Then, in front of Lottie, Max leant over and snorted the white powder from her flawless pale skin.

Lottie was mortified with embarrassment. Rooted to the spot she didn't know whether it would be ruder if she walked away or stayed put. She was still deliberating, her cheeks reddened with humiliation when Max lifted his head up and looked straight at her.'Sorry, that was unforgivably rude of me.'

'I was just going to fetch some food anyway –

under orders from Mary and Giles. I just wanted to thank you...' she trailed off.

'Charlie, will you escort Lottie back to the refreshment area, and bring me back something to drink. I'm in danger of sobering up here.'

Obediently Lottie followed Charlie out through yet another door and along an unfamiliar corridor back into the main entrance hall. 'Max and I are flying out to the south of France tomorrow night, for a two-week stag party on my parent's yacht, so Cindy's making the most of him this evening.'

'I guess they don't see much of each other. It must be hard,' Lottie answered, trying to sound like she'd recovered from the shock.

Charlie stopped. With a serious expression on his face, he turned to Lottie and spoke. 'Don't get too fond of Max. Although he'd kill me if he knew I was saying this, he does have a bit of a thing about you, but it's superficial. You are a lovely looking girl whose obviously smart and educated, but you aren't in his league.'

Lottie was immediately torn between embarrassment and indignation that this man was making assumptions about her status in life.

'Don't get me wrong,' Charlie continued. 'I'm sure you are going to make someone a great little wife, but the guy has booked one of London's top DJs, Ian Masters to do a spot tonight. I bet you can't even envisage how much that has cost.'

Lottie responded non committedly, 'I do have a pretty good idea how much chart-topping DJ's like the Master Mixer charge for a set.'

Having grabbed something to eat herself, Lottie collected a load of food on plates and carefully carried them back through to the show jumpers hang out. As she approached the group she received a cheer. Unfortunately, the size of the party had doubled as they had been joined by many of the overseas riders. Feeling in a helpful mode, Lottie went back and got some more plates.

By the time everyone had finished eating, Ian Masters, Lizzie's top DJ and business partner of Nick had arrived so everyone filed through into the ballroom for the evening's entertainment. Once the music started, the strobe lighting and special effects created a great ambiance. Lottie found she was having an amazing time as she danced alongside her show jumping heroes. Even Paul seemed relaxed and joined in with the group, jigging alongside Lottie and Mary.

Halfway through the act they were joined by Max who bounced towards them like Tigger on speed. He grabbed Lottie around her waist and swung her into him. 'Having a good time?' he shouted over the music. Dressed in black tie he looked gorgeous. As he pulled her towards him, Lottie thought she could feel his heart hammering in his chest. Under the violence of his gaze Lottie almost forgot how to breathe. As the music slowed down into a beat syncing link he whispered in her ear, 'I'm really glad you came. It means a lot.' He gently raised his hand up and brushed her hair off her face before kissing her gently on her cheek. Moments later he was gone, swallowed up in a mass of jiving bodies.

Making sure that both Max and Charlie were in sight, Lottie made her way up to where Ian was doing his DJ set. Having spotted her, Ian came out from behind his decks and gave her a huge bear hug. After a quick explanation from Lottie as to why she happened to be inside the house of Russian mafia, he had to carry on, but dedicated the next track to her.

An hour later the session finished, and everyone went back to the seating areas for a rest. Lottie was tired and ready to go home. She hadn't seen Ed for ages but thought she ought to at least warn him she was intending to leave. Dragging herself out from the comfort of the chair, she went hunting for him. After a fruitless five minutes, she headed back to the room with the casino. It was one in the morning and the gambling tables had closed, but a mixed group of people were sitting around in a large circle apparently playing a game of truth or dare. Quickly scanning the group, Lottie spotted Max, Ed and Giles amongst the players.

Max's bow tie was undone and was hanging loosely around his neck. His hair was dishevelled, and he looked completely wasted, albeit in a sexy way. Giles was the first to notice Lottie, 'Come and join us,' he called.

'I was just coming to let Ed know that I'm going home.'

'Nonsense,' Giles said. 'Sit down and divulge your secrets.'

Lottie laughed nervously. 'I really need to go.'

Ignoring her protest, Max stood up and

127

grabbed a chair for her to sit next to him.'Right then', he said in a slurred voice. 'It's your turn, so truth or dare?'

As dare seemed to involve downing a tumbler of Vodka, Lottie plumped for truth.

'Right,' Giles said. 'Apologies to those of you not involved, but this is a bit of a specialist question. Lottie, prepare yourself....drum roll.' He banged his hand on the table. 'Have Yangtze chosen who they are going to sponsor yet?'

'How do you expect me to answer that?' Lottie complained. 'You know its top secret.'

'Come off it Lottie, you must have an idea.'

Feeling herself going bright red, she flustered, 'All I do know is that they haven't made up their mind?'

Max piped up, 'Am I still in the running?'

'Of course you are, but so are Paul, Marcus, Mary and Giles.'

'Who's top of the list – surely you can tell us that.' Giles persisted.

Lottie wondered how to avoid answering but couldn't see an easy way out. 'Who do you think is top?'

'Marcus I suppose.'

Lottie's lack of denial was taken as confirmation, and she was left alone.

Once she was out of the limelight Lottie started to find the confessions very funny. When it got around to Max, one of the arty people asked him whether his father would make a good politician.

'Fuck no. He'll just be using it as a stepping-stone up to the House of Lords,' Max replied, but then poured himself a shot of vodka anyway.

When it got back to Lottie, Charlie piped up with a question. 'Whose is the most influential mobile number you have stored in your phone?'

Lottie thought for a moment, 'I guess the Chairman of the Conservative party.' To prove it, she dug out her phone and scrolled down until she reached Crispin. 'Here it is,' she announced, before hurriedly putting it back safely in her pocket.

The same question then went around the room. Ed jokingly said, 'the head of sponsorship for Yangtze,' to which the other riders laughed.

'Obviously, my father,' Max said as he fumbled for his phone. One of the arty types snatched the phone from Max's hand, 'Yes I confirm that,' he said laughing.

Before long, the party started to break up and Lottie slipped away to call for a taxi. She was exhausted, but she'd had a great evening. Her interaction with Max however had left her feeling confused. She found him incredibly sexy, and he'd made it clear that he fancied her, but his behaviour scared her, mainly because he reminded her too much of her stepfather. His blatant drug taking also reawakened the dilemma of whether she should allow the Yangtze Board to choose Max, the sexy poster boy, but potential time bomb, over the boring but reliable Paul.

Chapter 11

It was late morning when Max was rudely woken by one of his father's minders. He'd fallen asleep on a sofa and was now feeling incredibly stiff in addition to suffering a raging hangover.

'You'd better call your father back pronto,' came the order.

Feeling dazed and dizzy, Max started to hunt around for his phone.

'Here,' said the minder, thrusting the phone at Max.

Max sat back down before he fell over. Trying to focus on the small screen, he called his father's number. His father answered immediately, and Max just sat and listened to the tirade of abuse.

'You nebladogarnyy mudak,' his father's voice boomed down the phone. Do you have any idea how your stupid twitter comments have damaged my political career? Well you've ruined any chance of me being elected now.'

'I'm very tired and hungover and have no idea what you are talking about. I haven't tweeted for weeks?' Max snapped crossly.

'Don't you dare lie to me.... Well that's it. We're finished. So just get out of my house before I get you thrown out.'

Max felt confused, and rather shocked. He staggered back to his feet and decided to try and reach a loo before he was sick. Whilst he threw up in the toilet, the minder waited outside for him.

Once Max re-emerged from the bowels of the bathroom, the minder frog-marched him towards the main entrance, before literally throwing him out the front door. Max cursed the fact that he didn't have his car keys. He was about to knock on the door and complain, but common sense prevailed as he realised that he was probably still way over the drink drive limit. Making allowances for his thumping head, he walked slowly towards the street to hail a cab back to Cindy's flat.

Sat in the back of the taxi, he scanned through his twitter posts. Sure enough there was a comment made at 2am that morning, which said that his father would make a lousy MP, and was just using it as a stepping-stone to the House of Lords. The tweet added that Ivan Tarasov was part of the Russian mafia, and Putin's mole. Max stared at the screen in disbelief. Most of the previous evening was a blur, but he would have sworn in a court of law that he hadn't written the tweet.

Feeling that damage limitation was in order, he sent a second post as way of apology, claiming that his phone had been hacked. He'd rarely experienced his father that angry before and thought that some diplomacy was called for before he set off on his two-week stag holiday with Charlie.

Max didn't hear any more from his father directly, but the press ran the story of his father's de selection as a prospective parliamentary candidate following some negative publicity. Max rang Lee to make sure that everything was OK at the yard, and then headed back to Cindy's to get ready for the trip.

Once Max was safely on the flight, sipping champagne alongside Charlie, his brother Quentin and their cousin George, he quite forgot about the row with his father, and got back into party mode. It didn't take long to get to the South of France, and then it was a short drive down to Monaco where the yacht was moored.

Max was tired, and slept solidly that night, not waking until gone mid- day the following day. The first thing he did was to check his phone for any messages from Lee, and hopefully no angry voice mails from home. Being off the coast seemed to have messed up his phone as it couldn't connect to a network. Giving up, Max dressed and made his way out on board to catch up with the others who were lying around on loungers, sharing a joint.

Slumping down beside Charlie, Max took a drag before sitting back and enjoying the effects. The sun was warm, but the sea breeze stopped it from being unbearably hot.

'I could get used to this,' Max said. 'Maybe I should give up show jumping and become a playboy, plying my trade around the Med.'

'We're going ashore later, so you can get in some practice,' Charlie replied.

'Why would you need to when you already have one of the sexiest girlfriends on the planet?'

Quentin asked.

'Cindy is bloody gorgeous isn't she,' Max grinned, as he leant forward to take the spliff. 'Trouble is she's getting restless. Hinting about marriage and babies.'

Charlie laughed, 'You'd make bloody lousy parents.' Turning to his cousin George he added, 'their staple diet is vodka and coke, and I don't mean Pepsi's rival.'

'I admit we'd never win parents of the year award,' Max agreed good humouredly.

'Anyway,' Charlie continued, 'Max's affections are rather divided at present.'

'I'm just thinking about the future – long term family planning I guess.' Max replied.

'Like the Yangtze manager Lottie.'

Max reddened slightly, 'Yes, her or someone like her. '

'What's she like?' Quentin asked.

Before Max could reply, Charlie butted in. 'Lovely looking in an innocent girl next door kind of way – Not in Cindy's league, but better childbearing hips.'

'Honestly Charlie, you are so bloody opinionated,' Max complained.

Ignoring his friend, Charlie continued. 'Actually mate, I don't know what to think about her. She gives off confusing signals. I simply can't tell whether she's a boring little office girl who's struck lucky, or whether she's deliberately underselling herself.'

'I know what you mean. I thought she was some sort of PA when I first met her, but during

133

the meeting she was actually quite intimidating.' He hesitated, 'but once I got to know her, I changed my mind. She's really nice.'

'Do you know anything about her background?' George asked.

'I've met her mum and her two brothers, and I liked them. The mum has a livery yard. One of the brothers is a journalist and the others an actor, who isn't well known, but has just landed some huge part in some TV production.'

'What about money? You don't want some little gold-digger after you.' Quentin quizzed, deciding to be blunt.

Max carefully considered his response. The trouble was he didn't know. It wasn't something he'd considered. Until recently he'd just wanted to have sex with her. Lottie as a future wife, where wealth was an important consideration, hadn't really occurred to him until now.'The brothers play polo, so I don't think the family are exactly bottom of the social pile, but that fact that we don't know the name Wilkins means they probably aren't anything special.'

'I know what you mean,' Charlie added. 'She's kind of a nobody, but last night she did come out with a couple of things which didn't fit?'

'Like what?' Max was curious.

'Well did you see the way Lizzies' star DJ greeted her like an old friend.'

'As in the night club?' Quentin sounded impressed.

'No a hairdresser in Hackney,' his brother replied sarcastically. 'Also Max did you see what was on her phone during the truth or dare game?'

Max shook his head, 'Don't even remember us playing any games.'

'You were pretty fucked by then,' his friend cuffed him jovially on the arm. 'Yeh, anyway, she only had Crispin Marchbank, the Conservative party chairman on speed dial.'

'How strange,' George said. 'Are you sure it wasn't just some random guy with the same name?'

'Well it was his picture, so I don't see why not. I think Lottie is a dark horse. I feel there are interesting times ahead.... You never know, we may be back here next year celebrating Max's impending marriage to the mysterious Lottie.'

Max thought it unlikely but didn't think it was the stupidest idea his friend had ever had. Later when they got ashore, Max tried his phone again, but it still wasn't working. Taking Lee's number off his contact list, he borrowed Charlie's phone but all he got was number unavailable. He could only assume there was a network fault. Reassuring himself that if there was a problem, Lee could sort it, he gave up.

Chapter 12

Lottie was in London at Yangtze's head office for a meeting with Simon and her boss Florian. With one week to go before the final sponsorship announcement, they were thrashing out the pros and cons of the individual riders. The Chinese directors were excited by the project and had finally allocated a budget of eight million, of which six would be split between three riders, with a further two million on the advertising campaign to support them.

On the tube journey to the Yangtze office Lottie was feeling sick. Although she didn't have the final decision, her opinion could hold sway. Every rational thought she had was to recommend that Max was dropped. Unlike the others, he didn't need the money, and if the press ever got hold of the fact he used cocaine – that would destroy her credibility. Yangtze had given her a great, well-paid job and they had put faith in her. Nevertheless, her heart ached at the prospect – her whole marketing plan had been based on the beautiful, talented Maxim Tarasov.

The meeting started promptly. The decision to select Marcus Wallis was universal, but choosing the other two riders was harder. Simon wanted to choose Giles, as he was such a reliable rider, although Florian thought a female may broaden the appeal.

'Would the directors object to sponsoring the Gilmar Stud, then it's more a case of two for the price of one?' Lottie suggested.

Florian hesitated, 'That's certainly a solution, what do you think Simon?'

'I don't normally agree with husband/wife deals, but Giles and Mary are such a great partnership, I think it's a good plan.'

'So it's now between Paul Denton and Maxim Tarasov for the final place,' Lottie's boss said. Again, over to you Simon.'

'This is a hard decision to make,' Simon said. 'Maxim is the better rider and has a world class horse. And although I don't personally fancy him, he is very handsome. On the other hand, he only has one decent horse whereas Paul has a whole yard to choose from. Paul doesn't have poster boy looks, but he is stable and consistent.'

'Are we going for Maxim?'

Lottie started to sweat, and her heart began to race. This was it, she needed to speak up now. She opened her mouth, 'Um,' but Simon interrupted her.

'Well there is the issue over Maxim's tweet at the weekend. I don't know if you are aware of it?'

'A little. Didn't he tweet that his father would make a terrible MP, and on the back of it he was deselected? Um, yes, that could cause a problem,' Florian mused.

'I was there when the incident happened, and I would swear under oath that it wasn't Max who sent the message, but rather one of his girlfriend's arty, lefty friends.' Lottie felt she needed to defend him on this count at least.

'I must admit; I don't think his girlfriend is

good for him. She is well known for using drugs. Did you see any evidence of drug use at the party Lottie?' Simon asked.

Lottie bottled out. 'Yes, although I don't think any of the show jumpers were involved,' she answered guiltily.

'Well let's see how the next few days pan out and make the final decision on Maxim versus Paul on Friday. Meanwhile Lottie, if you'd like to let the others know the good news, just make sure they keep it under their hat until the press launch.'

Lottie found a spare desk and logged onto her computer so she could work out what to say to Marcus and the others, knowing she needed answers to the barrage of questions she'd be asked. She had no idea whether the riders were even in the UK, but taking a chance she rang Marcus's land line. Tracey answered the phone, and as soon as she realised it was Lottie, she rushed out into the yard to fetch her husband. She arrived back moments later sounding out of breath, 'He's just coming,' she said.

'Oh good, I'd half expected him to be away competing.'

'He's home for two weeks doing some UK based shows, then it's off to the Netherlands for the next leg of the World Series. Anyway, here he comes.'

'Lottie, lovely to hear from you. Did you have a good time on Sunday night?'

'Yes, thanks Marcus. It was a great party, and hopefully you will have something else to celebrate soon. It's all very hush hush until next weekend, but I've been given permission to let you know that you've been selected for a two-million-pound sponsorship from Yangtze.'

Lottie sat quietly, smiling to herself, as Marcus and Tracey shrieked with delight. Finally, after they'd danced around the kitchen, Marcus spoke again. 'That's amazing news, and the timing couldn't be better. I've had Ivan Tarasov's office on the phone offering me the opportunity to buy one or more of Max's horses.'

But, ... I mean why? How come.?' Lottie was lost for words.

'From what we gather, the tweet incident was the last straw. Max's old man's had enough. Its Ivan's company that owns the horses, and he says he's no longer prepared to support his son.'

'What does Max say? Surely he's putting up a fight?' Lottie was horrified.

'The official line is that Max has decided that without financial support he can't carry on, so has gone abroad for a couple of weeks whilst the horses are sold.'

'I don't claim to know Max very well, but I can't see him being so indifferent to the fate of his horses – he certainly seems to adore them.' Lottie felt her professionalism slipping, her hopes dashed. She then remembered that Max was away on Charlie's stag party. It occurred to her that maybe Max wasn't even aware of what was happening.

'Tracey and I feel the same. We reckon that his father is doing it behind his back. I've tried calling Max, but his phone isn't working. Poor Lee has been out of his mind. He's been desperate to contact Max but hasn't been able to get hold of him either.'

'Are you trying to buy one of the horses?' Lottie thought that at least Marcus would give them a good home.

'I'd have loved Zhivago, but he's already been promised to Lady Hardcourt for one million.'

'I'd have thought that was cheap,' Lottie said.

'It is, although the horse isn't an easy ride. Still there is a lot of potential in stud fees. Also Ivan wanted the deal done quickly, otherwise I assume he'd hold out for at least two or three times that. Lady Hardcourt is a wonderful supporter of British show jumping.'

'What about the other horses?'

'Frederick Seipp is buying Lenny, and the 2-year-old filly Roxy. I've provisionally expressed an interest in Harvey. He's still a bit green, but age wise he will be ideal to take over from Sid when I retire him in a couple of years. I was going to sound out my other sponsors, but thanks to you I can make my offer official now.'

'Do you have a contact number for Lee? I know someone who may be interested in the brood mare.' Lottie asked.

Armed with a new mobile number for Max's groom, Lottie quickly called him to get the full story.

'Oh God, I'm so gutted for Max.' Lee was in a terrible state. 'I've been desperate to get hold of him, but his father has shut down all our phones, and issued me with a new number.'

'So Max doesn't know? I was discussing it with Marcus, and we thought the official line about him giving up was false.'

'Although I work for Max, I'm employed by Tarasov Industries. They also own all the horses and the vehicles, and they lease the yard, so they have absolute control. I just hope that Max doesn't blame me for letting all this happen.'

'As he knows his father better than anyone, he'll understand how powerless you are.' Lottie said sympathetically.'Are the horses actually sold yet?'

'They're all still here, but I think the deals have been made. Why?'

'Because there is still a 50% chance that Max will get the 2 million sponsorship deal. If I can persuade his father not to sell Zhivago for a few more days, Max may be able to buy him himself.'

It's worth a final shot I suppose,' Lee sounded doubtful. 'I know Ivan's in his office in Canary Wharf all this week so you may be able to talk to him. Good luck.'

Once Lottie was off the phone, she googled Tarasov Industries and scribbled down the address on a post –it note. It was only then that she remembered that she still had to ring Giles and Mary to tell them the good news. Again, she took a chance and rang the their land line. Mary answered and promptly burst into tears.

'Are you OK?' Lottie asked hesitantly.

'Yes....thank you,' Mary sniffed. 'I can hardly believe it.'

'You both deserve it,' Lottie was smiling.

141

'It's going to make such a difference to us. We will be able to pay back our bank loan and do the urgent repairs to the stable roof.'

'You're not going to put an offer in for one of Max's horses then?'

'No, we have plenty of horses. The most important thing for us is to have a rainy-day fund,' she hesitated, 'So is Max selling some of his horses?'

Lottie explained what had happened, and this time Mary cried again.

With her pleasant work done, Lottie hopped on to the tube and headed off for Canary Wharf. She didn't really have a plan of action and decided that the greater likely hood was that she would be refused entry, but she felt that she had to try.

After an hour of travelling she was feeling hot and dishevelled as she reached the entrance to the high tech, glass fronted skyscraper which was the home to the European arm of Tarasov Industries.

Deciding that her best chance of entry was through a confident attack, she strode up to the reception and insisted upon meeting the chairman, Ivan Tarasov, and explained that she was head of marketing for Yangtze Motors.

'Do you have an appointment?' came the predictable reply.

'No, there wasn't time. It's' about a major sponsorship deal that Yangtze are offering, but it's critical that I firm things up today.'

Taking the bait, the receptionist rang through to Ivan Tarasov's office. Much to Lottie's surprise she was told that he could spare her 5 minutes and someone would come down to collect her shortly.

A few moments later there was movement from the elevator at the far end of the foyer. As the lift doors opened an attractive, if slightly effeminate young man in an expensive looking suit appeared and made his way across to meet Lottie.

'Are you the lady from Yangtze?' he asked in a public school educated voice.

'Yes hello, I'm Lottie Wilkins.'

The young man extended his arm and offered a handshake. 'I'm Peter Tarasov.'

'Presumably you are related to Maxim.'

'My half-brother, but he pretty much acts like I don't exist most of the time.'

'In all fairness, I don't know Maxim well enough for him to discuss his family life.'

Lottie followed Peter into the lift. Standing beside him as he concentrated on the floor numbers, she was able to study him. Unlike his brother, he had neat, gleaming black hair and an almost feminine beauty, with high cheek bones and long eye lashes.

The lift stopped on the top floor where the doors opened into a magnificent reception area with wood panelled walls, antique paintings and lavish furnishings. Huge windows gave a panoramic view of London. A pretty, thirty something female personal assistant manned the desk.

'If you would like to go on in, Mr Tarasov is waiting for you.'

143

Peter opened a door behind the reception and ushered Lottie into the plushest, executive office she had ever seen. Immediately in front of her was a huge, highly polished mahogany table, where at one end was placed a high-tech computer and numerous screens.

Staring at her from across the room was a heavily built man in his late fifties, with dense jet black hair and bushy eyebrows. He was attractive, in a heavy, masculine way, however his eyes were dark and penetratingly suspicious.

'You have 5 minutes,' he said in a deep, stern voice with a perceptible accent.

'Thank you for sparing the time to see me.'

'Yes, yes, now get on.'

'My name is Lottie Wilkins and I am the head of UK sponsorship for Yangtze Motors. I don't know how much Maxim told you, but he is in the running for a 2-million-pound sponsorship deal with us.'

Ivan Tarasov grunted, which in light of any other comments, Lottie took as confirmation. 'The thing is that the directors need to make their final decision this week, but we've now heard rumours that Maxim's horses are being sold, which of course would make him ineligible. I can't get hold of Maxim for confirmation, hence why I've come to you as owner.'

'All the horses will be sold by the weekend.'

'That's rather sudden.'

'My son needs to learn a harsh lesson.'

Lottie braced herself, 'Is it because of the tweet incident?' He didn't answer, so swallowing

144

nervously, she continued.'It wasn't Maxim's fault. I was with him, and I would swear in a court that he didn't send the tweet. We were all playing a game, and his phone was being passed around the group. Somebody else had to have done it.'

'Miss Wilkins, I appreciate your defence of my son, but my mind is made up.' Ivan stood up, indicating that she should leave. 'Peter will escort you. I don't suppose we will meet again. Good day.'

Lottie knew she was defeated. With no other plan, her only recourse was a dignified exit before she gave way to tears. Giving her a sympathetic look, Peter followed her out, and accompanied her back down to the foyer.

'Do you fancy joining me for a quick coffee?' he asked.'It's not much, but I do want you to cheer up. At least you tried to help. It's more than I've done.'

'Why's that?' Lottie realised that it verged on the edge of rude, but curiosity had got the better of her.

'I've always played second fiddle to my older brother. He's sporty, famous, and most important of all, not gay. Although I worked hard at school, read corporate law at uni, and dedicated myself to the family business, I've been practically invisible. It's always been about Max.'

Peter walked over to the reception desk and signed them out of the building. 'There's a Starbucks just around the corner,' he said. Lottie obediently followed. As she couldn't save Max's career, there was no rush to get back to her office.

Taking charge, Peter ordered two lattes, and they found an empty table where they could carry on the conversation.'I don't want you to think I am heartless, but I don't see the point of me burning my bridges with father, in an attempt to stick up for Max, when quite frankly my brother has brought it on himself.'

'Fair enough,' Lottie shrugged.

'For the first time in my life, my father is taking notice of me, and although I would never wish my brother ill, it does make a nice change for me to be on top for once.'

'Are you and Max very close?'

'Not now. We got on well as children, but our lives are very different now. I guess we don't have time for each other.' Peter paused and took a sip of coffee.

'We have different mothers of course, so technically we are only half-brothers. Max's mother had terrible post-natal depression, and killed herself when Max was still a baby. She had been a real beauty, but very highly strung. Effectively this meant he was brought up by a series of nannies until he was seven. My father married my mother Ruth when Max was a toddler. He and Ruth travelled around the world together, and when I came along, I tended to go with them at Mum's insistence, whilst poor Max was left in London with the hired helps.'

'No wonder Max is like he is.'

'Yes. It explains a lot... although my mum did her best for him. Of all Dad's wives she was the most ordinary, and homely. I think after Max's mother's death my father was looking for comfort and understanding rather than glamour. My mum didn't believe in abandoning children to nannies and boarding schools and insisted on bringing me up herself. Of course my father disapproved. He blames her over-protectiveness for making me homosexual.'

'That's ridiculous.'

'That's his way. My mum had to wait for my father to be away before she could give Max any attention. Max adored her, but as my father didn't want him turning into a wet, mummy's boy, it was hard. When my father eventually got bored of my mum, and divorced her, Max continued to keep in touch. He would come and stay in the holidays. There we were allowed to be brothers. I reckon it was thanks to my mum that Max didn't totally go off the rails.'

'I hope the loss of his horses doesn't push Max over the edge now.' Having seen Max's casual approach to drink and drugs, Lottie was worried. Max had been kind to her, and she didn't want him ending up destroying himself as her stepfather had done.

'I'll do my best to make sure he's OK, 'Peter promised.

Once Lottie was back at the office, she called Lee, having failled with Ivan.

'At least you tried. Max will appreciate that,' Lee replied.

'What's happening to Max's broodmare Tilly?' Lottie asked hopefully.

'She wasn't officially on the books. She only has a value if she is carrying Zhivago's foal.'

'Is she in foal at the moment?'

'She should be. She was running with Zhivago, but she hasn't been tested.' He paused. 'Why do you want to buy her?'

'It kind of depends on the price..... I had this silly idea of taking her back to Devon, then gifting the foal to Max, so that he still has a link to his beloved Zhivago.'

'That's very kind of you.' Lee answered.

'We've plenty of land at home, so keeping her won't be an issue, but I can't just get hold of thousands of pounds by this weekend.'

Lee hesitated. 'There is a solution,' he paused again. 'As she isn't on the books, then she doesn't have a proper value. There's no proof that she's in foal, so technically I'd just be offloading a retired horse..... if you can pay £500, just to keep things above board, I can go back to Ivan Tarasov with a clean conscience.

Chapter 13

For the first few days of the trip, predatory females hounded the stag group wherever they went, but by the Thursday the Grand Prix teams began arriving. Soon every bar and club in the town were packed full of the Formula 1 travelling circus of teams and their huge support crews.

That evening, sat in the corner of a crowded hotel bar, Charlie, George and Quentin sulkily nursed their drinks. Having now found themselves being practically invisible, they needed to seek alternative amusements. Max was still confident, so Charlie insisted on a bet. 'The next woman who comes into the bar – I'll bet you 100 euros that you can't get her into bed.'

'Done,' Max grinned.

Moments later, the support crew from one of the motor racing teams walked in. Amongst the male mechanics was a rather plain, dark-haired woman in her early twenties, dressed in jeans, and a blouse.

'There you go,' Charlie laughed. 100 Euros if you shag her.'

'She's hardly my type,' Max looked dismissively at her.

'Are you about to lose the bet?' Charlie challenged.

'No of course not. I just need a bit of stimulation.' Max headed off to the loos to do a line of cocaine. He made his way back to the bar and drank a couple of shots before approaching his target.

The girl, who he found out was called Brittany, couldn't believe her luck.

'I recognise you,' she said. 'Are you a cricketer?'

Max laughed, 'No I'm a professional show jumper, and my name is Maxim Tarasov.'

Brittany beamed. 'Of course, so what are you doing here?'

'On my best friend's stag week,' Max pointed towards his friends, who all waved.

Max looked at Brittany's flat, freckled face, and her lank hair. She had a large arse, but quite nice tits. Her Midland's accent was annoying too, but Max reckoned that so long as he focused on her breasts, he'd probably manage an erection later.

He tried to show polite interest when Brittany introduced him to the rest of their team, but the cocaine hit had made him restless, and quite frankly these people were boring. Every time he glanced across at Charlie and the others he saw them laughing. Determined not to lose the bet, he persevered.

After a couple of hours of buying drinks, and boasting about his own beloved Aston Martin, Max got to see the inside of Brittany's hotel room. Feeling very drunk, his next problem was getting an erection. Brittany was obliging, if rather inexperienced, and after half an hour's fore play, she was moist and willing. Focusing on her breasts, Max managed to rise to the occasion, and soon slipped comfortably inside her tight vagina. He smiled to himself – one could drive a carriage and horses up between Cindy's legs, and still have room. At least the ugly girls generally had lower mileage and tried harder.

Having satisfied her, Max allowed himself to come. Having quickly dismounted, he headed into her bathroom to shower. He dressed and headed back into the room, ready to make his escape. Brittany was sitting, partly dressed, texting on her phone.

'Thank you,' Max said. 'Maybe I'll see you around.'

'Is that it?' she sounded shocked.

Max looked confused. 'Well yes. What else were you expecting?'

'Well more than just a quick one-night stand.' Brittany's angry face glared at him.

Unmoved, Max merely shrugged. 'My girlfriend is one of the most beautiful women on the planet. She is all I need. Now, it's been a pleasant evening, but it's over.'

'You bastard,' she shouted. 'Just get out.' Picking up her purse, she hurled it across the room. Hurriedly, he shot out the door.

Max headed off down to the bar. The others had clearly got bored and headed back to the yacht. He decided to have a few more drinks before he followed them. He was on his second double shot when he realised that he was the subject of some interest from Brittany's mates. Eventually two of the male members of the group came over to challenge Max, having been messaged by Brittany.

'You bastard. You just used our friend,' they said in a threatening voice.

'On the contrary, I made sure she enjoyed herself. It's not my fault I left her wanting more.'

'She thought you wanted to be her boyfriend.'

Max nearly choked on his drink. 'Oh, come off it,' he mocked. 'Your friend Brittany needs a reality check. Does she seriously think I'd fall in love with someone like her?' To make a point, he turned his back on the two guys and ordered another drink.

Soon Max started to feel tired. He was extremely drunk and just wanted to get back to the yacht. Not entirely sure of the direction to the marina, he fell out the hotel entrance and started to weave his way up the street. He heard the noise of footsteps running. The sound was getting closer. Turning around, he saw a group of Brittany's friends bearing down on him. Seconds later they had surrounded him. A menacing group, Max started to panic. He was too drunk to fight one person, let alone four or five. If they beat him to a pulp, it could mean the end of his career. He hurriedly contemplated running. He was fitter than them, and he just needed to get back to the hotel and get help, but he wasn't sure his legs would co-operate.

Suddenly coming around the corner came a police car. Max immediately waved to get their attention. Max nearly cried with relief as the car stopped by the group of lads. 'I'm being

152

threatened,' he shouted in French. As one of the officers got out of the car, the lads slipped away, leaving Max standing alone on the pavement. Having decided that they didn't want yet another drunk Englishman getting into trouble they offered to give him a lift.

Sunday culminated with the main Grand Prix race. As Charlie was a huge fan, he had purchased VIP tickets for the Paddock Club. This meant the four men could spend the day close to the centre of the action, but with the comfort of a bar and a decent lunch. The race had been on for twenty minutes, and with the initial excitement over, Max was starting to get bored. 'How many laps are there in total?' he asked.

'73', Charlie answered.

'Good God, seriously. Why?' Max replied, unimpressed.'I mean, other than the first and last laps who cares?'

'That's hardly the spirit,' Charlie shook his head in despair. Max headed off to the bar to get another drink. Whilst he was there he nearly collided with a former England rugby player, who was one of the celebrity sportsmen guests brought in to entertain the VIP area clients.

'Sorry mate,' the man muttered. He then gave Max a hard stare as he tried to work out whether they'd met before. Max kept quiet, and slipped past him, as the bar seemed more interesting. Having picked up drinks for the four of them, he was carrying them back when a rather pompous man turned to Max and insisted that Max pose for

153

a photograph with the man's wife.

'Can't you see I'm carrying a tray of drinks?' Max was astounded.

'I don't care. I've paid good money for these tickets, and it includes meet and greet with former sporting heroes.'

Max, called over to George, 'Will you take these off me?'

Having freed himself of the tray, Max squared up to the flabby jawed English businessman. 'Firstly, I am not a former sporting hero, I'm very much a current sportsman. Secondly, I too am here as a guest, and am not being paid to be a performing monkey to please the likes of you and your wife,' he said icily.

The following day, with the motor racing over, Charlie arranged for the boat to set off, and for them to explore further along the coast, including heading towards the Greek islands. The trip, in glorious weather, was four days of bliss. Max relaxed on board deck, drinking cocktails, and lying in the sun. Sometimes they stopped for a swim in the beautiful clear water and ate the most amazing food prepared by the on-board chef. They got back into Monaco the day before they were due to leave and went on one final wild night of drinking and partying.

Although Max was keen to get back home, it was with great reluctance that he left the boat, as the stag party headed back to the airport. The flight back went smoothly, and in no time at all they were back in the UK.

Feeling exhausted and vowing never to touch alcohol again, Max said goodbye to the others before making his way across the airport terminal to where he'd arranged to be picked up by Lee. He was eager to get back to see the horses and hoped that Lee hadn't forgotten. His phone still wasn't working, so it wasn't as if he could even call. He scanned the sea of faces as people called out to loved ones but couldn't see his head groom anywhere. He was just about to give up and call a taxi when he spotted his brother rushing through the entrance door.

Peter waived frantically, 'Sorry I couldn't get away. Do you need a hand with your luggage?'

Max shook his head. 'Where's Lee? He was supposed to be meeting me here.'

'I've come instead of him. A lot's been happening, so I offered to come and fill you in.'

Max was curious. He rarely had any dealings with his brother. Psychologically he braced himself. The news had to be momentous for Peter to get involved.

Once they were away from the crowds and heading towards the car park, Peter turned to his brother and said, 'I have no idea what is the best way to tell you, so I'm just going to come out and say it. Father has disowned you. In the last 7 days he has sold your horses and cut off all ties with you.'

Max felt as though he'd been punched in the stomach. 'Excuse me, I think I'm going to be sick.' Stopping beside the roadside curb, he vomited.

Peter felt sorry for his brother. Although Max

could be a spoilt brat, he didn't deserve to have his world destroyed. 'I'm so sorry. Would you like me to drive you down to Surrey? Your stuff's all at your girl groom's flat.

'Yes please,' Max said quietly.

Fortunately, Peter had the forethought to have brought one of the companies jags rather than his little sports car. Max spoke very little on the journey down to the yard, other than to give directions. His mind churned over with a hundred horrible scenarios as to the fate of his horses, and of Lee and Fran. When they arrived in the village, Max directed Peter to Fran's cottage, hoping that she would be there. He needed to know where the horses had gone, no matter how painful.

Fran had been looking out for them, and as soon as the engine was cut she opened the door. 'Max, I'm so sorry,' she sobbed. As he got out of the car, she ran over and gave him a tearful hug. Seconds later, her Jack Russell came tearing out the house, delighted to see his old friend. Max scooped the little dog up into his arms, and kissed him, whilst tears rolled down his face.

'Shall we go on in?' Peter suggested, not wanting there to be a public scene.

'Yes, please do.' Fran bustled them into the house and through to the sitting room.

'Do you want a drink?' she asked, but both brothers shook their heads.

'I must know what's happened to the horses.' Max got straight to the point.

Fran sat down on the arm of the sofa. 'Your

dad's orders were to get the horses gone within five days. He wanted a decent price, but the most important thing was that they had to be gone before you came home. It was a hell of an ask, and we were desperate to avoid any of them being sold to the Middle East, so Lee rang around the Brits and the Germans.'

Max felt slightly relieved, but then he knew that Lee and Fran would always put the horses' welfare above everything.

'Marcus has taken Harvey,' Max nodded approvingly, 'And the Seipps sent a transporter over for Lenin and Roxy. 'Again, these were good homes, which Max could accept.'What about Zhivago?'

He'd hoped that one of them would have bought his precious stallion. 'He was bought by Lady Hardcourt, and Lee has gone with him.'

'At least he'll be staying in the country. 'Oh god, I bet she's given the ride to that wanker Denton. He's such a ham-fisted oaf, he'll never cope with Zhivago.'

'You never know, if Paul can't cope, she may offer him back to you?'

'I doubt that,' Max said miserably. 'Once I was rude to her horse face daughter, and she hasn't liked me since.'

Ever the optimist, Fran said, 'Yeh, but she's also a shrewd businesswoman, and if she thinks you will protect her investment...'.

'What about Tilly?' Max asked.

'Who's Tilly? I don't recognise that name from the sales list?' Peter sounded severe.

'The old retired mare. Lee has sold her, but she's been added to the bottom.' Fran added quickly. 'She's worthless, but Lee managed to get £500 for her.'

'That sounds very cheap?' Peter sounded suspicious.

Max was about to add that she was worth a lot more than that as she was in foal to Zhivago, but Fran hurriedly made a face at him, so he shut up.

'Ten years ago she was worth £500,000, but she's in her twenties, crippled with arthritis and miscarried the last time we put her in foal, so £500 is good as she is just meat money.' Fran explained.

'I'll just grab my iPad from the car, to check.' Peter said.

Whilst he was gone, Fran whispered, 'Lee did a deal with your friend Lottie for Tilly. She's taken the mare down to her place in Devon. Lottie has promised that if Tilly successfully produces a foal, it's going to be gifted to you.'

'That's kind of them,' Max mumbled. It wasn't that he wasn't grateful, rather it was just that he felt sick and numbed by overpowering emotions. Now he knew his beloved horses were at least safe, he needed space to think. He had to get his head in order. He didn't want to be sat around being polite and making civilised conversation. The only option was to get back to Cindy's flat.

'I need to get myself sorted, then I'll be back for the few belongings I have left if that's OK?' he

158

said to Fran.

'Yeh, of course. It's no problem. Just take your time,' Fran said, standing up and giving Max a hug, and bursting into tears, 'You take care of yourself,' she sobbed.

Two hours later, Max found himself alone in Cindy's flat. He stared out the window, watching boats travelling up the murky waters of the Thames. The world that he knew had been destroyed. He had a thousand thoughts flooding into his head, all churning around like the water beneath him. He needed to think logically, but it was too difficult. Standing up he walked over to the drinks cabinet. Grabbing a bottle of vodka, he poured a large measure into a whisky tumbler. Having taken a huge gulp to steady his nerves, he leant heavily against the wall, and promptly burst into tears.

Chapter 14

Two days later Cindy arrived back from Paris, feeling particularly tired. She'd had a very trying couple of days. What with tetchy models, and a very highly strung designer to deal with, she'd had enough. There had to be easier ways of making a living. It didn't help matters that her gorgeous, rich boyfriend had just had his livelihood destroyed by his revengeful father. As she sat in a taxi crawling through the rush hour traffic, she wondered whether she'd find Max holed up in her apartment once she got home. She half hoped he wouldn't be there. She did love him, but with her biological clock ticking, she wasn't prepared to waste what time she had left. Without his horses, Max only had his pretty boy looks, and the effects of drink and drugs would soon destroy them.

The taxi drew up outside the smart wharf side apartment block. Cindy paid the fare and then made her way into the beautiful glass fronted foyer where she was greeted by the security warden. She loved living here, it was her expensive, luxurious sanctuary. Morally her home was half Max's. He'd put down 50% of the money, but the title deeds were only in her name. It had been a convenient mistake by the solicitor during the conveyance, but she'd never bothered to rectify the error. At the time Max had said he didn't care – he had access to as much money as he ever wanted, and the apartment was his way of committing to her.

As Cindy made her way up in the lift, she started to form a plan in her head. She'd have to be tough, but she had to set boundaries. She'd give Max one month to sort out his life, and learn to support himself, otherwise he would need to go. Bracing herself, she opened the apartment door. Immediately she was aware of the sound of sports commentary coming from the living room. She called out Max's name but there was no answer. Dropping her bags, she followed the noise of the TV.

Max was curled up on the sofa in a drunken stupor, still clutching a nearly empty vodka bottle. The floor was littered with empty junk food wrappers and clothes, whilst British Eurosport was replaying old footage of some show jumping competition. Cindy sighed. He looked so beautiful lying there sleeping peacefully, with his golden hair flopping over his face, partially covering his long blond eye lashes and exquisite bone structure, but without his father's funds he was nothing. 'I must be strong,' she said to herself as she walked over to the TV to turn it off, accidently kicking an empty wine bottle against the sofa, and making the dregs dribble out onto the cream carpet. She cursed loudly, which had the effect of waking Max. He cautiously opened one blood shot eye and tried to focus. He grunted in recognition but couldn't quite get it together sufficiently to speak.

Having cleared up the mess, Cindy made her

way through to the bedroom to have a shower. As she sat at her dressing table blow drying her hair, she decided that if Max was to stay in the apartment, he'd have to pay his way. Once her hair was dry, she opened her laptop and opened the file with her household expenses. Going through the service charges, utilities and food, she estimated that Max needed to pay her five hundred a week. She didn't know if he had any money. Peter had warned her that every account and card had been frozen, and all the vehicles sold. She reckoned she could get Max some modelling work, after all she had no intention of keeping him.

Over the next couple of days, they bickered and argued, mainly about money. Max had found out that his prize fund bank account hadn't been closed, as it wasn't one that either Ivan or Peter had access to. This meant that he was £40,000 better off than he'd thought. Immediately Cindy started demanding money for his keep, but he had other plans. The money would by him a basic horse lorry and a couple of novice horses – all he needed was somewhere to keep them.

Whilst Cindy was out visiting clients, Max was left alone to plan. His quickest route back into international show jumping was to get a job with one of the other professionals. Most jobs came with equine as well as human accommodation, and he would have time to bring on his own horses too. The only major flaw with this idea was that there were very few professionals who would touch him with a 10-

foot-long lunge whip. There were also only a handful of riders who Max could bare to work under. His most obvious choice was to try to get back working with Frederick Seipp and his team.

He needed someone else to talk to, taking a gamble he called Lee on his new phone. Alas Lee was busy, and being the newest member of staff, was under close scrutiny. Lee hurriedly reassured his ex-boss that Zhivago was well, and suggested that Max speak to Lottie, and offered to text her number.

Max cursed himself for not thinking of her earlier. He'd been meaning to call her to thank her for rescuing Tilly, and it would be good to hear her friendly voice. As he dialled her number however, he started to feel slightly panicky, and when she answered, he blurted out, 'Oh hello Lottie. Umm its Maxim Tarasov here. Er.. I just wanted to thank you for saving my dear old Tilly.'

'Oh Hi Max. Tilly's happily ensconced at home. I'm just so sorry I couldn't do more. The trouble was that by the time I found out, all your other horses had been promised to other people. I did try to get your father to hold off the sale of Zhivago until the sponsorship was agreed, but he wouldn't wait. I feel really bad that I didn't stop him.'

Max felt such warmth and gratitude towards his friend. 'Please don't blame yourself. If I hadn't been such an idiot.....Just for what you did for Tilly, I shall be forever grateful,' he added.

'What are you doing now?' Lottie asked, her curiosity getting the better of her.

'Bumming around in Cindy's apartment, wondering what the hell I'm going to do with the rest of my life.'

'I see. Do you want to carry on show jumping?'

'It's all I want to do,' he added firmly. He then mentioned his plan to get a job as a groom.

'It will be an awful comedown for you, being bossed around by people whose riding skill and knowledge is inferior to yours.' Lottie stated.

'But what else is there. Work in a riding stable on minimum wage for the rest of my life? Horses are all I care about. I'm desperate to get out of London and back into the fresh country air.'

'At the risk of sounding controlling, you would be most welcome to come down to our yard in Devon. We've only got a handful of full liveries, so since our last groom left, Mum's been managing them herself. I know she's desperate for a break, so you'd be doing us a huge favour. In return there's a cottage for you to live in, and plenty of room for a few horses. We couldn't afford to pay you, but we do have a decent arena if you wanted to make a living by teaching.'

Max hesitated. In his present circumstances, it sounded like a great option. Devon was a bit of a backwater, but he could quietly bring on a couple of horses, and with Lottie's contacts, eventually get some sponsors. 'It sounds great,' he replied.

'No need to decide now. Why don't you come down this weekend, and see what you think? You may hate the place, but at least make up your mind after you've had a look around,' Lottie replied.

Max readily agreed, and arrangements were made for him to get the train down to Plymouth on Friday afternoon, where Lottie would collect him from the station.

The next day, against his better judgement, Cindy bullied him into doing a modelling job. It paid quite well, and just involved him standing around in underwear for a fashion shoot. It wasn't hard work, but Max hated every second of being there and it did little to help his failing confidence levels. The only consolation was that he got paid in cash, money he handed on to Cindy for his share of their living costs.

Although Max and Cindy were getting on each other's nerves, and Cindy kept threatening to evict him, she seemed equally cross when he announced that he was travelling to Devon to see about picking up the shredded remains of his career. They ended up having a huge row, with Cindy accusing him of being a total loser. He too said things he would later regret, but it was obvious to both of them that their relationship wasn't strong enough to survive his newly acquired poverty.

Max found himself counting down the hours until he could escape London, but as he headed for Paddington station he started to feel nervous. From being a confident, arrogant man in full control of his life, he had morphed into a nobody. Lottie had gone from being inferior to him, to now being totally out of his league. She had the power and control and he had almost nothing to contribute in return.

To boost his ego, Max splashed out on a first-class ticket. He saw it as a final little luxury before his life changed forever, which was inevitable bearing in mind his lack of potential to generate more cash. Max had hoped for some peace and quiet, but the carriage was busy with commuters and day trippers returning home for the weekend.

Max gazed out of the window and watched as the landscape transformed from grey city to the green fields of the countryside. Gradually he became lost in thought. Every horse paddock that flashed by reminded him of the horses he'd adored, that due to a stupid drunken night were lost to him. He wondered whether they too missed him. At least Zhivago had the familiarity of Lee, but for the others everything was strange. His father had disposed of them without any regard. Max had always cared about his horses' feelings. As a little herd they were close. Now they'd been sold on, the horses who had been friends, were sent away with their fate unknown. Hurriedly Max wiped away a stray tear and ordered himself to get a grip. Luckily everyone around him was too busy with their own lives to take any notice.

Max had just managed to pull himself together when the steward approached with the refreshments. Having lost his appetite, Max ordered a vodka and tonic. He reckoned that a bit of Dutch courage wouldn't be a bad thing given his ordeal. Once again he was left in peace to nurse his drink and give him time to plan.

He began to think about Lottie. He considered the irony that for months he'd been desperate to bed her, and now that he probably stood the greatest chance of having her he couldn't risk it. Lovers never made good business partners, and former lovers were even worse. When he thought back over all the friends and acquaintances he'd made over the years, she'd been the only one there when he really needed it.

Unable to help himself, his mind fleetingly reverted to its old arrogant self, wondering whether Lottie was just another pathetic, devoted fan who only lived her life through others. Admittedly she had a good job, and her family seemed nice and respectable, but it didn't mean that they didn't live in a council flat in a dead-end market town. Her lorry was ancient, and she did only have one decent horse. Maybe he shouldn't have been so hasty in rushing off after her, just because she'd been kind.

As the train reached Bristol Temple Mead, half the people in the carriage got up ready to leave, much to Max's relief. As the train emptied, Max's attention was drawn to a photograph on the cover of a discarded magazine. Getting to his feet, Max walked over to investigate further. The *Tatler* magazine headline read, *'Britain's most understated eligible bachelor.'* Underneath the headline, Max recognised the person in the photo as one of Lottie's brothers.

Hurriedly flicking through the publication,

Max found the supporting article. There was a lovely photo taken in the grounds of a country house of Tom, Lottie, their actor brother, their mother Beth, and their infamous father Nick Marchbank, night club owner and younger brother of the Tory Party Chairman, the Duke of Chiswick. The article explained that studious academic Tom was the Earl of Martley. Although he spent his days doing research, and his evenings as a freelance society journalist he was shortly to inherit Dewerstone, a stately home along with a 10,000-acre estate in Devon.

Max was horrified. It was certainly karma for the disparaging thoughts he'd had only moments before, and he felt both chastened and distraught by what he'd learnt. He wondered why Lottie had a different surname, but at least the conflicting snippets of information he had on her now made sense.

Max wasn't familiar with Devon, so took great pleasure in the journey as the train wound its way along the edge of the coast. He sat, sipping his 3rd drink as he gazed out to sea. Before long, the train travelled back inland and the scenery changed to the beautiful but starkly different view of the Dartmoor hills. After the confines of London, Max's spirits began to lift as the glorious county unfolded in front of him.

By the time the train pulled into Plymouth station, Max was not entirely sober, but the numbing effect of the alcohol helped to subdue his nerves. As he was only carrying a small bag, Max was one of the first to alight, and after a moment's confusion, found the exit signs. For a rural station, it was surprisingly large and busy, and as he passed through the barrier there were people everywhere. Finally, he spotted Lottie, who waved cheerfully. She looked relieved and he suspected that she'd half expected him to have bailed out.

Max had a moment's uncertainty as to how he should greet her, so plumped for a kiss on the cheek, which seemed to be the right thing to do. She responded with a brief hug, 'So glad you made it. Did you have a good journey?' she said enthusiastically.

'It's good to see you again, and thank you for the invitation,' Max replied, as he followed her outside to a mud sprayed Range Rover.

As they reached the car, Max decided to tackle Lottie on the article he'd seen. 'Why didn't you tell me you were part of such a glamorous, and prestigious aristocratic family?' he asked accusingly, sounding more aggressive than he intended.

Lottie cringed. 'You've being doing research?'

'No I haven't,' Max sounded like his old arrogant self. 'Someone left a copy of *Tatler* on the train, and your family were plastered all over it.'

'Ah, I see.' Lottie replied, trying to hide her irritation. 'Well don't get your hopes up, because we don't have any money.'

Max stood rooted to the spot. 'Nobody has any right to accuse me of being a gold digger,' he flashed angrily.'Is that why you didn't tell me –

you dared to think I might be desperate enough to want you for your inheritance?'

Lottie had had enough. 'No – It's because my parents are boring, middle-class professionals, and my only links to the aristocratic side of the family is through my mother's second marriage. Let's face it, if it wasn't for my job with Yangtze, you wouldn't have given me a second glance.'

'I did get more propositions than a person could reasonably be expected to handle,' Max answered more consolatory.

'You of all people should understand why I have to be careful,' Lottie replied bitterly. 'Girls fell in love with you because you were famous. Well to a lesser extent, I too have been a victim. So many people who think I'm a Marchbank automatically assume I'm an heiress with a drug habit. My brother Tom is an Earl and inherits a 10,000-acre estate when he's 25, but as for the rest of us.... My stepfather Nick blew most of his fortune on drink and drugs. The Dewerstone Estate owns our house. Only the livery side is ours, well Mum's, and Ben will one day get the share of Lizzies night club. I'm lucky that I've got a good job, but I'm not rich. Just have good contacts.'

'I'm sorry I was rude,' Max replied softly. 'Please can we start again... I am grateful for the chance to get back into horses. I don't even know why I over-reacted to the *Tatler* article.'

Lottie smiled, 'That's fine, now get in the car and I'll take you home to meet my disreputable family, rather than the airbrushed image of them you are imagining.'

170

Max sat back in the car seat and closed his eyes. The friction between them had at least had the effect of sobering him up. He had surprised himself by his oversensitivity, but he guessed it was down to his new-found poverty. He looked across at Lottie who clearly hadn't made much of an effort to impress him. She was wearing dirty jeans, muddy Jodhpur boots, and a well-worn shirt. Her hair had been hurriedly tied back, and bits had come loose. He couldn't decide whether to be flattered that she didn't feel the need to put on a pretence, or disappointed that she didn't care sufficiently to try.

After about fifteen minutes they left the city and headed up over the moors. Soon Lottie turned off down a narrow lane, surrounded by high hedges, brightly emblazoned with pink campions, cow parsley and foxgloves. The road dropped down into a valley, passed neat little cottages, orchards, and lush fields. Lottie slowed down to drive over a granite bridge, before climbing a steep winding hill. As they reached the top, the countryside opened up. Ahead was a stunning granite house, surrounded by a small park and woodland. The dramatic effect was enhanced by the wonderful backdrop of a large granite topped Tor- a Dartmoor hill covered in bracken and gorse, with scatterings of what Max thought were rocks, but could have been sheep.

Moments later they reached the estate entrance. As they went through the large iron gates, Lottie pointed out the lodge where she lived. She didn't stop but carried on towards the main house. As the car came to a stop, Max spotted a huge grey dog coming hurtling towards them, barking frantically. 'Christ, it's the hound of the Baskervilles,' he muttered, reluctant to move from the safety of the vehicle.

Lottie jumped out of the driver's seat and rushed around to greet the dog, who jumped up affectionately, wrapping its huge paws around her waist. 'Don't worry,' she called to Max. 'Shadow is really friendly.'

Max cautiously got out of the car. 'What the hell is it?' he asked.'She's a deerhound,' Lottie grinned, as she absent-mindedly caressed the dog's head. Shadow headed over to Max, and leant her body into him, demanding a stroke.

'She's so huge, I could practically ride her,' Max muttered. 'All I need is a saddle.'

'Come and meet everyone, and then I'll show you to the guest suite. Once you have freshened up, I bet you will be desperate to see Tilly,' Lottie said enthusiastically.

Beth warmly greeted Max, but neither Nick nor Ben were to be found, so Max followed Lottie and Shadow up to the guest wing of the house, which overlooked a small lake. Max's bedroom was large and airy, but the furnishings were designed more for modern comfort than elegance. The large bay window gave the room a spacious feeling and offered fantastic views of the Devon countryside. Conscious that he was keeping Lottie waiting, he dumped his bag on the bed, and hurriedly splashed some cold water over his face before following her back downstairs.

Lottie led him passed a huge kitchen, and out into a courtyard. Going around the back of the garages, a path led down to a pretty stable yard, across from which was a neat, moderately sized cottage. Ignoring the human accommodation, Lottie headed into the feed store and grabbed a handful of pony nuts, which she slipped into the back pocket of her jeans.

'I'll take you to see Tilly,' she announced. 'Her field is a couple of minutes' walk away. She's sharing with a retired ex-racehorse gelding, whom she bosses around terribly.'

With both Max and Shadow following her, Lottie strode off down a grassy track, passed a large horse schooling arena, and through a gate into an empty field. Shadow ran around the boundary of the field on the lookout for rabbits, but Lottie headed straight through the middle, directly towards another gate, half-hidden by a large beech tree.

As they reached the gate Lottie called out, 'Tilly, look who's come to see you.' Max saw in front of him his first ever top senior level showjumper, now greying and showing signs of multiple pregnancies, lift her head and nicker appreciatively. Slowly, Tilly turned and ambled up towards the gate, her equally elderly black companion following closely behind her. Lottie opened the gate and they headed off down to meet the two horses.

Max put his arms around Tilly's neck and buried his face in her mane, whilst she nuzzled his back with her nose searching for treats. 'I'm so

173

sorry Tilly,' Max mumbled. 'It so great to see you my darling, I've missed you so much.' Lottie, who had been deliberately keeping her distance, and making a fuss of Tilly's companion, produced the now slightly warm nuts from her pocket, and handed half to Max to give to his beloved mare. She pretended not to notice the tears in his eyes.

'They have a shelter at the bottom of the field, and if the flies get too bad, we'll stick fly rugs on them. I've also bought Tilly a couple of turnout rugs. She has stud mix once a day, but normally the lady who owns the other horse feeds her, so they get fed at the same time. When the weather gets too bad, we will bring her in at night. So hopefully you think she is in good hands with us.'

In a slightly croaky voice, Max replied, 'To be honest, I'm not sure how to ever thank you.'

Relieved, Lottie replied, 'Oh that's easy. You can repay me with some lessons on Taggart if that's OK with you. After all, you are one of the best show jumpers in the world. Sparing time to give me some advice – well, for us mere mortals, that's a dream come true,' she laughed, hoping to lift his mood.

They walked back up to the yard, and Lottie showed Max around the cottage that went with the groom's job. Originally a farmhouse, it was larger than Max had expected. Typically, the house had a large kitchen, together with a separate cold store, a scruffy, but comfortable looking sitting room, and a sparsely furnished dining room. Also downstairs was a boot room, with an old stone sink and an ancient washing machine.

Max followed Lottie up the faded staircase to the landing, off which there were 3 bedrooms and an old fashioned, but functional bathroom. 'I'm afraid the accommodation isn't exactly palatial, but everyone who has stayed here says it's comfortable.' Lottie said, apologetically.

'No, it's great. In fact, it reminds me a bit of the house that went with Lark Rise Stables. That had a similar feel to it. I had some good times there,' he mused.

'Anyway this is yours if you want it,' Lottie retorted. 'We only have six horses in full livery, so the rest of the time you'd be free to teach or bring on your own horses.' She glanced at Max, hoping that he was going to say yes.

He smiled. 'I'm really grateful for the opportunity to escape London, and this is my best chance of getting back into jumping. If you don't mind then thank you, I'd love to.'

'And I can have some lessons off you?' Lottie smiled appealingly.

'It will be a pleasure,' Max replied warmly.

They headed back to the house, and Max went to his room to shower and change for dinner. He'd travelled light, so didn't have anything particularly smart to wear. He had anticipated grabbing a meal at a local pub, certainly dining with aristocracy hadn't been part of his game plan. He pulled out his least crumpled top, and chinos, and had a wash and shave. Feeling underdressed, and in his new state of poverty, he nervously headed back down to meet the family.

Much to Max's horror, everyone else was dressed formally for dinner, putting him immediately at a disadvantage. Beth came over to him, seemingly genuinely pleased to see him, gave him a warm, comforting hug.

'Come and meet my husband Nick,' she said.

Sat in an armchair, by a large bay window, was a handsome man in his fifties. He pulled himself to his feet, smiling, he extended his hand, 'Pleased to meet you Max. I'm Nick Marchbank, Lottie's stepfather.'

'I'm so sorry I didn't bring anything suitable to change into.... Lottie didn't warn me.'

'We could lend you a dinner jacket, but to be honest, I only dress for dinner, because it saves me having to think of what else to wear, so if you are happy to stay as you are, then its fine by us. To be honest, we would normally have had supper on a tray, but we thought we'd make an effort. It's not every day we get to play host to the son of a Russian Billionaire.'

Max cringed, 'I'm honoured, but now I feel a fraud, bearing in mind I've been dis-inherited.'

Much to Max's surprise Nick just laughed. 'Lottie told me about tweet gate. Your father really needs to get things in perspective. I've lost track the number of times it happened to me. Compared to what I used to get up to you're a saint.'

Max instantly liked Nick and started to relax. 'It wasn't just the tweet I'm afraid. I also slept with the wife of the Constituency party chairman of the seat my father was hoping to stand for.'

'Really,' Nick roared, 'Oh, you are amusing.'

Max was handed a gin and tonic, by Lottie's brother Ben, together with a warning that it was from the family's own distillery and was lethal in large doses. Max cautiously took a sip, anticipating the bitter taste of a poisonous home-made concoction, but was pleasantly surprised. The liquid warmed his throat and was strangely comforting. He drank quickly and was immediately offered a refill.

Lottie had been talking on her mobile when he'd entered the room, but when her conversation finished, she made her way over to see him. Dressed in a body-hugging blue silk dress, Max considered how stunning she looked. Relaxed and happy, she seemed so different from the stern, intimidating woman he'd first met all those months before. He inwardly cringed, as he remembered his arrogant treatment of her.

'Sorry about my clothes, I just wish you'd warned me.'

'I was planning on taking you down to the village pub, but earlier Mum insisted that we joined them. Dad, as in Nick, says he's been dying to meet you, as we've allegedly been talking about you non-stop for days now.'

'I hope I'm not a disappointment,' Max replied uncertainly.

'You've nothing to worry about,' Lottie reassured him.

'But I'm practically penniless.'

'So is he nowadays. At least you were

disinherited. Nick drank away all of his, so relax. No one is going to judge you.'

As Lottie topped up his drink, Max said, 'So doesn't anyone in your family drink alcohol? I seem to be the only one working my way through the drinks cabinet.'

'Nick may have a glass of wine with his meal, but any more than that and his doctor will shout at him. Neither mum, myself nor Tom drink. Mum never did, and we've been brought up with Dad's little problem so it kind of put us off. Ben being the youngest missed the worst of it, so isn't quite so hung up on the drinking thing. He doesn't tend to really drink at home, but I suspect that when he's not here.... Well you get the picture.'

Moments later dinner was called. Nick slowly, and stiffly made his way through to the dining room supported by Beth. Max was conscious of the numbing effects of the gin starting to take hold as he followed Lottie, whilst her younger brother took up the rear.

The dining room was large and airy, in contrast to the heavy antique furnishings. As expected, Nick made his way over to the head of the table, whilst Beth sat on his left. Nick beckoned Max to sit on his other side,

'Come, sit next to me and join me in having a glass of wine,' he ordered.

'Thank you....' Max hesitated. He panicked, not knowing how he should address his host.

Noticing Max's discomfort, his host added, 'please just call me Nick. Of course, I'm part

Russian you know. My Great Grandmother was related to Tsar Nikolas, which is how I got my name. She married Crispin Marchbank, who my elder brother is named after. Their son served as Prime Minister, and we've had a Tory minister in the family ever since. My brother is Party Chairman, and now heads the party in The Lords. I blame my Russian ancestry for my love of vodka, but alas my wife won't allow me to drink it any more,' he added wistfully. 'I assume you are an aficionado of the grain?'

'Very much so,' Max grinned. 'Alas the excessive appreciation of it has got me into trouble more than once.'

Whilst the family ate, the conversation slowed, and gave Max time to sit back and take stock of his situation. He'd drunk just sufficient alcohol to get a warm, contented feeling. Right now he loved the Marchbank family. They were so incredibly welcoming and non-judgemental. He'd never grown up within a stable family unit and longed for acceptance from Lottie and her relations. His father would have been delighted by the connection, and the irony wasn't lost on him.

He sat and listened as Ben and his sister discussed the characterisation of Sebastian, the role he gathered Ben was rehearsing for. Beth then joined in, blaming the character's drink problem on the guilt felt at being homosexual whilst trying to live within the confines of Catholic teaching. Ben counteracted by blaming the fearsome controlling nature of Sebastian's mother. Meanwhile Lottie said it was genetic, and that Sebastian was merely following on from his father.

Max had never read the book or seen the film, so had no opinion. Although this left him unable to contribute to the discussion, he found himself enjoying listening to intelligent reasoned conversation. Not something he'd experienced a great deal of since leaving school. He decided that now was his chance to become more cultured. He had no idea how long he'd be able to stay with the Marchbanks', but he was determined to make the most of every minute.

Chapter 15

Three days later Max and Lottie drove a rental van up to Surrey to pick up the remains of Max's possessions. They arrived shortly before lunch and headed straight to Fran's cottage. Fran had rushed back to meet them in her lunch break, so had little time to gossip, but admitted that now she was at the racing yard, show jumping news was sparse.

'The rest of your stuff has been put in the old foaling shed at Lark Rise,' Fran explained.

'Is there a new tenant yet?' Max asked.

'Yeh, another showjumper, but I can't remember his name. He's not very well known.' Fran answered.

Max started up the van whilst Fran waved then off. 'Oh, I've just remembered the name of the guy who's taken over the yard. It's the tosser that went to Germany with you last year – Ed Carter.'

Fortunately, when they pulled up in the yard there was no one around. Lottie was relieved, as it spared Max more humiliation. Max walked across to the ricketiest looking stable which was home to his possessions.

'Let's get on with it, so we can get out of here as soon as possible,' Max ordered gruffly.

As he opened the door, Lottie peered into the

gloom, and to the pile of belongings unceremoniously dumped on the dusty floor. Max marched in and grabbed an armful of clothes, before hurriedly heading back to the van. Lottie bent down to pick up a couple of expensive looking riding jackets, emblazoned with the names of competition sponsors, when she noticed a couple of beautiful, framed photographs of Max on Zhivago thrown down and smashed in the corner of the stable.

Climbing over the rugs and saddles she carefully picked up the photos, shaking away the loose splinters of glass. Lost in sad reflection of better times, Lottie didn't hear Max returning.'What's it like picking over the carcass of my previous life?' Max asked sharply.

'Sorry,' Lottie was slightly startled. 'I'll get new frames.'

'What's the point? The person in that photo no longer exists.' Max sounded close to tears.

Feeling awkward, Lottie turned, and gently touched his arm. 'I realise how painful this is for you. Why don't you get back in the van and leave this to me?'

'No you are all right.' Max braved a weak smile. 'Besides which you'll be too bloody slow.'

They carried on robotically walking to and from the van, with armfuls of stuff. The last things to pack were Max's saddles. They were covered in dust, but as Lottie picked up the first one she admired how beautifully handcrafted it was. 'This is gorgeous, 'she announced in admiration. Max stopped to look.

'That one was Zhivago's.' It was particularly comfortable. Taking a closer look at it he added. 'I reckon it would fit Taggart. If you aren't going to be offended by the offer of second-hand goods, I'd like you to have it.'

'But that's too generous.' Lottie was shocked. She didn't feel worthy accepting the saddle worn by one of the greatest showjumpers on the planet.

'Nonsense,' Max said. 'I'd rather it was used, and besides, I have so much to thank you for – this is a poor repayment.'

As they started their journey back to Devon, Max's mood lifted. Lottie had taken over the driving, and Max was scanning her IPad searching for horse lorries for sale. Of the £40,000 he had left in the bank, he decided that he would splash out half of it on transport, and the balance on horses. 'Would you object if we made a short detour?' he asked. 'I've found a moderately OK lorry in my price bracket I'd like to have a look at. It's a bit old fashioned and basic, but will do for starters,' he added, having read the advert out loud.'

'Everything's relative,' Lottie muttered, thinking that it sounded the height of luxury, compared to her own twenty-two-year-old bone shaker.

The next morning Lottie drove Max to the bank, so he could arrange an electronic transfer to the owners of the 18-tonne ex eventer Scania lorry. Lottie stood back and flicked through sales brochures but couldn't help overhearing the conversation between Max and the bank clerk. She heard the note of horror in Max's voice, when he was told he only had £25,000 remaining in his account.

'I don't understand?' Max sounded confused.

'There was an American Express direct debit for just over £12,000 Sir,' came the reply.

Chapter 16

As Ben entered the room he felt terrified as everyone turned and looked at him and to make matters worse he was late.

'I'm dreadfully sorry, there was a hold up on the Central Line,' he apologised, feeling his cheeks reddening.

'Well hurry up and find a seat, we're already behind schedule thanks to you,' snapped the officious looking woman he remembered from the audition.

A rather camp looking man in his late twenties immediately stood up, 'come and sit next to me. You MUST be playing Sebastian.'

'Yes,' Ben answered gratefully, sitting beside his new friend.

'Pleased to meet you,' his companion said in a hushed voice. 'Julian,' he extended his hand.

'Ben.'

'Delighted to make your acquaintance.'

The director got to his feet, 'When Anthony Blanche has quite finished flirting, I will begin.'

The room fell silent. 'We will start filming at Castle Howard next week, starting with Charles first visit, and then the summer holiday section where Sebastian has broken his foot. The students leave college in 3 weeks' time, so then we move down to Oxford, and have just 8 weeks to get the bulk of the filming done covering the first third of the book.' He paused. 'Everyone clear so far?'

There was a general mumbling of agreement.

'Excellent. Well for the rest of today, I want you to all get to know each other. Later we will start running through a few scenes, but the next few days are mainly for the costume and make up departments to sort you actors out with your look. The only thing we haven't done yet is to find a venue to film the Marchmain House scenes. If anyone has any ideas, then let me know. It's not a major part of the book, so won't be too intrusive.'

Desperate to win back some brownie points, Ben put up his hand. 'I could ask my uncle if we could use his house for filming.'

'You are familiar with the book I assume?' Ben recognised the owner of the voice, as that of Damian King, an arrogant heartthrob who'd had roles in everything from Rom-Com films to TV detective drama.'Marchmain House is meant to be a stately home, not a terraced house in Wandsworth.'

Deciding he had to defend himself, Ben answered, 'You don't have to concern yourself. Old money you see. You can look us all up in Debrett.' Around him the cast and crew started laughing. Ben grinned. By paraphrasing Sebastian, he'd managed to get his point across. Although he was the least experienced of the actors, he was determined not to let Damian push him around.

'Thank you for the offer Ben. If you think His

Grace, The Duke of Chiswick would consider allowing us access to his home that would be excellent,' the formerly scary woman sat next to the director answered.

Whilst the director continued with his briefing, Ben surreptitiously scanned the room. Rather to his horror, the woman playing his mother was a formidable Bafta winning actress, plus Lord Marchmain was being played by one of the most treasured actors in the country. The girl playing Cordelia, the youngest sister was unknown, neither did he recognise the stunning beauty playing his sister Julia Flyte. Although in the story, he was supposed to fall in love with Damian's character Charles Ryder, he couldn't take his eyes off the beautiful girl meant to be his sister.

At the risk of coming across as cocky, Ben was desperate for an opportunity to impress the girl playing Julia. Just before the meeting broke for refreshments, the director raised the question of stunt doubles for the hunting scene involving Brideshead, Cordelia and Sebastian. The actor playing Brideshead said he couldn't ride, but the young actress playing Cordelia said she was OK if it didn't involve jumping hedges.

'Don't tell me.. You've ridden to hinds since you were 5,' Damian put on a mock upper-class accent as he deliberately challenged Ben.

'As it happens I was three when I went to my first meet. I also play polo, so no I don't need a stunt double thanks.' Inwardly Ben was delighted. Damian was sat far too close to the girl playing

Julia, so any chance to make his own presence known was vital.

Once they broke for lunch, the formidable Bafta actress came over to Ben and introduced herself. 'I hear you're not long out of RADA?'

'Ten months,' Ben answered. 'Although I was very lucky to walk straight into a theatre role, so I've kept busy, and haven't needed to wait tables yet.'

'Well if you need any advice, I'm always happy to help,' she offered.

'Thank you. It would be an honour,' Ben answered with sincerity.

As the Bafta actress moved on, the Julia actress came over to Ben. 'Sorry about Damian. He is rather in love with himself....I'm Sophie by the way.'

'Pleased to meet you,' Ben shook her hand. 'Ben Marchbank,'

'Yes I know. After finding out the cast list, I've been stalking you on the internet,' Sophie grinned.

'Well I'm embarrassed to say, that I've wholly neglected to research anyone, so I'm afraid that I'm not familiar with your CV.'

'I've been in a couple of TV dramas, but they were shown on BBC 2, so barely registered with the great viewing public.'

'Well that just means that the director must have seen your incredible talent, and thought you worthy above all the more famous names.'

Sophie smiled warmly, 'Ditto. Damian is rather irritated that he had to work hard to get the part of Charles, despite being well known, and yet you've practically walked straight out of drama school and breezed into playing the part of Sebastian.'

'I just wish it was you I was supposed to fall in love with. It's going to take all my very limited acting skills to convince anyone that I'm gay.'

'I'm glad you aren't. And as we are the new kids on the block, I think we should team up make a pact to stick together.'

Ben looked into her eyes and in a very serious voice announced. 'I, the Honourable Benjamin, Silas, Felix Marchbank do solemnly swear that through thick and thin, through the rough and the smooth, for better or for worse, whether richer or poorer, in sickness and in health, that I will stand by you throughout the making of this film.'

Sophie grinned delightedly, 'Thank you kind, noble Sir. In the face of such a valiant gesture, I'd better swear allegiance too.'

Over the next couple of weeks Ben started to settle down into his role. He and Sophie continued to be good friends, plus he was getting to know the rest of the cast and crew. It was once they got to the third week that things started to go wrong. They were filming the scenes where Sebastian starts to fall in love with Charles. No matter how hard he tried, the director wasn't satisfied with Ben's performance, and by the end of the day the other cast members were showing signs of impatience.

By the time Ben got back to his hotel room,

any self confidence in his ability as an actor had been decimated. Feeling homesick and alone, and filled, in equal measure by self-loathing and frustration, he did something he'd never done before. He raided the mini bar.

The next morning Ben arrived on set feeling both physically and emotionally sick. His head was pounding, and he was gripped with fear. He just wanted to lie down in a darkened room, and the thought of actually having to act was almost too awful to consider. Luckily the weather was terrible, so the plan to film outdoor scenes between Charles and Sebastian were scrapped, and Ben was given a stay of execution, whilst the crew switched to filming a scene between Charles and Julia.

Over lunch Damian made a few digs in Ben's direction. Ashamed by his weakness as a human being, and his ability as an actor, Ben couldn't bring himself to retaliate. He was sure that they all despised him and regretted their decision to cast him. He couldn't imagine a time when he'd felt more miserable. Ben had little appetite, and picked at his food, whilst trying to be invisible. After a brief lull whilst he ate, Damian then restarted with the snide remarks.

Suddenly the Bafta winning actor Michael Forman, who was playing Lord Marchmain, turned to Damian and said, 'I don't know why you are being quite so cocky. It isn't so long ago that you murdered the part of the prince, when I was playing Prospero at The Old Vic, whereas I hear young Ben here is extremely good in live theatre productions.'

Ben just sat opened mouthed. One of the greatest actors in the business had just defended him. Michael turned and spoke to Ben. 'Meet me in the hotel foyer at 7pm. I'm taking you out to dine, and we can talk through the elements you are finding tricky.'

'Thank you,' Ben muttered, almost lost for words.

Michael was as good as his word. His driver took them to a quite restaurant in York, where they were able to chat in peace. Michael was happy to impart advice on how Ben should play being in love with Charles. As the evening wore on Ben confessed his guilt over his drunken binge.

'Dear boy,' Michael looked amused, 'I'm not saying that it will be easy. You have the risk of genetics, mixed with a career where the personality needed to succeed also involves a predisposition to excess. But you have such an inbuilt fear of sliding down the slippery slope, and that will be your protection.'

Buoyed by Michael's belief in him, Ben cheered up immensely. The next day he went back on set with a new sense of confidence. Having followed Michael's advice, he got through the dreaded romantic scene. It wasn't going to be the best performance of his life, but it was sufficiently convincing to be acceptable, and he finished the day safe in the knowledge that he was going to survive.

Chapter 17

Once Max had moved into Lottie's cottage, he wasted very little time in getting on with the rebuilding of his life. From the precious pot of prize money which was his only capital, he spent twenty thousand on a moderately acceptable lorry. Compared to the luxury of the Tarasov's Scania, his new lorry looked scruffy and old fashioned, and very much of the level of amateur riders. Being a HGV it carried 4 horses, slept 4 humans and had a bathroom and a cooker, so in theory it would at least allow him to compete in the UK. Although Max felt decidedly underwhelmed by his purchase, he couldn't afford better, and Lottie's childlike enthusiasm and excitement over the lorry made him feel rather guilty.

Max's next purchase was a little hatch back car, followed by the buying of his first horse – an extremely well-bred but sensibly priced, unbacked four-year-old colt, obtained from a small stud in Cornwall. The colt, which had been born on Midsummer's night, he named Oberon. He was a stunning animal, with a sleek dark bay coat, and a look at me attitude. He floated across his new field, oozing the confidence of his famous ancestors. He'd be given a couple of months of groundwork training, and then Max intended to back him.

The days passed quickly. What with his new role as an instructor, riding Taggart, helping with the liveries and training Oberon, Max lost track of time. Suddenly he realised that his friend Charlie's wedding was less than a week away, and he had made no preparations.

The invitation had been for him and Cindy, so the first thing he did was to text Charlie and ask if he could bring Lottie instead. Charlie replied seconds later, saying it was fine with him. That evening when Lottie got home from work, Max plucked up the courage to ask her to accompany him.

'It should be a glamorous occasion. Both families are loaded. The service is in the local village church, then the reception will be held in a marquee in the grounds of Arabella's family home. It's one of the nicest houses in Gloucestershire,' he added by way of an extra selling point.

'They don't mind you bringing me and not Cindy?'

'Already checked with Charlie and he's cool. He never really liked Cindy anyway.'

'Gloucestershire is too far to get there and back in one day.'

'It's sorted. I booked a room at a rather smart local hotel months ago. I've checked and they can turn the double into twin beds if that's OK. If you'd rather have your own room, they may be able to arrange something.'

Lottie hesitated. She was pleased that he hadn't just expected her to sleep with him, but she wasn't sure she was even ready to share a room.

'I promise I will behave honourably,' Max smiled, sensing her uncertainty. 'I won't get undressed in front of you, and I shan't complain if you snore.'

'Well in that case you're on, thank you.' Lottie grinned.

Fortunately for Max, his brother had managed to rescue the majority of Max's wardrobe, including his expensive, Italian designed morning suit. He had also paid for the hotel room at the point of booking it, at a time when money had been so plentiful. He was just congratulating himself on his good organisational skills when he remembered that he hadn't got Charlie and Arabella a wedding present.

He logged onto the wedding Facebook page and downloaded the gift list. He scanned the list in horror. Lottie peaked over his shoulder.'OK so where's the section which lists the £29.99 John Lewis kettle or the set of knives? Christ, who puts a £5000 garden sculpture on their wedding list?'

'People like Charlie and Arabella unfortunately,' Max replied as he frantically scrolled down the list looking for something under £100.

Lottie was delighted that Max wanted her to join him, and she was determined to make a special effort; it was the first time he would be back in society following the break with his father. She therefore arranged with her boss at work to borrow Yangtze's flashiest sports car for the weekend. She desperately wanted Max to feel good about himself.

They set off early the morning of the wedding, the sports car eating up the miles. As they got close to the church, Lottie pretended that she was tired, and asked Max to drive. The plan worked well. They arrived at the church at the point when most of Max's acquaintances were milling around outside and spotted him getting out of the flash motor. Dressed in his beautifully tailored morning suit, he looked rich and powerful, and the paparazzi homed in on him and Lottie as they walked towards the church.

Charlie was standing, waiting nervously in the church porch, along with his brother Quentin, whilst his cousin George was inside directing people to seats.

'You're looking well,' Charlie said. 'Thought you'd be living in the gutter once your old man kicked you out, but seems I was wrong.'

'God, you're such an arrogant arse, 'Max replied, slapping his friend jovially on the back. 'Anyway, congratulations mate.'

'You must be Lottie,' Quentin slipped behind his brother in order to shake her hand. 'Thank you for bringing Max.'

'It was the other way around actually,' Lottie answered. 'I haven't been to a decent wedding in ages, so I'm delighted that he invited me.'

'Surely not. You're one of the Marchbanks'. You must be practically tripping over the floods of invitations dropping daily on your door mat.'

Lottie laughed. 'You'd think... but no one's getting hitched or anything exciting like that at the moment.'

She felt a hand on her shoulder. 'Come on let's get inside,' Max said gently. Having been seated, Lottie flicked through the order of service leaflet, whilst Max was turning around, chatting to his friends. She was just thinking how very 'Four Weddings and a Funeral' it all was, when she heard Max exclaim. 'Christ what's she doing here?' She turned to see Cindy standing in the doorway, clearly planning her entrance. 'It's the ghost of girlfriend's past,' Lottie said rather louder than she'd planned, much to the amusement of the surrounding guests.

Soon the church was packed, and once the ceremony began, Lottie forgot that Cindy was even there. The bride looked stunning, and although Lottie didn't particularly like Charlie, he was handsome, and the two of them looked good together. Once the service was over the photographer took charge, which meant lots of standing around. Lottie couldn't help feeling a little bored, as she didn't know anyone, and Max wasn't great at introductions. Whilst he chatted away merrily, catching up on old school friends, Lottie was left making small talk with elderly aunts.

The reception was being held a couple of miles from the church, in a marquee in the grounds of Arabella's parent's house. As Max still had the car keys, she let him drive. There was a short delay as the cars entered through the large driveway gates as security guards were meticulously checking invitations. Eventually they parked up and walked down the gravel drive toward the garden.

Max studied the table plan and announced that they were on table 3 along with a bunch of Max and Charles old school friends, together with Charles' cousin George and his wife. As they reached the table, Lottie was about to sit down but she couldn't see her place name. The one next to Max had Cindy's name on it. Behind her she could hear Cindy calling across to a friend, 'It looks like I'm stuck on the table with Max, and his boring friends; we'll catch up later darling.'

'Max,' she hissed. 'We have a problem.'

'But I told Charlie I was bringing you.' Max trailed off, looking confused.

'Well he's a man. He probably didn't think to pass on the message. Besides which, you should have un-invited Cindy.'

'Oh crap. Look you stay here. I'll ask the caterers to set another place or move Cindy or something.'

'No.' Lottie stood firm. 'It will cause a great deal of fuss and confusion, and the last thing we need is the wedding breakfast being disrupted. I'll slip back to the hotel for a couple of hours, and pop back later when the evening guest arrive.'

'But that's not fair. I can't let you do that, after all you've done.'

'It's quite fair. You stay here where you're needed. I'll be fine.' Lottie gave him a determined look, before grabbing the keys and setting off back to the car, desperate to leave before things got embarrassing. Once back in the car she reset the satnav for the hotel and sat crossly cursing her

197

rotten luck at having spent a week's wages on an outfit that had barely seen the light of day.

Lottie's mood improved slightly when she reached the hotel and realised how smart and luxurious it was. It wouldn't be too much hardship; there were worse places to be killing time. The young male receptionist was very friendly and she let slip her predicament. He must have felt sorry for her, because as she was unpacking her case, he called to offer her a heavily discounted afternoon spa package, which she gratefully accepted.

Although not what she had planned, Lottie spent a lovely afternoon eating a cream tea, and having a massage and facial. She then went back to the bedroom, and having bagged the bed nearest the window, changed into her evening wear, a little black Frank Usher dress.

Back at the reception Max was not having anywhere near such a relaxing time, mainly thanks to Cindy.

'So how are you managing, living with little miss chastity?' she sneered contemptuously.

'We're just friends.'

'Oh come off it Max. You've given more rides than a London taxi. Now you're telling me that you and Lottie skip hand in hand through the meadows, like something out of fucking Jane Austen.'

'Not every relationship is built around sex.'

'If something has two legs and a vagina and has ventured within ten feet of you then you've screwed it. That's the way you are. So what is it?

Are you living with a dyke?'

'Will you shut up?' Max snapped, glaring at her. 'Firstly, I didn't say I was celibate, and secondly, I don't want to rush things with Lottie. I have too much to lose.'

Moodily Max left the table and made his way over to the bar. He was already feeling angry over the place settings, and having Cindy attack him was the last straw. It hadn't occurred to him that Cindy would still have come. It wasn't as if she liked his friends, and now she was here being spiteful, whilst Lottie was stuck in a hotel room. He ordered a double vodka, and having knocked it back, ordered another on the basis that getting drunk was the only way he was going to survive the afternoon.

Lottie left the hotel shortly after 6.30. It was only when she drove up to the entrance to Arabella's house and saw two thick necked security guards that she realised that Max had both invitations. Pulling up at the gates, she smiled sweetly and tried to explain about the paperwork mishap.

'With respect love how do I know you aren't just some journalist trying to get a scoop?'

Lottie was slightly taken aback, 'But why would I. I mean they're quite rich, but it's not as if they are Brad and Angelina. They are a respectable, attractive Gloucestershire couple who've got married. It's not exactly front-page tabloid news.'

'Well it's our job to keep people like you out so it don't appen,' the second man answered in a gruff voice.

Realising that she was getting nowhere fast with the Cotswold's answer to the Mitchell brothers, Lottie grabbed her phone out of her handbag and tried calling Max, but there was no signal. Feeling frustrated, she started the car engine, and reversed back into the side of the lane out of the way. She then got out of the car and waved the phone in the air until she managed to get a bar of signal. Now practically climbing the hedge, she re-dialled Max's number.

After three abortive attempts the phone started ringing, but Max didn't pick up. Realising that she was wasting her time, she turned to make her way back to the car, but as she tried to move forward, she realised that her expensive silky black tights had been snagged by brambles. As she tried to free herself, she stung her hand on some nettles, and then the tights ripped.

Freeing herself, she got back onto the road, but now her shredded tights and bleeding leg made her look like a Friesian cow who'd recently lost an argument with a cattle grid. Limping slightly. She made it back inside the car, before ripping off the remains of her tights, and dabbing her blooded, pale bare legs with some scrappy old bits of paper serviette she found in the bottom of her bag.

Having tidied herself up, she thought she'd have another go at getting into the party. Again they refused, meanwhile graciously waving through those fortunate evening guests who had their invitations.' Exasperated, Lottie tried her last available option. 'Why don't you let me in, and then one of you escort me to my table? Once I'm there I can produce my invite and my partner will vouch for me. If I'm lying, then you can call the police.'

Reluctantly the older of the two men gave in. Whilst his sidekick opened the gates, he got in the passenger seat of the car and Lottie drove through into the grounds.

Having quickly found a parking space, the security guard stuck to her like glue as she made her way across to the marquee. She was relieved to see that Max was sat where she'd left him, although as she got closer, it was obvious that he was totally wasted. Aware that she was coming towards him, he stood up, swaying, to greet her.

'Thought you weren't coming back. You've been so long.'

'I've been trying to get inside for over an hour, but you had the invitations so they wouldn't let me in. I did try ringing.'

'I'm sorry,' he slurred. Unsteadily stepping forward, he wrapped his arms around her, and gave her a hug. Lottie gently rested her hands on his back, enjoying the sensation of warmth and security of having his body so close to hers. Her bare arms felt the smoothness of his beautifully tailored clothing, and she breathed in the smell of his expensive aftershave. Drawing her into him he kissed her purposefully on the lips. 'I've really missed you,' he added.

Lottie glanced around, but the security guard had slipped away. Turning her attention back to

Max, she again recognised the tell-tale signs of recent drug use in his blood shot eyes. That was Cindy's influence, she thought bitterly. 'Would you like a drink?' he asked.

'Tell you what, why don't you sit back down while I get us both a coffee.'

'Good idea. Feel a bit wrecked,' he muttered, thumping back down in the chair.

It took Lottie ages to hunt down coffee, and by the time she had carefully manoeuvred her way back to the table with two very full cups, Max had fallen asleep, his head slumped forward, resting on his arms.

'Would anyone like a cup of coffee?' she asked. 'I appear to have one going spare.'

One of the male guests, readily accepted, which acted as a handy ice breaker, being that the only person Lottie actually knew out of the two hundred or so guests, was unconscious. She sat down in Cindy's empty chair and carried on the conversation.

Much to Lottie's frustration, Cindy arrived back at the table a few minutes later. Scowling at Lottie she said, 'I see you've managed to bore him to death already.'

Having been messed around all day, Lottie was in no mood to take bitchy comments. 'I've only just arrived. It must be your intellectual wit and conversation that's comatosed him.' As she finished speaking, she was aware of polite titters from around the table.

'From what I hear Max may as well be asleep. He says you are a frigid, stuck-up little princess.'

'Better than being a litmus stick,' Lottie snapped back crossly, her thoughts suddenly in overdrive.

'I know I am probably going to regret asking, but what is a litmus stick?' Coffee drinker man asked.

'You know - a thin, shapeless bit of card used for testing drugs and measuring acid.'

'Stupid cow!' Cindy snarled before flouncing off.

The conversation started up around the table, and although Lottie tried to be sociable, her attention was being constantly drawn to Max. She wished he would wake up. Those few seconds of intimacy had left her aching for more. She also hated to think that he thought she was frigid. She had plenty of passion inside her, but what curtailed her was a crippling fear of history repeating itself.

As the wedding guests started to leave, Lottie managed to arouse Max sufficiently for him to stagger out to the car. Then again, he managed to stagger into the hotel lobby and into the lift. Finally, Lottie managed to get him onto the bed. She helped him partially undress, and then left him to sleep.

It was still early when Lottie woke the following morning. Max was still asleep, so she quietly dressed before making her way downstairs for breakfast. She was sat in a quiet corner drinking coffee when he finally appeared, his eyes still bloodshot hidden behind designer sunglasses. Gingerly lowering himself down onto the sofa next to her, he moaned. 'I just want to curl up in a ball and quietly die.'

'Good morning to you too,' Lottie replied sarcastically.

'I'm sorry. I can't even act as your boyfriend for 24 hours without turning the whole thing into a disaster.' Max groaned self pityingly.

Lottie thought his description of their relationship a little odd, but chose to ignore it, at least for the time being. 'It wasn't your fault over the place settings. In fact, I had a lovely time here yesterday, having some relaxing spa therapy.'

'You probably had a nicer time than me,' Max replied, before turning to catch the attention of a passing waiter.

'Cindy says you think I'm a frigid, stuck-up little princess,' she challenged.

'It sounds like the sort of thing I'd say,' he replied, seemingly unfazed.

'Thanks a bloody lot,' Lottie hissed crossly.

'Admittedly that would have been when I first met you. I was pretty pissed at having my advances rejected.'

'Just because I wouldn't sleep with you, you assumed I must be frigid.'

'Pretty much,' he added wearily. 'Look, I think my head's about to split in half. Can we carry on this conversation later when I'm more alive?'

'No. It doesn't work like that. Can't you understand that I couldn't have sex with you – it could be seen as compromising the selection process? I was being professional NOT frigid.'

'What about afterwards,' Max decided to defend himself. 'You haven't exactly been throwing yourself at me.'

'Well for a start you've never shown any interest yourself. Plus, you are such a player, who knows where you've been?'

'My body is a temple,' Max answered, leaning back into the chair and closing his eyes.

'A temple to worship the Gods of STD no doubt.' Lottie stopped abruptly as she saw a waiter fast approaching with a plate of toast and a cafetière.

'If you must know, I've always been very careful.' Max replied sulkily.

Lottie felt that she'd sufficiently made her point, and it was now time to make the peace. Delving into her handbag she retrieved a packet of painkillers, which she tossed to Max.

'Thanks,' he muttered appreciatively.

Chapter 18

It was a glorious summer's evening. Lottie was sitting in the beer garden of the local village pub along with various members of the riding club, enjoying a relaxing drink, following an arduous day's training. In the middle of the group, holding court, sat Max, laughing, and joking as if he didn't have a care in the world.

Lottie was delighted at how well he had settled in. He was proving to be an excellent teacher, and his diary was filled with instructing and training sessions. Membership within her own riding club branch had swelled since Max had become a regular instructor, and he seemed to have an endless supply of females throwing themselves at him. That evening was no exception, and a rather sexy divorcee in her early thirties was clinging to Max in a very unsubtle way.

When Max had first arrived in Devon, Lottie had just been pleased to see him happy and contented as it meant more chance of him staying around. The more they had got to know each other, the greater their bond had become. Max had become a close friend, and they worked well together. Her only regret was that there was no sexual chemistry between them. She had always fancied the pants off him, but hid her feelings, less it put Max in an awkward position. It was better to have him around as a long-term friend, than to have a full-blown relationship that would inevitably not last. The trouble was that Lottie felt a stabbing pain every time Max got himself another woman, and watching him now, with the sexually confident divorcee, was torturous.

Being a typical riding club, the conversation naturally gravitated towards the annual summer area competitions. Lottie had been a keen team member of both the show jumping and dressage teams for several years, but now, because of Max, things were different.

'Lottie, why aren't you jumping next week?' Steve, one of the few male members asked.'Suppose you're too good for us now you're partnered up with Max here.'

Lottie reddened slightly, 'Well kind of. Since Max has been training us, Taggart has improved so much he has gained too many points to be eligible to compete at riding club level. I'm gutted that I can't join you guys next week. Guess I'm just going to have to look for something else to ride.'

'We'll miss you,' one of Lottie's friends added. 'Make sure you get sorted soon.'

Max interrupted, 'Before you all feel too sorry for Lottie, may I say that she has qualified for the Foxhunter final at Horse of the Year show.'

'Have you? Wow.' Various club members expressed their surprise. Impressed by the news. Lottie smiled. 'It's all thanks to Max. I'd never have managed it without him.' She wasn't being generous. It was true. It had been her lifelong ambition to ride at Britain's top horse show, but it had always been a pipe dream. She had only qualified the previous weekend, and it was still sinking in.

The only downside was that this chance would probably be her one and only opportunity to go. She'd always known that it was her lack of confidence and ability that was holding Taggart back. He wasn't exactly close to being in the same world class league as Zhivago, but he loved jumping and had sufficient talent to find Lottie's goals underwhelming. As much out of guilt towards her horse, as in sympathy for Max, she'd made a promise to him that he could compete Taggart whilst he waited for other opportunities. It was inevitable that within a very short time, Taggart would be winning too much to be eligible to compete in the types of classes she was capable of riding. The obvious answer was of course to buy another horse.

It had been all very well boasting about going out and getting another one, but in the cold light of day, reality had kicked in. Scanning through the online horse adverts, there wasn't anything in Lottie's price range that wasn't a baby, a pensioner or so small she could have used her feet to stop. Although not exactly broke, first buying Tilly, and then forking out a small fortune on a wedding outfit, had left a huge hole in Lottie's savings account. It also wasn't long until she was off to the USA for the World Equestrian Games, so horse purchases would have to wait.

Since Max's arrival, Lottie felt she had neglected her family. For weeks Tom had been messaging her, to ask her to keep in touch with their pseudo cousin Verity. Lottie thought it was a rather strange request, and hadn't bothered to make an effort, but when she saw a Facebook post from Verity asking if there was anyone with transport who could help her collect some garden furniture she'd purchased off eBay, she volunteered her services.

The following Saturday, Lottie and Verity set off in Lottie's horse box, heading for a house north of Lydstock. As it was still early, Lottie had decided to risk driving through the town centre but was now regretting the decision as there was far more traffic congestion that she'd expected. Suddenly a man ran up to the truck, waving frantically. Lottie wound down her window and asked, 'Can I help you?'

'Have you lost a horse?' he asked, sounding out of breath.

'No, why?'

'There's a horse tied up to the gate around the back of the RSPCA charity shop.'

'Well it's not mine,' Lottie replied dismissively.

The man looked disappointed, so with curiosity getting the better of her she added, 'Has it been abandoned do you think?'

'Yes, reckon so.'

Lottie turned to Verity, 'Is it OK with you if we make a bit of a detour?'

'Yes fine. The sellers said they would be in all morning.'

Turning right at the next junction, Lottie

drove the horse box around to the charity shop, parking on double yellow lines. A small crowd of people had gathered at the back of the shop and were staring at a large painfully thin chestnut gelding. One of the onlookers turned to Lottie, 'Is this your horse?'

'No, I've just been flagged down. I have a livery yard, and my lorry is empty, so I'm happy to take him back with me until the owner can be located.'

'Oh, would you? 'asked another lady who introduced herself as the shop manager.

'I'll give you my contact details,' Lottie offered.

She went back to the lorry and pulled down the ramp, ready for loading. She grabbed a lead rope and stuffed some pony nuts into her jean pocket.

The horse had clearly been tied up for a long time. There was poo everywhere, trampled into the ground where the horse had been twisting and turning trying to escape. Whoever had left him there had used a chain, rather than a rope, so the poor horse was trapped.

It flashed the whites of its eyes and attempted to back away as Lottie approached. Instinctively she extracted some nuts and stretched out her hand as an offering. Hunger overpowering fear, the half-starved horse tentatively stretched out his neck and nibbled the food, allowing Lottie to get close to his head. With soothing words, she managed to clip her lead rope onto the horse's tatty head collar and then released the metal chain. Cautiously she led the horse out of the yard and towards the horse box. Verity had opened the partition in readiness and now stood inside tentatively shaking a feed bucket containing the remaining handful of pony nuts.

The horse allowed himself to be taken to the bottom of the ramp before hesitating. Lottie watched as he considered his options, torn between running off in a bid for freedom and complying and being trapped. Fortunately, hunger was the deciding factor, and much to Lottie's relief he headed inside, diving his head into the feed bucket. Lottie quickly shut the ramp before he changed his mind. She always kept a water container in the lorry, and having filled a bucket, offered the horse a drink. As she lifted the bucket to within his reach he nickered in gratitude.

Within half an hour the horse was settled in a stable at home, with a huge haylage net, and standing on a bed of soft shavings. Whilst Lottie and Verity continued their journey, Beth arranged for the vet to come and give the horse a health check.

It was mid-afternoon by the time Lottie was back on the yard, just as the vet was getting back in his car. 'I've left instructions with your mother to worm him tomorrow. The poor chap is very underweight but luckily, he was abandoned before it became critical. I suggest you keep him stabled for a week, and then gradually build up the time he is turned out each day. There doesn't seem to be anything else wrong with him. He has been microchipped. I've taken the data and should be able to get some history on the horse soon.'

Lottie was still gazing over the stable door, watching the big chestnut horse, with the white blaze quietly munching away when an RSPCA van appeared in the yard. The horse looked so contented, she hoped that they wouldn't now take him away. She was so relieved when the inspector agreed that the horse could stay with them.

'He's going to need a name,' Beth said. 'We can't just keep calling him the horse.'

'I think we should call him Hope. As in faith, hope, and charity shop,' Lottie announced, grinning.

Max had been away teaching, and so had no idea about the new arrival on the yard. As he got out of his car Lottie excitedly headed him off and explained what had happened. Max followed her over to Hope's stable and gave a cursory glance inside before heading off back to his cottage. Lottie stayed outside Hope's stable.

'You could show a little more interest,' she exclaimed, unable to hide the disappointment from her voice.

Max turned around and snapped. 'What's there to get excited about? Just another bloody useless horse to feed. Well don't expect me to look after it. I've got enough to do.'

'Why are you being so hard?' Lottie was confused and disappointed.

'Don't you get it?' Max shouted. 'You just can't fucking help yourself can you. Miss bloody lady bountiful, going around rescuing lost causes. Makes you feel good doesn't it. Well, I didn't ask to be rescued. I don't need your sympathy and I'm not having anything to do with that bag of bones.' With that he stormed off.

Lottie burst into tears. Going into Hope's stable, she hugged the horse, burying her wet face into his scraggy mane. 'It's not your fault you've been ill-treated,' she sobbed. Hope turned and looked at her, wondering what the fuss was all about.

'Don't worry, you're safe now,' she whispered, gently patting his neck.

Early the next morning Lottie and Shadow headed off down the driveway to the yard to check up on Hope. She'd barely slept. Max's outburst had upset her more than she'd cared to admit. She'd spent most of the night tossing and turning, her mind racing as she tried to work out what had gone wrong. She peered over his stable door, 'Hello Hope,' she said, but at that moment realised that the stable was empty. Confused she looked around the yard. It was only then that she noticed a red chestnut horse shaped animal in the field with Taggart. Both horses looking relaxed and happy.

Taking his feed out to the field along with Taggart's she was feeling increasingly puzzled. There was no way her mum would have turned Hope out, so it had to be Max. Having fed the horses, she strolled back into the yard, contemplating starting the mucking out. Deep in thought, she turned the corner and went headlong into Max, making him drop his saddle. Max cursed under his breath.

'Sorry,' Lottie replied hurriedly, as she went to retrieve the feed buckets which had rolled into the nearby drain.

'Did you turn Hope out this morning?'

Max scowled, his eyes flashing moodily. 'Is that what you've decided to call it? I've already told you, I'm having nothing to do with it, so to answer your question. No I didn't OK.'

'But how did he get in the field?'

'No doubt he sprouted wings and flew out the stable,' Max replied venomously.

'Whatever,' Lottie sighed. She was too tired to argue.

Having changed, ready to leave for work, Lottie was just feeding Shadow when there was a knock on her front door. Greeting her were her mother together with a photographer and journalist from the Lydstock Herald newspaper, come to get a photo of Hope. Fortunately, Lottie's start time was fluid, so she was able to escort everyone to the field, where she was made to pose next to her skinny new friend.

Unfortunately, once the story had broken locally, news of Hope's rescue spread rapidly. The following day Lottie received a call from her contact at Horse and Hound wanting the low down on Max Tarasov and the Charity Shop horse. Lottie tried desperately to keep Max's name out of the story, and repeatedly emphasised that Hope was nothing to do with her business partner.

Alas the story was too good, and Max and the Charity Shop nag went viral.

When Lottie got home from work the next evening, a furious Max greeted her. 'How dare you humiliate me as a cheap publicity stunt to make yourself look good,' he yelled.

'All I did was to rescue a poor neglected horse. Setting out to deliberately embarrass you was the last thing I wanted.' She paused, hating the fact that they'd fallen out. 'Have you seen how beautifully he moves? He may make a half decent competition horse once he's back to full strength.'

Max looked like he was about to explode, 'You're fucking priceless. You seriously think I would lower myself to ride that thing. Oh, you'd just love that wouldn't you? Both your rescue cases teaming up... well you can forget it. I'd rather go back to modelling for Cindy. I'd have more self-respect than being your charity case.'

'Why are you being like this?' for the second time in two days, Max was about to reduce Lottie to tears.

'Because I don't want your charity. If you want to bestow yourself onto someone, then save it for your little mate Ed Carter. I'm sure he'll lap it up. If you're really lucky you may even get a good seeing too in return.'

Not allowing her a chance to respond, Max pushed passed her, and headed off down the yard.

Chapter 19

For the next couple of weeks Lottie made a point of avoiding Max. Despite still feeling upset with him, the last thing she wanted was to drive him away completely. Hope was starting to fill out, and he'd really settled in. Even better, he was now officially hers. The RSPCA inspector had turned up the week before to check up on Hope. Lottie had put him in his stable, to save the inspector a walk, and whilst they were chatting, Hope jumped out over the top of the stable door, cantered off down the yard before jumping the five-bar gate back into the field.

The inspector gasped in surprise, however he then admitted that he should have expected it. With the help of a donation from a national horse magazine, they'd managed to trace some of Hope's history via his microchip. He had been born eight years before at a top Hanoverian stud in Germany before being sold as a three-year-old to the UK. The trail had gone cold two years ago, so it wasn't possible to locate an owner. Technically Hope hadn't been officially registered with the RSPCA, so Lottie asked if she could officially take ownership. Following a phone call to the charity's head office it was agreed that Lottie would take official ownership for a donation of £300.

The one advantage of Hope's sudden celebrity status was that he was showered with gifts. On a daily basis he received presents of feed, carrots, tack, and rugs from all sorts of people from pony mad girls to a group of elderly ladies. Lottie created Facebook and Instagram accounts for Hope and loaded the site with photos of him standing next to his gifts. Soon she was posting little Tik Tok clips of him which she shared on social media.

As Hope's health improved Lottie started taking him out for walks, and she began lunging him in the sand arena. She learnt to her cost, to only handle him in a bridle. The only time she attempted to lunge in a head collar, Hope simply pulled away from her, jumped out of the arena, and back down to his field, the lunge rope trailing dangerously close to his hind legs.

Max continued to avoid Hope, and barely spoke to Lottie. His only comment upon watching Lottie leading Hope towards the school was to mutter. 'I hope you don't intend riding that thing. It will probably kill you.' He then disappeared before Lottie could reply.

Although Lottie hadn't intended to ride Hope, he was getting so much stronger, it seemed such a waste not to do something with him. Taggart's jumping saddle seemed to fit OK, so one late summer morning when Lottie took him out for a walk, she got to the edge of the nearby village where there was an old stone mounting block. Hope looked relaxed and happy, so gingerly Lottie mounted.

Hope didn't seem at all concerned about having a rider on board, and when Lottie squeezed his sides, he obliged by walking on, his huge stride eating up the ground. Lottie had assumed that Hope had been broken to ride, and this confirmed it. Riding through the village, Lottie started to enjoy herself. Coming out the opposite side of the village, Lottie asked Hope to trot. He responded instantly. Lottie found the powerful action difficult to rise to, and soon pulled him back to a walk.

Knowing that Hope wasn't fit, at the next junction Lottie turned for home. It meant a steep hill climb, and Lottie decided to risk another short trot. She was just asking Hope to come back to a walk when she became aware of some rustling in the adjacent hedgerow. Hope snorted suspiciously. Suddenly a deer scrambled over the hedge, practically landing on top of them. Horrified, Hope shot forward into a gallop, heading for the safety of home. Lottie tugged frantically at the reins but Hope just set his jaw and simply ran through the bridle.

Terrified that Hope would run headlong into a car, or slip on the tarmac, Lottie started to panic. Ahead of her was a sharp bend, and directly ahead on the start of the bend was a field gate, if she could get him into the field, then she could safely run him until he exhausted himself. Although she was frightened, Lottie steered towards the five-bar gate, knowing that Hope was at least expert in jumping them.

Hope didn't question the command, and headed for the field entrance, unfortunately he wasn't balanced, and as he took off he twisted his body. He cleared the gate, but at such an awkward angle that Lottie slipped sideways in the saddle. Seconds later she felt herself falling, and a blur of hooves thundered above her head as she landed painfully on the hard, dusty ground.

Moments later, feeling sick and dizzy, Lottie knew she had to get back before Hope hurt himself. She tentatively moved each limb, and having satisfied herself that she was in one piece, she painfully struggled to her feet. As she tried to walk however she felt a searing pain in her left ankle. She didn't want to risk taking off her boot in case she didn't get it on again. She suspected a sprain rather than a break, and due to her concern for Hope, she decided to struggle on in his wake.

Having hobbled across the field, she followed the hoof prints through a gap into the next field. There was no sign of any large chestnut horse, just an open gate leading back onto the lane. It took her ages to limp across the field, all the time, sobbing both because of the pain, but also due to her feelings of guilt. If anything had happened to Hope, she could never forgive herself.

As Lottie reached the gate, she could hear a car coming racing down the road. She stood in the gate way waiting for it to pass, glad to rest her throbbing foot. As it came into view she recognised it as Max's car, which came to a screeching halt beside her.

'I told you not to ride that bloody horse,' Max shouted through the open car window.

'Is Hope all right?' Lottie asked.

'He's fine – safely back in his field.'

Lottie felt so relieved. 'Thank goodness,' she

replied.

'Just get in the car will you?' Max ordered, leaning across to release the passenger door catch. Limping badly, Lottie pulled back the door and climbed in.

'It wasn't Hope's fault. A deer practically landed on us, and he panicked.'

'And then you couldn't stop him I suppose.' Max muttered disapprovingly.

'How do you know?' Lottie challenged.

Max hesitated. 'Well, it's obvious,' he responded coldly.

Max drove her back to the lodge. 'Do you want any help?' he asked.

'No it's OK,' she replied quickly, not wishing to inconvenience him further. She opened the car door and slid her feet onto the gravel driveway. As she eased herself up onto her feet, her swollen ankle gave way and she nearly fell. Not waiting for another refusal, Max jumped out of the car and rushed around, offering his arm as support.

If Lottie hadn't been in so much pain, she would have thoroughly enjoyed being held by Max. Not since the wedding had she got within such proximity. He smelt of a mixture of horse, and expensive aftershave. He was so strong that he practically lifted her up the steps into the house, before helping her into her small sitting room. As soon as she was seated, he made to rush off.

'Sorry Max – could you help me get my boot off please?' Lottie pleaded.

'Yes, of course,' Max muttered, clearly not comfortable playing the role of carer.

Kneeling at her feet, he unzipped her riding boot, and gently eased it off.

'You look like you are about to propose?' Lottie joked, trying desperately to get him to smile. Max scowled moodily before getting back to his feet. 'Well if you are all right I'd better get back. Just make sure you get your ankle checked out.' With that he shot out the door like a scalded cat.

Lottie looked miserably down at her bruised and very swollen ankle. She was still certain that it wasn't broken and hoped it would have improved before she left for the USA only three weeks away. She was equally upset with Max, or more specifically her relationship with him. Only a few weeks ago, he'd practically become her boyfriend, yet now he could barely stand spending more than a few minutes in her company. She missed the closeness of their friendship, and her longing for a more physical relationship remained undiminished.

Lottie was still trying to summon the strength to move, when the front door opened and she heard her mother's voice. Seconds later Beth and Nick appeared in the doorway carrying bandages, ice, and chocolates. Having treated her ankle, Beth went into the kitchen to make Lottie a drink and a sandwich. Nick sat down beside his adopted daughter and said, 'We've just had a call from your brother Ben. He's coming down to stay this weekend and he's bringing a woman, plus his

221

producer.' He smiled, amused at the prospect of vetting his youngest son's girlfriend.

'And what do you make of this? We are also being honoured with the presence of Verity Horton Thomas and two of her friends. They are coming to meet up with Ben and get this. Verity is representing Tom. Who'd have thought it?'

Beth walked back in with food and drink for her daughter, 'Do you know anything about the connection between them?'

'I was aware that they had become close friends, but I don't know quite how close.' Lottie answered.

'But with Tom being the next Earl of Martley he must have dozens of beautiful heiresses practically throwing themselves at him.' Nick exclaimed. 'I don't mean that Verity isn't a nice girl, but she's no oil painting, and I'd have thought a bit too earnest for Tom who must have so much choice.'

'Don't forget, he's your son,' Beth reminded him. 'You preferred the innocent girl next door to the spoilt rich heiresses too.'

Nick gazed lovingly at his wife. 'Very true my darling. And at least he knows for certain that his girlfriend will love Dewerstone.'

'I believe it's their shared passion for nineteenth century romantic literature that cemented their friendship,' Lottie added. 'I think it's sweet.'

Once Lottie was finally alone, a mood of depression descended. Although she was looking forward to seeing her baby brother, the fact that even he now had a girlfriend really made her feel on the shelf. Her mum and Nick had fallen in love at seventeen and were still devoted to each other. Here Lottie was in her late twenties, with only the scars of one terrible past relationship to show for it. She had secretly hoped that something would have happened between her and Max, but now that was looking like being a lost cause.

The lost cause did send her a text later, saying horses fed. It wasn't exactly the most romantic gesture, but at least it showed some consideration. She texted back a thank you along with a smiley emoji, but he didn't respond further.

The following afternoon, having obtained a pair of ancient crutches, Lottie was mooching around the yard, along with Shadow, and pretending not to watch Max schooling his young horse Oberon, when one of the livery girls called across, 'Lottie, you have visitors.'

Coming up the track from the main house were Verity, her friend Indira and her brother Ed Carter. 'Sorry to arrive so early,' Verity said breathlessly, 'but Ed wanted to pick your brains. I hope it's OK.' She then looked down at Lottie's bandaged foot. 'Oh my, what have you done?'

'Riding accident. First hack out on Hope. It was all going well until a deer jumped through the hedge and landed on us.' Lottie smiled, delighted to finally have some company. 'Anyway, as I am somewhat incapacitated, I am completely free and all yours.'

'It's good to see you Lottie,' Ed came over and kissed her on the cheek, before giving her a hug.

'Apart from your leg, are you well?'

'Yes. Loving my job and having Max around has been entertaining.'

'Oh yes, I'd forgotten,' Ed lied. 'Is that him in your school?'

'Yes, it's a four-year-old he bought last month. Very promising. Also, once I've been up to Hoys, he's going to take on my horse Taggart, whose talent is wasted on me. Anyway, how about you? Heard you've been winning quite a bit.'

'Yes, Trooper has really improved. He and I are the travelling reserves for the world equestrian games.'

'That's wonderful news. Well done,' Lottie said enthusiastically.

'It's in part thanks to the new sponsors you helped me get. I've been able to rent a yard and afford to compete at all the top show. I've also been given the ride of one of Lady Hardcourt's horses, a wonderful grey Holstein. The reason I'm here is that I'm hoping to be selected for the next Olympics, but I was wondering whether there was any funding available – Like the National Lottery fund.'

'It isn't my field of expertise. I know that the National Lottery fund is only for community projects, but it may be worth contacting UK Sport. They provide funding for potential Olympic sportspersons. Why don't we do some internet research?'

As they headed off back to the house, Max halted Oberon watching them disappearing into the distance. He'd seen the delight on Lottie's face when Ed arrived. What made it worse was that Ed was off to the world equestrian games. Only a few months earlier, Max could have annihilated Ed, but now here he was, no better than a glorified groom, whilst those less worthy, were heading for glory.

As he quietly rode around the arena, waiting for Oberon to cool down, his head was fully of a thousand thoughts and emotions. He was angry with Ed for using Lottie, angry with Lottie for needing to rescue things, and angry with himself for being so nasty to her, the one person who was trying to help him. He was jealous of Ed, both for his sporting success, and his friendship with Lottie. He was also full of self-pity because everything that had gone wrong in his life was his fault. There was the death of his mother, and the destruction of his career. He was now destroying the only relationship in his life that really meant something, but he simply couldn't stop himself.

Max didn't really want to join the dinner party. He would have preferred to head off to the local pub and get totally wasted amongst his newly acquired drinking buddies. The thought of spending the evening making polite small talk was almost unbearable. Beth had been so insistent that he join them, and as he was so fond of her, the last thing he needed was the guilt of letting her down too.

He arrived late, and half drunk. Fortunately, they hadn't started eating, but were already seated at the dinner table, so he was forced to sit between Verity and Ed Carter's sister. Ed was directly opposite him, next to Lottie. At the opposite end of the table were Beth and Nick together with their youngest son, a stunning looking girl, and an older bearded man who looked very arty.

As the delicate salmon mousse starter was served, Ben started explaining to his father that the night club booked for the filming of the Old 100th scenes had let them down. As Nick was still a significant shareholder at Lizzies, Ben hoped his father could pull some strings. They planned to film there over a couple of evenings, and host a real party, using guests as extras.

As soon as the course was cleared away, Nick called his business associate Ian. The BBC producer was handed the phone, and they discussed timings. Much to Lottie's delight, the party night was set for the evening prior to her departure for the world equestrian games. Not only would she be able to attend, but it meant she could invite the team riders, including Ed.

The conversation moved on to more detailed planning such as music. Verity passed on Tom's thoughts, and as he reckoned he had some useful contacts, she was given the task of securing the services of a band. The BBC were to sort out the set and provide costumes.

As Lottie was intending to travel straight on to Heathrow the morning after the party, Max reluctantly agreed to take his car, and to give her and Verity a lift. Nick had no intention of going, but offered to speak to his brother to ask if Lottie and her friends could stay at the Mansion House.

Crispin had already agreed for the house to be used for the film set, so Nick reckoned a little more disruption wouldn't hurt.

Whilst everyone was distracted, Ed leant forward and quietly spoke to Max. 'Look mate, I don't want to piss on your territory, so I need to know if you and Lottie are an item? If not, I may ask her to partner me to the party.'

Hearing her name mentioned, Lottie decided to listen in to the conversation. Max's mood had blackened further since he'd been drinking. 'She's not my girlfriend, we're just...' he hesitated, unsure of how to describe their relationship. 'It's strictly business, and very limited pleasure,' he added spitefully. 'Anyway, I only date supermodels, not pen pushers.'

'Ouch, that was brutal,' Lottie said in an unconvincingly jovial tone. Although Max was drunk, he still noticed Lottie's pain as she put on a brave front.

Ed glared at him. 'That was bloody unnecessary. You can be such a bastard sometimes,' he hissed. Max didn't bother replying. He felt terrible. He didn't want to keep punishing Lottie, but he couldn't help himself.

Having had a few seconds to recover, Lottie then added, 'You say about the super models, but didn't yours ditch you?'

'We had a falling out, but she's always texting me asking me to go back.'

'Well good luck with that then,' Lottie responded sarcastically.

Once dinner was over everyone moved into

the drawing room where coffee was served. Lottie made a point of sussing out Ben's friend Sophie, who she noticed was standing on her own.

'Hi Sophie, I'm Lottie, Ben's big sister.'

Sophie extended her delicate hand, 'Ben's told me about you. You're the head of UK sponsorship for Yangtze Motors.'

'Yes, hence the higher-than-expected population of international showjumpers in the room.'

Sophie giggled, 'So which one is your boyfriend. It is the tall dark macho one that looks like he's a US fighter pilot come off the set of Topgun? Or the beautiful moody drunk one, who looks like the 1980's TV version of Sebastian Flyte?'

Lottie laughed, 'Technically neither. 'I met Topgun man at a New Year's Eve party. We sort of went out together for a bit, but he's looking for a richer woman than me who can bank role his show jumping career. He occasionally pops up looking for advice, and he's a useful stand in date.' Lottie took a sip of coffee. 'The moody drunk one is the son of a Russian billionaire, but they had a massive bust up, so he's staying with us until he either gets a huge sponsorship deal or makes the peace with his old man. I wouldn't mind him being my boyfriend, but no such luck I'm afraid.'

'He's gorgeous, but he doesn't seem very nice.'

'Max can be lovely, but he's been crabby for weeks now, and being drunk just makes him worse. It's the world equestrian games coming up

228

in a couple of weeks, and Max was desperate to go. He would have been selected if his father hadn't sold all his horses in revenge.'

Sophie gave a shudder. 'Remind me never to get involved with the Russians,' she said. 'Although, I'm hardly going to be tempted when I have your gorgeous brother to look after me.'

Chapter 20

As Max would be spending the night at Crispin and Felicities house, Lottie did wonder whether it was worth broaching the subject of Ivan Tarasov. She reckoned that Ivan would be impressed if he were to be targeted by the party chairman directly, and for Crispin, it meant a potential very rich party donor. If she could convince everyone that the whole idea was Max's, then his father may forgive him. The trouble was that Max was still barely speaking to her. In fact, over the previous few days the only comments he'd made were bitter snipes about her and Ed. If she dared to mention his father, she knew she'd simply get her head bitten off. Tired of fighting, and with her mind supposed to be on sorting out flights and entertainment for Yangtze directors, she decided not to bother trying to fix things between the Tarasovs'.

When the day of the party arrived, Lottie put her cases in Max's boot, but when she returned a few minutes later, she found he'd petulantly thrown them out onto the floor, saying that it was too much to carry. Lottie stormed off back to the house to get her own car keys and bumped into her mother. Beth was always a glass half full type of person, and gradually Lottie calmed down.

'Why's he being so horrible Mum?' Lottie

whined. 'I know he's upset about not going to Kentucky, but that's hardly my fault, and he shouldn't be taking his frustration out on me.'

'I think it's more than just the horse thing,' Beth replied. 'He doesn't like Hope because he now reckons that you just have a burning desire to go around rescuing things. He no longer feels special and thinks he's just another of your projects.'

'But it wasn't like that,' Lottie was nearly despairing.

'I know that darling, but he doesn't. Nick and I also both agree that he's jealous of you and Ed. People generally lash out at those closest to them, those they really care about when they are in pain. You can see the hurt in his face every time he looks at you and Ed together, so just be patient.'

'Do you really think so?' Lottie dearly hoped her mother was right. The bitterness between her and Max was awful, and she longed for it to stop.

Verity suddenly arrived breathlessly at the door. 'It's all sorted. Max says that as long as you don't mind travelling in the back with 'your' cases, he'll drive.'

Lottie desperately didn't want to leave her car in London for ten days, nor to drive home jet lagged, so she agreed.

Max made a point of only engaging in conversation with Verity on the long drive to London. Verity made frequent attempts to bring Lottie into the discussion, but it just made the situation more socially painful. When they finally got through central London and reached the

Mansion House, Tom rushed out to greet them, and to help carry the bags to the guest suites. He warmly hugged both his sister and Verity, and enthusiastically shook Max's hand, oblivious to the tension.

'Uncle's still at The House, but Aunt Felicity says to pop in and say hello before we all leave,' Tom enthused. 'She's organised a light buffet so we can have something to eat, so I suggest we meet up at eight o clock.'

Although Lottie needed a shower, and had to apply fresh make up, she didn't have to dress up. It didn't seem right going to a club in casual clothing, but the females were all being issued with costumes on arrival, whilst the men were told to come in black tie. Despite Max's attempts to ignore her, she knocked on his door and offered to escort him to the dining room. He didn't show much enthusiasm or gratitude, but he accepted her offer.

Max was in awe of Nick's brother's home. Although his father's house was full of riches, it didn't have authenticity, class, or a sense of history. There were liveried staff, magnificent artwork, and priceless furniture and artefacts. It was how he imagined a palace to be. He followed Lottie through a maze of corridors, and they finally ended up in the dining room, where a beautiful lady in late middle age moved gracefully across the room to meet them.

'Lottie, it's so lovely to see you,' she said, as the two women kissed.'And you must be Max Tarasov. Welcome.'

232

'Thank you, Your Grace. It's kind of you to put us up in your beautiful home.'

'It's a pleasure. Please help yourself to some food. One of the footmen will get you anything you would like to drink.' She then turned back to Lottie, and started quizzing her about her job, leaving Max to slip away and grab some food, and a large vodka.

Soon he found himself chatting to Tom who explained that his brother was already at the club as they'd been filming there most of the day. 'We're just needed for a few background scenes, so it shouldn't be too onerous,' he added.

Just as they were about to leave, Crispin arrived back from the Lords. Lottie hurriedly introduced him to Max, and explained to her uncle that Ivan Tarasov may be worth engaging with as a future party donor. Max was furious at Lottie's blatant attempts to stir things up with his father, but he was far too intimidated by the duke to make a scene.

The chauffeur then drove Max, Lottie, Tom and Verity from Kensington to Lizzies which was situated in Mayfair. Max had been determined not to enjoy himself, but following half a bottle of vodka, and some splendid aristocratic hospitality, he felt a rush of excitement as they entered the club. He waited with Tom whilst the girls were transformed into flappers. When Lottie reappeared looking like a nineteen thirties throwback, Max couldn't help laughing, but secretly he thought how beautiful she looked. He wanted to whisk her off her feet, and dance the night away, but stubbornness prevented him.

They walked through into the main area, where they immediately noticed Ben and Sophie waving at them from a corner table. Ben and a couple of his male associates stood up as Lottie and Verity reached the table Ben then took it upon himself to do the introductions.

'Everyone sitting here are my acting colleagues,' Ben explained. 'It's probably easier if I just refer to the guys by their acting names, so we have Charles Ryder, Boy Mulcaster, Bridey, Effie, Death's Head, and Sickly Child.'

'Isn't that a bit rude,' Max replied, not having read the book, and thinking that the poor girls deserved better. Both girls giggled. It was only then that Max realised that one was his current favourite famous female singer, Millie. 'I'm Max Tarasov,' he announced, feeling slightly star struck.

'Oh my God,' Milly replied. 'My kid sister's got your poster on her bedroom wall.'

'I'd rather be in your bedroom,' Max said cheesily.

'Play your cards right darling, and it may happen,' she replied. 'I've just got a quick celebrity cameo part in the film. I think we've finished, so maybe I'll join you later.'

Lottie was delighted by the attention she received from Ben's friends, and in particular the actor playing Bridie, who asked if she would be free for a dance later. As the actor table were waiting to hear whether they'd finished for the night, Lottie led her group away to continue

234

socialising, as she needed to track down her guests.

As the band started to play again, she and Max came across Giles and Mary, who were having a great time. Moments later they were joined by Marcus, Tracey, Ed and his sister. The show jumpers made a huge fuss of Max and seemed genuinely pleased to see him again.

'So I take it Paul isn't coming?' Lottie shouted, trying to be heard above the noise.

'Said it wasn't his thing.' Giles replied. 'Doesn't know what he's missing,' he added cheerfully before grabbing Lottie by the hand and whisking her down onto the dance floor. Having danced to one song, Ed stepped in and eagerly swung Lottie around. They kept going for nearly 20 minutes, before Lottie admitted defeat and insisted that she needed a break.

Slipping through the crowds, Lottie sought out Max. She found him leaning against the bar, swigging out of a bottle of champagne. As he saw her approach, he removed the bottle from his lips, before placing it down on a nearby table. 'Would you like to dance?' Lottie asked. 'Maybe try a truce, even if just for tonight.' 'I don't want to get between you and lover boy,' he snarled, taking another swig from the bottle. He then wiped his mouth with the back of his hand defying her to challenge him.

'We're just friends. Ed is not my boyfriend, and he certainly isn't my lover.' Lottie snapped back.

'Oh come off it. You are about to fly off to the

235

States with him. You'll be jumping into bed with him before the week is up.'

'No I won't,' Lottie shouted.

'Go on then. Tell me why not?' Max challenged, his eyes flashing menacingly. Lottie hesitated, so Max grabbed the champagne bottle, and pushed passed her aggressively.

'I won't have sex with him because I'm too frightened to,' she shouted at his retreating back.

Verity was having a far more successful evening. With her slightly old-fashioned look, together with her handsome aristocratic partner Tom, they became the focal point for filming. Ben and Sophie were still hanging around, waiting for Ben to be stood down. As the production team hunted down suitable couples for filming, they deliberately bypassed Lottie, not that she minded, as she was enjoying herself dancing with Ben's actor colleague playing the part of Bridie. As Bridie was purposely not meant to be at the club with Sebastian and Charles, he was kept well away from the cameras.

Max spent the next couple of hours flirting with Millie and her friend. He drank copious amounts of champagne, and Millie even produced a couple of wraps of coke, much to Max's delight. Despite having fun, he couldn't completely get Lottie out of his mind. He'd heard her closing comment, but chose not to react, mainly because he didn't know how to. He'd assumed that she would have spent the evening attached to the leach-like Ed and this was partly why he'd justified his decision to give her a wide berth. The trouble was that every time he managed to catch a glimpse of her, she was dancing with someone other than Ed.

When Millie invited him back for a naughty threesome with her lesbian friend Kerry, Max couldn't resist. Drunk, horny, and still under the influence of half a gram of coke, there was no question of him refusing. Millie's home was in a smart refurbished area in Chelsea Harbour, and Millie's record label had laid on a car to whisk them across the city. Once inside her designer apartment, Max gratefully accepted another line of coke. As he leant over to inhale the drug, Millie started to remove his trousers. She gently started to suck his balls, and the sensation was electric. With his erection at maximum, he returned the favour. Millie's body was small and muscular, except for her breasts, surgically enhanced, they stood out like perfect pert balloons. Kelly was taller, and athletic, and although not quite as attractive as her pretty pop star mate, she made up for it with her suppleness, and willingness to please.

The two girls were used to male models, and even the occasional pop star, but had never experienced the strength and stamina of a professional rider. Having given Millie the best orgasm of her life, he quickly recovered, and Kelly was tempted into having a go. 'OMG, if sex could always be this good, I could convert,' Kelly yelled, breathless with exertion and pleasure. Eventually exhaustion overcame Max, and lying between the two naked girls, he fell asleep.

Back at Lizzies, the evening was coming to a close. Lottie was tired and her feet were throbbing. She'd had a fun evening, and for a while at least, she managed to forget the hurt of Max's rejection. Everyone had been so great, but as the music drifted away, once again, the pain returned.

Ben and Sophie headed off back to their hotel, along with the remaining members of the cast and crew. Meanwhile Tom and Verity waited with Lottie for Crispin's chauffeur who was coming to collect them. Most of the showjumpers had already left, as they had an early drive down to Heathrow to supervise the loading of their horses onto the transport plane.

Once Tom and Verity arrived back at the Mansion House, Tom quietly led Verity to his private apartment in the west wing of the house. Verity was still a virgin, and Tom was desperate not to rush her, but he knew she was ready.

'Have you had many lovers?' Verity asked.

'Not many. When I was seventeen my father took me to a high-class prostitute. His plan was that I should be educated by a more experienced woman, without the complications of a relationship.'

'Really? Verity was amazed, but then she'd always been captivated by the legend that was Nick. Throughout her life, she'd heard such shocking tales about Tom's father that she supposed that this was just another element in a history of surprises.

'Other than that, I'm very boring really.

238

Anyway, I understand this is your first time. At any point you want to stop, just say. I really don't mind.' Slowly he started to undress her, building up the foreplay as he went. As he caressed the back of her delicate pale neckline she shuddered with delight. 'Slowly does it;' he whispered. 'We have all night. Don't feel embarrassed, you are beautiful.'

As Verity started to relax, Tom quickened the pace, less he explode. Finally, he was inside her. She was so tight, that the sensation was amazing. He suddenly thought about the analogy of backing a young horse. With his momentary lapse of concentration, Verity winced in discomfort. 'Oh I'm so sorry my darling,' Tom apologised. 'Should I stop?'

'Are you kidding?' Verity replied breathlessly. 'You're the only man in the world I want to do this with.' They carried on for what seemed like hours, then they lay together, hot, and exhausted, just holding each other. Tom looked across at Verity and saw tears in her eyes. 'What's wrong my darling? Are you hurt?'

'No not at all. In fact, I keep thinking this is all a dream. You are so kind and handsome. You could have any woman you wanted. I know I'm plain and a bit dull, so why choose me?'

'Because I don't think you are dull or plain. You have a natural untouched beauty, both inside and out. You are highly intelligent, and you are the only woman, other than my direct family, who I can have a decent conversation with.' He kissed her playfully on the tip of her nose. 'And as for me

– I'm not that great a catch. I may tick the obvious boxes, but I'm boring. Other than playing a bit of polo and the odd days hunting, I do nothing remotely dangerous. I shall soon be living in deepest Devonshire, with very little social life. My life's work is academic, and if I'm really daring, I may when I'm older get a non-exec directorship on the board of some charity. Most heiresses would be bored to sops within weeks of marrying me. I don't want an unhappy wife, so you see, I need you.'

'I will never be bored, especially if we do this every night,' she giggled. 'My only issue is that your father terrifies me.'

Tom laughed, 'Oh Dad's a pussycat. He's got this wild rebel image, but actually he's the sweetest person. It just such a shame that our parent's loath each other.'

'It's all very Montague and Capulet,' Verity concluded. 'Let's just make sure that we don't end up reliving the same tragedy.'

'The only thing tragic about me is my terrible taste in music.' Tom sniggered.

Chapter 21

Max cautiously opened his eyes. He still felt a little dizzy, and there seemed to be a naked breast poking into his left ear. Re shutting his eyes, he tried to recall the events of the previous night, which had led to him waking up in a strange bed surrounded by naked female limbs. At least they seemed like female limbs – if they were male limbs then he really was in trouble. On the other hand, he could feel more female limbs than was natural, so either he'd fucked Octopussy, or he was sharing the bed with Little Mix.

Cautiously he sat up and gave a little squeak of surprise to find the former X factor winner sleeping naked next to him, whilst her renowned lesbian lover was lying on his opposite side. Trying not to disturb them, he slid down to the end of the bed, before padding around the room in search of the bathroom. He was aware that he reeked of sex, so quickly took the opportunity to dive in the girl's shower, before towelling himself dry, and going on a hunt for his clothes.

He finally located his pants and trousers behind a large sofa, whilst his shirt, jacket and shoes were in the kitchen. Opening the fridge door, he helped himself to a glass of milk, and then decided to make his escape. Not to seem rude, he left them a note, and added his phone number at the bottom, more out of politeness than intent. He was relieved to find that he still had his phone and wallet, but less thrilled that his wallet was almost empty. He started to think back and remembered ordering copious amounts of champagne. Well now he didn't have enough money left for a taxi, so that meant taking the tube.

Max got some very odd looks as he took a seat on the central line. He looked dishevelled; and stank of stale alcohol. His hangover hadn't yet kicked in, but he suspected that he was still a little drunk. When he eventually reached street level, his phone started to ring. It was Millie.

'Sorry I had to leave,' he quickly blurted out. 'I have to get my car before its clamped.' He doubted that this was the case, but it sounded convincing.

'I just wonna warn you not to do a kiss and tell on me all right.'

'I'm hardly going to do that Millie. It wouldn't be a gentlemanly thing to do after you provided such generous hospitality last night.'

'Well, Kerry checked out your phone, and you've got that society journalist Tom Marchbank's number.'

'Believe me, he's the last person I'd be bragging to about my wonderful night of passion with an X factor star.'

'Why?' she sounded suspicious.

'Because I'm living with his sister.' As he finished his sentence the line went dead.

As Max got back to The Mansion House, Tom and Verity were in the entrance, about to leave.

'Where did you get too last night?' Tom asked.

'You really don't want to know,' Max replied. 'Let's just say that in a drunken fit of jealously I ended up going home with someone from the TV production team.'

'I personally don't care what you get up to, I just don't like it when you mess my sister around.'

Max grimaced. His hangover was starting to kick in, and he was already plagued with guilt. 'I know I need to make it up to her. Perhaps I could meet her at the airport on her return.'

'I'd said I'd collect her, but if you promise to turn up and not let her down then I think she'd appreciate it,' Tom replied sternly.

Once Max had retrieved his belongings and his car, he slumped into the driver's seat and promptly fell asleep. He awoke sometime later, barely able to move his neck, which had stiffened terribly due to the odd angle of his sleeping position. Having recovered fully he called his brother's mobile.

'Hi Max. What do you want?' Peter sounded weary, bracing himself for an awkward, embarrassing demand.

'Good to hear your cheery tones too,' Max replied sarcastically.

'Look, some of us are at work with jobs to do, so can you get to the point?'

'I really need some relationship advice,'

'And you immediately thought of me?'

'In as much as I need Ruth's current phone number and address.'

Sat in Heathrow terminal 5 waiting for her flight, Lottie called home. Her mother answered, keen to hear the gossip from the party. Lottie told her about her dancing with Ben's actor friends, and how she suspected that Verity and Tom were now officially a couple.

'Max went off with last year's X factor winner, but only after he threw his toys out the pram over his fantasy that Ed and I are an item.'

'I hope you weren't too upset darling.'

'Well at least it shows he cares- OK so it's not the most romantic gesture, but he must have feelings.'

'You know Max reminds me a bit of Nick,' Beth answered.

Lottie sounded horrified, 'Surely not. I know Max drinks quite a lot, but he goes for weeks without touching a drop.'

'I wasn't thinking of that, although I agree that Max is a bit of a playboy who knows how to party. No, it's that little rich boy arrogance that I see in them. They expect to get their own way, and although they don't mean too –they take people for granted.'

'Yes I can see that.' Lottie conceded.

'Of course, they are fundamentally different in one significant way. Nick always found it hard to express his feelings – he hid behind the bottle – only opened up when drunk. Max on the other hand lets his feelings be known. I guess it's his Russian heritage. He doesn't have repressed English emotions, just lets it all out.'

244

'I guess that's healthier,' Lottie answered. 'He's certainly easy to read – maybe a bit too easy. But saying that, Nick's quite open and talkative.'

'Only thanks to tens of thousands of pounds' worth of therapy,' Beth concluded.

Max punched the post code into his satnav, and headed off up the M1 towards Watford, and the home of his stepmother. He arrived in the quiet cul-de-sac as the mid-day news came on the radio. Having parked the car, he tentatively walked up the neatly flower-bordered garden path, and he knocked on the front door. Seconds later the door opened.

'Max. What a lovely surprise.' Suddenly Max found himself swamped by a powerful bear-hug. 'Oh, it's such a treat to see you.' Ruth kissed him on the cheek. Standing back, she ushered him inside her home. 'Come and sit down. Would you like a drink?'

'Coffee please.' Max was delighted by the welcome.

He sat and watched as she rushed around, clearing magazines off the occasional table, and plumping up cushions. He hadn't seen Ruth for a couple of years. Now in her late forties, she had put on weight, but it suited her. As the second of his father's wives, she'd been the kindest, and a natural mother figure. Although Peter was her own flesh and blood, she was the only one who treated Max with equal affection.

'You are looking well.' 'How are you?' Max asked.

'Your father still gives me a good allowance, so I'm able to live comfortably without having to work. I help out three days a week in a local charity shop, but otherwise, I have a quiet life. Peter rings me regularly, and I usually see him at least once a month.'

'Peter told me all about your fall out with your father. I was so sorry to hear what happened. I've been really worried about you. Ivan can be very cruel sometimes.' She rested her hand on his knee. 'I am very relieved you're OK'.

Max put his hand on Ruth's and patted it affectionately. 'To be honest, I got what I deserved.' He could barely believe what he was saying, but he'd done a lot of soul searching lately. 'I was ungrateful and unappreciative. And just like everything else that's good in my life – I end up destroying it.'

'Oh darling, you can't say that.'

'Yes I can. Just look at my life – It was my fault that my mother died, I then destroyed my career and now I'm turning the only decent relationship I've ever had into some sort of car crash. I don't want to, but I can't help myself.' Max gave Ruth a look of such desperate hopelessness she wanted to cry.

'Now just you look here,' she replied firmly. 'Your mother had post-natal depression. That's why she killed herself. You were just a tiny baby. If it was anyone's fault, then it's the health professionals that were to blame. It certainly wasn't you.' She gave him a hug. 'Promise me you'll never think like that again.'

Max nodded. 'I just wish you'd been allowed to be my mother.'

'So do I darling. It broke my heart when you were sent away to school at seven. Poor little mite. But your father said I molly coddled you and I would make you soft. He didn't see you as the vulnerable little boy in need of love and affection.'

'Does he still blame you that Peter's gay?'

Ruth smiled. 'It wouldn't be fair to say yes, but there were occasions when he insinuated as much, but it's you we're discussing not me. If you don't blame your father for selling your horses, then I suppose that's something. But you were so good. It's such a shame. I hope you don't give up completely.'

'No, horses are too deeply a part of me for me to give up without a fight, but that leads me to my final problem.'

Ruth sat patiently as Max explained his friendship with Lottie.

'It started off as pure lust, with me wanting to get her into bed and her resisting me. We then became really good friends, and for a while that was fine. The trouble is over the last few months these feelings have been creeping up on me, and it's getting unbearable.'

'What feelings Max?'

'I love her.' Max stopped. 'There I've said it out loud. Now it's real.'

'But she sounds like a lovely girl. So what's your problem?'

'Because I have nothing to give her. She deserves someone who can look after her, and yet

247

she spends her time caring for me. That's not how it should be.'

'Do you know how she feels about you?'

'She must care I suppose – she's done so much for me. I think she enjoys my company, but am I special to her, or just another of her projects? I just don't know'.

'You need to talk to her.'

'I know,' Max wailed in frustration. 'I want to tell her how I feel, but I want to build my career back up first – so she'll know that I love her for herself rather than what she can do for me.'

'Will she wait for you?'

'That's the fucking million-dollar question isn't it. There's someone else sniffing around her – another show jumper, and he's not good enough for her. The trouble is I've been so jealous that I've been acting like a total dick. Now she's flown out to the States, feeling angry with me, and that bloody gold digger will be there offering a shoulder to cry on.'

'Oh Max, you are in a mess aren't you. Just as well there's an easy solution.'

Max looked puzzled. 'What's that then?'

'You send her a message. Say you're sorry and tell her you care.'

'Do you think that will do any good?'

'She sounds like a kind, genuine soft-hearted girl. I'm certain it will do some good.'

Taking his step mother's advice, Max sat and composed a text. It had never taken him so long to type so few words, but finally he plucked up the courage to send it. He then spent the next hour stressing because she hadn't replied.

'Oh God, she hates me' Max's voice was full of despair.

'What time was her flight?' Ruth kept calm, 'Perhaps she's still on the plane with her phone switched off?'

'Yes of course. God I'm such an idiot,' Max felt a wave of relief. 'Thank you.'

Chapter 22

Lottie had checked into her hotel room before she got around to turning her phone back on. Feeling jet lagged, she really needed sleep, but had promised to message her mother to say she'd arrived safely. The first text message was from Max simply titled 'sorry'. She felt sick. Was this it, and he was saying he'd had enough of her and Devon. Tentatively she clicked on the message, and immediately nearly cried with mix of exhaustion and relief.

'I'm so sorry for being such an idiot. Please forgive me. The last thing I want is to damage our friendship. Will make it up to you once you are home. Have fun and take care. Love Max xxx'

After a few minutes' consideration, Lottie replied, *'No worries. So pleased we are still friends. Love Lottie.'*

Lottie spent the next few days running around Lexington like a Russian athlete on performance enhancing drugs. When she wasn't catering for every whim of the Yangtze directors, she was trying to herd the show jumpers for photo shoots and press interviews. Having decided that she should have been born a border collie, she finally stopped on the last day of the team show jumping where the British team secured a silver medal, being pipped to gold by Frederick Seipp's

German team. It also happened to be her birthday.

She had one tense moment, when she received an email from one of the livery girls who kept her horse on their yard. It said, *'While the cat's away,'* and it included a video attachment. Lottie instantly felt a stabbing pain in her chest, but knowing she must find out, she clicked on the video. She immediately burst out in relieved laughter. It was a clip showing Max schooling Hope.

Max knew Lottie's birthday was soon, but was horrified when, having finally arrived back from the pub at one o clock in the morning, rather worse for wear, he checked his phone and Lottie's birthday notification popped up on Facebook. He sent her a message, but it seemed inadequate bearing in mind their closeness.

Back in Kentucky, it was the team chef de quipe Simon who told the team that it was Lottie's birthday. Following his team's success, he'd offered to take everyone out for a celebratory meal. When Lottie received Max's message, she was sat in a restaurant having a meal with the jubilant British team. She responded by sending him a group photo and a message asking him to Skype.

Max was delighted to hear her voice. When he spoke he tried not to slur, but it wasn't easy. It had been a pub quiz and he'd been in a team along with some of the riding club members. Afterwards they'd had a bit of a lock in. Now the room was spinning, and it was hard to focus. He rubbed his tired eyes, trying to get them to focus on the screen. He asked how the team had done. He could tell from their elated faces that they'd been successful. Flashing their silver medals at Lottie's tablet, Mary said, 'Giles and Marcus got double clears, I got 4 and Paul 8 – overall team silver.'

'Well done, that's great.' Max replied. 'And Lottie, when you get home, I'm going to cook you a celebration meal.'

'Don't accept Lottie,' yelled Giles. He's a bloody awful cook.'

'Ignore him, he doesn't know what he's talking about.' Max complained.

'I'd love you to cook me a meal thank you', Lottie shouted over the noise.

'Seriously he is terrible,' piped up Marcus. 'He cooked for me once at Aachen and nearly burnt his bloody lorry to the ground.'

Max couldn't defend himself on that particular charge, so just laughed. Professional show jumpers could be such a cliquey insular bunch, and he felt so thrilled that he was being included in the banter, even though he was thousands of miles away. In competition terms there was an even greater disparity but just for a moment he felt like he was still their equal.

Despite having a thumping hangover, Max got up early to ride Hope. He'd been schooling the large chestnut horse for about ten minutes when he heard a voice. He halted and turned to see Beth standing at the gate watching him.

'Don't let me put you off,' she called across. 'Lottie will be delighted to see what you're doing

252

with him.'

Max rode across to her, 'I would do more jumping, but he gets so wound up, he just ends up leaping out the school, and carts me back to his field. He's just so strong, I can't stop him.'

'Would you take some advice – it's just that many years ago now I had a similar problem with a fjord thoroughbred cross who was a bolter. I turned to a classical trainer for help, and the results were amazing.'

'Go on,' Max said encouragingly.

'This classical instructor used to ride his horses in pelhams – but just used the curb rein. With a heavy-handed rider, that could do a lot of damage, but of course his hands were so gentle it was fine. Anyway, the principle is that the rider uses only the lightest touch on the reins– it's just an ask-release action, which lasts barely a second, using the fingers, or a twitch of the wrist. Because the horse has nothing to lean on, it can't take hold of the bit – it has nothing to fight.'

Max could see the logic, so Beth slipped off to the tack room and returned a few minutes later with her bridle. Max dismounted whilst they changed Hope's tack. 'Why don't you get on and show me?' Max offered.

'Only if you agree to do all the mucking out for the next few months if Hope throws me off and I break something.'

'You'll be fine,' Max said as he helped her to mount.

Beth then gave him a quick demonstration. Max was impressed by how quiet Hope was, as he gently responded to her aids. Having brought him back to a halt from canter, Beth slid off and handed Max back the reins. He climbed back on board and began to ride, following Beth's instructions.

Fifteen minutes later Max was jumping Hope, and for the first time he was in control. Following his orders, Beth increased the height of the fences up to the top of the wing. Now manageable, Max could effectively alter the striding to place the horse where he needed. Correctly positioned for take-off, Hope soared effortlessly over the jump, and Max whooped with delight.

Chapter 23

Lottie arrived back in Heathrow tired but happy following the success of the trip. The team had acquitted themselves well with their team silver, and with Marcus also getting individual bronze. The Yangtze directors had also returned back to China contented. Whilst everyone was focused on horses, she'd persuaded her boss to give her an additional two hundred and fifty thousand to spend on a horse lorry decked out in Yangtze colours. As a long term strategy it would be quite effective, driving up and down the motorways, and parking in prestigious venues to promote brand awareness. She'd already had initial meetings with a top name horse lorry conversion company who were prepared to put together a package using one of their nearly new 17 tonne lorries, and a top paint job for the price agreed.

Max had got to Heathrow far earlier than he'd needed, but he'd been so scared that he'd get held up in a traffic jam and was desperate to convince the family that he could be trusted. He was feeling very nervous, having parted on such bad terms.

He could have done with a stiff drink, but that was impossible, so instead he bought himself a packet of cigarettes. He wasn't really a smoker – just the occasional one when at school, and sometimes when drunk. He stood out in the road

255

and smoked two straight off, and immediately felt sick. Throwing the rest of the packet in a nearby bin, he headed off to the waiting area.

Having waved goodbye to Simon, Lottie headed for the terminal exit, where Max was patiently waiting for her. 'Did you have a great time?' he asked kindly. Before Lottie could reply he put his arms around her and pressed her body against his. He kissed her gently on the forehead, enjoying the warmth of her, and the sweet smell of her hair. 'I've really missed you,' he whispered.

'I missed you too. I had a lovely time, but I wish you'd been there competing – that would have made it complete.'

Max picked up her case. 'Let's get you home, you must be exhausted. Oh, and by the way, I'm sorry for being such a miserable bastard over the last few weeks. I was stupid and jealous, but I've given myself a good talking too and I promise to behave much better in future.'

'I'm so glad we're friends again,' Lottie replied. 'And I'm really pleased that you are riding Hope.'

'That was supposed to be a surprise!' Max sounded disappointed.

'It's been one of the worst kept secrets in history.' Lottie laughed.

'He's a bloody amazing horse.' Max enthused. You just have to see him jump. He's world class.'

'I'm so pleased.' Lottie stopped and gave him a hug. 'I would have rescued him even if he'd been a donkey, but the first time I watched him jump over his stable door, I knew he was special.'

The following evening, having recovered from her jet lag, Lottie made her way over to Max's house for a belated birthday meal. She was extremely hungry but had resisted the temptation to pig out before hand in spite of her doubts as to his ability as a chef. The last time an eligible male had cooked for her had been whilst she'd been at university. That time had ended up in embarrassment all round, when the chef seemed to assume that sexual favours were an automatic right as a repayment for cooking. She was nervous that history was about to repeat itself. It wasn't that she didn't want Max to make love to her; in fact, her body ached for him, but the fear was too great.

When she arrived, she realised what an effort Max had gone to. The dining table was properly laid out with a crisp white tablecloth. Soft music was playing on the iPod and there were numerous lit scented candles, dotted around the room. On the sideboard there was an open bottle of wine, plus a bottle of Lottie's favourite Schlur drink.

Having poured her a glass of sparkling grape juice in a crystal glass, he helped himself to some wine. 'Dinner will be ready in a few moments. Meanwhile, I have a birthday present for you. Sorry it's not much, and it's late.' He handed Lottie a carrier bag. 'Oh yes - sorry it's not wrapped.'

Lottie opened the bag and took out an expensive riding coat. 'Oh, Max it's lovely. Thank you so much... and such a thoughtful generous

257

gift.' Placing the jacket on an adjacent chair, she placed her hand gently on his upper arm and kissed him on the cheek.

Max looked relieved. 'I couldn't help notice that your jacket has a tear in the pocket. – and what with you going up to Hoys in a couple of weeks, it's important that you feel the part.'

'It's the nicest present, I've ever been bought by someone who isn't related to me.'

'I guess I've always had high maintenance girlfriends. It didn't matter when I was being bankrolled by my father, but no one I've ever dated would be contented with just a jacket.'

'You've obviously had the wrong girlfriends then.'

In the kitchen the cooker dinged. 'Ah, dinner's ready.' Max said. 'Sit down and I'll bring it through.'

Lottie sat quietly, amused by the sounds of banging, clanking and cursing coming from the kitchen. A few moments later he appeared carrying two plates. Placing her meal down in front of her, Lottie saw fish fingers, oven chips and peas.

The food tasted OK and have eaten Max once again disappeared into the kitchen to fetch dessert. What he brought back in made her laugh out loud. 'Oh I'm sorry – you must think I'm so rude, but has the trifle been involved in a road traffic accident?'

Max looked embarrassed. 'It was my favourite treat as a child. Ruth used to make it for me. I assumed it would be easy to make, but the jelly wouldn't set, and the custard was too hot when I poured it over the top. Then finally I put too much milk in the powder cream packet.'

'I'm sure it will still taste the same. I know it's the fashion for food to be served deconstructed – well this is the opposite of that. – The trifle equivalent of an Eton Mess,' Lottie replied, tucking in. 'Actually, it tastes fine.'

Once dinner was finished, Max made some freshly brewed coffee and they moved to the sofa where it was more comfortable, having evacuated Shadow who'd made herself at home.

'Lottie, I need to know what you meant when you said you were too frightened to have sex with Ed.'

'I didn't think you'd heard me.'

'I guess I just didn't know how to respond.'

'So, you went and shagged someone from X Factor.'

'Don't forget her lesbian mate. I had her too.' Max smiled. 'And before you say anything, yes it was crass and stupid of me, and I instantly regretted it. But less we get side tracked by incidental trivia, my question still stands.' He looked at Lottie, who was now squirming uncomfortably. 'Sorry. I don't mean to upset you, but it's obviously something really important, and as your friend it would help me to understand.'

'Oh dear, this is so awkward.' Lottie went bright red.

Max stood up. 'Come on let's go for a walk. It isn't dark yet, and you'll find it easier to talk with outside distractions, rather than feeling you're in some sort of court room in here.'

'I don't want you to think badly of me.' Lottie sounded choked.

'There is nothing that you could do or say, that would change how I feel about you. You're my dearest friend.' Max replied gently.

Lottie got to her feet, and with Shadow following on behind they walked out into the quiet Autumn evening. It was dusk and the birds were starting to roost as they headed off down the track to the fields.

'Well I guess I'd better start,' Lottie said. 'It all happened when I was at Uni. Taggart was still a youngster, so I decided to join the polo club as they provided the horses. There I ended up falling in love with Esra, a half Armenian shipping millionaire's son. He was captain of the team, handsome, clever and a playboy.'

'So not dis-similar to me then,' Max grinned, trying to keep the mood light.

'Anyway, we ended up in a relationship and for six months it was amazing. I was in love with this fabulous guy, and he was fun and exciting. I guessed that he wasn't entirely faithful to me, but I was so naive that I was blind to his infidelity.' She hesitated.

'Then you found out and beat him to death with his own riding boots,' Max interrupted. Lottie smiled, 'If only. No I found out for certain when I discovered that I had chlamydia.' She stopped and covered her face. 'This is so embarrassing,' she said looking into the distance.

'It's itchy and annoying, but there's worse.'

Max said.

Lottie turned and looked at him. 'You've had it as well?' Max threw his hands up in mock surrender. 'With my sexual history what do you think? Been there, had it, have the tee-shirt to prove it.'

Lottie was so stressed she answered, 'why would anyone want to wear a tee-shirt broadcasting the fact they'd had an STD?'

'Like durr,' Max laughed. 'So it that it?'

'Not quite, in fact that was only the start of my problems.'

'You have a secret love child?'

'No of course not. Now will you shut up and let me finish. It's hard enough for me as it is.'

'Sorry. Please carry on.'

'When I told Esra he went nuts and accused me of sleeping around. I told him that he was the only man I'd ever had, but he claimed that he didn't believe me. That's when things got nasty.'

'But it had to be his fault – that's ridiculous... again sorry for interrupting.'

'He decided to punish me and started posting horrible things about me on social media. It started off with posts that I was a dirty little slut riddled with STDs, then the posts changed to him accusing me of being a gold digger and lying about who my family were. He said that I was just the pathetic child of dull boring accountants and nothing to do with the aristocratic family I claimed to be part of. It went on for weeks. I was so ashamed and humiliated; I almost gave up my degree.'

'What a bastard. Oh, you poor thing.'

'My friends were all wonderful and supportive, and of course, after a week or so everyone had forgotten about me, but it destroyed my confidence, and I haven't had a proper relationship since.'

Lottie felt the comforting warmth of Max, as he gave her a reassuring hug.

'Have you seen him since you left uni?' he asked.

'No thank goodness,' she replied, giving an involuntary shudder.

'If your paths ever cross and I'm with you, I'll teach him a lesson he won't forget. How dare he treat you so badly!' Max was horrified by the story, but his mind was now in overdrive. It explained so much about Lottie.

Chapter 24

Ten days later Max, Lottie and Taggart set off for Birmingham and Horse of the Year Show. Max's lorry had been rather unreliable, but fortunately it started, and they managed to arrive in plenty of time to give Taggart a quick leg stretch ride before settling him into his stable. Max was being amazingly supportive, and Lottie really appreciated it, especially as she was sensitive to the pain he would be feeling at returning as a groom rather than a competitor.

As she rode around the temporary sand arena Lottie could feel Taggart's tension in the strange surroundings. Tracking up to the top corner of the school, Taggart suddenly shot sideways, nearly crushing a delicate little show pony coming in the opposite direction. The mother of the child rider glared at Lottie, but it just made Lottie giggle, especially as Max pulled his cap down over his face in mock embarrassment.

Once Taggart was back in his temporary stable, Lottie and Max went in search of some food. As they walked into the shopping mall, Lottie touched him gently on the arm, 'Thank you so much for coming with me. I know how hard it must be for you. I really appreciate your support.'

Max grinned. 'You're my best friend, of course I'm going to be here for you. But if it's OK with you, I'd rather keep a low profile. I'd be lying if I said it didn't hurt. I just hope that Paul doesn't bring Zhivago.'

Dressed in jeans, a plain jacket and a baseball cap, Max managed to remain incognito, and they made it back to the safety of the horse lorry. Max put on the little portable television, and they cuddled up together on the fold down bed. A couple of hours later, Max insisted that Lottie try to get some sleep. 'Not that I want to get rid of you, but you have an important day ahead of you tomorrow,' Max insisted. 'I've made up the bed above the luton for you.'

Lottie slowly dragged herself off the bed, 'Urggh, I was so comfortable.'

Max smiled. 'I'd love to spend the night with you properly, but I'm not going to rush you.'

'Thank you. I know it's rather a case of the elephant in the room. It's better if we just agree now that nothing is going to happen.'

'I know you aren't as slim as the models I've been used to dating, but calling yourself an elephant is a bit harsh.' Max grinned.

'Who's to say that you aren't the elephant,' Lottie replied petulantly.

Max laughed. 'Anyway, if I do ever seduce you, I'd rather it was somewhere luxurious and romantic. Your first time for many years needs to be special, not a bunk up in the back of a horse lorry.'

Lottie was taken aback by his sudden show of sensitivity. 'I'm impressed.'

Max smiled. 'I can be thoughtful. Not often

admittedly, but you're worth it.'

Lottie's competition wasn't until early evening, but she was on edge from the moment she woke up. Unable to relax, she kept taking Taggart out for walks to stop him getting too bored. Her mum and Nick arrived at lunch time, and they forced her to eat a sandwich. Later in the afternoon, Max acted as trainer and stood on the side of the warm-up arena giving her last-minute tips. He was still trying to keep a low profile, but everywhere he went, people were monitoring him, wondering whether they should say anything.

Minutes before Lottie was due into the arena both Marcus and Paul rode into the collecting ring on young horses, having qualified for the same final.

'Hello Lottie. Nice to see you on a horse,' Marcus called across cheerfully.

'I think I'm going to be sick I'm so terrified,' Lottie replied.

'We all get nervous. You just need more practice.' Marcus answered before turning his horse towards the warm-up fence.

'Not a bad looking animal,' Paul muttered as he passed a critical eye over Taggart whilst overtaking Lottie, who'd now brought Taggart back to a walk.

Marcus then spotted Max, 'Good to see you Max. Let's catch up for a drink. Are you coming to the party later?'

Max was about to say no, but Lottie interrupted. 'We haven't been invited?'

'I'll make sure you're both added to the guest list.'

Moments later Lottie was called forward by one of the stewards. By now she was shaking with nerves. She'd never jumped in front of such a huge crowd, and she was certain that Taggart would be unsettled by the massive arena. Her mum and Nick had got tickets and would be watching her but she half wished her mum was beside her. She needed a shoulder to cry on. As she walked around waiting for the previous competitor to finish, her legs felt like jelly, and she questioned how on earth she was going to find the strength to ride.

Max looked at her kindly. 'It's OK to feel scared. Forget about everyone else around you. Just go in and enjoy yourself.' He gave her a reassuring pat on her leg. 'Just pop Taggart over the practice fence once more, then in you go.'

Lottie did as she was told. After so much schooling from Max, Taggart was jumping so much better, and he sailed confidently over the fence, but as Lottie headed towards the tunnel leading to the arena, her beloved grey horse started to tense. He'd never been great in new surroundings, and the size and noise of the crowds were almost more than he could cope with.

Lottie pushed him on as best she could, given that by now her whole body had turned to jelly. Taggart crept cautiously into the arena, and immediately shied at the TV camera. Snorting, and with his neck set like a stone statue, he carried on, his eyes out on stalks, and barely aware of the jumps. 'Come on Taggart, it's OK,' Lottie spoke to him. He momentarily flicked back an ear to listen to her, before once again staring out into the seating area. The countdown clock started, giving Lottie a mere thirty seconds to get Taggart in the zone. She pushed him into canter, and they headed on a scenic route towards the first fence.

Taggart only had half his mind on the job as he approached the first fence. He got in too close and had to twist himself awkwardly to avoid hitting it and made them both look like complete amateurs. Luckily he got back into a half decent rhythm and managed to get over the next four fences without incident. Then Lottie needed to bring him around passed the entrance towards a wide spread. Three strides before take-off, Taggart again spotted the TV camera and shied. Giving himself no chance to then jump, Lottie had to pull him in a circle, to represent, costing her both valuable seconds and penalty points.

She was vaguely aware of sympathetic mutterings from the crowd. Unfortunately, Taggart was now unsettled and unbalanced, and knocked both that fence, and the following one. They did manage to complete the rest of the course and left the arena to polite clapping and the announcement that they had 12 jumping and 2 time faults.

As soon she spotted Max, she jumped off, throwing the reins and a carrot at him, before rushing off to the loo where she was violently sick. Having composed herself, she went back to the collecting ring, where Max was walking Taggart around, cooling him off.

'Are you OK?' he asked.

'I'm so sorry I let you down. I did try, but Taggart had stage fright. He was so solid in his neck I could barely ride him.'

'You didn't let me down,' he replied gently.

'You've been training him beautifully for months. I've dragged you up here to help, and for what. I'm hopeless,' she sobbed.

'It's fine. That's horses for you.' He gave her a reassuring hug. 'Do you want to try again next year? We could take him to some bigger venues during the year and get him used to them.'

'No. He's yours to compete. That's if you still want him after today's performance.' Lottie sniffed.

'Well if you're sure. I'd love to. Other than the emotional loss of my precious horses, the hardest part of what my father did was to deprive me of the chance to compete. It's all I've ever wanted to do, and how I define myself. Without it I'm lost.'

They walked Taggart back to his stable. Lottie wished they could just load him into the lorry and leave, but Marcus had got them tickets to the show jumper's party that evening, so felt obliged to stay.

'Are you coming to the party later?' Lottie asked.

'I'm not sure. I am just here as a groom. Maybe I should find out what Lee and the boys are doing this evening.'

Having filled up Taggart's haynet, they set off

in search of Lee. Having turned the corner of the stable block they nearly collided with Marcus.

'Hi Lottie – hear your horse was a bit camera shy, still well done. Did you enjoy it?'

'I was too scared to enjoy it. Max is going to take over competing Taggart, but we just need to expose him to some larger venues so he can get used to them.'

Marcus turned to Max. 'Good to see you mate. I'm jumping in twenty minutes, but it would be great to catch up later. Did you get the tickets for the party this evening?'

Max hesitated, 'Yes, we got them thanks, but I'm no longer entitled to go to a party for riders.'

'Nonsense. I'm inviting you as my guest, so now you must come.'

Max smiled weakly, uncertain of whether to refuse. 'I mean it,' Marcus added, noticing Max's hesitation. 'I shan't take no for an answer. I know which is your lorry, so if you don't show, I shall bloody well come and get you and drag you there myself.'

Once Marcus had left, they carried on hunting for Lee. They finally found him coming from the warm-up arena carrying a rug. Without saying a word, Lee dropped the rugs, before giving his old boss a hug, and slapping him on the back.

'all right boss?' he said.

'Been worse. You OK?'. He hesitated, 'Zhivago?'

'I'd rather work for you, but Paul's all right. He's entered Zhivago in this evening's class so you'll see him. He doesn't suit Paul's riding style, but they kind of muddle along. Zhivago's well cared for. He's always been a grumpy bastard, but doesn't seem any worse, so I guess he's fine.'

'If you hear that Lady H wants to sell him or move him on, will you tip me off. Not that I've got a hope in hell of raising the money to buy him, but you know...' Max trailed off. He still loved the bad-tempered stallion and hated the thought of not knowing the horse's destiny.

An hour later Max watched cringing from the sidelines as Paul hauled Zhivago roughly around the show jumping course. Zhivago wasn't enjoying himself and made a couple of careless mistakes. He hadn't lost his ability, but his passion for the job seemed to have died. Lottie could sense her friend's pain. As soon as Paul left the arena, she said, 'Come on let's go and get a drink.'

They headed off to the bar, where Lottie bought Max a large vodka. He sat staring moodily into the middle distance.

'We've got so far. We just need to work on a plan to buy back your horse,' Lottie said, trying to raise Max's spirits.

'Other than winning the lottery I don't see how,' Max moaned.

'I haven't got an immediate answer, but I'm not giving up.' Lottie was determined. The obvious answer was to get Ivan Tarasov on her side, but she'd need Crispin's help. Failing that she thought about approaching an owner's syndicate. Currently however the horse was not for sale, so there was nothing to be done.

Half an hour later, Lottie was leaning against the outside wall of the men's loos waiting for Max, when she became conscious that she was being watched. Huddled together like bullies in a school ground were a small group of riders whom she'd been competing against earlier in the Foxhunter class. There were a couple of girls, around her own age, both wearing designer riding gear, with matching long blonde hair tied back in ponytails. There was a male rider in his early forties, and there was the ringleader, Spencer Holland, a moderately well-known semi-professional in his early thirties.

Spencer had never quite managed to break through into the major league, but up to 1 metre 40, was one of the most successful riders on the circuit. Being that he was one of the few male competitors who was under forty, not gay, and good looking, he tended to be idolised by up-and-coming young riders. Lottie only knew him by sight, having never actually spoken to him. She'd always considered him to be out of her league. Their paths rarely crossed, so she'd never given him a great deal of thought. Wearing a fitted black jacket, and expensive leather boots, with a baseball cap, he was frequently mistaken for one of the grand prix riders.

Egged on by the group, Spencer came across to Lottie. Lottie smiled nervously, but he didn't react. Getting as close to her as he dared, he half whispered. 'So how come none of us have ever heard of you, yet you seem to be on first name terms with half the British show jumping team? he asked in a slightly sinister tone.

'I have actually been competing for a number of years, - it's just I don't generally leave the West Country. Admittedly it's not my riding prowess the likes of Marcus are interested it, but I don't see that it's anyone else's business.'

Spencer scowled, irritated by Lottie's unhelpfulness. 'Are you the latest team bike?' he snapped rudely.

'My relationship with the team should be obvious,' Lottie retorted, referring to her jacket emblazoned with the logo *Yangtze Motors Supporting British Show Jumping.* Spencer looked confused.

'You aren't exactly Poirot are you?' Lottie challenged him. 'If you're so desperate to find out about me why don't you do some research, rather than marching over here being rude and boorish?'

'I don't like pushy little upstarts OK?' he glared at her. Unable to help herself, Lottie smirked, amazed by the fact that she found the situation funny rather than intimidating.

Suddenly from behind her, Lottie heard a familiar voice.'Are you being picked on by the school bully? Never mind sweetheart, the head boy's here to save you.'

Max marched up to her and putting his hand on the small of her back, guided her away to safety. Turning back to look at Spencer he added, 'Don't let me catch you picking on my mate again, or you'll be sorry.'

Lottie glanced backwards, looking at an

affronted looking Spencer, and two fed-up looking girls and burst out laughing. 'Have you worked it out yet Poirot?' He didn't reply.

Chapter 25

Max was reluctant to go to the party in the function suite, and by the time Lottie had pleaded and cajoled him into getting ready, they were running late. Luckily they arrived with Simon Palmer, and were allowed in without question. Lottie was starving and headed straight for the buffet, but Max was not in the mood for a party and headed straight to the bar. Having downed a couple of large vodkas he started to feel slightly better.

Most of the riders seemed genuinely pleased to see Max; he was inundated with offers of drinks including from many of the foreign riders. Just as he was starting to get some self-confidence back, Paul kicked up a fuss.

'This is a party for competitors, not washed-up has-beens and grooms,' he announced in a loud voice. 'Will someone call security?'

Marcus stood up, 'I invited Max. He's here as my guest, so lay off him Paul.'

Despite being defended by Britain's leading show jumper, Max couldn't help but feel deflated. Max was under no illusions that Paul was a dickhead, but what hurt was the fact that Paul was stating the painful truth, that Max no longer had the right to be there.

Suddenly one of the HOYs officials entered the room and headed straight for Max. 'This is it. I'm going to be asked to leave,' Max muttered, bracing himself for the humiliation. Lottie, who'd been chatting to Simon, instinctively excused herself, and headed towards her friend, to provide moral support.

The official looked awkward as he spoke. 'Mr Tarasov, could I have a word with you in private?' He ushered Max towards the back of the room and into an empty office, with Lottie following in hot pursuit. 'We're together,' she announced, 'as guests of Marcus,' she added.

The official ignored her, and said, 'This is all rather embarrassing, but on behalf of the organisers, we need your assistance.' Max, who'd been preparing himself for eviction was too stunned to talk, but merely nodded his head.

'For tomorrow's matinee performance, we'd decided to trial a bit more of a family friendly fun competition this year. It's a pro-am celebrity rescue relay. The professional rider starts off with a short course of fences, then the amateur, celebrity rider takes over and jumps a course of about 70cm. Should either rider have a stop or a knock down, they are rescued, by their partner.

Max looked confused so the official continued. 'For example, we have Giles paired up with the ex-supermodel Jade. If Giles knocks down his fence 5, then Jade has to take over on her course. She starts from her jump 5, until the course is completed, then she starts her own round. If she has a stop or a pole down Giles rescues her. It's all against the clock, and the fastest pair wins.'

'Sounds fun, but how does it involve me?' Max asked.

The official reddened slightly. 'When we were

275

looking for celebrities to take part, we contacted the English, Hollywood based actress Melissa May, as we'd been told she was a fair horsewoman. We never heard back and thought that was it. This morning her office called to say that Melissa is flying to the UK tonight and is turning up here tomorrow morning with a half a million-pound horse, she bought just to do the competition.' He cleared his throat, before continuing. 'She is quite a demanding lady, and she is insisting that she is partnered with you,' he said looking at Max.

'But I don't have a horse. How high would I have to jump?'

'We didn't want the celebrities' fences to look too tiny, so the course builder is making it 1metre 40.'

'Could you do it on Taggart?' Lottie asked.

'If you don't mind, then yes, I've actually jumped him at home bigger than that.'

'I just hope he behaves for you,' Lottie added.

The next morning, instead of heading off home, Lottie plaited Taggart's mane, and re washed his tail and legs to remove the stable stains. Taggart was bored of being stuck in a stable, and longed to get back to his field, and this made him grumpy. When he wasn't grabbing brushes with his teeth and throwing them across the stable, he was trying to nip Lottie.

'I'm sorry darling. Just a few more hours and we can leave,' she told him.

By the time she'd finished preparing him, his tail shone like it had been streaked with silver and

276

he looked amazing. She hadn't seen Max for ages. He'd shot off in a taxi into Birmingham muttering something about a costume. He arrived back late, missing the course walk, and with the first riders about to start.

First to go were Giles and the former supermodel, Jade. When Giles saw the former page three girl riding towards him he gasped in astonishment, unable to take his eyes off her voluptuous chest. 'I hope those beauties are well strapped down, otherwise you'll get a black eye every time you go over a jump.' Although Jade was primarily a show rider, she jumped a slow but accurate clear round, and they left the arena with a good clean score.

Next to ride were Paul and a famous female radio DJ. They were hot favourites, and both jumped fast clear rounds. 'At least Paul was matched with someone who could understand his Yorkshire accent,' someone commented.

Mary went next teamed up with a former male Blue Peter presenter, but he was rather rusty, not having ridden for a few years and twice needed rescuing. The pretty German Corrina Seipp was next to jump alongside a singer from a boy band, and the teenagers in the audience went mad with excitement. Jacq, the sexy French rider, and father of Karen's baby, followed on, accompanied by an actress who'd starred in Downton Abbey.

Marcus and a former Olympic gold medallist cyclist then managed to knock up the fastest time of the competition before the commentator Mike

Tucker announced that there was a surprise late entry.

'Having just flown in from Hollywood, whilst in the middle of filming Highwayman 2, please give a huge welcome for Melissa May.'

The crowds, especially the dads, went wild as the gorgeous, beautiful Melissa coolly cantered into the arena on a sleek jet black mare. She waved to the crowds before coming to a halt in the far corner. Lottie, who didn't have a ticket, rushed over to the competitor's seats and managed to slip in next to Marcus.

'Who's her partner?' riders were asking, as the lights dimmed and the theme tune from Highwayman one began playing. Seconds later, Max, heavily disguised under a hat and cloak, cantered into the arena on Taggart. Taggart's eyes were on stalks. He'd never seen so many people, and so much noise. He was considering slamming on his brakes and running away, but he was aware of a black mare calmly watching him. Unlike his mistress whom he'd felt shaking with fear, Max was calm and determined, so Taggart decided not to bail out, but to go with the flow.

Max cantered around the fences, enjoying himself. Although was he making the most of being back in the limelight, his main reason was to take the opportunity to get Taggart acclimatized to the noise in the arena. As the music slowed, he pulled up alongside Melissa, whipped off the cloak, and, from inside his coat, produced a single red rose, which he presented to her. Lottie had to admit that he did look so handsome, and it was wonderful to see him sat on her precious horse.

'Oh my God it's Max Tarasov,' someone in the audience screamed, and again the audience went mad. Lottie held her breath, but fortunately Taggart was far too concerned with flirting with Melissa's mare to take any notice.

'Is that your horse?' Marcus asked.

Lottie was far too stressed to speak, and just nodded, as she gripped the barrier.

Max found he had to give Taggart a sharp jab with his spur to get him moving, as the horse was far too interested in his new friend to listen. Startled by the unexpected dig in his side, he gave a small buck before springing into action. Having got Taggart's attention, Max prepared him for the first fence. He was apprehensive, as the fence was higher than Taggart had generally jumped in competitions, and if he wasn't concentrating then Max's comeback would end in disaster before it had even started. Fortunately Taggart locked onto the fence, and making a concerted effort, jumped cleanly.

In such a tight arena, and with fences bigger than he was used to, Taggart really had to work hard. Being naturally obliging, he did his best. There were a few hairy moments where poles rattled, but aided by Max's superb riding, they jumped clear.

Melissa then set off, on her beautiful black mare. Max watched intently, praying that they would jump clear, as he didn't want his luck to run out by asking Taggart to jump again. The

279

mare was extremely talented, and more used to jumping at the highest level, and totally over jumped the tiny fences. Melissa was sufficiently competent to cope, and much to Max's relief they made it around the course without error.

The commentator cheerfully announced that they had come 3rd. Max was so happy he could feel tears welling up. His old self would have thought him mad, getting so thrilled about getting placed in what was only a novelty class, but so much had happened. For the first time in months, he finally realised that he really had been given a second chance. Max patted Taggart's grey neck. 'Thank you boy, you've been amazing,' he said softly.

After the prize giving, Melissa jumped off her horse and hugged Max. 'Darling, we were wonderful.'

Max grinned, 'We do make rather a good team. Turning, he gave her mare a stroke on her neck. She's a beautiful horse; only eclipsed by the beauty of her owner.'

Lottie, who was out of sight behind Taggart, feeding him carrots made vomiting actions; the only person who spotted her was Ed Carter, who grinned.

'The horse is named Santa Cruz. I only bought her for the competition today, and I have to fly back to the States tomorrow. The previous owners delivered her here. I'm not sure what to do with her. Would you like to take her on?

Max could barely believe his luck. 'I'd love to. Thanks. If I can compete her for a few months, then when you're next in the UK, you can decide whether to keep her.'

Melissa turned, and spotting Lottie said, 'Max get your groom to sort out the horses, while I take you for a late lunch to celebrate.'

'Hang on a moment – what am I supposed to do with your horse?' Lottie asked.

Melissa simply ignored her, linked her arm through Max's and led him away, leaving Lottie standing angrily, holding the two horses.

She led them both back to the stables, where she shoved Taggart back in his stable, and then used his head collar to secure Santa Cruz. With the black mare securely tied up, she untacked both horses. Making two trips, she then trudged back to the lorry, and put both sets of tack into one of the outside lockers. She then looked in the feed locker and realised that the haylage was nearly all gone. It wasn't surprising, as Taggart should have been due home by now. Not only would it be at least four to five hours before they got back, she now had two of them to feed.

Lottie went back to the stables, and took out one of Taggart's water buckets, so the mare could have a drink. Lottie then headed off to the trade stands where she knew there was a chance she could buy a bale of feed. Having reached the stand, she noticed that they only had display stock. She tentatively asked the business owner if he had any stock for sale.

'No. We've sold out,' he said gruffly.

'I'm desperate. Could you sell me one of your open sacks?'

'You should have been more prepared,' he answered unhelpfully.

'I've had Melissa May's horse dumped on me. We should have left this morning. Now I have 2 horses and no food.'

Grumbling, the man relented. Charging Lottie £10, he handed her an opened bale. Although she was grateful, he made no further offer to help transport it, so she was forced into hauling the 25kilo bale back through all the crowds, and then a further quarter mile back to the stables. It took her ages, as she had to keep stopping. Her back ached and she got cramp in her hands, but finally she made it back. Both horses were hungry and snatched at the haylage.

'At least you are grateful,' Lottie said to them.

Leaning exhausted against the stable door, Lottie was just wondering how long Max would be when the stable manager approached her. He was an officious looking man in his late fifties, wearing a suit and carrying a walkie talkie.

'We've been wondering when you were going to turn up,' he glared at Lottie. 'It's against the rules to leave a horse outside the stable unattended.'

Lottie was in no mood to take any grief. 'Well if you can tell me which stable this black mare is supposed to be in, I'll happily put her there.'

Having given the stable manager the horse's name, he checked on his list. 'This horse was never issued a stable. I also need to see its passport, otherwise I'm afraid it will have to be removed from the premises.'

Lottie sighed. 'I don't have her passport. As I explained, she was dumped on me by her new owner Melissa May.' The lack of reaction meant the man neither knew nor cared who Melissa May was. He had a job to do and that was that. 'I am waiting for you to remove the horse.'

'She isn't my horse to remove?' Lottie said, trying to control her temper.

'So where's her owner?'

'I assume back in her hotel room. She muttered something about lunch, but that was ages ago.'

'You'll need to contact her and get her to come back here immediately.'

'At the risk of sounding awkward. I don't have her phone number.' Lottie then explained how she'd come to have Santa Cruz dumped on her.

'Can't you load the horse in your lorry? I assume you have transport.' The stable manager sounded exasperated.

Lottie cringed. 'It's my friend's lorry. He has gone off with the keys, and without them I can't work the electronic ramp. I've tried calling him, but his phone is switched off.'

'Well you can't leave the horse tied up here.'

Lottie was tired, emotional, and losing her ability to remain calm. 'What do you recommend then? I can hardly slip her into my handbag, so what do you suggest, because I am out of ideas?'

'If that's your attitude then I am going to have to call the Police.'

'Really! You don't think they may have

283

something more important to do?' she asked.

He ignored her, turned, and walked off, shouting into his walkie talkie. Turning her attention back to the horses, Lottie saw that the black mare was getting cold. The only spare rug she had was Taggart's muddy turnout rug, but it was better than nothing. Feeling exhausted, and emotional, Lottie then burst into tears.

Max had been having a wonderful time with Melissa. After a fabulous lunch, they'd gone back to her hotel room, and had the most glorious sex. Melissa had a fabulous body and knew how to use it to her advantage. Melissa also found pleasure in Max's fabulously fit physique, and endless stamina. She was so used to the steroid pumped, chemically enhanced men of LA; it was great to spend the afternoon with a male body which was so naturally beautiful.

It was nearly 4pm before Max realised how late it was. Kissing Melissa on her perfectly rounded breasts he said, 'I must go. I've got to drive the horses back to Devon.'

'Can't your groom take the horses? I want you to stay the night. I fly back to LA in the morning?' she pouted sulkily.

'Sorry, but Lottie isn't licenced to drive the HGV lorry.' Feeling guilty he added. 'And technically she isn't my groom. She owns the horse I was riding, and she also happens to be my landlady.'

Melissa lay back, her bronzed, naked body calling Max back to bed. He looked at her with anguish. His body ached for her, but he owed it to

Taggart to get him home. Hurriedly dressing, he said, 'Now you're my sexiest owner, you must pop over and see me regularly. I want to ride for you in more ways than one.'

As he was about to leave, he remembered to ask for Santa Cruz's passport. Fortunately, Melissa had it, as Max needed it to register himself as the mare's official keeper with British Show jumping. Having stuffed it in his jacket pocket, he rushed away. He arrived out of breath a few minutes later just as a police car pulled up outside the stables.

'Where the hell have you been?' Lottie shouted at him.

'You know where. I've been spending time with my newest owner,' he said, irritated by her snappiness.

'You've never given me that much consideration?' Lottie retorted. 'It's been hell here. Melissa's horse had no hay, no passport and no stable. The Hoys authorities have called the police, probably thinking I've stolen a horse, whilst you've been off enjoying yourself.'

Max glared at her. 'I've got the passport here,' he said, retrieving it from his pocket. 'I didn't know we'd run out of hay, and I'd happily have fucked you if you weren't so bloody frigid.'

Lottie turned, and entered Taggart's stable, trying not to cry. She'd had to buy a spare head collar, which she now put on Taggart. He was as cross and fed up as she was and tried to bite her. 'O come on give me a break,' she whimpered.

285

With the correct paperwork in place, the police went away satisfied, and relieved. The last thing they wanted was the responsibility for a horse. The stable manager was pacified, and Max headed off to unlock the lorry. Lottie then led the two horses, whilst struggling to carry the water buckets and half eaten hay nets back to the lorry. Taggart jumped up the ramp, eager to get home. Cruz quietly followed.

Once Lottie had climbed up into the cab beside Max, he immediately apologised. 'Sorry,' he said. 'I didn't mean to be so long. I understand why you were so cross. I'm also sorry about what I said.'

'It's OK,' Lottie replied in a small voice. She was hurt, and upset, but saw no point in carrying on the argument. After all, she decided, he was a man, and one who happened to be being pursued by one of the most famous, male- fantasy women in the world. It wasn't his fault that she felt so bitter and jealous. What was it about all these A list celebrity females, who kept coming after the man she'd hoped to make her boyfriend.'

They travelled in silence for nearly an hour before Max spoke. 'Oh, I nearly forgot. I owe you £2,500 which is your share of the prize money.'

'That's generous, and unexpected. Don't you need it?'

'Melissa gave me her share.'

'Well in that case I'll use it to buy Hope a decent saddle. Thanks,' Lottie replied.

Chapter 26

Over the next couple of weeks, Max upped the number of competitions, keen to jump both Cruz and Taggart at a level where he would be able to claw his way back up the rider rankings in time for London. He was also keen to bring on Hope and Oberon but was limited by a lack of a groom. The lorry was also regularly playing up, and Max was reluctant to travel more than two horses at a time in case they needed rescuing from the side of a motorway.

Lottie helped as groom for weekend competitions, bringing Shadow with her for company, whilst quietly working on a solution. With Hope's social media followers increasing daily, he was attracting commercial interest. The day before Max's birthday, Lottie popped up to London to Yangtze HQ where she signed off the contract on the new lorry which was now ready to be delivered. She then headed off across town to the central office of one of the largest equine sports companies who had offered a substantial sponsorship package for Hope, the funding of which would pay for a groom.

Lottie took the crowded Friday evening commuter train back home and spent the first half of the journey standing in the corridor. She used the time to phone various family members.

Ben, Max and Nick all had birthdays within a week of each other, so the plan had been to hold a joint birthday and firework party at Stapletor the following evening.

The planning was very last minute due to the dependency on the weather, but with a clear, bright night forecast, Lottie and Tom hurriedly rung around friends, confirmed with the caterers and the fireworks company, and finalising the arrangements. Luckily Beth had pre-arranged for all the guest rooms to be prepared as Ben announced he was bringing down half the people from the film set.

The next morning, once the horses had been sorted, Lottie dragged Max off to a very posh horse shop, thirty miles away, borrowing Nick's Range Rover for the journey. Hope's sponsors Horsetek had given her a load of retail vouchers for their products. Lottie had also used some of her Hoys prize winnings to order a new pair of Italian handcrafted leather riding boots as a birthday present for Max.

On the way, Lottie broke the news of the sponsorship deal to Max and explained that there would be sufficient revenue to employee a couple of junior grooms.

'What's the catch?' Max asked, not sounding very grateful.

'Horsetek want me to keep going with the social media for Hope. When he starts competing, he needs to wear their branded boots, saddle cloths and rugs. I also need to set up links to their site on your website.'

'And for that they are paying £50k a year. That's not bad.'

Lottie cringed. 'I did suggest that they may like to run a competition, to win a visit to the yard, and to meet you and Hope. I hope you don't mind?'

'I'm not really in a position to say no, am I?' Max replied. 'Can we make sure that we employ at least one hot young female groom?'

Having reached the saddlery shop, Lottie handed over her vouchers, and the shop produced the full Horsetek range of horse clothing in Hope's size. She'd ordered Max's boots when they'd come to fit Hope's saddle the previous week, having briefly pinched his old ones to ensure the correct fit.

As the sales assistant appeared with the new handmade boots, Lottie turned to Max. 'This is my birthday present to you.'

He turned around, a look of surprised delight on his face. 'Thank you. That's so kind.' He immediately wrapped his arms around her, kissed her on the cheek, before squeezing her in an affectionate hug.

'I'd noticed that your old ones were worn out, and when you shared that prize-money with me, it gave me a chance to treat you.'

He tried them on, and fortunately they fitted perfectly. 'These are just great,' he said, parading around the shop, much to the amusement of fellow shoppers. Lottie glanced at her watch. 'Sorry Max, we're going to have to shoot. I've got to get to Exeter services by one.'

289

Max looked puzzled. 'Why?'

Lottie ignored him, but headed out to the car, carrying all the new horse equipment. Once they were in the Range Rover she said, 'I've got a second surprise for you. Yangtze are letting me have a vehicle for you to drive. Its logo'd up with their sponsorship I'm afraid, but it's yours to use as much as you want.'

'Is it an Intrepid?' Max asked, feeling it would be rather nice to have a smart four-wheel drive to go around in. Thinking quickly, he also wondered whether it would be worth getting a trailer to cover his lorry's more unreliable days. 'How long will I have it?' he asked. 'I guess I'll have to give it back at the end of the Olympics? At least by then I should be in a better position financially.'

'I haven't actually seen the vehicle,' Lottie replied truthfully. 'It may be a long-term sponsorship. After all, one vehicle is a lot cheaper, and thus a more sustainable marketing option. I reckon that if you stay high profile in the sport, they'll let you keep it.'

They arrived at the services with ten minutes to spare so Max rushed into the shop to buy them lunch. They'd just finished their sandwich, when Lottie noticed the beautiful Yangtze coloured lorry heading for the HGV Park. Hurriedly she fired up the engine. 'Whoops wrong car park,' she said.

As they turned into the lorry area, Max noticed the horse lorry. 'Oh my God. Is that it?' He sounded like a little boy.

'Yes. Sorry it's not an Intrepid,' she joked.

'Is it really for me to use whenever I want?'

'Pretty much. There may be a couple of times in the year when we are asked to use it for purely promotion purposes, but yes, it's yours to use. And the more you use it, and get it seen out and about, the happier they'll be.'

Max jumped out of the Range Rover and rushed over to meet the driver who was climbing down out of the cab. Max was given a tour of the technical elements of the vehicle, whilst the driver's mate drove up in a support car, ready to take his colleague back to Yorkshire. Once the two men had done their handover, Max and Lottie explored the living area.

'I love the extendible living area,' Lottie said as she pushed the button and the side of the lorry glided outwards.

'It's got a drinks cabinet. It's even posher than the Tarasov Holdings one.' Max exclaimed.

'At the risk of stating the obvious, with your new lorry, and a couple of grooms, you'll be able to go out and properly compete now,' Lottie said.

'You are the most amazing person I've ever met, Miss Lottie Wilkins. I don't know how I'm ever going to thank you.' He kissed her gently on her cheek, and then, wrapping his arms around her, held her tightly.

Lottie loved the feeling of his body against her. It was warm and reassuring. 'Thank you,' he whispered. 'I'll make sure that I repay your faith in me.'

Later that evening, as Max stood with a glass of vodka, watching the fireworks, he mused to himself. It had been the best of days and the worst of days. His father had never been great, but his PA's had always made sure that Max was sent a card and a decent present. This year Ruth had sent a card, but that was it. There wasn't the usual coke and an amazing shag, which Cindy had always provided. He had very little money and was back at the bottom competitively with his career.

Despite being failed by his family; Max had rarely had such an amazing birthday. His adopted family treated him like an equal, and the beautiful, clever, resourceful Lottie; his best friend; had given him back his hopes and dreams. As the fireworks exploded, lighting up the house and garden Max felt his own inner glow of contentment.

A fortnight later two grooms joined the team, both blonde, attractive and in their early twenties. Dizzy came from working in an event yard in Somerset, whilst Pippa was a recent graduate in equine studies. They were to live in the house in the old servants' quarters. Although the girls were employees of the Marchbanks', it quickly became apparent that they only considered Max to be their boss and tended to ignore Lottie.

For Pippa it was her first proper job, and of the two, she was the more willing and knowledgeable. Dizzy had left home at sixteen, and worked in numerous jobs, and subsequently was far more streetwise. Max was delighted to have the girls. It meant that he could get on with schooling his horses, leaving them to clear out the stables of his competition horses and the full liveries.

Other than when she was away, Lottie had always looked after Taggart herself, and since Hope's arrival, she'd included him in her daily routine. Having owned Taggart since a foal, she'd been very close to her big, lovely grey horse. He always neighed with excitement when she arrived on the yard, and recently Hope had begun to copy his friend. Lottie jealously protected her relationship with her horses, and thus the arrival of the girls made very little difference to Lottie's workload.

Chapter 27

Within a few days of the girls' arrival, Max was made an offer which made their presence essential. A pre-Christmas 'Up Close and Personal' tour had been arranged covering ten equestrian centres, starting at Gleneagles and finishing in Devon, featuring two young male eventers. Unfortunately, a fortnight before the start of the tour, one of them broke several ribs in a rotational fall. Max was therefore asked to stand in. Having been offered a lucrative share of the proceeds, Max felt it was impossible to turn down. Secondly it also meant a useful training ground for his inexperienced horses.

Lottie was also delighted by the opportunity as it was great for the sponsors. Hope's Facebook page announced his forthcoming trip, and Lottie taught him to walk around holding an RSPCA collection bucket between his teeth, so he could do some charity fundraising during the interval.

Pippa drew the short straw and had to stay back and look after the liveries, but on the understanding that she would get to go to London. Both Lottie and Dizzy were to travel with Max, as he intended to take all four horses. He looked on the tour as a chance to bond with Cruz, and to give the other three venue experience. As part of the demonstration involved showing how to bring on a young horse, Oberon would get good exposure.

Lottie had never travelled to Scotland, and was amazed by how beautiful it was, albeit cold. They arrived at the Gleneagles Equestrian centre the day before the first performance. Having settled the horses in the stables, Max and Lottie joined the tour organisers for a meeting, along with Max's co-star Joe.

Joe was in his early twenties, tall with dark wavy hair. His face was a little long and narrow, but he had good cheek bones and an arrogant, confident air. He'd just started competing at 5-star level and had a huge social media following. Bankrolled by his wealthy but unhorsey parents, he had dozens of horses to choose from, as well as numerous instructors.

'We need to have some structure,' announced a tall thin blonde woman who was coordinating the event. 'Are there specific in-jokes between eventers and show jumpers we could use to hang the script on?'

'Eventers are generally seen as posh Southerners and show jumpers as working-class Northerners,' Joe suggested. 'And generally better looking,' added his hard-faced mother.

'Although in this situation that comparison is hardly relevant,' Lottie interrupted, thinking mainly about Max's beautiful, arrogant face.

'Isn't it?' Joe's father looked sceptical.

'Most people's interpretation of a working-class Northerner is rather more Yorkshireman with whippet than Russian Mafia,' Lottie teased.

'My father isn't bloody Mafia,' Max muttered

through gritted teeth.

'I suppose he's more Rupert Murdock with a Kalashnikov.'

'Tarasov Industries is a well-respected media empire. The fact that my father just so happened to upset Putin is probably a good thing when it comes to the moral high ground,' Max added.

'Event riders are generally much more athletic and fit than showjumpers,' Lottie contributed as she slyly compared whippet like Joe to the rather more well-built Max. I gather that's why showjumpers stick to traditional saddles, rather than monoflap event ones. The showjumpers are too stiff and fat to bend over to reach the girth straps.' The grooms giggled, and even Joe failed to hide a smirk. 'So maybe we could hold a 100-metre dash,' Lottie laughed. Max glared furiously.

'Ooh, so not popular with the showjumper,' Lottie mocked. 'Maybe my last suggestion will be more acceptable. What about going down the route of show jumpers being one trick ponies, so to speak?' Lottie offered with a giggle. 'You two could you a dressage face-off.'

'That's not a bad idea,' the coordinator lady agreed. She looked at Lottie, 'See if you can get a judge for each of the venues- make it a proper competition.'

'That will be good won't it Joe,' his mother interrupted. 'Joe has weekly lessons with the Huttons', so he's bound to do well.'

'What test do you want for tomorrow?' Lottie asked.

'Surely we should be focusing on the bigger picture, and not get bogged down with incidentals,' Joe's father glared at Lottie.

She glared back. 'I need to get a judge to match the level, I'll have to order the tests and the score sheets, and the boys will need to learn it. There are also lots of levels. I assume you want to show collection and extensions, as they are good to talk about regarding elasticity training for jumping. But can either of you produce a piaffe for example?' she added with a hint of sarcasm.

Max turned to her. 'Look through the tests and choose one with simple flying changes, and as you said, collection and extension work. I'd imagine that's medium or Advanced Medium level?' Joe nodded in agreement. Leaving the meeting, Lottie went off in search of dressage judges.

As Gleneagles Equestrian Centre was part of the hotel complex, everyone involved was invited to stay for free, including Lottie and Dizzy, although they had to share a room. That evening, once the horses had been fed, everyone met up for dinner. Joe came with both his annoying parents and two grooms; the skinny female event manager joined them together with local radio presenter who was to act as compeer.

Dizzy wasn't used to fine dining and kept dropping her cutlery and moaning. Joe's grooms gave her sympathetic glances, although Lottie suspected that it should be they that deserved the sympathy. Joe's parents held court during the meal, and acting as if it were their show, whilst talking down to everyone including their own son. Joe, used to being upstaged when they were around, remained quiet. Max was determined to make the most of the hospitality and enjoyed the free food and alcohol, getting louder and more amusing the more he drank.

Having noticed Joe's parents glaring at Max whilst he entertained the diners with tales from the show jumping circuit, Lottie asked the mother, 'Are you staying for the whole tour?'

'Possibly. We do like to support Joe as much as possible, however I may need to pop back to Surrey with Joe's Daddy.'

Lottie glanced at her husband, 'Oh sorry, I assumed you were Joe's father?'

'I am,' he answered gruffly.

'My mistake. It's just that as Joe isn't three, the use of the third person would imply that his father wasn't here,' she replied bluntly.

The room instantly fell silent. Joe's mother sat mute; her lips pursed in disapproval. Finally, after what seemed like minutes, she said, 'And what gives you the right to give me English lessons young lady?'

'It wasn't so much your use of English I was highlighting, but rather the child-like way in which you address your son,' Lottie calmly replied. She quickly glanced at Joe who sat open mouthed.

'Let's not all fall out guys. We have a lot still to discuss,' the organiser added hastily.

During dessert, Max got up to use the bathroom. Whilst he was out the room Joe asked Lottie whether Max was Russian.

'Half Russian. Oligarch father who owns a media empire. Mother was English but she died. He doesn't like talking about it.'

One of Joe's grooms then piped up. 'I heard Max Tarasov had given up show jumping. We were really surprised to see him here.'

'He did have a huge bust up with his father and they went their separate ways. Because all of Max's horses were owned by his father's company they were sold. It's just meant that Max has had to start all over again. Of the four he has brought here, two are mine, one is Max's, and the black mare belongs to Melissa May.'

'Are you his girlfriend?' Joe asked.

'She's officially my business partner,' Max answered, walking back into the room at that second. 'She's also the head of marketing for Yangtze UK, and the smartest and most resourceful person I've ever met. Technically she isn't my girlfriend, but I guard her jealously.'

Joe looked offended. 'I wasn't fishing, just wondered where your feisty, opinionated friend fitted in?'

During coffee Lottie asked Joe, 'So, returning the enquiry Do you have a girlfriend? It's just good to know how everything fits in.'

'Not at present,' Joe replied stiffly.

Lottie couldn't help herself, 'Parents chase the girls away, do they?'

'Joe needs to concentrate on his career. Plenty of time for girls later. Besides, he must be careful,' Joe's father replied.

'I know how you feel.' Max squinted

drunkenly at Joe. 'Horsey female fans can be a bloody nightmare. I've had them throwing their underwear at me whilst I've been in the ring or hung on the stable doors attached to notes with phone numbers. I used to get love poems posted onto the side of my lorry. My groom Lee once entered the stable at a show and found a girl, stark naked, sat on top of my horse Lenny.'

'Just as well she didn't try the same stunt with Zhivago,' Lottie added.

'That could've been messy,' Max laughed.

The next morning was spent in a dress rehearsal, as they ran through the proposed sequence of events. Lottie and Dizzy were kept busy as each horse needed tacking up before being worked in the warm-up arena, ready for Max to jump on. Lottie rode Hope followed by Taggart whilst Dizzy took Oberon and Cruz. By the end of the morning everyone was exhausted, but the show was in place.

Over the lunch break everyone sat around eating sandwiches. Lottie quietly watched Max, as he discussed the final running order of events. He looked so happy and confident, just like his old self, when he was one of the top riders in the world. His passion and enthusiasm was contagious, with even the aloof Joe beginning to express himself.

At six thirty that evening, the local horsey population started pouring into the equestrian centre. All around could be heard the excited buzz of conversation. Max's entrance was to be on Cruz, so whilst Dizzy trotted her around the smaller indoor school to warm her up. Lottie flitted around making last minute preparations. As she came around the corner of the stable block she nearly bumped straight into Joe. He looked deathly pale.

'First night nerves?' she asked sympathetically.

Joe nodded.

'Just be yourself – that's what people have come to see. You are an amazing and talented rider, and horsey people are looking for tips and advice.'

'I'm sure most of them just want to see Max. He's far more of a showman.'

'Well, that's not true. Most of the tickets were sold before his appearance was even announced. To most of us mere mortals, 5-star event riders are like Gods. You could turn up dressed only in a loin cloth, with a rose between your teeth and people will still think you're awesome.'

'Coming from you that's praise indeed. Thank you,' Joe smiled weakly. 'I suppose I'd better find my horse. And before you ask, yes this is more terrifying than riding around Badminton.'

At 7 o clock the show started. The arena was plunged into darkness, and under a single spotlight Joe made his entrance on his top horse, cantering around to Robin Thicke's Blurred Lines, and lots of screams. As his music stopped, he paused in the corner of the school whilst Max made his entrance on the glossy black mare to

Robbie Williams' "Party Like a Russian".

Lottie, who was stood holding Taggart, giggled, and turning to the group of grooms stood next to her. 'Well, Max may have lost his wealth, but he clearly hasn't lost his sense of irony.'

The lights went up in the arena, and the two riders began their first mini lecture. Their first section was about control. As a demonstration, they had put together a game of musical chairs. Each time the music stopped both had to jump a row of chairs. As the music restarted a chair was removed. The game finished when one horse ran out.

The audience got excited, and the tension rose as the riders both got down to one chair. In the practice session both horses had swerved the final chair, not recognising it as a jump. The audience held their breath as Joe approached. This time his horse jumped the chair, much to the delight of the crowd. Cruz, also headed for the jump, but at the last second twisted her body away, jumping to the side. Joe was announced the winner.

The second section featured the dressage test. A local British Dressage judge was brought into the arena, and seated on a chair, whilst the arena party hurriedly laid down dressage markers and white boards. Meanwhile Max quickly switched onto Taggart, and the two of them started talking to the audience about the importance of teaching flexibility in striding through extension and collection work.

Joe was the first to ride the test, which on his

Badminton horse looked good. Lottie then held her breath as her beloved Taggart entered the arena. Despite the crowds, he seemed relaxed as Max popped him into collected canter. When Max had first arrived at Stapletor, Taggart had been the only horse available to him. The regular schooling that Max had given him had clearly paid off, as Taggart performed movements that he'd never have previously managed. Lottie looked on lovingly at his kind, honest face, with his ears flicking backwards and forwards as he concentrated on Max's instructions.

With the tests completed, both riders demonstrated the benefits of stride flexibility by jumping a series of fences, all with irregular distances. The dressage scores were then called out, with Max narrowly beating Joe. Lottie shrieked in excitement, thrilled with her boys' success. She could hardly believe that her beloved horse had won.

During the interval Lottie led Hope around to the side of the arena where the audience were browsing the trade stands and purchasing food and hot drinks. With his collecting bucket in his mouth, Hope walked around with Lottie. Within minutes Hope was swamped with attention. As people started stroking him and offering polo's Lottie had to grab his bucket, which was filling up fast with spare change.

'What's he like to look after? Does he appreciate being rescued?' a young girl asked.

'I hope he does, but he is very naughty. He loves jumping over his stable door and running back to the field. It was watching him clearing the big 5 bar gate back into his paddock that made us realise what an amazing jumper he is.'

Following the interval, the third section involved working with the young horses. Oberon, with his gleaming dark brown coat, glistening under the spotlights, cantered around confidently as if he'd been born to perform. Joe's four-year-old was nervy and highly strung and threw in some very challenging bucks. Joe sat quietly, and without making a fuss he reassured his young horse. Whilst Max dropped his reins, mid speech, Oberon took a step forward and poked his head over the barrier and into the crowd. He was rewarded with strokes and mints, which delighted the audience, and did wonders for his confidence.

Lottie watched from the side-lines, still holding on to Hope, who was nibbling affectionately at her hair. With fifteen minutes to go, Lottie mounted him and began his warm-up process, and trying to avoid colliding with Joe's horse, as it bucked and shied around the arena. She was relieved that Hope tended not to jump around too much. His problem was his sheer strength, but with the Pelham in his mouth, he had nothing to lean on, which helped enormously with both steering and stopping.

The final section of the evening involved both riders highlighting their skills. Some portable cross-country fences were brought into the arena for Joe, whilst a row of show jumps were arranged for Max. Within seconds of Max riding Hope into the arena, Hope's large chestnut ears locked onto the fences and he started to bounce on the spot in anticipation of jumping them. When Max blocked him, he stood sulking until he realised that he had an audience. As Max stood at the side to give Joe room, Hope distracted the front row of the audience by shoving his head over the barrier and nudging peoples' knees, hoping for attention.

Joe rode his horse around the mobile fences, whilst chatting to the audience about the unique way in which to tackle each obstacle. Once it was Max's turn, he popped Hope over the show jumps at a metre ten, before raising them up until they were Grand Prix height. Lottie looked on with huge pride as the horse she'd rescued only a few months earlier, soared over the massive fences, with a look of sheer joy on his face.

As the evening ended, the lights went down. With the spotlight on Joe, he did a final lap of the arena. He was handed a spear, and as he jumped his last fence, he raised up the spear and pierced a balloon. As it popped, it released thousands of little glitter stars that fluttered down into the arena much to the delight of the audience.

Max then cantered back into the arena on Hope, who was loving all the attention. The music switched from "Blurred Lines" back to "Party like a Russian", and as the spotlight fell on him he cantered up to a strategically placed jump. As Hope took off over the fence, Max pulled out a pistol from his pocket. As Hope landed, Max immediately pulled him up. He pointed the gun directly ahead, where a bottle of champagne had been placed on a table. Firing the weapon, he blew the cork off the top of the bottle, spraying champagne all around him, as the crowd cheered.

Having completed his lap of honour, Max left the arena at a canter, before pulling up next to Lottie, with a huge grin on his face.

'How did you learn to shoot like that?'

'My father insisted on us learning. I rather think he upset the Russian mafia at some point in his career.'

'Um.. OK... Well Hope was amazing.'

'I've been secretly training him for a couple of weeks. He was a good boy.'

'Well done. It was a great show.'

'Yes. I think it was, and thanks to you for making it all possible.' Leaning down from Hope, he grabbed her hand and gave it an affectionate squeeze.

The following day, Joe and Max began the journey south and on to the second of the ten venues. Social media was full of praise for their performance. One person had recorded large parts of the initial performance and played around with it -dubbing the voice over the top, they called it the sex on horseback show.

The Horse and Hound team visited the London leg of the tour and interviewed both riders. Lottie was delighted to find that they had printed a wonderful photo of Taggart and Hope. The article headline was 'The Russian is back.'

Chapter 28

Once Max was back home, the preparations began for London. Although Max wasn't sufficiently high up the rider rankings to enter the World Cup qualifier, he was eligible for most of the classes. Boosted by the success of the tour he entered Taggart, Cruz and Hope. A week later Max, Lottie and Pippa set off up the M5 towards the show.

Lottie found Dizzy hard work, but Pippa was easier to get on with, especially when she was on her own. During the tour, Lottie and Dizzy had sat in the cab alongside Max the driver. Dizzy had said very little, but Lottie and Max had a fantastic time in each other's company, playing silly games and singing badly.

This time it was Max who was quiet and sullen. The closer they got to London, the quieter he became. Pippa and Lottie tried to keep the mood light, but by the time they reached the A4, it was possible to cut the atmosphere in the cab with a knife.

In an attempt to be helpful, the girls took it in turns to climb through into the living area to make Max cups of coffee and treat the horses to a carrot. The horses were infinitely more appreciative than their rider. Lottie was then forced to concentrate as they navigated their way through into the Docklands. When Lottie nearly directed them the wrong way up a one-way street, Max nearly ripped her head off. Under normal conditions she would have shouted back, but the thought of driving a HGV in such trying conditions made her think some diplomacy was called for and bit her tongue.

They arrived on site at mid-afternoon, and the horses were unloaded and put into stables which would be their home for the next five days. Normally Lottie would have felt guilty about keeping Taggart in for so long, but with his friends in stables either side of him, he seemed content. A special anti-weave bar was erected on the door of Hope's stable, otherwise he would simply have jumped back out again.

Once the horses were settled, Lottie suggested to Pippa that they grab a taxi and pop up to Harrods for some Christmas window shopping. Pippa had never been so was delighted. Max refused, muttering about there being a hundred better ways to kill time.

Lottie and Pippa had a great time in Harrods. Most of it was spent admiring the beautiful decorations, but Lottie did pick up a few treats in the food hall to take home. Pippa then popped into the book section and came back a short time later with a brown paper bag, which she presented to Lottie.

'You've been so kind to me, I wanted to get you something to say thank you.'

Lottie unwrapped the present, and grinned. Inside was a copy of Jilly Cooper's *Riders*. 'I've never read this, but I have a feeling that I'm going to enjoy it. Thanks.'

'I loved reading it when I was a teenager. I wanted to marry Billy,' Pippa smiled.

Having bought a few more small treats, the girls flagged down a taxi to take them back to the lorry park. Max was nowhere to be seen, so whilst Pippa topped up the horses' hay nets, Lottie started cooking. Having no luck getting hold of Max, Lottie just prepared food for the two of them. Whilst they were eating Pippa asked if Lottie knew any of the other grooms.

'Dizzy knows loads of them. She says they have parties and stuff. I'd like to join in, but I feel a bit awkward,' Pippa confessed.

'I only know Max's ex head groom, Lee. He now works for Paul Denton. If he's here I'll introduce you.'

Once they'd finished eating they headed off to the stables. They checked up on their horses before setting out to find Lee. Lottie had no idea which block of stables housed Paul's horses, so they wandered up and down the rows until Lottie recognised the stunning black head of Zhivago looking over one of the doors. Walking up to him, she said, 'This horse used to belong to Tarasov Industries, but Max's father sold him last June.'

Pippa went to stroke him, but true to form, Zhivago flattened back his ears and went to bite.

'You're still a miserable sod I see,' Lottie said to him. 'Typical bloody stallion.'

'What the hell are you doing here? Get out before I call security.'

Lottie spun around and glaring at her, hands

on hips was Paul's head groom.

'I'm looking for Lee?' Lottie replied calmly, glancing at Pippa who looked like a rabbit caught in headlights.

'What du want wiv im? What are you up too?'

'We are not UP to anything. Pippa here has just started her first job as groom for Max Tarasov. She doesn't know anyone, and as I know Lee reasonably well, I thought he may be able to help her. I was just telling her about Zhivago when you appeared.' Lottie defiantly stood her ground.

'Well, he's not here so clear off.'

'Can you tell me where he is?' She got no response. 'So that's a no then is it? Guess I'd better text him instead.'

'I told you to clear out?'

'We are going, although we both have the appropriate passes for this area, so we actually have a right to be here.'

'You're not a groom or a rider.' The head groom challenged.

'No but I am an owner, and the head of sponsorship for Yangtze.' In front of the angry groom, Lottie then called Lee, and arranged to meet. 'Who's the short, bad-tempered guy with a red jacket?' she asked. 'Ryan you reckon. Well, he's been very rude to us. I may be having words with his boss. Anyway, see you in ten minutes.'

Putting her phone in her pocket, she beckoned Pippa, before passing scary Ryan. With a wave, she said, 'A tip for you. Don't instantly go into aggressive mode —one day you may piss off someone really important - -you know, like a major sponsor for example.'

Once they were out of earshot Pippa squealed. 'Oh my God, you were so awesome.'

'I must admit I did enjoy it.' Lottie confessed.

Max had left the complex and headed down the road to the nearest bar. Feeling sick with fear, he'd escaped in search of some Dutch courage. Now, surrounded by raucous, happy groups of workers on their Christmas party nights out, he felt very alone. In the background, he could hear Hallelujah being sung, a song he adored, but it merely added to his black mood.

He was terrified of letting Lottie down after everything she'd done for him. Melissa was flying into London to see him too, and would expect results, but he had three inexperienced horses to ride against the best competition in the world. For the first time in his riding career he felt truly scared. What made it worse was that he was no longer part of the inner circle of riders who gave each other support and encouragement. He was steadily getting drunker, but it wasn't helping. Admittedly the terror was subsiding, but the gap was filled with self-loathing and a sense of failure.

He felt his phone vibrating furiously in his jeans pocket. Having retrieved it, he squinted to focus his eyes on the screen. There were three missed calls and two text messages, all from Lottie, begging him to call her. He gave a weak smile before replacing the phone in his pocket, aware that two girls were eyeing him up. He needed consoling and they seemed willing to help.

It wasn't long after 1am when a phone call woke Lottie. Drowsily she answered it, seeing that the caller was Max. 'I'm at the gates. Can't find my pass. Buggers won't let me in,' he slurred.

'OK give me five minutes and I'll be with you.' Lottie closed the call, cursing as she frantically groped around in the dark for the light switch. 'Sorry,' she whispered to Pippa. 'Just popping out to retrieve Max.' Having shoved her feet in her boots and wrapped herself up in a thick coat and woolly hat, Lottie quickly checked to see that Max's pass wasn't still in the lorry, before grabbing her own, and a torch.

The cold night air had the effect of properly waking her up. She trudged across the lorry park and towards the gates. Ahead of her she observed two guards, dressed like Robocop, staring down at someone seemingly asleep on the ground. Once she was within close proximity, she announced her presence. 'I'm afraid I don't have his pass. It must be on him somewhere. If we really can't find it, can I vouch for him?'

The guards muttered non-committally so she knelt beside Max and said 'Your pass must be on you somewhere.'

As she reached into his pocket, he suddenly came too. 'Get your hands off me, 'he said; his unfocused eyes barely recognising her.

Lottie knelt beside him. 'Come on Max, it's me Lottie,' she whispered. Without thinking, she leant forward and gently kissed him on the lips. He opened his eyes and smiled groggily. She reached inside his jacket, to look for an internal

312

pocket. Delighted that her hunch had paid off, she retrieved the pass, and waved it triumphantly at the guards. Speaking softly, she placed her hand on Max's shoulder. 'Come on. It's too cold for you to stay down here. Let's get back to the lorry.'

Rolling onto his side, and then on to his knees, Max managed to get unsteadily to his feet. Swaying dramatically, he started walking, but it was slow and hazardous. Lottie succeeded in getting him as far as the start of the lorry park, but then he overbalanced, and fell to the floor, pulling her down with him. She landed in an undignified heap on top of him, the commotion causing curtain twitching from a nearby lorry. Lottie rolled over and rubbed her now sore left knee. Max managed to shuffle around and get himself in a seated position.

'I'm sorry. I'm so sorry,' he mumbled. Lottie moved across to sit beside him, as she felt the icy cold from the floor penetrate her layers of clothing. 'It's OK,' she said.

'But it's not OK' He gave a muffled sob. 'I'm scared. Really scared. Don't want to let you down. What if I fail?' He looked like he was about to burst into tears.

Trying to ignore her freezing rear, Lottie put her arm around his shoulders to comfort him. 'You've got two very inexperienced horses, and one speed horse. No one is expecting anything from you. If you want to just go home tomorrow, then we will. What you've achieved in such as short space of time is incredible. No one will think

313

any less of you if you want to put the brakes on.'

Max wrapped his arms around her and buried his face into her chest. In the pale light reflecting from the couple of car park lights, Lottie glimpsed his profile. Even now, with his dishevelled blonde hair, and tear-stained face, he looked beautiful. She lifted his hair from covering his eyes and kissed him on his forehead.

Once the cold had become unbearable, Lottie managed to coax Max into moving, and slowly they made their way back to the lorry. Lottie partially undressed him, before he slumped down on the bed and instantly fell asleep.

The next morning Lottie and Pippa got on with sorting out the horses. Lottie mucked out Cruz's stable, whilst Pippa lunged her, then they swapped roles, so Lottie got to lunge Taggart. Both girls then mucked out Hope, before taking him to the exercise arena, as they didn't trust him not to run off back to his friends. Once the horses were eating their lunch, Lottie and Pippa went off to the Olympia shopping village where Lottie treated Pippa and Dizzy to British Show jumping jackets for Christmas.

When they arrived back at the lorry, they found Max up and dressed, but looking very hungover.'Oh, you've finally got up then,' Lottie said, stating the obvious. 'Do you want to leave, or should we get Hope ready for the pantomime stakes?'

'Why would we leave?' His voice sounded strained.

'I thought that was what you wanted. You

314

said so last night.'

'Did I? Can't remember.' He hesitated, 'No, we've only just come. I need to face up to the others at some point.'

'At least your first class isn't a serious one. Most of the riders will be saving their top horses for the higher prize money competitions. I know Hope's way too inexperienced to get placed, but if you can just get around the course that will be wonderful,' Lottie said, conscious not to put any pressure of expectation on Max.

'What is the Pantomime stakes class?' Pippa asked.

'It's a typical matinee jumping class, designed for less experienced horses. It's a fairly bog-standard jumping class, except for the fact that the riders have to jump in a fancy-dress costume.' Lottie answered.

Max said nothing but made himself a strong black coffee. He then grabbed his riding gear and headed off towards the stables. The girls quickly ate and had a tidy up before following him. The running order for the jumping class was up on the screen. Max and Hope were halfway down the list to jump. He'd been given Prince Charming as his character.

'Poor Giles, 'Lottie sniggered. 'I see he's the Pantomime Dame. Oh, and Paul Denton is the Evil Baron. Corinna Lissok is Snow White, Ed Carter is Dick Whittington and Marcus is Buttons.'

Max looked deathly pale as he rode Hope around the warm-up arena. Despite his fears, his fellow riders seemed genuinely pleased to see him, and a few stopped to shake his hand. As the riders congregated around the entrance where the costumes were hung ready for collection, they dismounted and handed their mounts to their grooms. As Lottie stood ready to grab Hope, Paul rode up on Zhivago. The black stallion immediately lunged at poor Hope, who jumped back in horror.

Paul sneered at Max. 'So, the rumours are true. You've made your comeback.' He hesitated and laughed. 'With one horse who gets stage fright, and one picked up from a charity shop. I presume this is the charity shop horse. Apply named, as you are certainly competing more with hope than expectation.'

Max glared but remained silent. He stroked Hope's neck, feeling the cruel irony that his former horse was the one upsetting his new one.

'He looks like a cracking horse. What's his breeding?' Giles asked, giving Hope the once-over.

'Tracey only ever gets me dead men's' jeans for working in the yard from charity shops. I wish she could pick up the odd Hanoverian Sport Horse at the same time,' Marcus added.

Paul dismounted, and handing a glowering Zhivago to his head groom, went over to collect his costume. When he reached the rail, he removed his black padded jacket.

'It's a miracle, Paul's been parted from his coat without it needing to be surgically removed,' Giles called out, much to the amusement of those

316

around him.

As Paul put on the black cloak of the evil baron, Lottie said loudly. Careful of his jacket, it's probably a horcrux.' Paul turned and gave her a confused stare, clearly not familiar with Harry Potter, but there were sniggers from the competitors who had children including Marcus and the German riders.

As Max appeared dressed as Prince Charming, he received a few wolf whistles. At that moment Clara Barker arrived. 'Wow. You'll almost turn me on if you bend over in those tights,' she joked.

Even once the class started, the jovial festive mood continued. Only Max rode around the warm-up area looking haunted. As each rider entered, appropriate music played. Ed Carter was first into the arena, and in honour of Dick Whittington, he entered to 'London Calling' by The Clash.

After half an hour it was Max's turn. Initially, as he headed down the tunnel Hope panicked, spun on his haunches, and tried to run back. Max quickly stopped him, as Lottie ran up beside him for moral support. Lottie offered Hope a polo, and with the switch of focus onto his stomach, she could encourage him down the tunnel, where the music was predictably Adam and The Ants' Prince Charming.

'Good luck,' Lottie whispered to Max as they arrived at the entrance. Hope suddenly saw the audience. He'd enjoyed the attention from the crowds on the tour, so changed his mind about entering under the bright lights. He twitched his

317

ears happily as he listened to the cheers.

Max pushed him into canter and they rode around the arena waiting for the buzzer, although Hope was looking out into the audience hoping for another treat. Max's mind was in turmoil. He'd been nuts to enter such a novice horse in an international competition, and he could feel that Hope's mind wasn't really on the job. The buzzer sounded and Max turned towards the first fence, feeling sick with nerves. Suddenly Hope's concentration switched and he locked on to the fence. Max nearly cried with relief as he felt a huge surge in energy.

Seconds later Max was over the first fence and on to the second, a large oxer. Hope was now in his stride and practically towing Max into the fence. He now had to keep still and not pull. If it ended up in a battle of strength Hope would win easily. Keeping his riding soft, he managed to contain the energy and Hope soared over the big spread fence.

They cleared the third and fourth fences, and then it was onto the tricky fifth jump. This was a large upright of planks, coming off an awkward dog leg turn. Alas Hope's inexperience meant he slightly lost balance on the corner, and subsequently hit the top plank. There was a collective groan from the crowd as the plank crashed to the floor. Fortunately, the rest of the course jumped well, and Hope and Max finished on just the four faults.

The commentator said, 'An unfortunate four faults for Maxim Tarasov and Hope. Still, we are delighted to see Maxim back on the circuit. As many of you know Hope is the horse that was found abandoned outside a charity shop less than six months ago. This is his first major competition, and Maxim must be delighted with his performance.'

The crowds cheered even more, and just for a second Max broke into a smile before he headed back down the tunnel. He was immediately pounced on by Lottie and Pippa. They were laden with treats for Hope, who was delighted by all the attention. Max dismounted, and as Pippa grabbed the reins, Lottie wrapped her arms around him, kissed him on the cheek and gave him a hug. 'That was fantastic. You were both amazing'.

'We got four faults,' Max stated despondently.

'Yes, on a horse that's barely jumped in BS competitions and has gone straight in at international level.' Lottie looked at him in disbelief. 'By rights it should have been a car crash, but you are one of the best riders in the world, and Hope is just awesome.'

Max finally grinned. 'You are right as always.' He turned to Hope and patted him on the neck. 'I reckon you are going to be world class mate,' he said. Before he could escape to watch the rest of the class, Clara Barker grabbed him, and he was forced to talk on live TV about his comeback and the discovery of Hope.

Once he'd freed himself, he headed to the riders' area, keen to get a glimpse of Zhivago's round. Despite his frustration at the financial cost of having down the planks, he was delighted by

319

the response of his fellow riders to Hope's performance. One of the American riders, dressed in an elf costume asked Max to name his price, having spotted Hope's potential.

'Sorry, but he's not for sale. He belongs to my girlfriend, and she'd kill me.'

As he finished, he realised he'd made a Freudian slip. Then again it was about time he did something about Lottie before someone else got their claws into her. He just needed a bit more time to get his career back on track, and that would give him the self-confidence to make a proper move.

Paul went clear, but for Max it wasn't pleasant watching. Paul was too heavy handed, and Zhivago was swishing his tail in displeasure. For a horse of Zhivago's calibre, the course should have been easy, but it looked amateurish and lacked control or refinement. Max felt his heart ache as he watched his old friend being ridden so badly. The agony was made worse by the knowledge that it was all his fault, if only he'd been more appreciative of what his father had done for him.

Forcing himself to get a grip, Max made his way back to the stables to check on the horses. Having had a coffee and a sandwich, Max rested for an hour, it was then back to walk the course for the early evening jumping class. Taggart was fresh and put in a few bucks during the warm-up They weren't unseating, but it showed Taggart wasn't concentrating, which didn't help Max's nerves. Taggart had only just risen to the top level of show jumping grading, and certainly wasn't proficient at jumping the big, international tracks.

By the time it was Max's turn to jump, his nerves were again in tatters. Being a bigger, heavier horse, Taggart didn't have the stamina of the more thoroughbred types, and now the bucking had stopped, Max was worried that he'd tired him out. As they rode down the tunnel, he could feel Taggart tense. He gave him a reassuring pat, but it wasn't very convincing. Fortunately, as they entered the arena, Taggart relaxed slightly. The tour had been such a positive experience, Taggart had gotten to rather enjoy having an audience, rather than fearing it. Max asked him for canter, and they weaved between the fences, until the buzzer sounded. The course was trickier than the one for the earlier class, and Max hoped that Taggart had enough experience to cope. As they headed towards the first jump, Taggart's ears flicked forward, concentrating on the fence.

A minute later, the crowds clapped as Max landed clear over the last fence. There had been a couple of hairy moments where poles had rattled, but luck was on their side, and they were through to the jump off. He left the arena, and Lottie and Pippa were waiting with hugs and treats for Taggart. When Max dismounted, he hugged Lottie. 'Thank you for getting me back here,' he said, gently kissing her on her forehead.

Max hurried off to watch the rest of the first round, and to walk the jump off course, whilst Lottie and Pippa walked Taggart around, so he didn't cool off too quickly. There were twelve riders through to the jump off. Max had an early draw but for once he didn't mind. Taggart was too inexperienced to take risks with. His plan was to get a steady clear round and hope to pick up some prize money for a lower placing.

Taggart felt eager to jump again, and towed Max into the first fence. Time spent on schooling and balance meant that Max could now push him around the corner, but he still played it safe in not cutting in too tightly. Coming to the last line, they were down on the clock, but Max resisted the temptation to push on in case Taggart flattened. His approach to the first part of the combination was spot on, but Taggart over-lengthened his stride on landing, meaning he was too tight into the second part of the combination. Putting in a super-horse effort, he cleared the fence, but was too unbalanced to cleanly jump the third part, and inevitably hit it. The audience groaned in sympathy, as thousands of pounds of potential winnings evaporated.

Max couldn't be cross with Taggart. Again, it was just lack of experience which was the downfall. Max gave him a pat on his neck and leant forward to stroke the large grey ears. At the end of the tunnel he could see Lottie, who still looked delighted by the performance, despite the costly error. She ran forward and kissed Taggart on the nose. His gentle, kind face gazed back at her, as she delved into her pockets for more treats.

She glanced up at Max who looked miserable. 'Cheer up,' she said happily. 'It was such a shame

322

you had the last fence down, but you both did so well.'

'I'm cross with myself,' he said dismounting. 'It's the end of the first day, and I'll be lucky if I've won £200. That won't even cover our costs of being here.'

Lottie looked at him despairingly. 'And you need to put things into perspective. Today you've ridden two very inexperienced horses, neither of whom have ever jumped at this level before. It could have been a disaster, but it wasn't. They both jumped well, you gave them a good experience, and in the future your efforts will lead to success. So, don't you dare beat yourself up over a couple of poles.'

Max smiled. 'You can actually be quite scary, especially when you know you're right. It's just I'm so desperate to pay you back for all your kindness over the last six months.'

'You are – simply by being here and competing my horses. If it wasn't for you, Taggart would still be jumping at riding club level and Hope would be stuck in a field doing nothing. When I was younger I used to cry myself to sleep when Olympia was on TV. I so wanted to be a show jumper, but knew I didn't have the opportunity, courage, or talent to do it. The last twelve months have been the best in my life. OK so I'm not actually going over the jumps myself, but the fact that I'm here, with a purpose, and being part of it – well I'm kind of fulfilling my dreams. It's all thanks to Yangtze and to you.'

Max gave her a hug. 'Glad to be of service.' He

then hesitated as the results were given out. He'd come tenth and had just squeezed into the prize money pay out. As Max led Taggart back to the stables he bumped into Lee. Lee quietly let slip that Lady Hardcourt was dis-satisfied with Paul's lack of winnings on Zhivago and was potentially looking for a new rider.

'I know you and she never got on, but it may be worth you sucking up to her a bit. You never know.' Lee stopped mid-sentence as Paul's head groom approached.

'You ain't got time to stand around chatting.' Paul's henchman Ryan snarled. 'Especially not with 'im,' he added glaring at Max.

'I want Lee to come back and work for me... Get him away from arseholes like you. Alas his loyalties lie with my old stallion, so I'm going to have to wait.'

As Max turned to leave he added. 'I mean it Lee, any time.'

Chapter 29

That evening Pippa went off to a party with Lee and his mates, whilst Lottie and Max headed to the hospitality hall for a drinks reception for owners and competitors. As soon as they arrived, Max headed off to the bar whilst Team GB Chef de Equip, Simon Palmer accosted Lottie.

'I haven't seen you since the WEGS, how are you?' he asked.

'Pleased to be here again. Of course, this year I'm here as an owner.'

'Yes I particularly like that chestnut of yours. Do you actually own him or is he legally owned by the RSPCA?'

Lottie explained how she'd come to be the registered owner.

'I think you've got a world class horse there. I look forward to following his career. He has massive scope. Reckon once he's got a few miles under him, he'll be superb.'

Max seems to be pleased with him. The trouble is that he's still beating himself up over Zhivago. Especially given the recent poor form.'

'It's a shame Lady H won't give the ride to Max. She's desperate to have a horse in the next Olympics. Zhivago has star quality but he's quirky and very few riders can do him justice.'

'From what I understand, Max had a falling

out with her a couple of years ago. Maybe you could plant the idea in her head?' Lottie smiled sweetly.

'I'll see what I can do,' Simon answered. 'Now excuse me, but I must be seen to circulate.'

Lottie went over to join Max who was catching up on the gossip from Giles, Mary and Frederick Seipp. On seeing Lottie, he popped to the bar and got her a lime and soda water, whilst she relayed to Frederick the known history and breeding of Hope. Astounded, Frederick explained that Hope had come from one of Germany's elite performance studs, where even foals sold for serious amounts of cash.

Mary was just wondering whether Hope was related to her top stallion when everyone's attention was drawn to the arrival of Ed Carter, arm in arm with Lady Hardcourt's horse-faced daughter Olivia. 'He's only after one thing,' Mary whispered cattily.

'He was after me for a while, but when he found out that I don't have a substantial trust fund, I was dropped faster than a pair of tart's knickers,' Lottie added.

'A healthy trust fund is a strong incentive, especially in this sport where the costs are so high,' Giles mused. 'Can't blame the lad.'

'He is quite handsome,' Mary added.

'The Hardcourt gene pool is certainly in need of it.' Max chipped in. 'Lady H was trying to push Horse-Face onto me for a while, but I told her that I preferred my rides without a Roman nose.'

'No wonder she doesn't like you,' Lottie

replied.

'Look out they're coming,' Giles hissed, as Ed and Olivia wound their way around the clumps of guests towards them.

'Hi Ed. I haven't seen you for a while,' Lottie announced cheerfully.

Ed approached her and having given her a peck on the cheek said, 'Lottie, I must introduce you to Lady Olivia Hardcourt. Olivia, this is a friend of mine, Lottie Wilkins.'

'Pleased to meet you,' Lottie smiled warmly, but was met with insolent indifference. Olivia barely gave her a second glance.

'So how long have you two been together?' Lottie asked.

'We got to know each other at the World Equestrian Games,' Ed answered, confirming Lottie's suspicions as that tied in with the time when he stopped messaging her. 'Although we haven't been together very long, Olivia and I are hoping to announce our engagement soon,' he added. 'I know its quick, but sometimes you just know when things are right don't you.'

'Gosh. Congratulations,' Lottie replied.

'Thank you. I hope you aren't too disappointed,' he added, oblivious to the truth.

'No its fine. Besides, I have quite enough on my plate with Max,' Lottie smiled through gritted teeth.

'Mummy has said that she'll get Ed a horse as an engagement present,' Olivia replied, whilst slipping her arm territorially around Ed's waist.

'That's nice. Anything in particular?' Lottie

asked out of sheer nosiness.

'I may ask for Zhivago.' Ed said, raising his voice so Max could hear.

Max immediately spun around. 'Surely you're not serious,' he asked, trying to hide the contempt in his voice.

'And why not? He belongs to Mummy,' Olivia snapped, tossing her head back so her ponytail swung around like an angry horse.

'Because it would be going from the frying pan into the fire.' Max bit back.

'Thanks a lot,' Ed sounded hurt.

To avoid an argument, Lottie stepped in. 'Max isn't implying you are a bad rider or anything,' she said, slightly crossing her fingers. 'It's more that Zhivago is quirky and only likes a certain style of riding. Unfortunately for Paul, the way he rides doesn't suit Zhivago, hence why they haven't really jelled as a partnership. Because you studied under Paul and his dad, the techniques you have adopted naturally mirror that of them. So unless you learn to ride Zhivago the way he likes, you won't fare any better.'

Simon had also overheard the conversation, so decided to tackle Lady Hardcourt directly.'I know he's very talented but is it worth you holding on to such a temperamental horse?' he asked her.

'I want a horse in the next Olympics, and I reckon Zhivago is my best chance,' she answered bluntly.

'But the partnership with Paul isn't working, so if you wish to fulfil your dream, you should possibly consider offering the ride to someone else,' Simon replied. 'And to be honest, I don't think young Ed is a good alternative. They are too similar.'

'Well who do you suggest? And don't say that arrogant young dandy Maxim Tarasov.'

'To be honest with you Lady Hardcourt, out of the British riders, he'd be the only one to really do the horse justice. Since the breakup with his father, he's grown up a great deal. It hasn't been easy for the lad, but he's a better person for it.' Simon watched as Lady Hardcourt hesitated, torn between ambition and dislike.

'Other than Max, there are two or three German riders' who'd do the horse justice. If you really don't want the talent to go to Europe, I guess at a push Marcus Wallis may be a possibility?'

'I'll have a think about it. I always appreciate your advice Simon,' Lady Hardcourt acknowledged.

Having nearly lost his temper, Max headed straight back to the bar, leaving Lottie to make the peace. She wasn't particularly fussed about staying friends with Ed, but determined to play Lady Olivia at her own game, she asked, 'Ed are you going to bring Olivia down for Tom's 25th next month?'

'If I'm still invited?'

'Yes of course. Indira is presumably still Verity's best friend, and you've become a friend to our family too.'

Once again, Olivia felt obliged to interrupt.

329

'Eddy and I are very busy with our own preparations, so I doubt we'll have time to attend. Where is the party going to be held?'

'We haven't decided on which house to use, but they are both in Devon.'

'That's a long way to travel for us.' Olivia replied, effectively turning down the invitation.

Although Lottie wasn't the slightest bit concerned whether they came or not, she was determined to make a stand. Turning to Ed she said, 'It should be a good party. It's not just Tom's 25th. On his birthday he inherits the Dewerstone Estate, and becomes the Earl of Martley, so there's that to celebrate too. Anyway, if you can both make it, it will be great to see you.' With that she turned away, but not before clocking the look of surprise on Olivia's face.

Later in the evening, Lady Hardcourt once again brought up the subject of Zhivago. 'I've been thinking about what you said Simon, but a change of plan simply isn't possible. I'm going to sort out Zhivago's temperament by having him gelded.'

Max, who was in earshot, spun around. 'That's insane. Half his value is in keeping him entire, and he's far too old for his behaviour to change,' his eyes flashed with anger.

'What I do with my horses is no concern of yours,' Lady Hardcourt snapped.

'I just don't you screwing up even more one of the best horses in the world.' Max sounded close to tears.

'Max, you've said enough, now calm down,'

Simon scalded him, worried that the situation may escalate, and frustrated that unwittingly Max was blowing any chance of getting the ride.

'I just care about him so much,' Max muttered, as he headed off back to the bar to drown his sorrows.

The next morning Lottie and Pippa cleaned out the stables and worked the horses whilst Max recovered from another hangover. During the afternoon performance, he had both Hope and Taggart in the Top score competition, and both jumped well, managing to end up in 6th and 5th place respectively. This boosted Max's confidence for the evening competition – a speed class in which he'd entered Cruz. It didn't help his nerves, when he learned that Melissa was in the audience, but the black mare was on top form. She liked Max's soft riding, and jumped her heart out for him, and they finished in a very financially rewarding 2nd place.

Melissa was delighted and once he'd done his lap of honour, Max got a text summoning him back to her suite at The Royal Garden Hotel. Max was on such a high, the thought of spending a night of glorious sex with an A list celebrity was only slightly spoilt by the guilt of letting Lottie down, having promised to take her out for a celebratory meal.

Whilst Pippa went out for a drink with her newly acquired bunch of friends, Lottie defrosted a microwave meal and got on with reading her

Jilly Cooper book. She'd got to the point where the kind, sweet Billy Lloyd Foxe was marrying the awful Janie, and Lottie was so frustrated she nearly threw the book out the lorry window. Lottie was a little bit in love with the fictional hero, whilst loathing his friend, the infamous stud Rupert Campbell Black. As she sat alone, listening to chatter and laughter coming from neighbouring lorries, she thought how typical it was that when it came to his horses, Max resembled the gypsy Jake Lovell, but with humans, he was Rupert.

Whilst Lottie sat quietly reading, Max was lying naked in bed, drinking champagne, and enjoying a post coital comedown. Melissa's long tanned legs were wrapped around him, and her perfectly shaped breasts sensually brushed his bare skin. He could barely believe his luck. Having lost everything only six months earlier, he was now back in the game, and had simply swapped one of the most beautiful women in the world for another, rather younger model. It was just a shame that Melissa didn't do drugs. A line of coke would have been just the thing to help enhance the mood.

Later, as they enjoyed a meal together, Melissa talked about her current film, and said how she hoped Max would be able to find the time to visit her in LA. Max agreed. He was under no illusion that Melissa was fickle, and once she became bored of him, he may lose a good horse. He needed to keep her sweet, at least for a while.

The next day the horses had a natural break,

with the main evening class being the Puissance. Max spent the morning with Melissa, before returning to ride the horses in the afternoon. Then, leaving the horses in the care of Pippa, Lottie whisked Max away to spend the evening with her brother and step uncle. The arrangements were last minute, so neither of them had brought clothes suitable for a formal meal with the Duke of Chiswick. Luckily Max had a suit and Lottie had a dress, so they didn't feel too underdressed.

Lottie felt surprisingly nervous during dinner. She wasn't used to being served by liveried footmen, and although Crispin and Felicity were charming hosts, they intimidated Lottie. After a couple of drinks, Max started to relax. Seated next to his hosts, he started to tell them about his father's business interests. To his surprise, Crispin seemed extremely interested in Tarasov Industries.

Whilst they were sat having after dinner drinks, Crispin explained his motivation. 'The BBC are currently expanding the world service. The idea is to broadcast in other languages and provide essential unbiased news and transmitting in countries where there isn't necessarily a good national service at present.' He took a sip of his drink, carefully considering his next move. 'As you are aware, the West isn't comfortable with Putin, and we certainly don't want another Ukraine type Russian intervention. The plan is to extend our broadcasting deep into the former Eastern bloc countries, but we need someone who has media influence and understands our target areas.'

'Speak to my father,' Max advised. He's no fan of Putin and has lots of contacts. It would also be a way for him to get involved with the Conservative government.'

'Oh yes. I'd forgotten that he put himself forward as a prospective MP. What happened?'

Max grinned sheepishly. 'My father told me to be nice to the constituency chairman and his wife at a party in NEC Hilton. So, when I went back to my hotel room and the chairman's wife followed me, I did the honourable thing and gave her a good time. It would appear however that I gave her to much of a good time, and when her husband found out, my father was dropped as the nominated candidate.'

The last afternoon of the show was a World Cup Qualifier, for which Max wasn't eligible, so he had to wait for the final class of the day. Once the world cup class was over, won by Frederick Seipp, the overseas riders headed off home, leaving just the UK and a handful of Irish riders to jump in the evening performance. As an incentive to encourage top riders to stay, the prize money was good, and the odds were fair, so Max had entered all three horses.

The course was rather big and challenging, and Cruz brought down the back rail on one of the wide oxer fences, however he managed two slow clears on the others. In the jump off Marcus set a fast time on Max's old horse Harvey. With neither of his horses having much experience, Max couldn't afford to push either of his remaining rides, and instead, opted for slow and hopefully clear.

He took Taggart in first, and everything went to plan, and they were rewarded with a clear round, and lots of praise from the commentator about his riding. He barely had time to feed Taggart his reward apple before it was time to jump on Hope and whisk him over a few warm up fences. He then had to dash back into the arena for the final round. Hope was starting to know the routine, and gave an excited fly buck, in anticipation of jumping again.

Max was desperate to really push on and really see what Hope was capable of, but the last thing he wanted was to over face the horse and destroy his enthusiasm, so again, he rode a slow, precise round, which wouldn't win any accolades, but it would be a solid foundation for the future. The crowds loved Hope, whose sorry tale had made him into an equine celebrity. His big chestnut ears were always pricked forward and his eyes sparkled with joy at being the centre of attention.

Having jumped two clear but slow rounds, Max achieved 5th and 6th place, and some decent prize money. Having ridden Hope and led Taggart into the prize giving ceremony, Max rode back out quietly whilst the four top riders did a lap of honour. As he came back to a halt in the collecting ring, one of the Irish riders, Kieran O Lacey approached him, asking about Hope. 'Two years ago, I sold a horse the spitting image of yours to a show jumping family in Wales. He was a strong, wilful bugger, but one of the most talented jumpers I'd ever ridden.'

Max told Kieran the little he knew, whilst the Irishman examined Hope. The horse I sold was called Jazz Time, but this could be the same horse. The age is right, but I don't understand why the microchip hasn't picked up more history.

Lottie had appeared, ready to grab Taggart. 'Do you reckon it's possible that he has two microchips? The one we found must be the original, which we traced back to the stud in Germany, but there is nothing past the age of two when he was sold to the UK.'

'I guess if they were on different sides of the neck, a scanner would only find one at a time so it's possible,' Kieran agreed. 'Well if it is the same horse, I got him jumping up to 1 metre 40 courses and got placed at Dublin International Horse Show. I would have kept him but money was tight, and I was made a very good offer from a family whose son was just moving up to seniors. I guess the horse was too much for the kid, and they just moved him on.' Kieran gave Hope a pat, 'Well I'm glad he has a decent home now.'

'I'll get our vet to check him when we get back,' Max answered. 'It would make sense that Hope had been jumped professionally before. He's simply too good at the job.'

Half an hour later, whilst the horses were being loaded in the lorry, ready for the journey back to Devon, Ivan Tarasov slipped away from the closing ceremony in preparation for a meeting with Simon Palmer. Impressed by what his son had achieved, and having spent a very fruitful day with The Duke of Chiswick, Ivan wanted to do something to help Max, but he wanted the assistance to be a secret, which was why he needed help from the team Chef de Equip.

As the two men formed a plan over a bottle of Chateau Margaux Balthazar, Cindy happened to be dining at a nearby table. As she tuned into their conversation, she started to form a plan which would guarantee to bring Max back to her.

Chapter 30

Whilst the horses enjoyed a post-show rest, Lottie rushed into Plymouth to do some last-minute Christmas shopping. Max waited around for the vet, who eventually located the second microchip, but found it to be faulty, so couldn't get a reading.

Later that afternoon Max drove into Lydstock to buy a few more presents. He'd never really spent Christmas with a large family and didn't know what to expect. Determined not to be caught out, he made sure he had a small gift for each of the Marchbanks, Dizzy and Pippa. He got back just as it was time to bring the horses in for the night. Lottie had been back for a while and had already headed out with Shadow to the furthest field to fetch Tilly and her companion.

Once the chores were finished, it was necessary to shower and tidy up, as they'd both been invited to the first family meal of the Christmas get together, both Tom and Ben having arrived earlier that afternoon.

The next morning was Christmas Eve, and the Marchbanks were hosting the local hunt meet. Nick no longer hunted, and as Ben was using his mother's horse, Beth and her husband rushed around with trays full of hot punch, mince pies and canapés. Lottie had Taggart, and Max rode

Hope. Tom borrowed one of the livery horses, whose owner spent most of their time in London. Meanwhile having helped with the food, Dizzy and Pippa were heading off to their respective homes for a holiday.

Max had never been hunting, and found he rather enjoyed the social side. The hunt wasn't the fastest, but it was good to ride on the moors, discovering places he'd never seen before. Hope got very excited and kept bucking, and squealing, much to the amusement of nearby followers. Taggart didn't hunt regularly, but had been out enough to know the score, and behaved beautifully.

Although the hardened hunters were happy to stay out most of the day, Max and Lottie decided that a couple of hours was quite long enough, especially as it had started to rain. Shortly after one o clock, they headed home, dropping down into the valley where it was more sheltered, as they made their way back through the lanes. Apart from the occasional cry from a pheasant, and the steady beat of the horses' hooves, the countryside seemed silent. There was a damp, earthly smell of rotting leaves, mixed with wood smoke from cottage chimneys.

When they arrived back in the stable yard, the horses were turned out into the field to roll, whilst Max and Lottie popped into the house to grab a sandwich. Beth was in the kitchen preparing that evening's dinner. She loved being able to fuss over her family, and the warm kitchen was full of the smell of spices, and meats. Beth handed them some mulled wine to drink, left over from the morning's meet. It was sweet and warming, and about the only alcohol Lottie, Tom and their mother would drink. Due to its lack of intoxication, Beth had heated up some brandy and mixed in with the glass she offered to Max.

Max and Lottie had just started to bring the livery horses in from the field when Tom and Ben arrived back. Both were splattered with mud, and their horses looked tired. Whilst the boys hosed down their horses' legs and checked for cuts, Lottie hurriedly forked down the bedding in their stables, before making up warm mash feeds, laced with molasses and carrots.

Once the horses were all bedded down for the night, and Shadow walked and fed, everyone got changed for dinner. It was the Marchbank family tradition to have a formal dinner, followed by a few party games, before heading to Lydstock for the Midnight Mass service. Ben's girlfriend Sophie had gone home to her parents, but instead had brought home his actor colleague, the screamingly camp Julian.

During dinner, Julian repaid the hospitality with bitchily, hilarious tales. Being an actor made him a natural orator, and he held the attention of everyone in the room.

'You are very amusing, you must come again,' Nick offered.

Julian gave a small bow in acknowledgement. 'Thank you, it's wonderful being in the company of such beautiful people.' He turned his head and gave Max a cheeky wink. Mellow with good wine, and in an exceptionally good mood, Max just grinned.

Beth turned to Max, 'I do hope you aren't missing your family too much. You are so much part of our lives now; I forget that you'd probably rather be somewhere else.'

'Believe me, at the moment there is nowhere I'd rather be.'

'That's very sweet, but you must miss Christmas at home?'

Max hesitated. He didn't want to overshare, but neither did he want them fretting unnecessarily. 'My father doesn't really do Christmas. He normally uses the break to head off to the sun for a fortnight, with the latest wife and my brother stays with his mates in town. For years now I've had my horses to look after. It's meant doing all the chores Christmas morning, and then heading off to my girlfriend's for a late lunch. One of my grooms used to live locally, so she'd bring the horses in, so I didn't have to rush back. My girlfriend wasn't exactly domesticated, so what we ate was generally out of a microwave.'

'I take it you two have split up,' Julian enquired.

'She kicked me out when I lost my inheritance.'

'Oh, how harsh, you poor boy,' Julian exclaimed dramatically.

Max laughed. 'She did me a favour. Now I'm having my first proper Christmas in eighteen years.'

Three hours later, after showing everyone

341

how terrible he was at charades, Max climbed into the passenger seat of Lottie's car, before the convoy set off to Lydstock for Midnight Mass. His hands and feet felt numb, but from the effects of the deadly Dewerstone gin, rather than the cold. Lottie put on Christmas CD, and together with Tom, sat in the back, they sang rather badly all the way to the church.

Max had been expecting a small village chapel, so was surprised when they entered the church, and it was the size of a small cathedral. The church was over a thousand years old, and lit by hundreds of candles, it seemed to capture centuries of spiritualisation. The organ music was beautiful, and when the choir sung, the sound soared majestically through the building. Max felt quite emotional. He finally felt the experience of a proper Christmas.

Lottie and Max got down to the yard the next morning, and hurriedly got on with the morning stable duties. They were soon joined by Tom and Ben, who helped change rugs, whilst Lottie chopped up apples and carrots to put in the horses Christmas morning breakfasts. Once the horses were all outside, Ben and Tom mucked out the stables, whilst Lottie filled the haynets and Max topped up the water buckets.

By ten o clock the chores were done, so everyone headed back to the house for freshly brewed coffee and a cooked breakfast. It was then time to hand out presents. Lottie was pleased at Max's delight when he discovered his new riding jacket, and high-tech stirrups. From her brothers' she received a voucher for a set of lorry driving lessons. She noted that her parents had been rather generous with their presents to her brothers, as both received Rolex watches, whilst she was given a pair of jodhpurs. They were very nice, but she had to hide her slight disappointment as she'd always wanted a posh watch.

As the family started to clear away the discarded wrapping paper, Beth suddenly stopped, a look of horror on her face. 'We've forgotten Lottie's present.'

'We need to go outside,' Nick announced. 'Your main present is outside. It's a collaboration and an equal share each from your mum, me, Peter and Max.'

There was a mad scramble for shoes and coats before everyone trooped outside. Nick, Beth and Max headed off towards the back of the garages and everyone else followed.

As Lottie turned the corner, she gave a squeal of surprised delight. Parked in the yard, decorated with a large bow, was a small shiny horse lorry. 'Oh my God, it's amazing!' she exclaimed.

'I could hardly have you driving around in a 25year old bone shaker, whilst I have my luxury HGV,' Max grinned. 'So when I sold my lorry, the dealer did a px on this new conversion. It's a 4.5 tonne, so still easy to drive, but it means you can carry two horses.'

Lottie couldn't stop beaming. 'You've all been so kind and generous. I can see now why I need to pass my lorry test. And there was me thinking it was just because you needed a co-pilot. Thank you.' She went around hugging everyone. As she got to Max, she hesitated, subconsciously making sure that he wasn't going to object. Max grabbed her and gave her a bear hug. 'I hope you didn't sink all your money into this. You need to buy more horses.'

'Don't worry, I didn't. That's why your family stepped in to help.'

Max was surprised by how good he felt inside. He'd given plenty of presents before, mainly to Cindy, but these were received with no great excitement, whatever their cost. This was the first gift he'd give, where he'd really put thought into it first, and where the reaction was such heartfelt delight.

The next day, whilst the boys went hunting, Lottie went off to see her biological father Peter. Normally she went begrudgingly, out of a sense of duty, but as he'd finally opened his wallet and helped pay for the horse lorry, she was pleased to have the opportunity to thank him.

Chapter 31

After a few days of taking it easy, Max, Dizzy and Lottie set off for the Liverpool International Show. This was the North of England's alternative to London and had a post-Christmas pantomime atmosphere. On New Year's Eve. Max jumped Taggart in the morning class and managed to get placed following a cautious double clear. Later in the afternoon he achieved a good result with Cruz, before trying out Hope in the Grand Prix class. Now he knew Hope had show jumped before, he was a little less reluctant to push him. Also, his winnings at London had nudged him up the rankings just enough for him to be eligible to compete in the more senior classes.

Hope's lack of experience meant that they clocked up a slow clear in the first round, just managing to finish within the allotted time. When it came to the jump off, Max again played it safe, but was delighted by Hope's determination to tackle the huge fences. Their lack of speed meant they only managed 8th place, but as the class included several world class horses, Max had shown that he was back as a serious contender.

Having settled the horses back in their stables, they were about to head off to get changed for the evening's activities when Dizzy asked about Zhivago.

'Shall we have a sneaky look at Paul's stables and see if we can spot him?' Lottie suggested.

'It would be good to see the old boy?' Max agreed.

It didn't take them long to find Paul's row of horses, and the end box contained the familiar black head of Max's beloved stallion. As Zhivago saw people approach he pricked his ears in curiosity. Once they got close, he flattened his ears, ready to bite, but stopped as he recognised his former master's voice. Instead, he nickered gently, pleased to see Max.

'Oh, my darling chap, how are you?' Max lifted his hand and affectionately rubbed the solid black neck. Then fumbling around in his pocket, he handed Zhivago a treat.

'I'm so sorry boy. Please don't give up on me. Somehow I'm going to get you back.'

'Oi what are you doin'? Get out of here before I call security.' All three of them physically jumped as Paul's head groom Ryan came storming towards them.

'I was just saying hello to my old horse,' Max replied calmly.

'Well he's not yours now so sod off.'

Ryan placed himself in front of Zhivago, legs astride, whilst slapping a leather whip against the side of his boot, so it made a cracking noise. Zhivago hated him, and flattening his ears back, he leant forward, and bit Ryan on his back.

Roaring with anger he spun around and lashed out at Zhivago's head with the whip. The stallion shot backwards, retreating to the back of his box, whilst Ryan screamed at him.

Aware that he still had an audience, he turned again, ready to chase them away, and use his whip if necessary. Suddenly Ryan felt a searing pain in his right jaw, and he fell backwards, as Max's right fist contacted it.

'Next time you hit a horse like that I'm gonna make sure you never work in the industry again.' Max yelled, shaking with anger. Turning to Lottie he added, 'Let's leave before I end up killing the bastard.'

Once they were out of earshot, Lottie said. 'Wow how did you learn to fight like that?'

'My father has always been worried about KGB agent attacks, so insisted that his children learnt how to protect themselves. That's how I'm able to handle a gun, as well as unarmed combat of course.'

'I can't see your brother Peter as a trained killer?' Lottie grinned.

'Well maybe him not so much,' he replied with a wry smile.

Alas, seeing his beloved horse again made Max feel wretched. Those not involved with the late evening puissance had all been invited to a party hosted by the event organisers. Paul was competing, but Marcus, Ed, Giles and Mary were in the mood to party, along with the German, Dutch and French contingents. Lottie had been invited in her capacity as an owner, but Dizzy had headed off to join her groom friends for a night out on the town.

Max sat morosely nursing a large vodka,

347

whilst Lottie did her best to be cheerful. She considered the oddity of starting the year with one international showjumper and ending it with another. Of course, twelve months ago, it had been Verity's birthday party, and she'd ended up seeing the New Year in whilst waiting in casualty with Ed. At that time, she loathed Max. Now they were inextricably linked in his career rebuild, and she loved him. She just hoped that he felt the same way.

'Cheer up Max,' she smiled. 'With Zhivago's recent poor form, at least his value is dropping. You just need to win a couple of rounds of the Longines World Series, and you'll probably have enough money to buy him.'

'Yes, but I need Zhivago in order to win that level of competition, so it's rather a Catch 22 position,' Max replied miserably.

'Not necessarily. I've had a word with Hope, and he reckons that with a bit more practice he'll be up for the challenge. Hope also promises that his owner won't ask for a share of the prize money.'

Max forced a weak smile. 'You're as mad as a box of frogs, Miss Wilkins, but I do love you for it.'

'Do you?' Lottie sounded surprised.

'Of course I do. Now come here. I need a hug,' he ordered.

Lottie didn't need asking a second time. Wrapping her arms around him, she breathed in his wonderful scent, as his muscular fit body enveloped her. Looking up at his face, she went to kiss him on his cheek, but he turned his head so their lips connected. Seconds later his tongue began to explore her mouth, and she felt a bolt of sexual energy rush through her body.

Just as she was getting to the point where she wondered how she was going to contain herself, Max abruptly stopped. Behind her, Lottie heard the voice of Simon Palmer. She turned, bright red, as Simon apologised for the interruption.

'I'm off shortly, but I wanted to congratulate Max on his performance.' Lottie looked blankly at him, wondering if he was surreptitiously judging kissing techniques. It took her a minute to realise he was referring to show jumping.

'That young chestnut horse of yours has got world class potential. Give him a few months' experience on a few of the bigger circuits, because in June I want you both available for the Nations Cup Team event in Aachen.'

'What really? Do you reckon we're good enough?' Max sounded delighted.

'Your horse just needs to clock up a few more miles and learn to cope with the trickier circuits, and yes, you will both be an asset to the team.'

'Thank you.' Max beamed with delight.

'Anyway, I shan't keep you two further. Best wishes for the New Year, and I'll catch up with you soon.' Simon turned on his heels and left.

'So you see – there is a chance you can win your horse back.' Lottie said.

At midnight they kissed again. A long, slow, passionate kiss that alas was interrupted when Giles grabbed Lottie from behind and insisted that Max share the Yangtze lady. By the time she'd extricated herself, Max had been grabbed by one of the German female riders, so she slipped off to ring home. Having wished her Mum and Nick a happy new year, she tried calling Tom. He'd taken Verity to London to see the fireworks and his phone wasn't connecting. She gave up and moved on to calling Ben. He was spending the New Year with Sophie and her family and sounded pleased to hear from her.

It took ages for Max to free himself from the clutches of numerous women. He arrived back some time later looking very dishevelled and seemingly far more drunk than Lottie had realised. Before long the party broke up, and they made their way back to the lorry. Dizzy was still out, and Lottie was just wondering whether this was the time that their relationship was going to move forward, when she realised that Max had fallen face down on his bed and was sound asleep.

Luckily it was a late start the following morning. Dizzy still hadn't returned, so Lottie dragged herself out of bed and went out to feed and muck out the horses. Her mind was still full of the night before and what nearly happened. A year before, and she would have run a mile from Max's advances but now she felt so differently towards him, her body ached for more.

The early afternoon session featured a light-hearted competition, in which the Puissance wall was used in a shrinking game. After each round it was made narrower, until it was simply a single column of bricks. As it was essentially a version of the musical chairs game Max had played with Cruz, it made sense to enter her. As the game was fresh in her memory, she realised what had to be done, and obediently jumped cleanly in every round, eventually winning the class.

Later Taggart jumped in the top score knock out and managed to win £2000. Finally Hope jumped two great rounds in the Grand Prix class and earned Max a further £5000 for coming 4th.

Having watched the class, Lottie started to make her way back to the stables but decided to take a detour past the trade stands. As she made her way through the crowds, a smartly dressed lady holding out a tray filled with glasses of champagne accosted her. 'Would you be interested in joining our owners syndicate?' she asked hopefully.

'No thanks. I already have two horses competing here,' Lottie replied, and went to make her way past, but then a thought struck her. Turning to the lady she said. 'Actually, I may be interested in hearing more about it.'

Having been seated on a comfortable sofa and had a glass of bubbly and some nibbles thrust upon her, the lady, who introduced herself as Caroline started her sales pitch. 'It's a bit like a unit trust fund which buys sports horses then,' Lottie summed up the explanation. 'Each owner has a very small share, which spreads their risk, gives them an interest to follow, and provides good horses for up-and-coming riders who otherwise can't afford them.'

351

'Yes, that's pretty much it,' Caroline agreed.

'So how many riders do you have?' Lottie asked, her mind working overtime.

'We are currently supporting one event rider, two dressage riders and one show jumper?'

'Who's your show jumper?'

Caroline mentioned a name Lottie hadn't heard of. 'Would you consider a second rider? I have someone in mind who may be of great interest.'

Caroline hesitated. 'We have offers all the time from riders. We haven't been established long enough to have sufficient horses for too many jockeys I'm afraid, so generally no.'

Undefeated Lottie continued. 'I think you may be interested in this rider. He's just come 4th in the Grand Prix on one of my horses. Due to unforeseen circumstances, he now only has three grade A horses and a youngster to compete, so would readily take on a horse or two for your owners.'

Caroline started to look more interested. 'Is this rider anyone I would have heard of? We only support British riders at present.'

Lottie grinned. 'Oh, I can guarantee you've heard of him. Shall I bring him over to your stand, say in twenty minutes?'

Caroline reluctantly agreed, so Lottie rushed off to find Max.

Max looked cynical, but reluctantly agreed to follow Lottie to the stand. It took them a while to reach their appointment due to constant interruptions from fans wanting autographs and selfies. When Caroline finally spotted them, she gave a little shriek, before ushering Max into a quieter area away from onlookers.

Once she'd regained her composure she said, 'Normally we put prospective riders through a thorough vetting process to evaluate their ability and potential, but in your case your record speaks for itself.'

She hadn't remembered the publicity over Max's fall out with his father, so he was required to explain how as a professional rider, he had so few horses.

Lottie then mentioned the gossip about Zhivago potentially going on the market. Caroline explained that their purchasing budget for any one horse wasn't huge, but the meeting finished with her promising to think seriously about putting in an offer.

Chapter 32

The next two weeks were quieter for Max. Almost all the professional riders had headed off to Dubai. Max had never been keen on flying his horses halfway across the world, forcing them to adjust to the hot climate even when money hadn't been a consideration. As Max had never had a massive string of horses, he'd always taken the opportunity to give them a break.

Whilst the three grade A horses had some down time, Max concentrated on competing Oberon who'd done very little since the tour. He also had plans to buy a couple of ex racehorses, with the idea of turning them into competition horses to sell on as a side-line. He also found time to catch up with some coaching, which was easy and financially lucrative.

He barely saw Lottie for the first week. Her employers had asked her to work on a campaign for their small hatchback, and this required her spending time in their London office. Even when she was at home, Tom's upcoming party was her focus. Max was surprised at how acutely he missed her being around him. It wasn't just that she was clever and beautiful and made him laugh. He had also taken for granted her boundless energy and resourcefulness, especially in her attempts to rescue his career.

Making rather a belated new year's resolution Max vowed to make sure that he secured Lottie for ever. She was far too important to him to let her slip away. What was needed was a big show of commitment on his part – he'd ask her to marry him. At least now he was winning, and more financially self-sufficient, he felt worthier of her love. The first hurdle to get over was her fear of physical intimacy. Maybe Tom's birthday party would be the time to try. It would mean giving up bedding Dizzy. Lottie wasn't the sort to put up with the loose, open relationship he'd had with Cindy, but the sacrifice would be worth it.

A week before Tom's birthday, Lottie received a distressed phone call from Verity. Finding it hard to understand what Verity was trying to say between sobs, Lottie invited her over for the evening.

Less than an hour later, puffy eyed and sniffing, Verity was seated on Lottie's sofa, whilst Shadow cuddled up to her. With Tom still up in London, Verity apologised for being such a nuisance, but she didn't know who else to talk too.

'I told my parents that Tom and I were planning to get engaged on his birthday,' she paused and gave a loud sniff. 'Dad went nuts and said if I married a Marchbank he would disown me and throw me out.' She stopped and burst into tears.

Lottie leant across and handed her a box of tissues. 'But that's ridiculous. He clearly hasn't thought that threat through.'

'What du mean?' Verity sobbed.

'Just think about it,' Lottie sounded clinical and rational. 'Tom inherits Dewerstone next week – your home, and Rupert's home. Even if your father were to disinherit you, he can't throw you out the house. As Tom's fiancé, you'll have more right to remain than he will.'

'I guess so.' Verity sounded a little happier.

'My little brother needs to grow some balls and go over and spell a few things out to your parents. He's back on Friday, and if it helps, I'll come over too.'

'Oh, will you?' Verity sounded pitifully grateful.

'Of course, your father isn't in a position to make such high-handed threats. It's just I think he needs a bit of a reminder.'

Lottie phoned Tom, and he promised to get down to Devon as early as possible and agreed to go and tackle his future in-laws.

Early on the Friday evening Tom and Lottie set off for Dewerstone. When they arrived, Verity was already waiting for them on the doorstep, before ushering them into the house. As they followed Verity down the corridor, Lottie glanced at her brother, and noticed how scared he looked. 'You need to man up,' she hissed disparagingly.

Verity led them through to the drawing room, where her parents were sat watching television. From the surprised look on their faces, it was evident that they hadn't been expecting the visit.

'Excuse me for interrupting your evening, but it's vital that we discuss my forthcoming engagement to your daughter.' Tom sounded calm and self-assured, although inside he felt sheer terror.

Rupert jumped to his feet, looking red and flustered. In his early sixties, he'd lost his floppy blonde hair, and now had a passing resemblance to Toad of Toad Hall. Meanwhile Marina rose from her chair and muttered that it was good to see them, before disappearing off to the kitchen to arrange for some refreshments.

'You'd better sit down,' Rupert spoke gruffly. He waved his hand in the general direction of a dark brown leather sofa.

Tom hesitated, so Lottie poked him sharply in his back with her car keys, which had the desired effect and he hurried over to the seat and sat down. Lottie followed and sat beside him.

Rupert moved his chair so that he was looking directly at Tom. 'I assume you've come to ask for my daughter's hand in marriage. It's out of the question. I've made my feelings perfectly clear. I will not permit any daughter of mine to marry the son of Nicholas Marchbank.'

Tom didn't immediately respond but Lottie couldn't help herself. 'Well, no one could accuse you of beating around the bush. You certainly get straight to the point.'

'I don't believe in wasting time. I'm a busy man.'

Lottie eyed him sceptically.

Tom cleared his throat, then rose to his feet. 'You do realise that I don't need your permission to marry your daughter. I merely

357

wanted to show some respect; however, your blind prejudice clearly makes civility impossible.'

Marina came back into the room but remained standing awkwardly in the entrance. Lottie glanced up and observed how nervous and worried Marina looked. She immediately felt pity for Verity's mother, who clearly hated the whole conflict thing, but loyally stood behind her husband's decision. For once Marina wasn't the elephant in the room. Instead, the elephant was out there in the middle of the room, cavorting around in a most unsubtle manner.

Lottie was impressed by her brother. Although in most ways he took after their mother, he had inherited his father's dislike of confrontation. Nick needed a litre of Glenfiddich before he'd say what he thought. As a non-drinker, Tom usually just kept his head down.

Lottie decided to add her point. Jumping into the conversation before Rupert could respond she said. 'We all know the history between you and Nick, and it's perfectly reasonable that you don't want anything to do with him, but my brother is a person in his own right and deserves to be treated as such.'

Rupert was going redder by the minute. Matching Tom, he also got to his feet before replying. 'Bad blood will out,' he snapped.

'But that's ridiculous,' Lottie retorted. 'Nick's the only family member with addiction issues. You couldn't ask for anyone more clean living than Tom.'

'If I may speak,' Tom turned and gave his

half-sister a stern look. He then looked Rupert straight in the face and said, 'I have never had the slightest urge to drink or dabble in drugs. I abhor gambling and my only passion is literature. Why can't you accept that, instead of assuming I am the reincarnation of my father?'

'Well,' spluttered Rupert. 'It's a case of lack of temptation. If you suddenly find yourself under pressure running the estate – there's a damned distillery in the cellar. That's when your true self will come out and God help my daughter then.'

'No Rupert, I'm sorry but you're wrong.' Lottie stood there defiantly, hands on her hips. 'When Tom and I say, we don't drink, we really DO NOT drink. It's not a case of temptation. What we experienced as young children has clearly had a long-term effect on us. Neither of us can even bare the taste of alcohol. We don't know what it feels like after a hard day to be thinking, oh I need a drink. It simply isn't part of us. So, Tom isn't suddenly going to become a dipsomaniac the day he marries Verity.'

Tom interjected, keen to push the point. 'What my sister says is true. There is no chance of us following our father down the slippery slope to self-destruction. I love Verity. We share the same ideas and values. We both see beauty in literature, and we both care about Dewerstone. Why can't you see that we are well matched?'

Marina came across the room and in a meek voice said, 'I know Verity adores you Tom.' Rupert glared at his wife, but he was running out of arguments. 'I think it would be best if we all calmed down. Marina, will you get someone to fetch us some refreshments.'

Once he was seated, Tom started again. 'Thank you. I know if we can discuss these issues in a civilised fashion, it will be easier.' He glanced at Rupert, who looked stony faced, before continuing. 'As everyone here is aware, next week I inherit the Dewerstone estate.' Again, this was met with silence from Rupert. 'Now I am not about to sweep in here and turn everything upside down. I want to start taking my responsibilities seriously, but I'm not ready to give up my life in London entirely.'

He stopped talking as a tray with tea and cakes was wheeled into the room. Marina busied herself with serving, so Tom continued. 'I suggest that for the first year, I carry on with my London work for three or four days each week and spend the rest of the week here learning the ropes. Rupert, I am well aware that you have been doing an excellent job here, and I have got an awful lot to learn. It's going to be far easier if we can all get on and work together.'

Rupert muttered a begrudging acceptance of what Tom was saying, then Marina asked?

'What is going to happen about the living arrangements?'

'As I only intend being here part time, I suggest that I take a few rooms in the West wing of the house. Once Verity and I are married, and I'm down here full time, then we will take over the main house. In the meantime, if you have plenty of time to decide what you want from me in

360

regard to your living accommodation. The most obvious options are either a wing of this house or choose another property on the estate.'

Tom's confidence was growing. Having finished speaking he sat down and took a sip of tea. Initially he'd felt rather intimidated by Rupert, but the more he took control of the situation, the more compliant Rupert appeared to be.

Sitting opposite him, Rupert remained silent, although his mind was racing. He felt defeated. As the reality of the situation dawned on him, the desire to fight his corner dissipated. It was evident that the young man wishing to marry his daughter bore very little resemblance to his playboy father. The provisions made in the previous Earl's will also meant that he, Rupert, was not in a position of strength when it came to bargaining powers.

Swallowing his pride, and in an attempt to retain some dignity, Rupert rose to his feet and acknowledged Tom. 'I was wrong to assume you were just like your father. Clearly you have your mother's sense and wisdom. I think I speak for Marina as well, when I say that it is a huge relief to us. It does make sense for us to work together for the good of the estate, and if you can make my daughter happy, then who am I to prevent the match.'

'Thank you,' Tom smiled, as a look of relief swept across his face.

'She is the most precious thing in the world to us, so please love her as much as we do,' Marina said, as she dabbed her eyes with a tissue.

'So, are you happy for Tom's 25th to also be an engagement party?' Lottie checked.

Rupert nodded. 'But we would ask if there could be a separate celebration here at Dewerstone for us and our friends and family to join in.'

Chapter 33

Lottie was away working in London all week, preparing for a media campaign, and arrived back in Plymouth train station on Friday evening where Max was there to meet her. As he jumped out of the car to open the boot she saw that he was dressed in black tie and looking wonderfully handsome.

'Hello you.' He smiled, before grabbing her bags. Having hurriedly dumped her case, he turned and gave her a hug. Dressed lightly, Lottie had started to shiver with cold. The warmth of his body was so comforting, and then he kissed her on the lips, and she shuddered involuntarily, as her body started to tingle with delight.

'You're cold,' he said, ushering her into the warm car.

'How are things at home?' she asked as she climbed into his passenger seat.

'I've done my best to avoid it all, but from what I gather, the guest list keeps growing. Some people are now being put up at Dewerstone, and your mum has had to get a marquee added to the side of the ballroom to accommodate everyone.'

'How are the animals?

'All four-legged creatures accounted for. I took Oberon to a BS event yesterday and he got a double clear in the foxhunter class. Other than that, the girls and I have just kept the others ticking over.'

'That's good,' Lottie snuggled down into the seat, enjoying the feeling of warm air as it blew over her cold face.

When they got home, Max dropped her at the lodge so she could get cleaned up and changed, as she was expected to join the family for a dinner party. Twenty minutes later she arrived at the dining room, and was immediately jumped on by an ecstatic Shadow, who'd been staying in the main house all week. Having been nearly flattened by 45kg of dog, she made her way over to the only empty seat, which was between Max and Ben's girlfriend Sophie.

The whole Marchbank family were in attendance, including Crispin and Felicity, their two sons, Rufus and Will, plus respective wives, and children. Tom was sat with Verity, and Rupert and Marina were also there. Ben had just brought Sophie, although Sophie said that many of the main cast and crew were due down the following morning.

Sophie leant across to Max and said, 'This is the first time we've met when you've actually been sober.'

'Really.' Max sounded surprised. 'That's not good. It will have given you a very false impression of me because I'm actually a responsible, clean-living kind of guy.'

Lottie raised her eyebrows in disbelief.

Max was soon being quizzed by the women on his right, whom Lottie guessed was one of

Crispin's daughters in law. She was an attractive blonde lady in her mid-thirties, however she had a dour look about her, as if difficult to please. She did however seem interested in Max's career, and next to her sat her pony mad nine-year-old daughter Emily so he found himself with a captive audience.

As Sophie was talking to Ben, this left Lottie with no choice but to people watch. She was particularly interested in Crispin's sons, as she saw them so rarely. Rufus was the older of the two brothers. Now in his late thirties, he worked as a diplomat, and had spent many years working abroad. He was charming and courteous. He had the Marchbank's good looks, but unlike his slightly eccentric, shabby cousins, Rufus wore beautifully bespoke tailored clothes, which were in keeping with his position as the next Duke of Chiswick.

Three years his younger, Will had always been mean spirited and disagreeable. Will was a guard's officer, and his arrogance hadn't been kept in check by life in the Army. Both Nick and Beth had actively disliked him ever since he was a child, and popular belief was that he hadn't improved with age. Lottie watched Will, half concentrating on his conversation with Rupert, whilst he ogled Sophie from across the table. Beth was sat next to her husband, who for once looked relaxed in his older brother's company. Nick was on his best behaviour and was even trying to be civilised towards Rupert.

Deep in contemplation, Lottie nearly jumped

out of her skin, as Max's hand suddenly arrived on the top of her thigh. She glanced sideways, and he appeared to be still deep in conversation with Will's wife, however his left arm, acting seemingly on its own accord, was under the table, lifting her skirt. The hand began to stroke her bare flesh as it gently worked its way up the inside of her leg.

Sophie turned and in a half whisper said, 'I see you went for the cheek bones rather than the chiselled jawline.' Guessing that Sophie was referring to Max and Ed, Lottie nodded. 'The chiselled jawline wanted someone with more money. He's coming to the ball tomorrow with the only daughter of Lady Hardcourt.'

'You don't mind?'

'Not in the least.' The pitch in Lottie's voice rose as Max's hand started to finger her clitoris.

Lottie turned towards Max, who turned and grinned. 'Are you OK darling?'

She nodded, barely able to speak. Will's wife then leaned across to Max and said, 'Why on earth is Tom marrying that plain ginger girl? He could do so much better.'

'Mummy, you can't say things like that,' her daughter complained in a loud, embarrassed whisper.

'I don't see why not. It's what everyone else is thinking,' her mother replied.

Max said, 'Initially I thought the same, but when you get to know Tom, then the attraction between them is more obvious. Tom is an academic. Left to him, his guest list would have been 90% Oxford dons. Verity is clever and bookish. They'll fill their evenings discussing Proust and dissecting the works of the romantic poets.'

Lottie sat motionless. Her nervous system felt like it was on fire, as her body, re-awaked after years of neglect, was reaching a climax of stimulation. As Max's fingers worked their magic, she was practically orgasming. She felt hot and flushed and was desperate to cry out in ecstasy.

'Lottie are you OK. You're looking hot. Do you think you're coming down with something?' Ben sounded concerned.

'No' she squeaked, 'I'm fine.'

'God, I want you so badly,' Max whispered in her ear. 'Say you're tired, and I'll escort you home.'

A further ten minutes later, once the main meal was over, Lottie feigned tiredness, and excused herself. Having had a long day, no one was suspicious, and she was able to escape without cross-examination, chivalrously followed by Max. They walked back down the drive to the lodge, with Lottie shivering with the cold. Lottie rushed upstairs to the bedroom and turned on the heater, whilst Max paced around the kitchen. She then led him into the sitting room. It was too late to light the wood burner, so she popped on the electric fire, and they huddled around it, trying to get warm. As the temperature started rising, Max started to massage Lottie's neck and shoulders. He then moved downwards to her small, firm breasts, which he gently caressed, making her tingle all over. Kissing her seductively, he slowly started to remove her clothing.

They moved upstairs, and once they were in the bedroom, they ripped off their clothes, before falling, laughing onto the bed. 'You're beautiful,' Max whispered. Lottie's eyes devoured his fit, lean body. She'd fantasised so long about this moment, and as he mounted her she wasn't disappointed.

At first, he entered her slowly, making sure he didn't cause her pain. 'Oh God,' he exclaimed. She was so tight and pure that he nearly came. He eased himself back, to make sure he regained his control. As Lottie's confidence grew, she relaxed and let her instincts take control. Max's movements came faster, and a surge of electricity shot through her body: an ecstasy of the like she'd never felt before. Seconds later, with a cry, Max climaxed.

Once they'd recovered Lottie popped to the bathroom to freshen up. Her period was due any day now, so they'd taken a chance, especially as Max had visited the health clinic for a check-up. She felt amazing. All tiredness gone. Max welcomed her back into bed with a kiss. 'I've wanted you for so long, it's been unbearable, but so worth the wait. You do feel the same?'

'Yes. I can hardly believe we've finally made it together. Of course now you've unleashed my inner sexual desire, I'm going to want you every night,' she laughed.

Leaning back against the pillow Max grinned broadly. 'My darling Lottie, your wish is my command.'

Chapter 34

The following morning they were late arriving on the yard, after Max had woken with an enormous erection he didn't want to waste. Hope was banging his door in frustration, demanding his breakfast. Lottie rushed around with feeds, whilst Max changed rugs. An hour later, Max saddled up Oberon and took him into the school, whilst Lottie continued with the mucking out, and filling water buckets. Lottie had just stopped for a quick chat with one of the livery clients, when she noticed Crispin coming across from the house, accompanied by Will and his family.

The party stopped by the arena and watched Max working in his young horse. The livery client took fright and scarpered, so Lottie felt she ought to go and greet them. She dropped off her filled buckets, and then made her way over to them, puzzling to herself that Crispin had never shown any interest in anything equine in his life.

'So how many competition horses do you and Max own?' Crispin asked.

Lottie explained who everyone was, and then added, 'Max really needs at least a couple more Grade A horses to complete for this be financially viable. Luckily we have a sponsor for Hope, but once that contract finishes, the operation will struggle to break even with just three money generating horses.'

Undeterred Crispin asked about the running costs, and the prize money on offer.

'The Longines Global Tour has fantastic prize money, and when the European legs begin in May, Max will compete. With limited funds, and the inexperienced Hope being his only Grand Prix standard ride, it simply isn't financially worth Max travelling to UAE for the start of the tour,' Lottie explained.

Crispin nodded in agreement. 'I'm glad to hear that you are both being financially responsible, but I guess that bearing in mind both your backgrounds, business sense comes naturally.' Lottie invited them to meet the horses, much to the delight of Will's daughter Emily, and even Crispin gingerly patted the noses of Hope and Taggart. Will's wife then asked if there was a pony that her daughter could have a ride on. Lottie hesitated, wracking her brains as to the best option, before offering to fetch her old pony Aragon. 'He's elderly, and doesn't have shoes on, but he's safe, and small enough for you to handle.' Half an hour later, Emily was riding down the driveway on Lottie's shaggy bay pony, accompanied by Lottie on Taggart.

By early afternoon guests were arriving in droves for the party. Pippa and Dizzy had returned so they did the afternoon stables with Max, whilst Lottie and Beth directed people to their sleeping accommodation. Meanwhile Ben and Tom drove those allocated to Dewerstone over to Rupert and Marina's.

The caterers then arrived, shortly followed by the sound engineers and stage crew. To escape the chaos, Lottie took Shadow for a walk, before heading back to the lodge to get changed. She'd bought an expensive elegant pale blue, slightly revealing designer dress, which had cost a week's salary. When she'd purchased it on one of her London visits, her only aim had been the seduction of Max. With that particular box already ticked, she mused at the irony, it had happened whilst wearing an old M&S favourite, and ancient granny knickers.

Max came to collect her an hour later. Dressed in black tie, he looked gorgeous. His blonde hair glistened under the artificial light, and his blue eyes twinkled with desire. He placed his hand on Lottie's back, to guide her towards the door, but within seconds, it had slipped down to her bottom. Putting his other hand on her shoulder, he stopped and kissed her seductively on her shoulder, making her shudder with desire.

'Do you think they'd mind if we were a bit late?' Max whispered?

'Probably, but only if they notice,' Lottie replied, already wet with anticipation.

Guiding her back towards the sitting room, Max hurriedly undid his trousers, and Lottie slipped off her dress and tights. Frantic with desire, they both came quickly. Conscious of the time, they hurriedly washed and re-dressed, and Lottie reapplied her makeup and tidied her hair.

The party had already started by the time they

371

arrived. Guests were eating and drinking, whilst the band played Jazz music in the background. Three large central chandeliers lit the ballroom, and all around the edge of the room candles flickered. All the best artwork had been brought in to hang on the walls, and at various points around the room there were neoclassical Greek statues, surrounded by flowers, and gave the room a very Georgian feel. Lottie and Max managed to slip in unnoticed and tag on the end of the buffet queue where they could check out the other guests.

As well as the entire family being present, there were mostly Tom's Eton mates and his society friends. The mix was made more eclectic by the inclusion of several Oxford colleagues, including research fellows and a handful of literature professors. There were various journalists amongst the guests, all officially off-duty, and a few of Tom's fellow polo players.

Ben and Sophie had arrived with a few of the other Brideshead cast, including Julian, and the friendly guy playing Bridie. Lottie had managed to get invites for a few of her riding club and livery friends, and some specially selected neighbours had turned up. Verity had arrived with her best friend Indira, who'd come with a boyfriend, and finally Ed and Olivia Hardcourt.

Nick was walking around, acting as the perfect host. Dressed in his dinner jacket, he still looked handsome. Unlike his rather reserved son, Nick had always preferred being the centre of attention, and loved nothing better than a party where he was in control. Normally banned from drinking, he'd permitted himself a night of freedom. He'd also managed to get his hands on some speed, and subsequently had boundless amounts of energy, and felt amazing. Ignoring the fact that he'd be regretting it in the morning, and probably not be able to move for days, he was determined to enjoy himself.

'Your stepdad certainly knows how to party,' Max said admiringly.

'When I was a child, there were parties all the time. From what I can remember, they were pretty wild, in a Downton Abbey meets Trainspotting kind of way,' Lottie replied. 'Aristocracy. A Listers and alcohol, celebrities, company bosses and cocaine, and not necessarily in that order. Of course, I was too young to really know what went on.'

'I sometimes wonder if I hadn't been into horses whether I'd ended up like your stepfather?' Max contemplated. 'Actually that's not the kind of thought I should say out loud in present company. It doesn't show me in a good light.'

'Do you really think so?' Lottie looked quizzically at her boyfriend.

'You've been to one of my parties, so you know I'm no angel. There have been countless time when I would have got totally wrecked, but for the fact that I've had a competition the next day.'

'And that's the all-important difference. You have an off switch. Nick doesn't. Even to the point that he knew what he was doing was killing him, he didn't have the willpower to stop. That's why I'm not worried by you.' Lottie spoke with confidence and authority.

Max smiled. 'Fair enough,' he wasn't going to argue as they'd just reached the buffet table, which was laden with wonderful, mouth-watering food. There were sides of salmon, and plates of cold meats. Canapés including caviar, and mini beef wellingtons. There were salads, cheeses, pasta and rice dishes, mini quiches and other savoury pastries, almost too much to choose from.

Max made sure he got some of the caviar. His father adored it, so subsequently Max and his brother had developed a love for it to. Since his first taste of poverty, Max hadn't been able to afford such luxuries, so took full advantage of the opportunity when presented to him.

Whilst they ate, Lottie started chatting to one of the neighbouring landowners. Max quickly lost interest in the conversation, as his mind began to wander. Looking around him, he considered how lucky he was to have been accepted by such a fabulous family, and how grateful he was to have secured the love of the awesomely clever and resourceful Lottie. She was everything he could have asked for. She was both beautiful and kind, intelligent and unspoilt, and it was finally dawning on him quite how much he'd fallen in love with her.

All he needed were a couple more top horses, start having regular, lucrative wins, and he'd be financially secure enough to feel worthy of asking her to marry him. He reckoned that with luck, he'd be properly solvent within two years, and then he'd be in a position to secure their future together.

They finished eating, and Max picked up Lottie's empty plate, and took them away, before heading to the drinks table. Despite the family's lack of drinkers, the drinks table was incredibly well stocked. Max helped himself to a large slug of decent Russian vodka, and a Luscombe's Elderflower presse for Lottie. As he got back to where Lottie was standing, he realised that she'd been joined by Ed and the horse face Hardcourt girl. To make a point, as he reached them, he handed Lottie her drink, whilst kissing her on the back of her bare shoulder and calling her darling.

'You two are officially an item then,' Ed commented, in a matter-of-fact voice. 'Took you long enough,' he challenged Max.

'I didn't want to rush,' Max replied.

The small talk continued for a few minutes, but Max noticed that Ed didn't look too pleased, and that his relationship with Olivia horse-face seemed decidedly cool. He was just wondering what had gone wrong when Ed let slip the issue. Lottie had innocently asked Olivia about their future wedding plans when Ed interrupted.

'Lady Hardcourt had promised me Zhivago as an engagement present, but Olivia told me earlier that her mother has gone back on her word.' He sounded bitter and resentful. 'She's been offered good money by some syndicate, and apparently, she's accepted. Just like that, with no regard to my feelings.'

375

'You know what Mummy said, it was too good a chance to get her money back. She's already promised you something else to ride.' Olivia tried to placate her fiancé.

Meanwhile Lottie's attention diverted towards Max. He looked devastated. The pain etched on his face said it all. Even to Olivia, momentarily distracted by her petulant boyfriend, it was obvious that Max wasn't involved with the mystery buyers. Mummy would be pleased, she thought to herself. The last thing her mother wanted was for the horse to return to the Tarasov yard.

'Who's buying him? Is he staying in the UK?' Max hardly dared to ask.

'We don't know who these people are, but it sounds like it's a family setting themselves up as a syndicate for tax reasons. And I know what you think of Mummy, but she strongly supports keeping talent in the UK, so yes, he's staying here, although I think its Scotland.'

Any faint hope that Lottie was harbouring that Caroline's syndicate had worked a miracle was dashed. She'd run out of time and had failed. She glanced at Max, who looked like he was about to cry. She gently placed her hand on his shoulder, but he ignored it. 'Will you excuse me?' he said stiffly, before turning away and heading off through the crowd.

Lottie's heart sank further. Not only had she failed to secure Zhivago, Tom's 25th birthday, which she'd been excited about for months, was now ruined as far as her personal enjoyment was concerned. Feeling that she still needed to be courteous to her guests, she remained in situ and continued to make polite conversation, but her heart was no longer in it.

Max couldn't bear for anyone to see him cry. Rubbing his stinging eyes, he made his way outside. Standing in the icy cold air, he called Lee. When Lee finally picked up the call, he knew less than Max. No one had bothered to tell him; he'd still been working on the basis that the black stallion was on his way back to Lark Rise, now Ed's base.

With no more information, Max headed back inside. He was no longer in the mood to party, but vodka would at least numb the pain. The band were playing the type of fast, furious music associated with the 1920's and 30s – plenty of trumpet and sax, with a hypnotic drumbeat. As the sound grew to a crescendo, he wanted to cry out in pain, desperate for it to go away. Grabbing a bottle of vodka, he poured himself a large glass full, knocking it back in one go. Refilling he did the same again. The liquid burned his throat, but quickly the soothing numbness started to take effect, wrapping him in an emotional comfort blanket.

Having done her duty with Ed and Olivia, Lottie went in search of Max, but her progress was slow. Every few feet she found herself being waylaid by friends and relatives, keen to have a chat or a gossip. She almost made it to the far end of the room when she was stopped by her brother Ben and his actor friends, who'd all been drinking and were in high spirits.

'Have you seen Max?' Lottie asked hopefully.

'He was by the bar about ten minutes ago, but headed off looking like the world was about to end. What's happened?' Ben asked.

'He was hoping to get back one of his old horses, but it's been sold on to someone in Scotland.'

'Seriously. Is that all. I thought that he'd just been told that a close family member had died or something... So he's upset over a horse?' Julian asked in disbelief.

'Yep. Admittedly it was a pretty special horse. Olympic prospect special, but the chances of him getting it back were always slim. He takes these things very hard.'

'In that case, would you do me the honour of dancing, so we can re-kindle our acquaintance?' the Bridey actor asked politely.

Feeling guilty, but powerless, Lottie admitted defeat, and accepted. If Max wanted to be left alone, then it wasn't her fault. The least she could do was to extract some vestige of pleasure from what remained of the evening. The Bridey actor, whose real name was Neil, was a moderately famous actor, who'd been in several Working Title films, and a couple of TV series. On their last meeting, in the gloom of the night club, Lottie hadn't recognised him, but under the ballroom lighting, she suddenly realised who he was.

He was five years older than Lottie, divorced, and living in London, with part time access to his two children. It was clear to Lottie that he rather liked her. He didn't have Max's looks, but he was amusing, and cultured, and good to be with. Lottie started to think, if Max hadn't come into her life, whether Neil would have been a suitable partner. She then dismissed the thought on the basis that their lifestyles were incompatible.

They had been dancing for a while when Lottie spotted Max hovering near the bar. Excusing herself she took her chance and headed him off before he disappeared once again. His eyes were bloodshot and glazed from drink, but he still sounded lucid when he spoke.

'You've found me then,' he said in a matter-of-fact tone.

'Just wanted to make sure you hadn't topped yourself,' Lottie planned to keep her tone light. She was rewarded with a weak smile.

Having dispensed with his glass, Max had acquired a bottle of vodka. Conscious of her looking at him, he raised the bottle to his lips and took a slug of the clear liquid.

'I don't suppose that's water in there?' she asked, trying to remain jovial.

'Yes, there probably is. Not that I've got any bloody idea how the stuff's distilled,' he muttered. 'Anyway, I'm determined to get very drunk, and whatever is in here is doing a good job.' He hesitated, trying not to sound too abrupt. 'There is nothing you can do or say that will make me feel any better, but this stuff is bloody brilliant, so go off and enjoy yourself.'

'I don't want to abandon you.' Lottie felt helpless, but knew he was right. She couldn't wave a magic wand.

He put his hand on her shoulder. 'I know you care, but this is a special time for your family. I don't want you to ruin your night. Please go and enjoy yourself. I don't mind. I'll catch you later. Now go,' he ordered.

'OK, I'll see you later.' Lottie planted a kiss on his cheek and left him alone.

Lottie headed back towards her own group of friends but was stopped in her tracks by her mother. 'Is Max OK?' she asked. 'Have you two fallen out?'

'We haven't fallen out, in fact quite the opposite, but he's just found out that his beloved Zhivago has been sold on. Rather than encroach on our fun, he's asked to be allowed to wallow in self-pity on his own.'

'What a shame. Poor Max. I'll keep an eye on him.' Beth paused, then smiled to herself. 'When we first moved here we had a huge party. As you can imagine, Nick got totally wrecked. I left him collapsed in a heap on the ground, lying amongst the geranium bushes.' Lottie giggled.

'Admittedly it was July, so probably best not to leave anyone outside tonight or they'll be a frozen block by the morning,' her mother added.

At that moment, the band stopped playing and Nick, who hadn't yet ended up in the shrubbery, grabbed a microphone. He thanked everyone for coming and helping to make Tom's birthday such a special occasion. He then spoke about how proud he was of his son, and that he wished him every happiness for the future. He

380

beckoned to Tom to join him on the stage. With everyone's attention focused on him, Tom publicly asked Verity to marry him.

As Verity accepted his proposal there were cheers from the guests. Ben and his friends, along with some of the old Etonian's started to wolf whistle and chant. Seconds later, a large cake was wheeled out, covered in candles. One side was a birthday cake, and the other an engagement cake. Lottie looked at her brother. She'd never seen him look so happy as he did at that moment. Beside him, quiet, unassuming Verity looked like she was about to burst with joy.

As Tom cut into the cake, from outside there came a loud bang, followed by another. Guests rushed to the window to see what the noise was. In the garden, one of the staff was letting off fireworks. Everyone made their way outside as the sky lit up with coloured lights. Lottie took the opportunity to look for Max, hoping he'd made it. Guests were still making their way out the doors, but finally he came, discretely staying at the back, propping himself up against the wall of the house.

As the icy temperatures started to take effect, many of the guests rapidly turned tail to watch from inside. Lottie started to shiver, and headed back, albeit via where Max was standing, still clutching his bottle. 'It's too cold to say out here,' she said, shivering slightly as she spoke.

'Come here,' he ordered.

As she reached him, he put the half-drunk bottle on the floor, and he wrapped his arms around her. The numbing effects of the vodka had made him mellower. 'I'll warm you up,' he slurred. He leant back against the wall and closed his eyes. 'God, I'm totally fucked.'

He held her tightly as the last of the fireworks soared into the blackness of the night. Once it was over they made their way back inside.'I need the loo, so you go on, and I'll see you.' He waived his hand in the general direction of the ballroom. Lottie watched him stagger off towards the bathroom before heading off back to the dance floor.

The band had packed up and one of the DJs from Lizzies had started his set. Many of the older family members had left, including Crispin, Felicity, Rupert and Marina. The ballroom lights had been turned off, just leaving the flickering glow from the candles, giving the room a gothic atmosphere. Lottie started to scout the room, looking for her friends or Ben and his group. Suddenly she was grabbed by Ed. 'Come and dance with us,' he ordered.

Reluctantly she moved onto the dance floor, joining Ed and Olivia. It was clear that Ed was still sulking and taking it out on his girlfriend for her mother's betrayal over Zhivago. Lottie was almost feeling sorry for Lady Olivia, knowing the truth that it had been Simon Palmer who'd been the influencing factor. As the music slowed, Ed moved in behind Lottie and started to rub his body against her, in an unsubtle and suggestive manner.

Lottie halted abruptly, and spun around, glaring at Ed. 'What the hell do you think you are doing?' she demanded.

'Just dancing. Why? Don't you like it?'

'No not really. It's inappropriate.'

Ed sneered arrogantly. 'You used to like it. Are you allergic to cock?'

Lottie was almost speechless with disbelief. 'In case you have forgotten, we are not a 'couple''. She used her hands to express speech marks. 'You are meant to be in a fully functioning adult relationship with Lady Olivia, and this stupid dance flirting is insulting to her, and also to me as you're just using me for your own petty revenge?' As Lottie ranted, Max came up behind her, unnoticed, with his bottle tucked under his left arm, and carrying a drink for her in his right hand.

Ed noticed Max. 'I gather you've managed to thaw Miss Frigid Knickers here.' Max stood speechless. He was far too drunk to react quickly and was straining to work out what was going on. Taking a swig from his nearly empty bottle, he then placed it on the ground before trying to focus on what was obviously an argument.

Having not received a response the first time, Ed tried again. 'Come on Tarasov, spill the beans. Have you managed to get a shag from the Ice Queen here?'

'What fucking business is it of yours?' Max slurred, as his brain suddenly tuned in.

'Just wondering mate that's all.' Ed responded. Beside him Olivia was looking increasingly upset.

'Read my lips. What fucking business is it of yours?' Max repeated. 'I don't ask about you shagging Horse-face cus' you're a bloody gold-digger.'

Horrified, Lottie looked at Olivia, who now looked close to tears.

Ed glared at his rival. 'You're in no position to lecture me, except in your case there is no fucking cus you're with miss frigid knickers.'

Max took a swing at Ed, trying to land a punch on his smug face. As his arm shot forward, it missed both of its blurry targets, and instead the punch landed in space. There was a blood-curdling scream, followed by the smashing of glass. Olivia stood crying, her face, hair, and clothes soaked in red, with liquid running down her face.

'Oh Christ I'm sorry.' Max looked at her in horror, 'Got the drink for Lottie. I forgot.... I'm so sorry. Are you OK?'

'Let me get you cleaned up.' Mortified, Lottie led Olivia away, calling to Pippa who was standing nearby to clean the mess off the floor.

As they walked through the crowded room there were shouts of 'Oh my god, is that blood?' and 'Did you see that girl, she's covered in blood.' Lottie overhead one unhelpful person say that he saw a girl being glassed.

Lottie took the sobbing Olivia up to her old bedroom. Whilst Olivia had a shower to wash off the sticky raspberry J2o, Lottie dug around in her overflow wardrobe for a suitable spare party dress.

Olivia appeared ten minutes later, clean and wrapped in a large towel. Lottie handed her a black and white spotted Jack Wills party dress,

384

which Lottie had outgrown, but she hoped would fit Olivia's slimmer frame. Luckily the dress fitted, so Lottie helped Olivia apply some make up and re arrange her hair.

Olivia was still as upset by the harsh words as from the drink incident, so Lottie tried to repair the damage. 'I'm so sorry about Max. I know the drink was a total accident, but he should never have been so rude. When he's angry, and worse when drunk, he can be a total bitch with no filter.'

Olivia looked miserably into the mirror. 'But he's right. My nose makes me look like a Norman Cob.'

'It is a little more prominent than some, but Max is being spiteful because he loathes your mother, and that's not fair. You could be an A list model, and he'd still find fault, because he'd be determined to undermine you.'

'Does everyone laugh at me behind my back? I guess it's obvious that Ed's using me.'

'I've never heard any comments, but then I'm no more of an insider than you are. Anyway does it matter what a few people think? If you are happy that's what's important.'

Olivia stood up, looking at herself in the mirror. 'Thank you for the loan of the dress. I think it looks good on me.' Certainly, the narrow waist, and the fuller skirt emphasised her hourglass figure.'I hardly know you, but you've been so kind.'

'That's OK Not only am I glad to have been of assistance, but I also need to repair the damage done by my idiotic business partner slash boyfriend.'

As they walked back down the staircase Lottie spoke again. 'I know it's none of my business, but from where I'm standing, Ed's lucky to have you.'

'But he's so handsome. I know that people see me and reckon I'm out of my league.'

'Anyone who knows you, will know better. Yes, Ed is superficially handsome, and he's a good sportsman. He's well brought up but that's it. One day he'll be old and flabby. You, on the other hand will always be from the rich aristocratic elite, and he can't compete with that. What's important to your relationship is that you have the same life goals. If you are a good team, you'll be strong. I mean look at my brother. He could have married almost anyone, but has chosen a shy, nondescript ginger girl. Looks had nothing to do with it, they fell in love over literature.'

Olivia giggled. 'You should be a marriage councillor.' She paused, and then added. 'Anyway, I need to apologise for how equally rude Ed was to you.'

'I'd forgotten that' Lottie mused. 'I've heard that accusation so often in my life. Mainly by bitter men who didn't get their way with me. Just because I don't just jump into bed with someone the moment they ask.'

'But why did Ed say it to you?'

'I first met him twelve months ago, at Verity's party. He came on to me, thinking I could help his career. I did give him loads of advice, but I drew the line at sleeping with him, partly because I

386

knew he was just using me, and partly because I loved someone else.'

'Max Tarasov by any chance?'

Lottie nodded. 'Actually, at first I loathed Max. Thought he was an obnoxious, arrogant shit, but enforced poverty has been the making of him.'

They arrived back at the ballroom and located Ed by the bar. He took Olivia in his arms and hugged her, a look of relief on his face. Leaving them together, Lottie headed off in search of Max. It didn't take long to find him. He was slumped on the floor, with his back against the wall, near the bar, looking totally wasted.

Lottie sat down beside him. 'Are you OK?' she asked.

He nodded gloomily. Beside him the bottle was empty.

'Olivia is fine. Had a shower and got changed. She's back, happy, in the arms of her beloved.'

Max mumbled. 'Good. Worried I'd hurt her.' He looked at Lottie, trying desperately to focus.

'No, she was just wet and sticky. She was upset by the horse -face comment, but she'll live.'

As she finished speaking, Max leaned over and rested his head on her shoulder. Seconds later he'd passed out. She tenderly stroked his head, as she studied his beautiful features. With his eyes closed, his long lashes made him look like a little boy and she felt such an overwhelming desire to protect him.

Noticing his step-daughter sitting on the floor, Nick headed unsteadily over to check she was all right. With his bow tie undone and hanging loosely around his neck, he had the sexy, dishevelled appearance which Lottie knew her mum found irresistible.

'Are you OK sweetheart?' he gently enquired.

'Fine thanks. It's been a fantastic party, but Max doesn't have your stamina,' she smiled.

'As long as you are good,' Nick looked relieved. 'I'd better go. People to thank and all that.' Lottie felt such affection for him. He was such a people pleaser, and genuinely cared about everyone, with the possible exception of Rupert. It was hard to tell quite how much he'd been drinking. Following years of hosting Lizzies, Nick was expert at looking like he was in complete control even when extremely drunk.

Lottie sat, listening to the music and people watching for what felt like an hour, but in reality was a far shorter time period. Unable to move without disturbing Max, people she hadn't had a chance to speak to, came to her for a catch up and to share news. Finally, desperate for a wee, Lottie was forced to move. Having relieved herself, she managed to get Max back on his feet, where she took him back to his bed, before heading home.

The next morning Lottie and Pippa did the horses. No one had seen Dizzy for hours, after she disappeared off with one of Tom's old school friends. Lottie popped into to Max's farmhouse to check he was still alive, before leaving him to sleep. Once the chores had been completed, the girls had breakfast. Lottie then drove over to Dewerstone to meet Olivia. Rupert had arranged clay shooting, which Ed was intending to join in, therefore Lottie offered to take Olivia riding on Dartmoor.

Olivia confessed to having never visited Dartmoor and appreciated the personal tour. She hadn't brought riding clothes, so once again Lottie kitted her out, and then gave her Cruz to ride, whilst she took Taggart. The weather was dull and mild, but there was no fog, so Lottie took them up across the moors above the Walkham Valley to her mother's favourite spot on Yennadon Down.

Having enjoyed a long gallop up the sloping side of the down, they halted when they reached the summit. Below them was Burrator reservoir, a large expanse of lake, surrounded by forestation and tors. Behind them the view was equally dramatic, with the beautiful Devon countryside spread out below them, and leading finally to the sea.

The horses suddenly spun around as a herd of wild ponies appeared over the brow of the hill and cantered off into the distance. Taggart had been brought up on the moors, so wasn't worried by the strange, short legged, hairy horse dwarfs, but Cruz gave a deep, suspicious snort.

'Are you OK?' Lottie asked Olivia. After all, she'd wanted to impress her, not scare her.

'Yes, I'm fine. I've ridden much worse. In fact, Cruz is beautiful. Is she yours?'

'No sadly. She is owned by the actress Melissa May.'

'That's a shame.' Olivia paused before adding. 'It's so pretty here. No wonder you like living in

Devon. It's rather like a mini-Scotland.'

'I suppose it is a bit. Only fewer angry red heads with chips on their shoulders, and not a kilt in sight.' Lottie giggled.

They headed back down the side of the hill, following a well-worn sheep track, until they reached the moor gate. They then made their way along deserted country lanes towards home. About a mile from home, Olivia's phone rang. She answered it, and to her surprise it was Chef de Equipe Simon Palmer.

'Hi Olivia, I've just heard about an incident last night, and was calling to see if you were OK, and not hurt.'

'Oh right. Yes, I'm fine thanks.'

Simon could hear hooves on tarmac. 'Are you riding?'

'Yes, I'm currently in a Devon lane, accompanying Lottie Wilkins on her big grey, and I'm riding Max Tararov's black mare.'

Simon quickly processed the information. It certainly didn't fit with what he'd just been told by a furious Lady Hardcourt, who'd rung demanding that Max be blacklisted by British Show jumping.

'So you weren't glassed last evening then?'

Olivia was tempted to play up the incident to get back at Max for his rudeness, but she could hardly lie in front of Lottie, especially after her kindness.

'No nothing like that. Max was drunk and tried to punch Ed but missed. Unfortunately, he'd forgotten that he was holding a glass of Raspberry

J2o in his hand when he went for Ed, and the drink went all over me. The sound of breaking glass, and the fact I was covered in red liquid, probably fuelled the rumour.'

Simon exhaled in relief. 'Thank you, Lady Olivia, you've put my mind at rest.'

Lottie overhead the conversation, and immediately her heart started racing. It was clear that someone from the party hated her boyfriend and was looking for an opportunity to destroy him. The most obvious candidate was Ed Carter. She decided not to share her suspicions, but in the future she'd certainly be more wary around him.

Chapter 35

Max didn't surface until late on Sunday evening, and then he still looked pale and ill. Lottie forced him to eat a meal, and they collapsed in front of the TV, with Shadow. The next morning Lottie had an early start, as she was working away all week on the latest Yangtze project, and meant travelling to the North of England, and visiting various franchises.

Max spent the first part of the week concentrating on Oberon and taking him to more jumping events. Then on the Thursday he and Pippa drove the smaller, less conspicuous lorry to Berkshire, for the racehorse sales. Max's plan was to buy a couple of cheap animals to retrain as jumping horses. His logic was that it would be a good challenge for the two girls. If the horses didn't make the grade for what he wanted, there was a ready market for well-trained jumpers at the amateur level.

When they finally arrived at the auction, Max was glad that Lottie was safely up country. She'd have felt so sorry for the sad, broken-down rejects, and she'd have rescued the lot. Max had to ignore his heart, and look for horses with a sensible price tag, and clean, undamaged legs.

His attention was drawn to Rosy Future, a pretty, chestnut mare of 16 hands. She'd done a bit of racing, both on the flat and over hurdles, but not living up to her namesake, had never really made the grade. In Max's mind that translated to a low mileage horse that could at least jump. She seemed sweet tempered enough, and her legs were unblemished, so he took a chance and bid for her.

Pippa then spotted a large brown horse, his head dropping despondently in one of the furthest away pens. As she approached the horse, he lifted his head and gave a friendly nicker. Having slipped him a polo, she called to Max.

'His legs aren't in great shape,' Max looked critically, 'but he has an excellent record over fences. He's 11, and a big, long-bodied horse, so it will take a lot to train him to rebalance and come off his forehand.'

'He seems so kind and gentle,' Pippa pleaded. I don't suppose he'll go for much. Please bid on him.'

'I'll see what he fetches,' Max replied, wishing he hadn't brought a sentimental girl with him. Taking a final look at Percy the gelding's kind, honest face however, he felt a stab of guilt. If the horse were genuine, he'd be easy enough to sell on as a hunt horse so maybe he was worth a punt.

As they drove home along the M4, Max concluded that he'd never make a horse dealer. He's purchased Rosy for reasonable money, and then ended up spending the rest of his budget on Percy, who was everything he'd wanted to avoid, but had taken pity on the sweet natured horse.

The next day he rode both horses. Rosy was sharp and keen with a snappy jump. On her forehand, and restless in her mouth, she would need schooling, but Max felt she would make a good event horse. Percy was incredibly laid back, had no concept of collection, but had a powerful, confident jump. He wasn't agile like Rosie but had some potential as a jumper.

Lottie arrived back home the following evening, tired after a long week of travelling around the country. As soon as she had changed, she donned her thick coat and a head torch, and walked Shadow up to the stable yard to meet the two new residents. Having fed them carrots, she had to speak to the others, especially Taggart who was known to get jealous. As she approached Tilly's stable, she realised something was wrong. The mare didn't come to the door, but remained standing at the back of the stable, her sides heaving, and dripping in sweat.

She wasn't due to foal for a few more weeks. Panicking, she rushed over to the farmhouse to fetch Max. She knocked frantically on the door, 'Max, I need you to come quickly,' she called.

'Are you that desperate for me,' Max called lazily from the kitchen.

'It's Tilly. I think the foal's coming.'

Seconds later, the door opened. Max was frantically shoving on his boots. 'I'm here.'

He tore across the yard, and into the stable. Lottie stopped in the doorway. 'Is there something wrong?' she asked tentatively. She'd never seen a foaling, but the mare looked too distressed for things to be normal.

'Lottie, call the vet, say it's urgent,' Max barked.

The wait for the vet seemed endless. Max stayed with his mare, gently stroking her, and trying to re-assure her, while Lottie paced up and down the yard listening out for the sound of a car. The practice's top horse vet arrived half an hour later and promptly examined Tilly.

'The foal has a very weak heartbeat but is breached. In my opinion the mare has probably got a womb infection, hence her distress and raised temperature.'

He turned to Max. 'It may be a case that I can only save one of them.'

Max had tears rolling down his face. In a chocked voice, he said, 'I owe it to Tilly to try and save her. She's given me so much over the years,'

The vet looked stern, 'You realise that she's an old mare, who won't be able to have any more foals after this.'

'This could be your only chance to have offspring of Zhivago,' Lottie reminded him. 'But I couldn't sacrifice an old friend either,' she added sympathetically.

'Look I'll do my best to save them both. I'll need to perform a caesarean, but the foal isn't full term yet, so I don't know if it will survive.'

The vet gave Tilly a mild sedative, to help reduce the pain, and they loaded her into the small lorry before heading back to the veterinary hospital. Twenty minutes later Tilly was led inside the operating theatre and given a tranquilliser. Tilly dropped onto the floor before lying peacefully. An airway tube was inserted and then two assistants, called in to help, put Tilly into a sling so she could be raised onto a special table. The vet scrubbed his arms, and then shaved the hair around the area where he was due to make the incision.

A short while later the vet extracted a slime covered, small black colt. Whilst he concentrated on cleaning and sewing up Tilly, one of the nurses attempted to get the foal to breathe by itself. It lay motionless for what seemed like ages, but suddenly its little lungs started to inflate, and it raised its head.

Whilst Max and Lottie knelt beside it, rubbing it dry, one of the assistants went to fetch some colostrum, and a feeding bottle. The foal was initially reluctant to drink, but eventually it took a couple of life enhancing gulps. Another hour past before Tilly was lowered back down onto the floor.

As Tilly finally fully woke up, she was encouraged to get to her feet before being led to a stable. The foal was extremely weak, so Max cradled it in his arms, and carried it behind Tilly. Once she was in the comfort of a stable, Tilly began to revive, and only then spotted her foal. Giving a gentle nicker, Max put the foal down on the floor beside her, and she started to stiff and lick the little creature, who was curled up in a ball at her feet.

Due to her lack of natural birth, Tilly hadn't started to produce milk, so a further attempt was made to bottle feed the baby. Satisfied that in the short term there was little more to do, the veterinary team went home. Lottie and Max then took turns to stay with the foal, whilst the other crashed out in the lorry to grab some sleep. Lottie went to bed first. It was midnight, and she'd been driving since 6.30 that morning, and was so tired she didn't know how she could stay awake a moment longer.

When her alarm went off three hours later, she dragged herself off the bunk bed, and walked across the vet's yard to the stable. Max looked exhausted, but the foal was lying with its head on his lap, whilst Tilly munched at some hay.

'He's managed to drink a whole bottle,' Max announced, and it looks like Tilly's milk is starting to come through. I just hope the foal gets to his feet soon.'

'Let me take over, so you can have a sleep.' Lottie ordered.

'No, you may as well go back and rest. I won't be able to sleep anyway. There's no point in both of us staying awake.'

Lottie went back to the lorry and made Max a hot drink. She grabbed a spare duvet and took it back to the stable. She was still so tired she didn't argue, and, dropping on to the bed, went back to sleep. She didn't wake up until 7. Feeling very guilty, she went straight out to the stable. Max had run out of bottled milk, so was holding the foal up so it could reach Tilly's own supply. The mare looked exhausted, as did Max. Lottie slipped her hand in, taking over supporting the foal's weight from Max. She insisted that he have a break.

Before long the veterinary team arrived back. Max and Lottie were sent home, and one of the nurses took over. Max drove the lorry home, barely able to focus on the road he was so weary. Once they were back, Max went off to bed, and Lottie checked to make sure that Pippa and Dizzy were OK with doing the morning stables. Lottie took Shadow for a quick walk before slipping back to bed for a couple more hours.

For the next week, Max visited the vets daily to check up on his mare and foal. It wasn't until the following Friday that the foal could stand unsupported. By the next morning, it was agreed that both animals were well enough to travel. Tilly was pleased to be home. She wanted to go straight back out in the field, but the foal was too unsteady on his feet to risk it. It wasn't until two days later that Max was able to let them both out in the paddock.

Finally, the foal was starting to gain strength. Initially he stayed close to his mother, but eventually he plucked up the courage to explore, and he managed his first trot steps. It wasn't until the end of the second week that Lottie came home from work to find the little chap galloping around the paddock, bucking, and jumping.

Lottie was so relieved, as it meant the foal was developing normally. She knew how desperate Max was for a Zhivago foal, and although he'd been putting on a brave face, this foal was Max's last hope. There was also the eye -wateringly huge vets bill, which would take every penny of what Max had left from the sale of his lorry. At least now the foal looked like surviving, he'd have something to show for his money.

Max hadn't initially named the foal, mainly because he didn't want to tempt fate. Now the foal was starting to develop normally, he decided to take a chance. He wanted to acknowledge the Russian heritage of Zhivago, so decided to call the foal Tolstoy in the hope that one day the small black creature would be a sought-after premium stallion like his father.

The whereabouts of Zhivago remained a mystery. Lee texted Max the day the horse left the yard, where it was rumoured, he was heading North to Scotland. Equestrian gossip started to spread new that the stallion had gone to former leading showjumper Scott Brady, who was well known for having wonderfully supportive owners, who kept him well supplied with top horses.

Scott's team quickly refuted the story, leaving people to speculate that the horse had been bought for some spoilt teenager coming off ponies, who'd probably be annihilated by the temperamental horse. At each false news story, Max felt fresh pain and a sense of hopelessness. A further week passed, and whilst Lottie was at work she received a phone call from Simon Palmer. Reassured that Max wasn't within earshot, he asked her to keep a secret.

'I have been in discussions with the syndicate who now own Zhivago. They purchased the horse with the sole intention of giving the ride back to

Max. 'The impression I get is that these are champagne swilling, London businessmen with pot loads of money, who've taken a liking to your friend. I don't think they know one end of a horse from another. With glamorous events, such as the Longines World Tour, these guys are probably looking for an excuse to fly off for the weekend to exciting locations to watch their horse compete.'

'He's going to be so thrilled.' Lottie felt so happy she wanted to rush off and tell him that instant.

'I thought it would be nice to keep Zhivago's name a secret, and let Max find out when he appears down the ramp of the lorry. I've arranged for Zhivago to come down from the Scottish borders next Tuesday. Due to the sensitivity of the deal, and Lady Hardcourt's opinions on Max, it has meant a great deal of subterfuge has been necessary, so the poor chap has been in hiding.'

'How come they bought Zhivago?' Lottie was curious.

Simon coughed, 'Um, His name may have inadvertently passed my lips once I knew Lady H was considering selling.'

'Thank you.'

'Of course, no one must know of my involvement. The transactions have all been handled through a London firm of solicitors. All I know of the owners is their syndicate name, TM Associates. If they should choose to contact Max directly in the future, it's their choice.'

Simon then called Max. After the usual social pleasantries, Simon got to the point. 'At the risk of sounding presumptuous, I've arranged on your behalf, for you to take on the ride for a London based syndicate. The horse arrives at Exeter services at Tuesday lunchtime.'

Max was taken aback, 'Is this horse any good? I know I'm desperate for rides, and at the risk of looking a good horse in the mouth... well you understand.'

'My dear chap, I wouldn't saddle you with something useless, especially without consulting you first. I'm not able to reveal the horse's details now, but let's just say, that as a combination, I will automatically short list you for the next Olympics.'

Max couldn't wait for Tuesday to arrive. Lottie had arranged to work from home that week, so she could accompany him on the drive to Exeter, wanting to see his reaction when he saw his beloved stallion. All the way, Max was speculating as to which horse he'd been offered, assuming it was coming from USA or Western Europe, but never suspecting the truth.

They arrived early, so headed off to the services for a coffee. They'd just arrived back into the lorry park when a luge liveried transporter came into view. 'Exeter Services seems to be the gift which keeps on giving,' he laughed, referring to the arrival of his lorry a few months earlier. The transporter pulled up alongside, and with a hiss, the air brakes were applied. The driver, with a broad Scottish accent jumped down from his cab, came across to confirm he had the right drop off point.

'The horse has come from Scotland then?'

401

Max was puzzled, having anticipated an overseas delivery.

'Yes, come from Midlothian. Picked him up on Thursday. Can't say I won't be glad to see the back of im. I'm not fond of stallions.'

His co-drive then appeared, and they headed off to lower the ramp, so Max did the same on his lorry. He then stood excitedly waiting for the horse to appear. Seconds later, the familiar black head appeared on the top of the ramp. Max burst into tears.

'Sorry, don't you like him? Is it the colour?' Lottie teased.

Wiping his eyes with the back of his sleeve, Max replied. 'Christ I must stop crying every five minutes. And don't you dare send him back.'

Zhivago had been feeling out of sorts. He'd been whisked away from his friend Lee and delivered to a strange, cold place with no familiar face to greet him. Now, another long, lonely journey to some strange place filled with fumes, and no horses. He then recognised a voice he'd never forget. Looking down at Max he gave a relieved neigh. Max rushed up to grab him, throwing his arms around the stallion's neck. For once, Zhivago stood quietly, appreciating the reassurance, and didn't attempt to bite. He then followed Max happily, hopping up the ramp into the lorry for the drive to his new home.

Having unloaded him, Zhivago lifted his head and breathed in the air. Max decided to turn him out in a secure paddock for a few hours, so led him towards the yard for a rug change. As Zhivago entered the yard he spotted his beloved mare Tilly looking out over her stable door. Practically towing Max, he rushed towards her nickering gently. Tilly squealed in delight when she saw her mate. Zhivago nuzzled into Tilly's neck, practically purring with pleasure.

Max finally managed to pull them apart, and then, having put a turnout rug on Zhivago, led him down the lane to a small paddock, enclosed by high Devon hedges.

'Once Tilly's stronger, I promise she can come out with you,' Max told his horse. 'Kissing him, he slipped of the headcollar and Zhivago galloped off bucking and spinning. 'I don't reckon he's been out free like this since he was sold last year, poor chap,' Max said to Lottie who'd followed them down the track.

Chapter 36

Forty-eight hours later Simon Palmer received a phone call from a furious Lady Hardcourt. 'Did you know that that bloody Max Tarasov was the intended rider for that black stallion you insisted I sell?' she demanded, slightly over-egging the truth.

Simon thought it was irrelevant who had the horse. She'd had her money, and the horse had, in his opinion, gone to a much more suitable home. For an easy life however, he was prepared to lie through his teeth. After all, it was the kind of lie that never hurt anyone.

'I'm as shocked as you Estelle. The syndicate gave me the impression that they'd given the ride to Scott Brady. They even took the animal up to Scotland for a fortnight. I naturally assumed he was going to his new home, not going on a sightseeing tour of the Highlands.'

Although Lady Hardcourt was desperate to vent her fury, she was essentially a pragmatist. Simon flattered her by reminding her how her purchase of Zhivago the previous year had at least kept the animal in the country, and that was vital to Team GB. Accepting the praise, she calmed down.

As the news broke across the equine grapevine, Paul summoned Lee to his office.

Sitting behind a dusty, paper -strewn desk, Paul challenged him. 'Did you know about that bloody Max Tarasov getting the ride back on Zhivago?'

Lee stood in the small dingy office and, unable to help himself, smiled broadly. 'What seriously. Max has his old stallion back.'

'Come off it. Don't pretend you wasn't in on it?' Paul's henchman, Ryan stood in the doorway, his large body filling the frame, snarling.

'If you don't believe me, check my phone messages. I haven't spoken to Max for ages.' Lee wasn't easily intimidated, but he was starting to wonder whether he'd be getting out alive. His skin was hot and sticky, and he could feel his heart racing. He tried to remain calm, but at only 5ft 9 and lightly built, Lee was no match for the bully-boy brute of a yard manager.

'I expect loyalty from my staff. You I don't trust.' Paul, who had been seated, got to his feet. 'I don't like spies in my camp, and you are Tarasov's man. I reckon you've been tipping him off all the time you've been here.'

'I haven't,' Lee pleaded.

Paul walked around the desk and stood with his face up close to Lee, so Lee could smell stale coffee on his breath. 'I don't believe you, and I want you gone. I'm giving you an hour to get your things and leave my premises.' Paul's normally red face had turned crimson with anger.

'What about the wages I'm owed?' Lee was scared, but if he were to be jobless, he'd need to eat.

Paul reached in the pocket of his notorious

black puffa jacket and pulled out a wad of notes. Counting out three hundred pounds, he thrust them in Lee's hand before ordering him to piss off.

With the yard henchman, Ryan, breathing down his neck like a pit bull on heat, Lee went straight to the mobile home, his base for the last 8 months, and frantically began packing. He didn't have much in the way of possessions. He could fit his entire worldly goods in the back of his ancient VW Golf. Having spent most of his childhood in care; one kind, horsey foster family had taught him to ride, he'd always had jobs which came with cheap, cramped accommodation.

As Lee hurriedly stuffed his clothes into bin bags, Paul's henchman watched. Luckily Lee's car was parked just behind the mobile home, so he didn't have far to carry his belongings. With his every move being monitored, Lee trudged to and from the car, until the little Golf was stuffed with boots and hats, jackets, and jeans. Lee popped back to the mobile home for his last bits which contained a photograph of his mother – the only thing he had of her. He picked up his precious bag and stepped out of the mobile home. As he turned to shut the door, he was knocked backwards, falling to the ground. There was a searing pain in his face and his nose was bleeding.

'Get up,' yelled Ryan.

As Lee went to move, Ryan booted him in the ribs, 'I said get up you little shit.'

Winded, and barely able to breath, Lee tried to get up, and again got a kicking for his troubles.

Accepting that he was going to die, Lee rolled himself into a protective ball and closed his eyes. He just hoped it wouldn't take too long.

Suddenly there was a shout from the yard. Ryan gave Lee's back another violent kick, 'If you tell anyone about this, I'll make sure you never work in the industry again,' he snarled before he disappeared off into the distance. Lee's survival instinct kicked in, and he managed to drag himself to the car. His precious photo lay smashed on the floor. Extracting the battered picture from what remained of its frame, he managed to get open the car and gently lower his body inside.

The nearest hospital was ten miles away. Although he could barely drive; his face was swollen and every breath was agony, he had to get away. Somehow, he managed to get to the hospital and park up. As he tried to make his way down the hill to the hospital entrance he blacked out.

Several hours later, Lee woke and found himself in a hospital bed. Bandages covered his head. He tried to raise his hand to touch them but cried out in pain. He felt he'd been in a car crash. A pretty nurse came over and reassured him that he'd make a full recovery. He suddenly remembered abandoning his car in the car park. Rather panic struck; how would he cope if his car containing everything he possessed was impounded. The lovely nurse assured him that she'd have a word with one of the security guards, and make sure it was safe.

Four days later, Lee was told he was being discharged, but he'd need plenty of rest, and were there friends or family he could stay with. Lee was too embarrassed to admit that there was no one. He switched on his phone, hoping for inspiration, and found a missed call and a text message from Max, asking whether Zhivago was any better at travelling with mares. Hobbling out into the day room, Lee returned Max's call, knowing that Paul had travelled the stallion safely with mares in the same lorry load on several occasions. As he spoke, Max cut across him. 'Are you OK mate, you sound strange?'

'I've fractured my jaw.'

'What happened, were you hit in the face by a horse?'

Lee hesitated, and Max immediately guessed that things weren't OK. 'Lee, what happened?' he sounded stern.

'If you must know when Paul heard you'd got Zhivago he was furious and fired me. Thought I was your spy. His henchman gave me a pasting to make sure I didn't come back'.

'Christ, that's terrible. Were you badly hurt?'

'I am about to be discharged from hospital. I've broken my ribs and have a fractured jaw and skull.'

Lee heard the horror in Max's voice as he relayed the news to whomever was with him; he assumed Lottie. 'Poor Lee, has he got anywhere to go?' Lee heard her ask. 'Paul's sacked him, so I doubt it?'

'I can't believe Paul would be so cruel. Lee

408

could come here. We couldn't afford a decent wage, but at least he'd be safe.' Lee heard Lottie say.

Max called down the phone. 'Did you hear that? Come down here. Are you OK to drive? Can you remember how to get here? Grab a pen and I'll give you the postcode,' he instructed.

Lottie then took the phone from Max. 'Have you spoken to the Police?' she asked Lee.

'They did question me, but I couldn't say anything. Paul's henchman said if I said anything, he'd made sure I never worked in the horse industry again.'

'Bollocks.' Lottie sounded cross. 'Max will take you on. Someone needs to stand up to thugs like him. Please don't be afraid to tell the truth.'

The thought of a long drive, whilst in so much pain, made Lee feel quite sick, but the alternative was to sleep in his car, provided he didn't die of hypothermia first.

Having been discharged, he set the satnav for Devon, and buoyed himself up for the hundreds of miles drive. Before he set off however, he called the number he'd been given for the local police station and told them the truth. Twenty minutes later he found himself in an interview room at the local station where DNA swabs were taken of his clothing.

Having been released, he grabbed a sandwich and a coffee and headed off down the M1. He knew he shouldn't be driving after a head injury. A few times he nearly fell asleep at the wheel, but he was desperate to get to the safety and comfort of Max's home, and the thought of a soft bed, and a hot meal drove him to keep going. It was late afternoon when he reached Devon, and half an hour later, just as the sun was setting over the hills behind the house, he pulled into the driveway of Stapletor.

Beth had been on the lookout for him, and standing in the driveway, she directed him towards the farmhouse. As he turned the engine off Lee almost cried with relief. He was tired beyond belief, and his body was writhing in pain and discomfort. Moments later, surrounded by kind, welcoming faces, he was escorted into a warm kitchen, before being led upstairs to a cosy bedroom.

An hour later he and Max were sat at the kitchen table, eating a hot chicken casserole made by Beth. The first decent meal, Lee had eaten for months. Lee had been too scared to take the pain relief whilst he'd been driving, but now they were starting to take effect, and he was feeling much better. While Max filled him in on life at Stapletor, Lee sat and listened, hoping that this was somewhere he'd finally be able to call home.

'I've got the two girl grooms working for me,' Max explained. 'I'm sure you've seen them around. There is sweet, innocent Pippa, who is smarter than average, and almost certainly a virgin. The only time I tried flirting with her she nearly burst into tears. Then there's Dizzy who's the total opposite. I call her the hump jockey cause she'll ride anyone.'

Max then excused himself, as he had loads to

410

sort out as he was about to head off to Spain with the horses. Taking advantage of the peace, Lee headed off to bed, where he slept for twelve hours.

The next morning Lee slowly and painfully made his way downstairs and out into the yard. He stood motionless, taking in the scenery, and amazed by the tranquillity. Unlike the manic business of Paul's yard, there wasn't a horse to be seen in the yard, as they were all out in their paddocks. The only noise was birdsong. Lee admired the beauty of Stapletor House, which nestled in the pretty valley, surrounded by moorland hills.

An enormous grey dog, trotted around the corner from the house, regarding him with polite interest. Having inspected Lee, it headed off to the back of the stables. Lee slowly made his way across the yard. Despite his pain, he felt strangely contented. There was an aura of well-being and contentment, and he wanted to be part of it.

Max and two young grooms were at the back of the stables, loading the lorry with equipment and food in preparation for the trip to Spain. Having spotted Lee, Max re-introduced him to a pretty, slim, innocent-looking, attractive girl who he remembered was Pippa, and a shorter, equally attractive, big chested, but harsher young woman whom he knew was Dizzy.

Lee immediately found himself apologising for not being able to help. Max turned and said, 'You're not to lift a finger until you are completely recovered. Dizzy and I are off to Spain tomorrow morning. Beth and Pippa will hold the fort here,

411

as will Lottie when she's not working. Just relax
and enjoy the girls' making a fuss over you.'

Although Lee reckoned the stallion would
behave himself, Max decided to leave Cruz at
home. He'd only booked four stables and was
desperate to take Zhivago. Bearing in mind the
long journey, he didn't want to risk his stallion
getting horny and trashing the lorry, especially as
it was also Oberon's first trip abroad. Max and
Dizzy set off after breakfast and drove up to Dover.
Luckily the crossing was smooth, and then it was
off to central France where Max had booked
overnight livery for the horses, so they could have
a proper rest.

After a decent night's sleep, they headed off
for Madrid, and the show jumping Sunshine tour.
Many of the British riders had already arrived
before Max, although shortly after Max got there,
Paul rolled up with two lorries full of horses,
shortly followed by Ed driving an older, shabbier
vehicle and carrying his three best horses.

It wasn't until the evening, when Max was
doing his final check of the horses that he bumped
into Paul. Seeing the dumpy, sweaty
Yorkshireman, Max saw red. He yelled at Paul,
calling him a bastard and a coward. Paul, turned
around in surprise. There was no love lost
between the two men, but Paul was confused.
Even by Max's standards, the sudden turn of
aggression was unexpected.

'What du want?' he snarled.

Max faced up to Paul, and then grabbing him

412

by his collar, slammed him against the wall of the nearest stable. 'What you did to Lee was fucking inexcusable, you cunt,' Max yelled in his face.

Paul had been having regrets over firing Lee. He'd over reacted, and had lost a good worker, but couldn't see why Max was so upset. 'What's your problem? I fired him,' he panted, wondering if Max had gone mad.

'You and your fucking henchman put Lee into hospital.' The hatred flashed in Max's eyes. 'You left him for dead you bastard.' Max's hold tightened, making Paul nearly choke. 'I didn't lay a finger on him,' Paul spluttered, his round red face getting pucer by the second.

'No, you just get others to do your dirty work,' Max sneered. He then released Paul. 'You disgust me.' He practically spat the words out. 'Well you're going to pay. The police are looking to prosecute – GBH. You'll never ride for the British team again after this.'

'I really don't know what you are talking about,' Paul wined.

Max pulled out his phone from his back pocket. 'Look at these,' he said, handing Paul the phone showing pictures of Lee with his face swollen and bruised. Paul handed the phone back to Max. 'I would never condone this. I had no idea. You have to believe me.' He sounded panicky.

For all Max's dislike of Paul, he had a gut feeling that Paul was telling the truth. 'Let's hope you convince the police,' he said before turning and walking away into the darkness, satisfied that he'd made his point.

413

The next morning, Spanish police, acting under instruction from the Yorkshire constabulary, arrested Ryan and Paul, and they were taken away for questioning. A while later Paul returned on his own. Shaken and humbled, he slunk back to his lorry to lick his emotional wounds.

Over the next two weeks Max was very successful. Grateful to have his old friend back on board, Zhivago jumped his heart out and won the most lucrative grand prix class of the competition. Hope also won his first grand prix, and Oberon was top young horse. Even the slower Taggart managed to earn some decent prize money with some lower placings. Max transferred some winnings to the mysterious TM Associates and arrived back home with a healthy bank balance.

Chapter 37

Once back home, Max turned his attention to his project buys. Pippa had fallen in love with Rosy and had arranged to take her to a few one-day events once the ground dried up. Beth, who'd pretty much lost her nerve, had found reassurance in the placid, gentle Percy. Between Beth, Lottie, and a riding instructor friend, they'd been schooling Percy, and he was starting to show signs of improvement in his self-carriage and balance. Lee was on the mend, and although his ribs still hurt, had started to do small jobs around the yard.

As Max had predicted, Melissa May had got bored of owning a horse, and he received an email from her P.A saying that she wanted to sell Santa Cruz. Fortunately, she was asking a sensible price, so Lottie contacted Caroline and the owners syndicate, and they quickly came up trumps. Max was delighted, as he'd grown very fond of the mare, and it meant the last of his little herd was now safe.

Once Percy was up to scratch, he started to compete opposite Cruz. With six competition horses, Max organised things so that he effectively had two teams of horses, dividing them by skill. He made a team of Zhivago as his Grand Prix horse, Percy as speed horse, and Oberon, as his ride for the lesser classes. Then he had Hope, Cruz and Taggart as his other grouping. This ensured the stallions weren't put in the same lorry as the mare and meant each set of horses had a decent break between competitions. The only complications were with quarantine regulations, which were a bit of a headache.

One thing Max obsessed over was his fear of over jumping horses. In the past, this had led to digs from other riders about him being too soft. He didn't care what anyone else thought. He'd seen many a leg weary horse ruined over the years. He wanted his horses to love their job, and if this meant they were underutilised, then so be it.

In April Max took Hope, Taggart, and Cruz to the Spring London International show. He remembered London only four months earlier, where he'd been so scared of failure. With a few extra months of experience behind them, and some lucrative wins in good company, Max was starting to gain confidence in his horses.

Riders such as Marcus and Paul, as well as many of the top European riders, had whole strings of horses to compete, and in the main season simply flew from city to city, whilst their fleets of lorries tracked their way across Europe, and sometimes even further afield. Marcus was an exceptional rider, who could quickly adjust his style to whatever he was mounted on. Even still, it wasn't the same as having just a few special horses, with which one had a strong relationship.

The way that Max operated suited his style. Keeping things small meant that his overheads

416

were also lower. Admittedly having fewer horses meant injury to any one of them was more critical, but as his horses were lower mileage, the risks were smaller. His horses were happy, and as a result had fewer off days, and generally performed to their best at the top shows. For Max this translated into getting as much prize money as some of his competitors, with only a fraction of the rides.

Max's more relaxed methods meant he was never likely to stay in the top ten of the international rider rankings – he simply didn't compete enough for that. When it came to the big-ticket events however, by being able to focus properly, he stood a better chance of winning.

After a successful London competition, Max was starting to get noticed again. Potential sponsors started to court him, and the equestrian press began to get excited. Hope's sponsors were delighted with the publicity and fame of the charity shop horse, and for the first time in a year, Max was financially solvent. He secretly began to plan a big romantic gesture to seal his relationship with Lottie. He'd been told by Simon that he was a certainty for the European Championships in September. Max was determined to win gold, and to present it to Lottie as a unique engagement ring.

May brought a busy period to Max's team. The Longines grand tour hit European soil, and with fantastic prize-money on offer, it was essential to be part of it. First, there was a show jumping competition at The Palace of Versailles.

With such a romantic setting, Max asked Lottie to take time off work to spend the weekend with him at the show.

They arrived the day before the competition began. The horses were unloaded, and taken to the fabulous stable block, made of the same warm, golden stone as the palace. Once the horses were settled, Max, Lottie and Lee went for a walk around the grounds, attempting to get their bearings. They left the stable area and headed around to what they guessed was the front of the palace.

Directly ahead of them was the most magnificent fountain any of them had ever seen. Below the fountain was a lake in which there were huge statues, mainly comprising a chariot, with horses rearing up out of the water.

'I'm glad we don't have Taggart, he'd have a meltdown if he'd seen them,' Lottie remarked.

'I don't think Oberon will be too impressed either,' Max added.

Fortunately, the show jumping arena was further down the tree line, so the statues weren't directly in the horses' line of vision.

Max and the other riders had been invited to stay in the Palace, and it seemed that most had accepted the hospitality, which, on the final night, included a formal banquet hosted by the French president.

'Don't worry about me. I'll be OK with my can of beans, and my radio. You two go and live the high life,' Lee mocked, although in truth was looking forward to having the lorry to himself for once.

Rather than take their bags through the visitors' entrance, and having to carry them through the state rooms, guides were available to escort the competitors to the private section of the palace. Even with help, Max and Lottie felt quite exhausted, as they trudged down miles of corridors, looking to find their allocated accommodation.

Their room overlooked parkland. It was furnished practically, with modern style furniture, an ornate mirror being the only nod towards the classical. Max carefully unpacked his riding clothes, and his dinner jacket. He then headed for the window. 'This is the life,' he said with a contented sigh as he looked out across the splendid parkland.

Later that afternoon, they took all three horses out for some gentle exercise. With Lottie on Percy, Max on Zhivago and Lee riding Oberon, they followed the markers which led them out across the parkland behind the lakes. Being in such vast open spaces, both stallions began to jog impatiently, and Oberon bucked as Lee asked him for canter. Meanwhile Percy ambled along beside them, seemingly oblivious to what was around him.

On the way back to the stables they stopped to let the horses graze for half an hour before they were shut in their boxes for the night. They were just discussing whether to bother remounting to get back to the stables, when one of Paul's grooms rode past, riding one and leading two others.

419

Looking enviously at Lee, sat on the grass, enjoying the sun, she called out. 'Good to see you're OK Lee.'

He got to his feet and stretched lazily. 'It's a tough job working for team Tarasov, but someone has to do it I guess.'

'Did you hear that Ryan's been sent to prison for six months, and Paul has fired him. After what happened to you, loads of stuff came out about his bullying and violence. Hopefully we'll never have to see him again.'

'I'm glad. And thank goodness Paul's seen sense. I don't know what Paul saw in him, but the bloke was untouchable.'

'Apparently, one of Paul's major sponsors emailed him, furious that he employed such terrible staff, and they felt it reflected badly on their organisation. After that Ryan was out on his ear.'

'I wonder which sponsor that was?' Lee looked around at Lottie, who grinned. 'I can't imagine' she replied.

After they'd eaten, Max and Lottie joined the other competitors for drinks. The Palace had in recent years become a wedding venue, and thus had permanent catering staff, and fully stocked bars. The French riders were all in fine voice, thrilled to be showing off such a spectacular venue, and seemed to be getting up the noses of the Germans and Italians.

'Christ, you'd think he could be separated from that bloody puffa jacket in a venue like this,' Max said loudly as he stood behind Paul in the queue for drinks. The rest of the British riders within earshot sniggered. With two days of heavy competition ahead, everyone was being careful not to overdo things, and consequently the evening ended early as riders sloped off to bed.

It took Lottie and Max half an hour of wandering the corridors before they located their room. Feeling desperately horny, Max practically threw Lottie on the bed the second they got the door open. Lottie collapsed on the bed, giggling in excitement. Their work commitments had meant they'd hardly been in the same room together for weeks and were determined to make the most of it.

Max knew exactly which buttons to push to get Lottie turned on, and within minutes she was moist with excitement. Max came far too quickly and was frustrated with himself. 'I take it as a compliment.' Lottie insisted.

Lying on his side, his left hand caressing her naked breast, he spoke purposefully, 'I love you Lottie, and when we're married, I shall make love to you every night.'

'You haven't actually asked me yet,' she replied dreamily.

'I'm waiting to do the grand gesture. I haven't decided yet, but it might take a few months to arrange, so bear with me.' He leant over and kissed her breasts.'

'Sounds wonderful,' Lottie murmured, as she started to get turned on again.

The next morning Max was up at first light, as he was in the early speed class with Percy. It was

421

the brown gelding's first attempt at an international class, and although he enjoyed himself, his lack of experience showed through, and he ended up with 16 faults. Max was quick to reward him, as the horse simply needed more time and practice at the job before he had a hope of being as good as Cruz.

A group of French riders had watched his round, most of whom had been on the previous Olympic team. The ringleader, Max recognised as being Karen Allen's old flame Jacq. Sauntering arrogantly up to Max, he cast a critical eye over poor Percy. 'Vie is it, zat you ride so vell, and have your uge lorry, yet you fill it vith.. how do you say it.. bargin basin orses?'

'Admittedly I only paid £800 for this chap,' but he'll be good once he has a bit more experience.'

'Vhy vaste your time with such rubbish? Haven't you got some charity shop orse? Plus your reject stallion. You are mad.' He shook his head, and without waiting for a reply, he walked away.

Later in the morning Max jumped Oberon in the 1.40 metre class. Oberon had the most amazing scope, but again, as with Percy, he lacked experience, and lost balance coming down the final line. Bearing in mind his age however, Max was really pleased with the young stallion. Zhivago probably only had four- or five-years' competition life left, and he hoped that Oberon would be able to take over by then.

That evening Max was subjected to more

ribbing by the French riders. Frustrated, and unable to help himself, he challenged them to a bet. The offer of €1000 was taken up by Jacq, that Max would beat him in the following afternoon's Grand Prix class. With mocking laughter, the Frenchman gloated that it was going to be the easiest money he'd earn that year.

The following morning, Max's luck turned. He'd entered Percy in the one-round, against the clock 1.45m class, just for experience, rather than with any expectation. The course designer, to please the French President, had built the course with the final fence being in the furthest corner of the arena, and the finishing timing camera right by the entrance. This meant a crowd-pleasing fast gallop to the finishing line, which suited the rangy thoroughbred.

When it was Max's turn, he started off moderately carefully, as Percy wasn't used to jumping off a tight corner, and consequently slipped a little behind the leaders on time. Percy clobbered quite a few fences as he jumped, but for once, the poles stayed in their cups. They reached the final fence two seconds behind the leaders. Buoyed on by the shouts of the crowd, and Max's sudden pressure, as Percy landed over the final fence, he physically dropped his height by a couple of hands, and surged forward, reminding Max of the Aston Martin's sport mode.

Max almost shrieked with delight as the laziest racehorse on the planet, suddenly ran as if powered by rocket fuel. The crowds yelled excitedly as the pair stormed through the finish line. Unable to stop, Max shot passed the next competitor, who happened to be Ed, and careered out into the parkland, where he eventually managed to pull up. Percy's sides were heaving after his exertion. With his job done, he plodded back to the collecting ring, his head low, like a trekking pony.   With the wonderful finish, Max and Percy ended up coming second; the prize money of €5000 more than covering Percy's purchase price of £800.

By the afternoon, the spectators had arrived in their droves to watch the major class of the day. With first prize of €75,000, it had attracted most of the top European riders, and especially the French, who wanted to do well in front of the home crowd. Max was well placed towards the end of the class, but the downside was that he had more time to feel nervous. Zhivago was fresh, and bucked his way around the warm-up arena, as if deliberately playing into the hands of the French. Paul glared at Max's back, as Zhivago's hooves came close to his horse's face. He'd never let the animal get away with such bad behaviour.

Max understood his horse far better than anyone else, and by the time they entered the arena, Zhivago had switched his attention and was ready to focus on his job. Consequently, the partnership produced a faultless first round, much to the delight of the small band of British supporters, who had already enjoyed clear rounds from Ed, Marcus and Giles.

The second round followed with an equally impressive round for Max. Paul got four faults, as

424

did Marcus. This meant that of the British riders, it was just Max, Giles and Ed in the jump off. This time Max had the worst of draws and had to go first. His only option was to try and set an almost impossible time, and hope the others made mistakes trying to beat him.

There were only seven fences, including a large spread, followed by a tight little upright, and finishing with a gallop to the second and third parts of the treble. Zhivago was old enough to know the game and felt like a coiled spring as he entered the arena. As the buzzer went off Max pushed him towards the first fence. The pair they turned as tight as they dared into a fence modelled on the Eifel Tower. Fence three was easy, but then came the huge spread, which needed to be jumped off three strides. Almost impossible for most horses, Zhivago's incredible power got them safely over.

He hurriedly brought Zhivago back under control as six strides later was the tight little upright, which had light poles which fell so easily. Then, risking it all and putting faith in his horse, Max asked for gallop, and the pair charged towards the final two fences. A less experienced horse would have been too flat to jump such huge fences, but as Zhivago hit his last stride he instinctively bunched himself up and sailed over the fences. The crowds, realising they'd seen something very special, went nuts. Max was so overjoyed by his darling horse, tears of gratitude streamed down his face as he slowed to a walk.

There were twenty other competitors in the

jump off, and one by one they failed to meet Max's target. There were some who thought that beating Max was pretty much impossible, and aimed for a safer clear, hoping to safeguard some decent prize-money Ed gambled on beating Zhivago, but with a lesser horse he crashed the final line. The French were determined to win on home ground and pulled out all the stops. Jacq rode hell for leather and going to the final two fences he was on an identical time. Not trusting his horse, he checked him a stride off the double, unbalancing it, and there was the sickening thud of a pole hitting the ground. The partisan crowd groaned in dismay.

As the results were announced, Lottie cheered, and turned to hug a delighted Max. As other competitors swamped Max, Lottie gave Lee a hug.

'We'd better go and fetch Zhivago,' he said, and the two of them hurriedly pushed through the crowds and ran back to the stables.

Zhivago had been dosing and was most put out when his tack was thrown on him by Lottie. Lee then mounted the disgruntled stallion, and trotted off towards the arena where the prizegiving was due to take place. Lottie walked back down the hill. Ahead of her, the arena party were stacking the show jump wings onto a large flatbed trailer, and staff were preparing the ground for the President.

As Lottie reached the competitors section, she flashed her pass at the security guard, and headed off in search of Max. She spotted him and made her way across the grass to where he was stood waiting for further instruction. As soon as he noticed her, he beckoned her over. As she got within earshot, he leant down and in a quiet voice said, 'Winning always makes me horny. I can't wait to rip your clothes off and give you the ride of your life.'

'Would you like to hand me your phone so I can take some pictures?'

'What – of my love making. Not sure the sponsors would approve of that darling?'

Saying nothing, but with a disapproving glare, she grabbed his phone out of his pocket – much to Max's amusement.

Within moments, the military band struck up a fanfare and the crowds cheered the French president. Then, in reverse order the riders were invited back into the arena. Ed rode in first on Lady Hardcourt's beautiful grey Holstein, followed by one of the French riders. Giles was 5th. The World Champion Frederick Seipp was 3rd and the oldest rider of the French team second. Bringing up the rear was Max on his stunning, gleaming black stallion.

As Max was handed his prize by the President, he looked so happy, Lottie almost cried. The FEI TV cameras whizzed overhead, and the lenses of the press were concentrated on the winners. Lottie hurriedly took some photos of her own for the website and blog and took some on Max's phone. She just wished she knew who TM Associates were, and whether they even knew what was happening.

Despite Max's promise, once they were back at the stables, he decided that the three horses should enjoy some more grass eating time before being shut away in the stables for the night especially as the following morning they were due to leave for Germany. Therefore, once Zhivago had been untacked, they grabbed head-collars, and led the horses back out into the parkland to munch on the grass. From their prime spot, they watched the crowds disbursing. Some of the riders were also heading off, although most had elected to stay for the presidential banquet.

Once the horses were satisfied, they were taken back to the stables. Lee, along with the other grooms, and many of the show-ground crew were due to attend a party in one of the barns. Max and Lottie then headed back to their room to get changed. Max hurriedly dived in the shower, and then appeared still damp, and naked. His muscular torso, enhanced by the shimmer of water droplets, gave him the appearance of an Adonis. His golden hair, sleek and swept back off his face, simply emphasised his cheek bones, and showed off his beauty. As he dried himself with a towel he spoke in Russian, telling her how much he loved and adored her.

Lottie, who was partially undressed, dropped her jeans, and shrieked with the sheer joy of the moment. 'Oh my god you are so sexy when you do that,' she said as she melted underneath him. Max gazed at her, totally in love with this wonderful girl who saw such pleasure in the little things in life.

In the past, Max would have been fired up by a line of coke, but there was no need; reality in its pure sense was thrilling enough to satisfy him now. He bit his lip hard, trying not to climax too early. Lottie was so powerful, she could make him come with just a few, well timed, squeezes. Luckily, he managed to hold himself together until both had been satisfied.

They dressed for dinner, Max put on his dinner jacket, and Lottie put on a slinky, silk dress. They headed down to the most amazing room. Along its sides were gold, Greek style statues and in each hand held a crystal candelabra. Matching chandeliers hung down from the ornately decorated arched ceiling. Uniformed waiters carrying trays of drinks and canapés wandered amongst the guests. The room led through to an equally splendid dining room. Here a long table ran the length of the room. At the end the table went into a T shape and was where the President was to be seated in full view of the guests.

Amongst the showjumpers and their partners, mingled sponsors and high-ranking dignitaries including various foreign ambassadors. Max soon spotted Jacq who now owed him a thousand Euros and headed him off before he reached the safety of his fellow countrymen.

Having initially pretended to have forgotten about the bet, he then tried to get out of it by pretending it had just been a joke.

'Had it been the other way around, you would have made me pay, so honour your agreement,' Max stood firm. Reluctantly he pulled out a wad of notes from his back pocket. 'Here, take it,' he said sulkily. 'It may be a bit short.' Turning on his heals he slunk off. Max quickly flicked through the €820 notes. Smiling, he shoved the money into his inside pocket, planning to share the spoils later with Lottie and Lee.

For most of the British riders it had been a lucrative couple of days, and they were in good spirits. The exception was Paul, who was feeling desolate. His pride was badly wounded by his failure with Zhivago. He'd been convinced that the horse was no good, but he could no longer kid himself. Max was a better rider. He watched enviously as Max kissed his lovely girlfriend. They looked so good together. He'd never minded about Cindy. She was beautiful, but also a bitch. Lottie however wasn't just attractive. She was kind, clever and resourceful, and the perfect wife for a showjumper.

Paul wished he'd made more of an effort with Lottie at the start. If things had worked out it could have been him sat with her by his side, rather than yet again, arriving alone. He had plenty of staff at his disposal, and amongst them there were always a couple of girls happy to bed him, but he knew they were after a few extra privileges, and boasting rights. None of them cared about him as a person.

Before everyone could get too boozy, dinner was called. As the winner of the competition, Max was invited to dine at the far end of the long table, within conversational distance of the President

430

himself, and Lottie was directed to sit opposite him. To Lottie's right, and at the end of the top table, was the British Ambassador, and on her left, much to her amusement, one of the corporate sponsors from Renault Motors. Max had the French President's wife to his left, and a famous French singer, rumoured to be the President's lover on his right.

Lottie had an easy time. The Renault man spoke good English and quizzed her on Yangtze. The British Ambassador knew her step-uncle Crispin, his sons, and Ivan Tarasov, which afforded plenty of opportunity for polite small-talk. Max's ability to speak French was limited to school-boy basics, and neither woman spoke much English. The French singer did speak passable German, so Max managed to converse with her. She wasn't easy to understand, but Max quickly got the impression that she was attempting to flirt with him.

Max only drank in moderation during the meal. As conversation with his neighbours was hard work, he spent time quietly people watching, and studying Lottie, who oblivious to his stares was deep in discussions over marketing strategy. He smiled indulgently, thinking how beautiful and clever she was, and how lucky he was to have her.

Suddenly conscious of her boyfriend's gaze, Lottie turned and smiled broadly. 'Are you OK?' she asked.

'Everything's great,' he replied.

Realising he was not engaged in conversation,

Lottie introduced him to the British Ambassador, resulting in a long discussion on Putin, and Ivan Tarasov's opinions.

The next morning when Max and Lottie reached the stables, Lee was already there, but looking extremely hung over. Upon seeing his boss, he moaned. 'How come you don't look like shit? You're usually worse than me?'

'I barely drank anything, that's why.'

'But....' Lee was temporarily lost for words.'Why?' he added feebly.

Max smiled smugly. 'I've grown up a lot over the last 12 months. I now have everything I could wish for, and don't need to get off my face to make my happiness complete.' Max headed into Zhivago's stable to check the horse's legs. 'Anyway,' he added, 'I don't know who TM Associates are, and I wouldn't want to frighten them off with tabloid horror stories of drunken disorderly behaviour in front of the President of France.'

After a final hack around the beautiful grounds, Max and Lee set off to Hamburg, following the rest of the show jumping travelling circus, for the next leg of the Longines Grand Tour. Lottie headed back home.

Chapter 38

Max and Lee arrived home a week later, with some more good prize money, and after a few days' recovery headed back to Cannes with Hope, Taggart, and Cruz. This time they took Dizzy with them.

After some useful placings in Cannes, they went to Monaco, and finally back to Brittany for a Nations Cup, where along with Ed, Mary and Paul, came 2nd in the competition, having been narrowly beaten by the Germans. Again, after a few days at home, Max, Lee and Pippa headed back to Paris with the two stallions and Percy before finishing in Berlin.

Max finished the month by taking Hope to Hickstead. Then in August saw the Longines Grand Tour come to London. The competition was hotting up, as there were several riders wanting to maximise their points to qualify for the final being held in Dubai in November. Max hadn't competed in enough legs of the tour to be in the running for the final and the $1m prize, but he really wanted to win the $500k top prize in front of the home crowd.

Since his win in France, Max hadn't really pushed Zhivago. They'd got plenty of placings, but Max didn't like to ask his beloved horse to give of his all too often. Zhivago was feeling better than he'd ever felt. The rotating with Hope meant he got a decent chance to rest between competitions, and having just spent a week on rich meadow grass, he was feeling explosive.

Lottie had brought Beth and Nick up to London to support him, and they watched nervously as Zhivago bucked his way around the course in the first round, narrowly avoiding rolling a couple of poles. Fortunately, by the second round the stallion was more settled, and focused on his job and flew around the course making the massive 1metre 60 course look easy.

By the time the competition reached the jump off there were still 30 competitors in the running, including all the top German riders, the Americans, and a couple of Qatari princes on the best horses money could buy. Lottie quickly slipped out to wish Max luck, and as she walked past the VIP corporate hospitality area, she glanced in the window and could have sworn that she saw Ivan Tarasov.

After his good second round, the book makers had shortened the odds of a home win, with Max as joint favourite with Frederick Seipp on his great horse Wolfgang, already winners of the Munich, and Mexico legs. Marcus was an early starter, but had to be content with a steady, accurate clear. His top ride was lame, so he'd brought the relatively inexperienced Harvey, who he'd purchased from Ivan Tarasov fourteen months earlier. Ed followed him on his horse Trooper. Although he was a decent jumper, he wasn't in the elite, and his lack of talent meant he had the bogey fence down.

Paul wasn't having a good summer and was convinced that karma was getting her revenge for his appalling treatment of Lee. He got clear, but as he was desperate for at least some prize money, didn't gamble and instead played safe.

Husband and wife team of Giles and Mary, both gave it their best shot, with Giles having won the London leg the previous year. Giles was on his top stallion and rode a superb round, knocking 3 seconds off the best time so far.

Finally it got to Max's turn. Giles was still in the lead, with one of the American's close on his heels in second place, Karen's former French lover Jacq in third and one of the Qatari princes was in forth. As Max rode back into the arena the mainly English crowd started yelling and cheering, which made Max feel quite sick with fear. Zhivago was an applause junkie and put in a huge buck, before springing into a high stepping passage trot as Max tried to ride him passed the judge's box, much to the delight of the spectators.

As soon as the buzzer sounded, Zhivago switched into work mode, immediately changing from high school dressage movements to his best, springy working canter. Zhivago was experienced enough to know this was the fast-jumping bit, after all this was the last round, and his rider always felt so much tenser. Seconds later he locked on to the first jump, and off he went, his ears flicking between listening to Max, and concentrating on the upcoming fence.

As they sailed over the first fence, Max felt

like shouting out with joy. Zhivago felt like he had wings. Trusting his horse implicitly, Max took every possible chance, cutting almost impossibly tight between the third and fourth fences. The whole arena fell into collective silence, barely daring to breathe, as Zhivago powered off the ground at the steepest of angles, shaving at least two seconds off Giles's time. With two fences remaining, Zhivago was starting to tire, but desperate for crowd adulation, he used every ounce of his remaining energy to power home.

As they landed clear, the crowds erupted in appreciation at the black stallion's superb performance. As his grateful rider pulled him back to a walk, Zhivago raised his head and looked out into the crowd, enjoying the moment. He quickly flattened his ears and glared as Wolfgang cantered passed him and into the arena.

Out in the collecting ring, Lottie and Lee were ready with a supply of treats, whilst Max, having risked kissing his horse on the nose, rushed off to the side of the arena to watch his old trainer at work. For the next forty seconds, Frederick and Wolfgang rode a round that was a masterpiece of control and balance. Although fast and beautiful to watch, he was half a second slower. Max had won the half a million Euros.

As Max and Zhivago left the arena for the final time, the stallion now had a beautiful red rug covering his quarters, and his bridle festooned with ribbons, Clara Barker asked for an interview. Max dismounted, and handed the reins to Lottie, asking her to take him back to the stables. Joined by Lee, who was equally delighted, having just won £500 on a bet he'd placed the week before, they weaved around the well-wishers coming to congratulate them.

'Hello Zhivago,' came a child's voice. 'You're Grandad's special horse.' Lottie spun around to see Crispin clasping the hand of his horse mad Granddaughter.

'How lovely to see you,' Lottie blurted out in surprise. Then, as something else to say, added, 'Lee, this is my step-uncle the Duke of Chiswick, and his son Will's little girl Emily. Lee looks after Zhivago.'

Cautiously approaching Zhivago, Crispin tentatively patted the horse on the shoulder. 'Hello Zhivago, I'm Emily,' said the little girl. Turning to Lottie she said, 'Can I sit on him please?'

'He's rather unpredictable,' warned Lee. 'Not exactly a riding school pony.'

Lottie's mind was working overtime. If Crispin really was a part owner, then it was important to keep the interest. 'If you do exactly as you are told, I will let you sit on him.' Giving the little girl a leg up she lifted her onto Zhivago's back. Normally he would have tried to bite, but he was tired, and ready for a hard feed and a rest, so he happily plodded back to the stable lines.

As they got to the security guards, Emily had to be lifted off. Even a Duke couldn't get to the stables without the right paperwork. There were too many valuable horses at risk. Lee took Zhivago to his stable, whilst Lottie escorted the

437

Marchbanks back to the VIP area.

'Have you seen Nick yet? He's here with my mum.'

'I haven't yet, but they are staying with us tonight so we can have a catch up later.'

'It's great that you were able to come today, especially with Max winning.' Lottie chatted cheerfully, hoping that Emily's childish indiscretion would reveal more information on TM Associates. Having failed, she turned to Crispin, and said, 'I'm sure I saw Max's father Ivan in the hospitality tent earlier. Of course I couldn't be sure. Did you notice him? Max will be thrilled if it was.'

As a professional politician, capable of outwitting any poker player, Crispin kept a completely neutral expression on his face. Without a flicker of doubt, he said. 'No sorry. I've only ever met him briefly so wouldn't easily recognise him.' Lottie gave up, offering to fetch Nick, thus relieving her of the obligation of further small talk.

Max finished the interview, and headed to the bar for a celebration drink, whilst catching up on the gossip. As he was walking back from the loos, his mobile buzzed. It was a text from Simon Palmer informing him he had a guaranteed place on the British team to go to the European Championships in October. Smiling to himself, he thrusted his phone into his back pocket. Not looking where he was going, he smacked headlong into one of the most beautiful women on the planet.

'Oh I'm so sorry,' he exclaimed. 'Oh Cindy, I didn't realise it was you for a second – how are you?'

'Hi Max. Good to see you,' she purred suggestively.

'Christ, you look well.' Dressed in the most flattering, figure-hugging dress, she looked stunning.

'Congratulations on your win.' Leaning into him, she slowly kissed him on the lips.

'Thank you, but it was my amazing horse. I've managed to get him back.'

'Yes I know,' Cindy took hold of his shirt sleeve, and led him outside where there were fewer people around. Once they were out of earshot she said, 'I missed you so much, I wanted to win you back, so I secretly bought your favourite horse off that terrible woman.'

'You're TM Associates?' Max was astounded.

Cindy paused. 'I got my lawyers to make all the arrangements. I didn't actually know what they'd called it.'

'And you did it for me?' Max gazed in awe at her. He could barely believe it. The vision of exquisite beauty stood beside him, had purchased his beloved Zhivago.

'I want you back. I thought this would be the most wonderful way to demonstrate how much I still care.'

A hundred different emotions ran through Max's head as he tried to take in the news. 'Cindy, I don't know how I can ever thank you?'

'By being mine,' she lifted her hand and

gently stroked his handsome face.

Max placed his hand over hers. 'But things are complicated. I love Lottie. I live with Lottie and her family. My business is integrated with Lottie.'

Cindy shushed him by kissing him full on the lips. 'I'll share you for now.' She paused. 'Just don't disappoint me, otherwise your horse will be sold.'

'Do you want to come and see him?' he asked, unsure of what else to say.

'No thanks. These boots cost ten thousand pounds. I'm not going anywhere near those smelly stables. Just come to the apartment later.'

Still reeling, Max headed back to the stables. They were meant to be heading home to Devon. At least Lee could take the lorry back. As he reached the stables, he suddenly remembered having seen a child perched on Zhivago's back. Lottie was cleaning out the temporary stables. As she heard his footsteps, she appeared at the stable door, her black jeggings covered in bits of shavings, and slobber stains on her shirt. Her hair looked like it hadn't met a brush for days, and she had mud on her cheek, but when she spotted him, her face lit up.

'What the fuck did you think you were doing using Zhivago for kiddy pony rides?'

'Crispin's granddaughter just sat on him as we led him back. There was no harm done,' Lottie looked confused. Then her face broke into an excited smile. 'I think I know who TM associates are. That's why I was being nice to my uncle. I'm

440

certain he's one of the investors.'

'You're wrong.' Stress and guilt had put him on edge.

'But you've got to understand. Little Emily said Zhivago was their horse. Why else would Crispin be here. He doesn't do horses. Plus I saw your father in the hospitality area. TM Associates must stand for Tarasov Marchbank.'

'Sorry to burst your bubble, but you are making something out of nothing. I found out earlier today who bought Zhivago.'

'So who is it?' Lottie asked impatiently.

'Cindy'

'Cindy! That can't be right. ... I mean... Why?'

'She says she still loves me.'

'But it doesn't make sense?' Lottie looked bewildered.

Max snapped. 'No, you just don't want to believe it. That's the truth.'

'OK, so I'm not ecstatic about the news, but it doesn't make sense that she should be the owner.'

'Well it's a fact, so you'd better start accepting it.' Max sounded far harsher than he meant too, but he had to get Lottie to see the truth. Irritated, he turned and headed off towards the lorry.

Chapter 39

As Lee and Lottie headed back to Devon in the lorry, Max took a taxi across the city to Canary Wharf. As the driver crawled through the dirty London streets, Max felt a pang of homesickness for Stapletor, but as he reached Cindy's apartment, his mood lifted dramatically. She met him at the door, naked except for a fur coat. Within ten minutes he was snorting a line of coke off her hard, pert bottom, before they had the most glorious sex.

Max felt he was on fire. Cindy has zero inhibition, and nothing was out of bounds. Having lain on the bed, watching the river traffic below, Max started to feel hungry. Wanting to thank Cindy, he offered to take her out for a meal, and then on to a club. Whilst they dressed Cindy asked, 'Have you managed to thaw miss Frigid Knickers yet?'

'Yes, and she isn't actually frigid – just scared off by a bad experience.'

Cindy sceptically raised a perfectly shaped eyebrow, so Max relayed the story.

'Sounds like a right drip. Can't see her being your sort of girl.' Feeling disloyal, Max said nothing in Lottie's defence.

After a great night of clubbing and catching

up with old friends. Max got out of bed at lunchtime and had a leisurely brunch before travelling back to Devon, getting to Plymouth train station in the early evening. Lee came to collect him, but on the journey back seemed withdrawn.

Having freshened up, Max headed off to the yard to see the horses. As he arrived, Lottie and Pippa rode into the yard on Taggart and Hope, having been for a hack. He slipped into Zhivago's empty stable to avoid a confrontation, but after the girls had turned the horses back out in the field, they went their separate ways, and Max took the opportunity to corner Lottie on her own.

'Sorry I had to shoot off yesterday. You got home OK?'

'Clearly,' she answered sarcastically.

Max felt a rush of irritation. 'Cindy's an owner, and we have to accept that she will have her demands.'

'I don't have to accept anything,' Lottie snapped. 'I don't believe she's anything to do with TM Associates, and I won't treat her as an owner.'

'Well how do you explain the fact that she knew Zhivago cost £1 million?' Max half shouted.

'I don't have all the answers, but the evidence points to Crispin and your father being the secret owners. Maybe Cindy knows someone who works for Tarasov Industries or Marchbank estates?'

'Well I know Cindy still loves me, and Zhivago is her way of showing it. She's happy to share me, so why can't you?'

Lottie looked at him in disbelief. 'You need a

serious reality check, if you imagine for one second that I'll go along with that.'

'Well what do you want?' Max yelled. 'Are you going to kick me out? If so, just fucking say it?'

'Of course I don't want to kick you out. You're still my business partner, even if you've dumped me for Cindy.'

'At least if you were screaming and shouting, and packing my bags, I'd know you cared.' Max glowered.

'In case you'd forgotten, this isn't all about you. There are three people relying on you for a job and a roof over their heads. Neither can you keep two stallions in a penthouse in Canary Wharf. My feelings for you don't come into it.'

'Why are you so fucking British?' Max practically spat out the words, before storming off back to the farmhouse. 'It's because I still love you,' Lottie replied quietly to his retreating back.

Feeling very hard done by Lottie called for Shadow and headed off home. Beth and Nick were still in London, otherwise she would have run to her mother. Desperate to unload, she called Tom. Luckily, he was at Dewerstone, and insisted on driving over immediately with Verity and offering to pick up a large box of chocolates on route.

Half an hour later, loaded down with comfort food, Tom and Verity arrived. They were met by a tear-stained Lottie, her eyes puffy from crying.'Oh, you poor thing,' Verity said sympathetically. Tom put his hand on Lottie's shaking shoulders and guided her back into the sitting room.

'Why don't you kick him out?' Tom asked. 'If you're scared, I'll do it for you.'

Lottie explained that it was hardly fair on the staff or the horses, and that her and their mum loved having team Tarasov on site.

'No, the problem is Cindy,' Lottie sniffed. 'I can't prove that she isn't Zhivago's owner, but I have some evidence that Uncle Crispin is.'

Tom looked shocked. 'Why would Uncle Crispin buy a million-pound horse? That's completely unlike anything he'd do.'

Lottie explained about the slip up with Emily. 'Also, I reckon that most of the money came from Ivan Tarasov. He probably feels a bit guilty about selling the horse in the first place, and then, having got his feet under the high table of the Conservative party, probably wanted to repay his son.'

'It was you that introduced Ivan to Crispin,' Verity said.

'Theoretically, but Max played his part, which is all Ivan will care about. Anyway, I think Ivan is too proud to just buy back Zhivago, hence all the cloak and dagger stuff.'

Verity looked puzzled, 'So how does you uncle fit in with this theory?'

'It's the cloak and dagger stuff. If Ivan is just part of a horse owning syndicate, then it's not so blatant that he has gone back on his word. Crispin has probably only invested a small amount, but enough to make the syndicate appear genuine. It

445

also adds credulity to Tarasov Marchbank Associates.'

Lottie felt better. Her brother and Verity didn't think she was mad, and the conversation switched to wedding plans. An hour later, Lottie's phone buzzed. Looking at the screen, it was a text from Max. She opened it hoping for an apology.

Lottie. Guess all you want is a showjumper to make you feel good. Paul Denton likes you and is getting desperate. Sure he'll have you. M

Lottie was determined not to take it to heart. She'd known Max long enough to realise how spiteful he could be, especially when drunk. Not wishing to end up in a text cat fight, she replied, *not the best chat up lines I've ever read. Btw your foreplay sucks.*

Lee got a call from Max, asking to be picked up from the local pub. Having just got to bed, Lee grumpily threw on some clothes before heading off in the car, down to the village. When he got there, Max was standing outside, looking cross. Climbing into the car, he slammed the door, and started his rant.

'After all we've been through, I thought Lottie would go nuts over Cindy, but no, not her. She's so fucking righteous,' he paused for breath. 'She clearly doesn't love me; else she'd have cared enough to react.'

'I saw Lottie earlier mate, and she's gutted. She ain't no spoilt little madam who's going to ruin our lives just to score points. From what I know of her, she'll be playing the long game.'

446

Max read out the message he'd sent to her earlier. Lee stopped the car. 'That's just cruel,' he snarled, not caring that Max was his boss. 'She don't deserve that.'

'I want a woman with passion and spirit.' Max answered dramatically.

Lee hated it when Max was in this mood. The drunken, cocaine induced comedowns made him unpredictable, impatient, and nasty. Since Cindy's exit, Max had become a much nicer person, but now the bitch was back on the scene, Max was reverting to type.

Having dropped Max off at the house, Lee excused himself and headed back down to Lottie's lodge. He'd seen that her light was still on, and wanted to make sure she was OK As he stopped his car, the door opened and Lottie's brother and girlfriend stepped outside.

'Good evening Lord Marchbank, Miss Verity,' Lee politely acknowledged them. 'I just wanted to make sure that Lottie was all right.'

'Thank you,' Tom answered gently, as Lottie stuck her head out to see who'd arrived.

'Hello Lee. I don't normally see you down here.' Lottie sounded surprised.

'I just been to the pub to collect Mr Tarasov. I'm so sorry about his text, that was bloody out of order.'

Lottie smiled weakly. 'Had he said it to my face, I'd have thrown something at him. Revenge by text isn't the same.'

'Don't take it personal, when he's on a drunken cocaine binge comedown he's always a cunt.'

Lottie laughed. 'Don't hold back there Lee. Say it as it is.'

Max never mentioned the text to Lottie. He simply switched to indifferent professional mode whenever they were together. The atmosphere was strained when they did talk, but then Max headed off to the Netherlands with Hope, Taggart, and Cruz - it made home life less tense for Lottie.

Max had some good wins, and Hope came 3rd in the final round of the Longines, which was quite a feat bearing in mind his lack of experience, but he so loved his work, that Max could push him a little bit more each time they competed. The RSPCA were delighted with their ten percent, and Hope's sponsors loved the publicity. It seemed to Lottie that she was the only one not benefiting from her precious horses.

Whilst at home, the charity promoting the retraining of racehorses came to interview Lottie and do a photo-shoot of Percy. He was still nowhere near as accurate as Cruz, but since his success in France, he'd notched up some lower placings in other FEI competitions, which made him somewhat of a superstar. With his adorable nature, Lottie had fallen in love with him, and had decided that if Max packed up his bags, and nags, and left, she would try to buy Percy for her and her mum to share.

Chapter 40

Max arrived back a week later, and immediately shot up to London to spend a couple of days with Cind y. When he returned to prepare for the trip to Aachen for the European Championships, he looked tired. Luckily there wasn't too much to do, as Lee and the girls had become expert at changeovers. Max was secretly pleased to be home. Cindy's appetite for partying was insatiable, and having been tired from his trip away, he'd then barely slept, and survived London on a mix of speed, coke, and coffee.

Lottie had been out for a hack on Percy. When she arrived back at the yard, she politely greeted Max. Having dismounted, she untacked, and slipped on Percy's headcollar, ready to lead him back to the field.

'May I join you for the walk?' Max asked tentatively.

'Of course,' Lottie felt a wave of optimism. He looked terrible, and she hoped that maybe he was already tiring of Cindy.

They were partway down the lane when Max cleared his throat. Lottie turned to look at him. He hesitated, looking awkwardly at the floor, he spoke.

'Cindy wants to come to Aachen to watch her horse compete. Given the circumstances, and your hostility towards her, I think it's best for everyone if you don't go.'

'Well that's too bad. I've got to go.' Lottie practically snarled in disgust.

'Why do you have to go?' Max demanded.

'Yangtze want me to wine and dine the directors and do some more publicity with the sponsored riders. You remember Yangtze? My employers? The ones who paid for the lorry you use?'

'Well if you have to go, then stay out of my way. I don't want Cindy upset.'

Lottie opened the field gate, handed Percy a carrot and released him into the paddock. Turning to face Max, she gave a half smile. 'Cindy get upset! That woman has the sensitivity of a nuclear bunker.'

'She doesn't like it that you don't believe she's the owner.'

'Truth hurts.' Lottie shrugged indifferently.

Max felt terrible. Cindy had made it clear that she didn't want Lottie around. Now Cindy had the ultimate hold over him, she could twist him around her little finger. Although she told Max how much she loved him, and had bought Zhivago as a token of love, she was also quick to use him as a bargaining chip whenever she wanted her own way. With the horse's recent success, Cindy regularly reminded Max that the stallion could easily be sold for a profit.

As utterly grateful as Max was for the chance to get his beloved horse back, Cindy was starting to extract a high price. He was now burning his bridges with the one woman with whom he'd wanted marriage and a family. He knew he was being a total shit, but he was trapped. Desperate not to carry on the argument, he hopped over the fence into Tilly's field, and headed off away from Lottie, his eyes stinging with tears. Lottie headed home, and having turned on her tablet, changed her Facebook relationship status back to single, and ditched the remaining packet of her contraceptive pills.

Max and Pippa headed off early for the European championships, as there was a warm up competition two days before in a large equestrian centre fifty miles from the Aachen show-ground Pippa had spent most of the summer at Stapletor, mainly because she was building up a relationship with Rosy. Having had some success at some local British Eventing competitions, her parents had asked Max if he'd sell them the mare. Not wishing to make a huge profit off the back of Pippa's dedication, he agreed a fair price and the deal was done. He then insisted that she come to Europe, as Lee needed a break, and he foresaw a clash between Dizzy and Cindy.

Having jumped a quiet, clear round on Zhivago, in the first class, Max headed off to the stands to watch the rest of the riders. Pippa had thrown a rug over Zhivago's back, and was leading him around the warm-up arena, to keep his muscles warm. Pippa was happily chatting away to the black stallion, not really concentrating, but happened to glance up just as

Paul's name was called by the ring steward. Paul raised his hand in acknowledgement and quickly turned and popped over the practice fence one more time.

As his horse landed, Paul suddenly slid sideways, and came off, falling heavily on his back. The horse shot forward, nearly cannoning into Zhivago who squealed in irritation. Pippa just managed to hold onto the stallion, and then, through pure luck, grabbed the rein of Paul's horse, yanking it to a halt.

Paul, looking red faced and cross had got to his feet, and limping slightly, headed over to Pippa. It was only as Paul, with a muttered thank you, took hold of the bridle, that Pippa realised his left stirrup leather had snapped – clearly the cause of the accident.

The unsympathetic steward was crossly telling Paul to hurry up or his entry would be scrapped. Thinking quickly, Pippa yanked one of the stirrups and leathers off Zhivago's saddle and gave it to the now very flustered Paul. Having taken the broken bits, Pippa gave him a leg up into the saddle, and he shot forward into the arena.

After the shock of the fall, Paul felt unsettled, but for the first time in months luck was genuinely on his side, and he managed a clear round. By the time he came out the arena, one of his grooms had torn back to the lorry to get a replacement leather, scared that they'd be blamed for not noticing the frayed stitching. As Paul came back to a halt, the groom braced himself for the inevitable bollocking, but instead Paul was calm and almost distant. The groom, assuming mild concussion, was just pleased to be getting away without punishment.

Paul dismounted, and having removed the loaned stirrup and leather, marched across the arena, and over to Pippa.

'Thank you. It was very good of you to help me. I just hope you don't get in trouble from Max for assisting the enemy,' he said kindly.

'I'm j-j-just glad you're OK,' Pippa stuttered nervously.

'Well I appreciated your help,' Paul gently patted her shoulder, regarding her as one would a wild deer, cornered in a country lane.

Having not pushed Zhivago, Max only came tenth in the jump off, but it was sufficient prize money to cover the channel crossing and his fuel, so he didn't mind. After his disastrous start, Paul had gone on to win the class, his first for months.

Once the competition was finished, everyone packed up and headed off to Aachen to get their horses settled in before dark. Pippa had tried to keep out of Max's way, scared of being rebuked for assisting Paul, but once they were together in the cab there was no escape. Almost sick with terror, Pippa sat huddled in the corner of the lorry hoping not to get noticed.

'Am I really that terrifying,' Max eventually asked, after half an hour of silence.

'I thought you might be cross over me helping Paul, especially after what he did to Lee,' Pippa's voice was breaking as she tried not to cry.

Max smiled, 'Its fine. I'm sure he wouldn't have done the same for me, but we can afford to be generous. This is sport not war. Just, whatever you do, never let me catch you helping out any of the French team. I can't stand them.'

Cindy loathed horses. They were smelly, dangerous creatures, but their riders and owners were even worse. They smelt as much of horse as their beloved steeds, but at least the horses kept their mouths shut. Why was it that horsey folk were so boorish and dull, with no sense of style or personal hygiene? Cindy pondered. Still, as an owner, she had to play the game, so before she caught her flight to Germany, she purchased some Dubarry boots and a beautifully cut tweed jacket to put over a white shirt. Together with her skintight trousers, she knew Max would be delighted that she'd made such an effort, whilst remaining sexy. Unbeknown to Cindy, travelling on the same flight, but in the cheap seats, was Lottie. Lottie had arranged to meet Florian, the European Sales Director at the airport, as he was in his home country.

As Florian stood waiting, he developed an erection at the mere sight of the beautiful, model like woman, who sauntered past him. As a handsome, tall, Germanic blond, rich, and newly divorced man, he could have his pick of women, but the vision that past him was something else. Following her, he headed for the taxi rank where he heard her ask to be taken to the same hotel. Delighted, he was determined to get to know her.

454

Lottie arrived ten minutes later, carrying a load of luggage, which mainly consisted of promotional material rather than clothes. Florian fancied his chances with her too. She wasn't in quite the same league as the model, but she was still hot, and a fair bit younger. Florian had done his research and knew she was related to an English Lord. He rather liked the idea of screwing the English aristocracy. Having been stalking her on social media, he also knew she'd broken up with her sexy Russian boyfriend.

Once Lottie had been checked into her room she freshened up and prepared to head down to the stables. She longed to see Max and Pippa but was worried about her reception. She still had a job to do however, and she had Giles, Marcus and Paul to brief about that evening's meet and greet function, and the photo opportunity. She was dreading seeing Paul, after what he'd done to Lee, and knew it would be hard to bite her tongue. As it was, Paul had only been second reserve after such a bad season, but Mary had a fall and dislocated her shoulder, and then as first reserve, Ed's top horse had gone lame.

Cindy wasn't in a rush to get down to the stables, so instead she headed for the hotel bar, where she quickly found herself in conversation with a handsome German wearing a very expensive suit. It didn't take long for her to realise that the man was Lottie's boss, and that she rather fancied him. When he invited her up to his room, she followed; partly curiosity, but also it wouldn't hurt Max to know he had some competition.

Florian thought he'd died and gone to heaven. Not only was Cindy the most beautiful woman he'd ever had, but she was also an excellent lover, and seemed interested in the business. In turn, Cindy, who'd never had a German, was pleasantly impressed. He was clearly infatuated with her, and she felt this could be useful in the future. They lay in bed, chatting for a while but then her phone rang, and it was Max asking if she had arrived. Hurriedly getting dressed, she headed down to the horse lorry park.

Max was sitting in the lorry drinking vodka when Cindy arrived. As she climbed up the steps, she spotted Pippa lying on her bunk bed reading a book.

'You, scram,' she ordered.

Pippa hurriedly climbed down, grabbed her jacket and boots and shot out the door. Cindy slowly took off her jacket and kicked off her boots before sitting down beside her younger lover.

Max felt his erection rise as Cindy started to rub her hand on his crutch, but as she got close to him, he realised that she stank of sex. They had never had an exclusive relationship but knowing that she'd clearly just left the bed of another lover shocked him.

'I've just been with sweet, spineless little Lottie Rollover's boss. A rather handsome German called Florian. He wasn't very discrete, and told me that once the Olympics are over, your friend's probably going to lose her job.' She smiled triumphantly and was also delighted to see that Max looked pleased by the news. She knew she was winning the battle to gain the sexy Russian.

'Lottie's boss said that they've reached their UK sales targets, so if Lottie wants a job she'll have to head off to Eastern Europe.' Cindy smiled, 'Perhaps you could give her a crash course in Russian. She could then go and work for Yangtze Siberia. At least then she wouldn't have to worry about her frosty knickers melting.'

Max poured himself another drink, wishing he could allow himself to get really drunk. The news of Lottie's job loss pleased him, but not for the reasons Cindy thought. Cindy's efforts intensely flattered him, and he would be eternally grateful to her, but the only person he could imagine marrying was Lottie. If Lottie no longer had a high-powered job, then maybe they could run the show jumping business together. Before that he needed to somehow buy Zhivago off Cindy. The chances were that by that time that happened Lottie would probably have already vowed never speak to him again.

Cindy used the lorry table to cut some cocaine. Having taken some herself, she encouraged Max to join in. 'I can't,' he responded bitterly. 'If I got selected for a random drug's test my career would be over.'

'You never used to worry,' Cindy replied sulkily.

'I've grown up a great deal in the last twelve

months,' Max replied honestly. Even so, looking down at the white line of powder, it looked so inviting, he began to crave a hit. Using Cindy as a distraction, he hurriedly undressed, and having pulled down her jeans, they had cramped, but amusing sex.

Lottie made her way around the horse boxes. Firstly, she called in on Marcus and quickly briefed him, and then hunted down Giles. He always made her laugh, and fed her biscuits, and time in his company always lifted her mood. Having done her briefing, she was about to leave when Mary came in through the side door of the lorry. Looking concerned, she asked Lottie if she was OK.

'I guess. It's hard having Cindy lording it over Max, but I dare say I'll get used to it.'

Both tried to answer, but Mary butted in first. 'No one here really believes she's actually the owner of Zhivago. It's been the main topic of conversation for weeks now, and as Paul says, Lady Hardcourt simply wouldn't have sold the horse to that slut.'

'But the buyers disguised their identity by hiding behind the name TM Associates. All the correspondence was done through lawyers. Lady H wouldn't have known,' Lottie said bluntly.

'She's nobody's fool and Cindy's too indiscrete. Her ladyship would have used her great Roman nose to sniff out the truth long before any contracts were signed,' Giles added.

'We're sure the truth will surface sooner or

later Lottie, so hang on in there. You're the best thing that ever happened to Max.'

Lottie felt herself blushing. 'Thank you, its very kind of you to say that.'

'All the riders think the same. Max used to be an arrogant little shit. Although nobody could fault his passion for his horses, he had no respect or consideration when it came to people,' Mary said.

'I think it may have been his sudden dive into poverty that was the most influential thing,' Lottie argued. 'Isn't it a case that he just learnt to appreciate what he had?' Lottie couldn't see that she'd made much difference.

Giles got to his feet ready to open the door for her. 'No you're wrong. Granted, the loss of funds gave him humility, but your kindness had a powerful affect. You taught him compassion and got him to appreciate humanity.'

'I'd better go before my head swells so much I won't get through the door,' Lottie joked. As she reached the steps she turned and added, 'Thank you, you have no idea how much better you've made me feel.'

Feeling a lot happier she headed off in search of Paul's lorry. Reluctantly she knocked on his door, expecting to receive a frosty reception, but he greeted her with unexpected enthusiasm, immediately making her wary. She finished her briefing, and was about to head off, but Paul stopped her. Panicking slightly, Lottie insisted that she had to leave, but Paul quietly asked, 'Can you spare a couple of minutes, I need some advice?'

'OK, as long as its quick.' Lottie sat back down.

Paul was looking flustered, and red faced. 'Can you give me the phone number of your groom? And tell me her name.'

Lottie eyed him suspiciously. 'Do you mean Pippa? The one that's here.'

Paul nodded.

'I don't think it's a good idea. You may think it's amusing to get one back on Max for taking on Lee, by pinching his groom, but Pippa is a lovely, sweet girl and I won't allow you to hurt her.' Lottie spoke harshly, making her disapproval clear.

'But you don't understand,' Paul blurted out, almost panicky. 'She was so kind to me when my stirrup leather snapped, and I haven't been able to stop thinking about her ever since.' He looked so desperate; Lottie immediately softened.

'Well I suppose that's different. I'll go and find her, and if she agrees, I'll text it to you.'

'Will you? Thanks,' Paul looked so vulnerable, Lottie suddenly saw a glimpse of the nice person hidden under the bluff, no nonsense exterior.

As she headed for the door, he spoke again. 'I will always hate Max Tarasov, but you two are good together. Don't stop fighting for him. We all want you to kick the bony ass of that stupid model bitch and get her out of his life for good.'

Lottie, who'd never heard Paul string two sentences together was momentarily dumbfounded. 'I think you may be in love,' she

460

smiled before shutting the door behind her.

Walking back to the hotel she passed the stables and noticed that the light was on in Zhivago's box. Worried that something was wrong, she headed over to the stable and peered inside. Zhivago turned and looked, and having decided she wasn't exciting, went back to his haylage net. Sat in the corner of the stable, wrapped in a rug, reading was Pippa, who looked horrified at having been found out.

'Are you OK?' Lottie thought the poor girl looked terrified.

'Cindy kicked me out the lorry. I didn't know where else to go.' Pippa answered.

'Would you like me to come back with you?' Lottie asked.

'But what if she comes back later?'

Lottie thought quickly. 'I have a twin room back at the hotel. Why don't you grab your things, and share my room?'

'Thank you,' Pippa answered, 'but I don't want to get in your way.'

'Well I can promise you that I won't be kicking you out of the room in the middle of the night in order to accommodate my lover. Oh, and whilst I'm on the subject of love, Paul Denton has asked for your phone number.'

Pippa looked terrified. 'But... I don't want to go and work for him. From what Lee says, it's horrible.'

Lottie smiled. 'I'm not sure groom duties were what he had in mind. Following your good Samaritan act the other day, I think he's developed a bit of a crush on you. Anyway, shall I text him your number?' Pippa nodded but continued to look scared.

'If you are going to meet him, make sure you aren't too far from help. Just let me know if he does anything to scare you and I'll come and rescue you, but I've known him long enough to think you should be fine. Underneath he's quite decent.'

They headed back to the lorry, and Pippa retrieved her bag. Luckily it was stored in one of the outside lockers, so she didn't need to go inside. They then went back to the hotel so Lottie could get changed in time for the reception and photo-shoot

Lottie invited Pippa, but as the groom had only brought jeans, she insisted that she was happy to stay in the hotel room and watch the TV. Whilst Lottie was drying her hair, she paused to text Paul with Pippa's number. Moments later, Lottie heard a mobile phone ringing.

Lottie headed off to the drinks reception early, as she had arranged to meet Florian. He was confident and charming, and put her at her ease. She made sure that the room was ready, and that there were sufficient staff to hand out drinks and nibbles. Meanwhile Florian met the official photographer, and they set aside an area of the room for the formal pictures to be taken. Having made sure that everything was in place, they stood quietly for a few moments, and Florian subtly began his charm offensive, hoping to score twice in one day.

Soon the guests arrived, who consisted of the team members from each country and discipline, including the eventers and the dressage riders. There were also the various team trainers and FEI officials amongst the crowds. Simon Palmer arrived looking slightly on edge. Lottie noticed that he was keeping a sharp eye on Max, to make sure he didn't overdo the drink.

Lottie was kept busy as hostess. As Yangtze were sponsoring the party it was her responsibility to ensure that the horse-world elite were kept topped up with food and drink. She needed to constantly circulate, and on her first circuit of the room, she was pleased to hear Max in a passionate discussion about dressage with one of Team GB's dressage team.

'The top riders and horses in any discipline should be capable of riding a test to Advanced Medium level,' the dressage rider argued. 'In fact, it should be made obligatory. It would ensure that riders don't take short cuts and make sure horses are properly trained.' Around him, various event riders agreed.

'Just hang on,' Max insisted. 'It's all very well, but before you all jump on the bandwagon, you have to appreciate that by Advanced Medium, there are certain training elements that go directly against what I need as a show jumping producer. My main issue is counter canter. As soon as my horses feel my weight shift, I expect them to do a flying change. The last thing I need is for them to head off to the fence on the wrong leg, just because it's a good balance discipline.'

Lottie moved away. She was grateful that he was at least talking horses, rather than drinking himself into oblivion. Moments later she bumped into Paul who looked very pleased with himself. 'Pippa's meeting me later for a drink in the hotel bar. Thanks for your help.'

'Just make sure you take care of her,' Lottie replied.

Having finished arguing, Max headed off to find a drink. The desperate cravings had gone, but he felt deflated. He'd spotted Lottie's German boss being rather too familiar with her, and it made him feel very uncomfortable. Watching her operate the room, he was impressed by how cool and professional she seemed. Certainly, she was giving the impression of being completely over him. Max half wished she'd been sat sobbing in the corner of the room, clutching an empty vodka bottle. At least that way he'd know for certain that she cared.

The next day the British showjumpers rode well. Paul rode like a man in love, and with his riding improved, and he was rewarded with a double clear. As expected Max jumped two brilliant clear rounds, and Marcus also managed a slightly slower double clear on Harvey. Giles had an unlucky pole down and that cost them the gold medal. The German team had managed a clean score sheet, and thus were crowned European Team Champions. The four Brits stood on the lower podium, holding aloft their silver medals, as the German anthem played.

It was then time for the individual prizes. Max climbed up on the podium and stood for the National Anthem. Once again, his beloved Zhivago had jumped his heart out and pipped the world champion Frederick Siepp. Waving to the crowds, Max was delighted. As he lifted his medal, the flash of cameras momentarily blinded him. It was only as he climbed back down, a wave of sadness came over him. This was the point where he'd planned to propose to Lottie. If he did it now, he would probably never see his horse again.

Chapter 41

When Max arrived back home, he only had a twenty-four-hour window before he was due to head back up to Birmingham for Horse of the Year Show. Lottie had flown to Bristol airport a few hours earlier and was already out in the yard when the lorry returned.

Max insisted on returning Zhivago to his field, before getting on with the task of re stocking the lorry. Lottie headed off to the shops to stock up on human supplies for the next trip, sadly knowing that she wasn't welcome, in case she upset Cindy. What made it more irritating was that it was Lottie's horses that were off to Horse of the Year show. Feeling cross, she went into the supermarket where her attention was immediately drawn to the newspapers.

Lottie arrived back an hour later, ready to restock the lorry food cupboards, and armed with two tabloid papers. As she went to open the side door to the lorry, it opened from the inside and Max appeared carrying laundry to put in the wash.

'Are you going to wash it yourself or would you prefer to wash it in public?' she asked.

Max looked bewildered. 'You haven't seen the front pages of the tabloids this morning?' Lottie questioned.

'Clearly not,' he drawled arrogantly.

Putting her shopping bags down, she

retrieved the papers from under her arm. 'Tabloid Slutwatch have been having a field day with your girlfriend. One shows the both of you, semi naked, coming out of the lorry. And the other shows her, again, semi-naked, coming out of the hotel with my boss.' Lottie hesitated, allowing Max to glance at the pictures.

'Does Cindy intend fucking my entire social network?'

'Probably,' Max tried to hide his irritation.

'Is it some sort of revenge porn in reverse?' Lottie ranted. 'Has the woman got no morals?'

'I don't know. Now if you will excuse me, I've got lots to do,' Max thrust the papers back into Lottie's hand before marching off across the yard.

Max set off again the next morning, and in the interests of her love life, took Pippa with him, knowing that Paul would be there. Lottie headed up two days later, as she had been invited to the owner's drinks reception which followed the leading rider competition in which Hope was entered. Lottie had booked a room at The Hilton which avoided any embarrassment over sleeping arrangements.

It was early afternoon, the day before Hope's major competition, when Lottie arrived. Luckily she'd managed to get hold of a security pass, and was able to watch Taggart competing in the afternoon class from the groom's area. She watched her beloved friend popping around the course, his large grey ears focusing on each fence. He would never be the fastest horse, but being

467

kind and honest, he always tried, and this pretty much guaranteed regular prize money and justified his inclusion.

When Max rode out for the final time, Lottie was there to meet Taggart. Max looked surprised, but pleased to see her, but within seconds of him dismounting, Cindy had appeared and in the manner of a bitch on heat, pissed on Lottie's territory.

Not wanting to make a public scene, Lottie quietly led her horse back to the stables. Realising he was being led by his owner, Taggart kept nudging her in the back, demanding attention, and horse treats. Rather than taking him straight to the stables, Lottie led him to the lorry, and having found one of her riding hats and some boots, mounted him and took him for a ride around the practice arena.

Taggart had already worked hard, so Lottie kept mainly to a walk, but simply enjoyed just being there on him. Watching other riders jumping the huge practice fence, she had no desire to join them. Lately she'd been taking more of an interest in dressage, partly brought on by the need to rebalance Percy. Max had been schooling Taggart well, and when Lottie asked, he performed a half pass across the arena.

Lottie's mind started to work overtime. After the Olympics she'd be out of a job. She also didn't know how long Max would continue to live with them. Certainly, if Cindy remained on the scene, there would be an almighty hole in her life.

'Taggart,' she whispered. 'I'm going to take

you back, and we are going to take up dressage together.'

'What the hell are you doing?' Lottie was brought back to the moment by a sharp voice.

'Isn't it obvious. I'm enjoying a few moments with my horse,' she snapped.

'Don't you think he's done enough?' Max called out, not disguising his irritation.

'I just fancied a quick ride, after all I don't get it anywhere else,' she replied. She dismounted and led Taggart back through the entrance towards the stables.

Max came up beside her. 'That's your choice,' he said arrogantly. 'What are you doing here anyway?'

Lottie turned and glared, 'As their owner, I've come to watch my horses compete. I was going to offer to help, but I guess I'm surplus to requirements.'

Max was then summoned by one of the stewards, and he managed to slip away without having to respond.

Max was back competing in the early evening class on Cruz, but as Hope was being saved for the following day, Pippa had taken him for a light warm up earlier in the day. The drinks reception wasn't until nine, when the majority of riders would have finished. With nothing to do, Lottie stayed in her hotel room until eight, but decided to head back early so she could say goodnight to the horses.

Lottie got to the stables ten minutes later, and once again poor Pippa was sat reading, having again been kicked out of the lorry by Cindy. Pippa was desperate to get back to the lorry to change as she had been invited as Paul's guest to the reception. Lottie was furious, and much to Pippa's embarrassment, stormed back to the lorry to confront Max. Without knocking, she opened the side door and stomped up the lorry steps. Max and Cindy were lounging half naked on the sofa, a nearly empty vodka bottle on the table along with the remnants of some white powder.

'I told you to stay out the way,' Cindy barked, assuming it was Pippa.

Lottie saw red. 'You have no right to be here. This is my lorry, and don't you dare ban my staff from having access to it,' she shouted.

For a fleeting moment Cindy looked stunned, but quickly regained her composure. 'I'd forgotten about you,' she answered snidely, as if Lottie were some sort of disease.

'I wish I could say the same,' Lottie snapped.

In the previous hour and a half Max had drunk half a bottle of vodka and snorted a considerable amount of cocaine. He had been feeling guilty, both for his treatment of Pippa, but also of Lottie. Meanwhile, terrified of upsetting Cindy, he was frustrated, wired and feeling very stressed.

Lottie concentrated on Max. Studying him, his eyes betrayed his recent drug use. Unable to help herself, pure rage simply overwhelmed her.

'If I ever find you riding my horses under the influence of drugs, you'll never use them again.'

'Well that's no bloody loss. None of yours are

any good,' Max flew back at her.

'Fine, if that's how you feel, but it won't stop with the horses. If you continue with illegal drug taking I'll destroy your career.'

Max shot to his feet, raised his hand, and slapped Lottie hard across her face.

Lottie was shocked. Her face throbbed, but she was determined not to cry. 'It's just as well you have dual nationality because by the time I've finished, the only country who'll want you to ride for them in the Olympics are the Russians. In fact, being a drug user is obligatory.'

Turning her attention to Cindy she said coldly, 'I've told you to leave. You have five minutes to get out, otherwise I shall call security.'

Turning sharply on her heals, she stormed out.

As soon as she was outside, she had to rush to the nearest toilets where she was sick. Still shaking uncontrollably from the rush of adrenaline, she walked around to the stables in an attempt to calm down.

'What happened?' Pippa stared at her boss who looked terrible.

As they walked back to the lorry, Lottie confessed to losing both her temper, and her dignity. By the time they reached the lorry it was in darkness. Pippa quickly changed whilst Lottie tidied up. Having carefully locked all the doors they headed off to the reception.

Fortunately, the mark on Lottie's cheek had faded, and in the artificial light could hardly be seen. Paul looked so happy, accompanied by a

471

radiant Pippa who was so pretty, and couldn't stop grinning. Lottie was determined to prove that Cindy had been lying and hunted down Ed and Olivia. She hadn't properly spoken to them since Tom's party and as she approached, she felt awkward. Olivia was very sweet, but not very helpful, explaining that her mother knew nothing about Zhivago's new owners.

Lottie was on the verge of despair, but Ed added, 'Simon Palmer was the middleman for the deal. He'll know who the owners are. Ask him.'

Simon wasn't at the show, but Lottie had his mobile number. Slipping out into the corridor where it was quieter, she called him, and explained her problem.

'I need to speak to the client. I must get their permission before I say anything. Give me a few days. Don't worry OK.' Simon then hung up.

By the time Lottie got back into the room, Pippa had told Paul about the incident, and it was now public knowledge. Lottie admitted to Paul that she just wanted to load up the horses and drive home.

'Just do it sweetheart,' Giles said having overheard. 'Teach Max a lesson.'

Lottie raised her hands in frustration. 'I would, but neither Pippa nor I are insured to drive the lorry, so we're stuck.'

Paul cleared his throat. 'At the risk of interfering, I have the phone number of a driver agency I use. They are based in Birmingham. Would you like me to organise someone to take you home?'

Lottie nodded. 'I may live to regret it, but yes please.'

Two hours later, Pippa and Lottie loaded up the horses, whilst the agency driver did his pre-drive checks. Soon they were heading off back to Devon. Lottie's only regret was that she wouldn't be there to see Max's face when he arrived back in the morning. After a four hour drive they reached Stapletor. There wasn't a train for another three hours, so the driver slept in the cab, and Lottie went to bed for a short sleep.

While Lottie was arriving back from Plymouth train station, at the NEC, a very hung over Max reached the lorry park, only to discover an empty space where his lorry should have been. His immediate reaction was to assume that the lorry had been stolen, but he then realised that he had an audience.

'That'll teach you to piss off Lottie,' Giles called out.

'There's a riding school down the road, perhaps they'll lend you a nice cob for the jumping class later,' Marcus joked.

'Just fuck off all of you,' Max yelled, before storming off to a backdrop of jeers and laughter. He headed back towards the hotel, but it wasn't until the others were out of sight that he allowed himself to burst into tears. Having recovered his composure, he went back to the hotel. All his clean clothes had been in the lorry. It was pure luck that he had his phone and wallet. Cindy was supportive, as for once she had the moral high ground and invited him back to her apartment for a few days.

Once they were back in London, Cindy had work appointments. Alone, and traumatised, Max went on a three-day drinking binge, and then took another two days to recover sufficiently to call Lee.

'Do you think the Marchbanks will set the dogs on me if I come back?' he asked.

'They haven't dumped your belongings outside the estate gates, so I reckon it's safe to return,' Lee replied. 'Just don't expect the fatted calf,' Lee added. Lee was relieved that his boss had finally got in contact with him. Max's relationship with Cindy worried him. Not only was she a bad influence, but he thought Lottie was a far better prospect, and he hated to see her being hurt.

Max's first meeting with Lottie was awkward and embarrassing. Mortified by his behaviour, but seeing no adequate way of apologising, he avoided her. When he finally came across Lottie in the yard, he looked down at the ground, unable to face her. 'I'm sorry,' he muttered. He then paused, waiting for her outburst.

'I'm not sorry for what I said, although I do have a tiny twinge of guilt over the moonlight flit,' Lottie replied.

'Can we go back to being friends?' he asked hesitantly.

'It will make life easier if we move on and get back to some sense of normality.' Lottie said, although Max was aware of the lack of conviction in her voice.

Later that day Simon sent through an email

to Lottie and Max. He'd sent as an attachment a statement from TM Associates, which read,

TM Associates is made up of a group of London based businessmen and a Conservative Peer, who are friends. One of the group has been following the career of Max Tarasov, and saw the purchase of the stallion Zhivago as a way of not only showing support, but also as a sound business proposition. TM Associates are delighted with the current arrangement and may look at further investments in the future. We can confirm categorically that the model claiming ownership of the horse has no dealings with anyone involved with TM Associates.

Lottie was relieved. Her instinct had been proved right, and it would mean the end of Cindy's poisonous influence. Her theory that Ivan Tarasov and Crispin were behind TM Associates remained a strong possibility too. She hoped that everything could get back to normal, except of course her relationship with Max. On a business footing it would continue unscathed, but she suspected that any chance of regaining the special bond they'd enjoyed, had been blown out of the water.

Max didn't initially contact Cindy. She'd flown over to Milan to a fashion show, so he waited for her to return to London. He decided that the best way to tackle her was face to face. Having missed jumping Hope at Horse of the Year Show, he managed to get a late entry accepted and drove up to the Midlands for a show jumping indoor derby. Hope adored competing, and as he got familiar with the pre-event routine, had started to anticipate the big competitions. As soon as he saw his saddle and bridle, the adrenaline kicked in, and he started trembling in anticipation. He'd grown to love the audience, and practically towed Max into the ring. Over the year, he'd developed in strength and balance, and now more experienced, Max was finally starting to trust Hope, to ask harder questions, and take chances on tight turns, and cutting out strides.

Each event saw a little more improvement, and at the Midlands derby, Hope won both his classes, plus critical acclaim from the horsey press. Having arrived back home delighted by the performance, Max then headed off by train to London to catch up with Cindy for one final time.

Lottie couldn't understand why Max was bothering to visit when an email or phone call would do, but Max wanted to see Cindy's face when he confronted her. When he arrived, Cindy seemed surprised to see him, having forgotten that he was coming. She'd arranged to meet up for a drink with Lottie's boss Florian, who happened to be in London for a couple of days. Having hurriedly texted Florian, warning him that she'd be late, she made it clear to Max that she had appointments, and couldn't spare him much time.

'It's OK, I only need a few minutes. I just want an explanation,' he responded abruptly. Fishing around in his jacket pocket, he pulled out a copy of the TM Associates letter. Shoving it in Cindy's hand, he said. 'Well?'

Cindy quickly read through the letter, 'I don't

understand. I'm the owner.'

'How can you possibly be?' Max was exasperated.

'This is a lie. Lottie must have written it to deliberately discredit me. You must believe me,' she demanded.

Max shook his head. 'This didn't come from Lottie. Look at the email address at the top of the page?' Max was exasperated.

Having failed to convince him, Cindy burst into tears. 'I'm sorry, but I only did it because I still love you and want you back.'

Max looked at her in disbelief. He could hardly believe how gullible he'd been. He'd allowed her to walk back into his life, and she'd nearly destroyed it for a second time. As it was, he'd thrown away the special relationship he'd had with Lottie, and he couldn't see a way of recovering it.

'You said you had a meeting; well, I shan't delay you any longer.' Shaking with suppressed anger, he walked back down to the ground floor, and out into the street. Without purpose, he flagged down a taxi, and headed for one of his old favourite bars.

Due to roadworks, the taxi dropped him at the top end of the street. Walking the short distance to the bar, he was deep in thought until he collided with someone coming the other way. Stopping to apologise, he suddenly realised it was Ben Marchbank. Ben briefly smiled as he recognised his sister's boyfriend, but then his face fell.

'Christ, you look like you need a drink. Come on. I'll treat you as way of an apology,' Max insisted.

Ben agreed, and they headed off inside where Max ordered two neat double vodkas. Once they were sat down Max asked what was wrong. Ben sighed. 'We've finished filming Brideshead, and everyone else is off to their next projects. That's everyone but me. I haven't had a single offer.'

'I'm sure you'll get something soon,' Max responded politely.

Ben shrugged, 'That's not the worst of it. What really hurts is how Sophie is treating me. For two years now we've been practically inseparable, and yet, now she's been offered a part in a Hollywood movie, I'm not featuring anywhere in her plans for the future.'

'Sorry to hear that. I thought you two were great together.'

Ben then listened as Max explained about Cindy's deceit. 'Again, the worst of it is that I've damaged my relationship with your sister.'

'Do you love her?' Ben asked.

'She's the one person I want to spend the rest of my life with.'

'I know that deep down, she is still crazy about you, so what's your problem?' Ben looked confused.

Max hesitated, feeling very awkward. Since the incident at the NEC, Lee was the only person to whom he'd mentioned anything. Downing his third double, he ordered a refill before taking a deep breath. 'At Horse of the Year Show, Lottie caught me with Cindy, in the back of the lorry taking cocaine, and she went nuts. I was drunk, and totally wired on drugs. I'm ashamed to say that in the heat of the moment I slapped her across the face.'

Max saw the look of horror on Ben's face. 'It wasn't a hard slap – I mean she was totally fine – it just made her even more cross with me.' He stopped talking and downed his drink. Max noticed that Ben was mirroring him. Oh God, Max thought, I'm driving one of the Marchbank's to drink.

As the vodka started to take effect, Max started to open up to Ben. 'After what I did to Lottie, I was horrified by the sort of person I'd become, and I made a vow never to touch the stuff ever again.' Ben nodded approvingly.

'Saying sorry just doesn't seem enough, by way of apology to Lottie. I've got to think of something really special...' he trailed off. 'Jesus, I'm feeling drunk. Really should have eaten something,' he added.

'Maybe we should order some food?' Ben suggested.'By the way, where are you staying?'

'No idea,' Max replied. 'Planned to get the train home. Guess it's too late now.'

'You can crash down at my place,' Ben offered.

'Thanks mate,' Max answered.

Being two of the best-looking men in London, they were constantly being bombarded by women trying to chat them up. Everyone from cougars' to suspiciously underage kids seemed to imagine that Max and Ben were fair game. Finally Max lost his temper, 'I'm trying to have a conversation with my friend so just bugger off,' he snapped at some girls out on a hen night.

'Let's head off to my dad's club,' Ben suggested sometime later. As Max was far too drunk to have an opinion, he happily followed Lottie's little brother out of the bar, and into the back of a taxi.

Chapter 42

For the next eight months there remained an uneasy truce between Max and Lottie. As business partners their operation was textbook, but their personal relationship remained distant. When it came to the discussions over the Olympics however, Max was insistent that Lottie accompany him on the trip.

Simon Palmer had selected Marcus on Harvey, Max and Zhivago, Giles and his stallion. The final place was hard fought, but the eventual selection went to Paul on one of Lady Hardcourt's Holsteins. Mary was still having problems with a niggling shoulder injury, so Ed was chosen as travelling reserve. As Simon didn't consider any of Ed's horses to be world class, Hope was brought in as reserve, on the basis that he was reliable and no longer considered to be a difficult ride.

In the weeks running up to the greatest sporting event on the planet, the press constantly sought out good news stories on the athletes. Horse and Country TV came to Stapletor to film Max at home and to meet the horses. The RSPCA made a huge fuss of Hope, and this attracted the local television network and Radio Devon to pay a visit. A photograph of Zhivago taken whilst jumping at The European Championships ended up on the front cover of Horse and Hound, and every time Max ventured out to the local shops or pub he was inundated with autograph requests or photo bombed.

Lee, Lottie and the rest of the grooms headed out with the horses twenty-four hours ahead of the riders. Two transport planes had been chartered. Lottie and Lee found themselves sharing with the other showjumpers, and three of the dressage team horses and travelling staff. Also on board each plane was a vet in case of emergencies. Over the years Zhivago had flown all around the world and was completely unfazed by the experience. Luckily his indifference acted as a steadying force for the novice traveller Hope.

It was lovely for Lottie to catch up with Pippa. Once her relationship with Paul had developed, she handed in her notice and moved up to his yard in Yorkshire. Lottie had remained Facebook friends with Pippa and had learnt about Pippa's engagement a month earlier. Pippa was keen to chat, and once the seatbelt signs went out, she came over and handed Lottie an envelope.

'It's a wedding invitation,' she said, grinning broadly. 'We're getting married in October. I so hope you can make it.'

Lottie opened the envelope, and saw that the invitation included Max. 'Thank you. I'd love to come, and it will be great if I can persuade Max to join me.'

'I know he and Paul don't get on, but it's you two I must thank for giving me a job. Without you both, Paul and I would never have met.' Her eyes shone, and she had a look of such sincerity, it would be hard to say no.

The planes flew into the Southern hemisphere, and into winter. Luckily the climate in the Olympic city was like the UK in Summer. It meant there was no need for the horses to acclimatize to the heat, and unlike with the Beijing Olympics, they didn't have to stay in air-conditioned stables. Following a long flight, Simon Palmer, along with the other team managers, had arranged for a fleet of horse lorries to pick everyone up from the airport for the thirty-mile drive to the equestrian section of the Olympic Park.

Initially the drive was along deserted, dusty highways, with dry, featureless landscapes. As they got nearer, it became possible to see the sea, and the huge bridge that spanned the mouth of the river leading into the city itself. Soon the lorries started passing shanty towns, and the traffic flow on the highway started to resemble the M25. The lorries headed across the magnificent suspension bridge, and ahead the city looked incredible. The road swung south, and they followed the coastal road around the bay and out to the Olympic Park, situated in a green, hilly area on the western side of the city.

Eventually they reached the Olympic Village. The stables were close to the high boundary perimeter fence, and a cool sea breeze blew in their faces as they unloaded the horses. Zhivago and Hope were exhausted after the long journey, and once they'd been put in their stables they settled down to doze. Lottie took photos to send to Max, reassuring him that both horses were well.

The groom's accommodation was in a hastily constructed block of flats adjacent to the stables. Lottie was glad it wasn't hurricane season as she wouldn't have rated their chances of survival. There were separate entrances for male and females. Lottie was pleased to find that she was sharing a room with Pippa, and another English girl who groomed for one of the United States team.

The rooms were very basic. The beds were narrow and hard, and there was one hand basin in the corner of the room. The nearest bathroom was down a corridor, and the plumbing rumbled badly whenever a tap was turned on. The windows didn't fit properly, and the cheap carpet was so full of static, it practically gave Lottie a hair perm as she walked.

Once they'd unpacked, they set off for the twenty-minute hike to the athlete's canteen. There were already a lot of competitors on site, mainly from African countries, but Lottie also recognised the sounds of Australian accents, and the Indian Subcontinent. The grooms all stuck together, and having obtained various food and drink items, they congregated in a large huddle at the far end of the huge dining hall.

Everyone took turns to say who they worked for. As Max had both Lee and Lottie, she felt obliged to hurriedly explain that she was looking after the reserve horse. Pippa then, unhelpfully added that Lottie was Hope's owner, and this led

484

to an uncomfortable silence followed by a snide remark from one of the event grooms that Lottie was obviously in the wrong place.

With all eyes on her Lottie explained that she was only the owner of an Olympic horse by chance. Everyone listened intently as she explained how she just happened to be driving through her local town in an empty horse box when Hope was discovered. She added that he was such a challenge that the RSPCA were happy to let her keep him for a few hundred pounds' donation, and Max had spotted the horse's talent. 'So I'm not in the same league as the proper owners,' she added.

'What's Max like to work for?' someone asked.

'I feel like I'm monopolising the conversation here,' Lottie answered, feeling awkward.

'Only cus our employers are all boring. Max is different,' one of the Irish girl grooms argued.

'Why did his father disinherit him?' her teammate asked.

'Is it true that he takes Class A drugs?' asked one of the dressage grooms.

'Ivan Tarasov was planning to enter politics by standing for election as a member of Parliament. Alas his ambitions were cut short due to Max's member entering the local party chairman's wife. It meant a sudden withdrawal for both of them.'

'Sounds a bit of a harsh punishment,' Pippa said.

'Ivan Tarasov is pretty ruthless, and very

scary.' Lee answered.

'As for the drug taking – it's a bit of an urban myth. Max's ex-girlfriend Cindy is notorious for living on a diet of cocaine and caffeine, so I guess he was getting tarred with the same brush. I'm not saying that he's never tried drugs, but when he's around horses he would never do anything like that,' Lottie said, trying to convince herself as much as her audience.

Max and his teammates arrived the next afternoon, and they were taken to their rather more salubrious accommodation in the athletes' village. Again, the rooms were shared, and there was a strict single sex policy. Max moaned to Giles and Ed that it was like being back at boarding school. He was relieved to find that he was not sharing a room with Paul, but rather was with Giles and a Team GB rower.

Having unpacked, he managed to locate a golf buggy and headed off to the stables to check on the horses. Lottie and Lee had hacked Hope and Zhivago out earlier in the day, and now both horses stood resting in their stables. They both seemed pleased to see Max and nuzzled his pockets hoping for treats.

Max texted Lottie to find out where they were and offered to meet up for a coffee. They both arrived minutes later, and having climbed onto the back of the buggy, Max drove them back to the athlete's dining hall. With the Opening Ceremony being held that evening, over the previous few hours, the village had filled with people from all nationalities. As they sat drinking strong, dark

486

coffee, Lottie gazed out the window in fascination at the assembling crowds.

The strange mix of supreme athletes from all sports made for an eclectic mix. She'd never seen so many enormously tall people in one place, especially amongst the Afro-Caribbean runners and high jumpers. Then there were the tiniest group of humans, whose fit, sinewy frames, made them look almost childlike. The equestrian teams and the shooters had the oldest competitors. It was also interesting to see people in ethnic dress, and the differing voices were like an orchestra of human sound.

'Are you actually listening to me?' Lottie's attention was brought back to the present by Max, irritated by her uncharacteristic lack of concentration.

'Sorry, switched off there for a moment. What were you saying?'

Max huffed. 'I was going through the diary of events for the rest of this week, but if you've got something more important to do that's fine,' he replied sarcastically.

Lottie had been planning to attend the opening ceremony with the Yangtze directors, for whom she'd got tickets. In preparation, she'd brought a posh dress with her, but a couple of hours before it was due to start Florian messaged her to say he was bringing a guest and needed her ticket. Lottie longed to make a fuss, but as she would only be an employee for a further two weeks, it seemed fruitless. Nor did she want to jeopardise her severance package, and large sales bonus pay-out. It was only when she found out that she'd forfeited her ticket to Cindy that she burst into tears.

Fortunately, huge television screens were erected in the massive canteen, and Lottie was invited to join the other support crews to watch the live feed coming directly from the main stadium three miles away. Meanwhile Max and the rest of the equestrian team spent an hour queuing to join the procession of athletes into the stadium. With the athletes entering by country, in alphabetical order, they'd hoped to be going in as Great Britain, but alas were forced to wait until practically the end as the official banner was for the United Kingdom.

Being in high spirits, the team members laughed and joked with each other as they entered the stadium and were greeted by a wall of sound, and thousands of television cameras trained on them. Max followed the others and waved, but as the only people he really cared about were in the Olympic Village with him, it seemed pointless. As they headed further into the stadium, following the path of the running track, they found themselves within flirting distance of other teams. Having clocked some very attractive young Swiss girls, and egged on by Giles, Max started chatting to them in perfect German. There were also a couple of sexy Latvian gymnasts, who called over to Max and his friends. Responding in Russian, Max again did his bit for diplomatic relations.

Once it was over the athletes filed back out, and then there was a rush to jump on the buses back to the village. As none of the equestrians were due to complete for a couple of days, and as they didn't have to have the physical discipline of the athletes, they headed straight for the bar. Most of the equine support crew were already in situ, including Lee, Pippa and Lottie. As Paul headed towards them, Pippa jumped to her feet, and rushed to give him a huge hug.

Max went straight to the bar, but waved across to Lee and Lottie, offering to get them drinks. He appeared ten minutes later with lager, a triple vodka for himself, and cranberry juice. Having taken a large swig from his drink he explained that he had some catching up to do. The British eventing team appeared to have had a major falling out amongst them, and the dressage riders weren't entirely cohesive. In comparison, the show jumpers were all getting along well. Since he'd been in love, Paul had mellowed, and without any animosity being directed at him, Max was also calmer.

As it came close to midnight the groups started to disband, as people started heading back to their rooms. Max was tired, but not sufficient for sleep to come easily. Far from sober, and desperate to settle things with Lottie, he asked her to join him for a walk, adding that if he took her back to her accommodation, they could pop down to the beach.

Max took one of the golf buggies and ordered her to jump on board.

'Is it wise to drink and drive?' she asked uncertainly.

489

'Just hurry up and get in,' he replied impatiently.

They managed to get to Lottie's accommodation block in one piece, having clipped the security fence and a wall. Lottie hastily exited the buggy, grateful to still be alive. They then headed for the guarded exit point where a steep pathway led down to a beautiful sandy beach. As they reached the bottom there was a sharp drop. Max jumped down first, finding it easy with his long legs. He offered his hand to Lottie to help her down.

'Surely I should be helping you. It's you that can't risk being injured,' she joked.

'I would never allow that,' he replied firmly.

Lottie gazed out across the sand, to the moon reflecting on the water, and thought how romantic it looked. If they'd been in a film, soft music would have been playing, and directing them towards a dramatic reconciliation. As it was, Max had clearly lost interest in her sexually, and was probably too drunk for anything precious and meaningful to happen.

'Shall we walk?' she suggested, as a way of covering up her feelings of awkwardness.

Max looped his arm through hers and led them down towards the water's edge. 'I'm so glad you've come here with me,' he said, breaking the silence.

'Well technically I had to come anyway for my final act as a Yangtze employee, but it is nice really being in the thick of it all. It's not something I'll ever forget.'

'I know the last twelve months haven't been easy for you. Well to be honest, for either of us. From the moment Cindy re-entered my life like some kind of destroying angel, I'm only too painfully aware that I just side-lined you. It wasn't that I meant to, but I was so scared of losing Zhivago, and she just played on my fears.'

'The hardest thing was knowing what to do,' Lottie explained, surprised at Max's lucidity, bearing in mind his earlier drinking. 'When I tried not to over-react and play the long game you accused me of not caring, and then when I finally lashed out, you punished me for that too.'

A look of pain flashed across Max's beautiful face. 'I want to rebuild what we had before, but an apology just never seemed sufficient. A bunch of flowers from a petrol station, a box of chocolates, and a cute card can't fix months of pain. That's why it's been so long. I'm just hoping that being in this special place will help me to win you back.' He stopped talking. The breeze was gently blowing loose hair across Lottie's face. He looked into her eyes hoping for absolution. Raising his hand, he gently moved the hair back off her face. Leaning in, he softly kissed her on the forehead.

Lottie smiled. 'I've missed you so badly. I just assumed I'd blown it. Of course, you're forgiven.'

Max felt so elated, he wanted to take her in his arms, and make mad, passionate love to her, but he was rapidly sobering up, and the Dutch courage was disappearing. Instead, the voice of sense in his head told him to show respect for her and hang on. If he played things right, they'd have the rest of their lives together.

Taking off his shoes and carrying them, he encouraged Lottie to do the same. Then, walking hand in hand, they made their way across the beach with the water gently lapping at their feet.

The next few days were spent gently exercising the horses, followed by equine massage therapy sessions. The riders all received physio and attended sports psychology sessions. The dressage riders then had their competition, and after four days of competition Team GB came away with a silver medal, plus individual gold and silver.

The eventers were next to compete, but after the dressage phase were only in fourth place as a team. They redeemed themselves on the cross-country course and pulled themselves back up to silver position. The final event was the show jumping, and although the jumps were small in comparison to those Max jumped, the event horses tended not to have any respect for flimsy pole fences and this made them careless. Added to this, they were tired from the exhausting second day all the teams had cricket scores of faults.

The Germans were the most disciplined and retained both team and individual gold, with New Zealand in silver, and the British riders in bronze. The British press were delighted that both equestrian disciplines had ended up with medals, but this only added to the pressure on the show jumpers. Overall Team GB were doing well in the tables and the news broadcasts were dominated by good news stories. Not to be outdone, the horsey press also got in on the act. Two days before the showjumpers were due to compete the magazine published a guide to the individual showjumpers most likely to get medals. They concentrated on Frederick Seipp as reigning world champion, Jacq the French rider who'd fathered Karen's baby, one of the US team, and Max.

To be helpful to their readers, they listed the riders by their FEI rankings. Frederick, the Frenchman and the American were the top three highest ranked riders in the world. Marcus was 10th, Paul 15th and Giles 18th. Max was way down at 35th. In the horse rankings however Zhivago was the highest ranked of Team GB in 10th place. The Horse and Hound writer then explained how the rankings only told half the story. Max had far fewer horses than the other top riders, and, according to their calculations, his horses only competed in half the amount of competitions. They concluded that if the rankings were based on prize money won per number of competitions entered, then Max and Zhivago would be number one in the world, due to their phenomenal track record.

The article thrilled Lottie, and it made her feel so proud. The book makers agreed with her, and the odds of Max winning were slashed. The positive news had the opposite effect on Max, who felt that it just compounded the pressure of expectation on him. For the next two days he was snappy and irritable with Lottie and Lee, biting their heads off for every little thing, and generally being a nightmare.

The one bit of relief came on the first evening when Lottie received a phone call from Ben. When she'd last spoken he'd been miserable. Seemingly the only member of the Brideshead cast not to have another job to move on to and having been ditched by Sophie. He'd spent a few months doing odd bits for commercials, and a few walk on parts in a comedy series, but nothing substantial. Now his voice was bright and cheery, and as he asked her about life at the Olympics it was clear he was desperate to impart his news.

'I've got a great job starting next month,' Ben practically shouted down the phone. Probably the most romantic leading role ever.' He paused for dramatic effect. 'I've been asked to join the Royal Shakespeare Company for their next production. Starts off in Stratford for six weeks, then going on a sixth month tour before ending up with a month at The Globe.'

'That's great news, but what's your part?'

'Oh didn't I say. It's Romeo and Juliet and I'm playing the leading role.'

'You'll make a wonderful Juliet,' Lottie laughed.

'Ha ha, very funny. Anyway, that's not all. As soon as my nine months' tour with the RSC is up, I'm going straight on to star in a film.'

'What film?' Lottie asked impatiently.

'It's a Working Title production. Very hush hush at present, but as you'll never guess in a

494

million years, I'll give you a hint. It's a remake of one of your favourite books, and I may need Max as a stunt double. Oh, and I'll need to bleach my hair blonde. Have you worked it out?'

Lottie hesitated, her mind working overtime. 'OMG Not Rupert Campbell Black!'

Ben laughed. 'Yes.'

'We'll have to get Zhivago to play Maccauley and Hope as Revenge,' Lottie added. 'You're going to have so much fun.'

'I do hope so,' Ben replied.

Lottie had decided not to mention the news to Max, who was so on edge he wasn't in the mood for such frivolity. The next day Lottie had to leave Hope under the care of Lee, as she had her final duty to perform as a Yangtze employee. As a completion to the sponsorship agreement, the company was hosting an early evening drinks reception in the Olympic corporate hospitality lounge. The British show jumping team were expected to attend, for final marketing photographs, and to be ready to meet Yangtze's carefully selected guests. Max was the only rider not officially obliged to attend as part of the original sponsorship arrangement, but as his lorry was officially theirs, Lottie insisted that he came.

Lottie spent most of the day either running around sorting out the catering arrangements, or making sure the marketing displays and TV screens were working and in the correct positions. She chased up unconfirmed guests, and double checked that the most important invitees were still intending to come. With half an hour to spare, she slipped into the ladies' loos to change, and re-apply her makeup.

The guests started arriving within minutes of Lottie finally being ready. Lottie was horrified when Florian turned up, yet again with Cindy in tow. As the showjumpers drifted in, they headed first for the champagne, before huddling together in a pack for safety. Max was the last to arrive, but Lottie was relieved to see that he'd tried to look smart and was wearing in his team blazer. She kept her eyes peeled on him, intending to watch his reaction when he first spotted Cindy.

Having helped himself to a drink, he waved to Lottie, but seeing she was busy, he headed off to join his teammates. As he reached them, he realised that they were being interviewed, so hung back. He then spotted Cindy with the tall blonde German, whom he recognised as being Lottie's boss. Shocked, a wave of mixed emotions flooded his mind. There was a hint of possessive jealousy, and the familiar twinge of lust, but equally as dominant was a rising bitterness towards her.

He glanced across towards Lottie, who immediately beckoned him over to her.

Smiling, he headed across the room. In a neat, figure-hugging dress, she looked so pretty and confident. Her smile was warm and genuine, and Max felt a surge of protectiveness towards her. Suddenly a wave of anger came over him. How dare Cindy gate crash Lottie's last corporate event.

'I'm so sorry about Cindy, didn't know she was coming,' they both said in unison.

Max rested his hand gently on Lottie's arm. 'Are you OK?' he asked tenderly.

She nodded, 'What about you?'

He smiled weakly. 'I'm far too busy shitting myself over the jumping to care about her.'

He then turned as he heard his name being called. 'Photo shoot,' yelled Giles. 'Come on stop chatting up your girlfriend.'

'Sorry, must go. You've done a great job here by the way.' He then headed off back to the group.

Once Max's corporate obligations were completed, he excused himself and went in search of Lottie. He couldn't see her in the main function room, so he headed off into the corridor. There were a number of smaller rooms, so methodically he poked his head in each room, hoping to find her. The first room he entered was full of photographic equipment, and a couple were having a serious discussion in the corner of the room. Unseen, he quietly closed the door, and then jumped guiltily as he heard his name being called.

Cindy stood in front of him. Her skin-tight dress, hugging her beautifully toned body, she smiled warmly. 'I'm so pleased to have found you darling. I so wanted to make things up with you, so I've brought you a little good luck present.'

'Thank you, but it wasn't necessary.' Max replied feeling very uncomfortable. If she was offering sex, then for the first time ever, he was about to turn her down.

'Come in here a minute,' she said beckoning him into an empty side room which joined the main function suite.

Reluctantly he followed her. She turned and closed the door behind her. Max held his breath, expecting her to get undressed, but instead, she dug around in her handbag and produced a small bag of white powder which she placed on the table. I thought you'd appreciate this to help boost your confidence, she announced as if offering a counselling session.

Max greedily eyed the cocaine. Cindy was right, it was exactly what he needed to perk him up. 'That's sweet, but I daren't risk it. What if I'm selected for a drug's test?'

'What are the chances?' she asked. 'How often have you been tested?'

Max hesitated. 'Never – well Zhivago was after the European Champs, but there is always a first time.'

'Seems pretty low risk. Come on. I could have been sent to prison for life if customs had caught me bringing this into the country for you.' She opened the bag and poured some onto the table. Then using a credit card, she scraped the while powder into a line. Max was torn. With the competition only 36 hours away, he would fail a drugs test, but it was a small risk against knowing how good the drug would make him feel.

Cindy rolled up a ten-pound note and handed it to him. He was just about to bend down and inhale when the side door opened and Lottie walked in. She realised in an instant what was happening, and charging forward, she swiped the precious powder line on to the floor. 'What the fuck are you doing? If you're caught the whole team will be eliminated.'

A look of fury on her face, Cindy lifted her hand and slapped Lottie across the face. Lottie stood her ground. 'What is it with you two?' she said witheringly. She then turned towards the open door and called for security. Simon appeared immediately, and in a louder voice yelled. 'Someone get the guards, we need this woman evicted immediately.'

Max raised his hand and gently stroked Lottie's red cheek. 'I'm sorry' he said. He then turned to Cindy, and grabbing her arm said sternly, 'Come on we're leaving.' Before she had time to object, he frog marched her out through the main function room, and didn't stop until they were well clear of the building. Meanwhile running in the opposite direction, were a group of security guards.

Using his security pass as a competitor, he grabbed a buggy. Max managed to get Cindy across the Olympic Park to the main visitor entrance near to the city where there were taxis so she could get back to her hotel. Once she was safe he told her he had to leave. Immediately Cindy's large saucer eyes filled with genuine tears. 'Please come back with me,' she sobbed. 'I still love you.'

For the first time in years, Max truly believed her. She wasn't the sort of person to ever betray weakness. Now, stood in front of him, her shoulders heaving with grief, he realised that she really cared.

Desperate to comfort her, he wrapped his arms around her, and held her close to his chest. 'I still care about you, but my life has taken a different course, and it's no longer possible for us to be together. You will always be special to me, but I'm marrying Lottie.'

Pushing him away, Cindy stormed off down the street. He stood motionless, watching her slowly disappear out of his life. He waited until she'd gone, then feeling like a total shit, he headed off in the opposite direction, and kept walking until he found a supermarket where he bought a bottle of vodka.

Lottie continued to put on a brave face. It was her last proper day in the best job she was ever likely to have, and it had been ruined by her boyfriend disappearing off with his ex. Two hours later, she said goodbye to the last of the guests, and started to pack away the Yangtze promotional materials for the final time. Having had his date run away, Florian had disappeared off in a sulk, and the Chinese directors had gone back to their hotel. Lottie kept checking her phone, hoping to hear something from Max, but it was rapidly becoming apparent that she had effectively been abandoned. Once everything was done, Lottie headed off on the long solitary walk back towards the stables accommodation block.

Half a bottle of vodka later, Max texted Lottie to say sorry for walking out. Immediately his phone rang.

'Where the hell are you?' demanded Lottie, sounding cross and impatient.

'Sat on a park bench outside the stadium with a bottle of vodka,' he spoke slowly, trying not to sound drunk.

'Are you alone?'

'I have my vodka.'

Lottie's voice softened. 'Are you OK? Shall I come and find you?'

'No,' he insisted. 'I'm tired, and about to head back. Just felt bad about earlier. Had to get Cindy away. Didn't want her arrested. Felt I owed her that much. She's gone now.'

Lottie felt a huge wave of relief. As usual she'd imagined the worst. A tiny bit of her had feared that reality had imitated fiction. In the book Riders, Jake Lovell had run away from the Olympics with Rupert Campbell Black's wife.

The next morning the riders had a final briefing with Simon Palmer, sat on a bench a short distance from the stables. Max sat quietly nursing a hangover, and hoping it was going to shift before the competition started. Having run through the arrangements and the team strategy, Simon dismissed them. As Max got up to leave, Simon said grumpily. 'I want a word.'

Simon then tore into Max regarding his previous night's drinking binge.

'I was upset,' Max retorted.

'Make sure you're recovered later or I won't

501

hesitate to bring in Ed, and you'll never get invited to ride for the British Team again.' Simon looked furious. Then, curiosity getting the better of him, he added. 'So why the hell did you run off with that bloody woman last night?'

'I was afraid that she'd get arrested, and I thought I owed it to her to get her to safety.'

'She's nothing but trouble – why even go there?'

Max sighed. 'I guess it was a final act of honour. I made it clear to her that we are finished. My life is with Lottie now.'

'Well thank goodness for that. She's far more suitable for you.'

Max headed back to his room, and caught up on a bit more sleep, whilst Lee and Lottie took the horses for a quiet hack. Two hours before the competition was due to start, Max dressed, taking care to look as smart as possible, before grabbing a buggy and heading off back to the stables. His headache had cleared, but his unsettled stomach from the alcohol had been replaced by nervous sickness.

He bumped into Giles who looked equally ill. 'I think we should join the Irish team,' Giles joked. 'At least then our complexions would match our green jackets.'

The stadium started to fill with spectators, meanwhile the FEI ground jury checked the fences. The riders were then allowed into the arena of the course walk. By now the wind had picked up and it had started to rain, which at least the British horses were used to.

Being the Olympics, and the greatest sporting show on earth, great care had been taken with the design to have a huge visual impact on the television screens. Although the fences were the official 1 metre 60 in height, some of the amazing features made them look even more enormous. The wall fence was designed in the style of the host city's stunning cathedral, with the East spire acting as one of the jump ends. There was an upright fence, coming off an awkward 5 and a half strides, where the filler was made up with Olympic rings.

The water fence had little boats bobbing up and down on the shallow water. There was another upright fence made of planks, resembling a sailing ship. A large oxer was decorated in the flag of the host nation. Max had to keep telling himself that this was no different to the dozens of other grand prix classes he'd ridden in over the past couple of years, many of which he'd won. Having the least experienced horse on the team, Marcus was worried that Harvey would take exception to the most garish of the fences.

Soon it was time to start, and the riders began filing back to the stables and collecting areas to get ready. The host nation were the first to go, and their rider got around with three fences down. Following this the next four competitors also racked up large faults. It was left to Frederick Seipp, and his fabulous horse Wolfgang to show them how it was done. As current world champion, he rode a textbook round which was both fast and clear.

Marcus was first to go for team GB. Max watched nervously as Harvey, previously his own prodigy, rode into the enormous stadium. Two years on from when he'd been sold, Harvey had grown up considerably, and produced a steady, careful clear. Half an hour later, a terrified looking Giles headed in on his clever, bold stallion Gilmor Emperor. Having produced another excellent clear, the British team were starting to feel hopeful. At the half way mark, they were tied in first place with Germany, USA, France and Netherlands. Italy, Ireland and Australia were all close behind with once fence down.

While Paul rode into the stadium on Lady Hardcourt's Grey Holstein Esmeralda, Max was starting his warm up, but heard the gasp of dismay when a hoof landed in the water. Having finished on four faults, this put huge pressure on Max to go clear. As usual, Zhivago pratted around in the warm-up arena. Not having been properly worked for a fortnight, he was full of himself, and bucked and shied his way around the practice area, annoying the other riders.

By the time Max entered the stadium the rain was coming down in sheets, and the wind was blowing into a gale. To the relief of the organisers, he was the last rider to go, as some of the fences were starting to rock. If Max went clear, there would still be a tie, as only the 3 clear scores would count. The medal positions would then be based on the collective time difference. A group of plucky Brits screamed in delight, and waved their flags as Max rode passed them. Giving them a wave, he headed off down past the judges box at a collected canter.

The rain was driving into Zhivago's face, but he was oblivious to it. He loved jumping, and with his ears pricked forward he eyed the fences with delight. Recognising the sound of the buzzer, Zhivago gave a huge impatient buck, before settling down to do his job. High up in the stands, Ivan Tarasov nervously gripped the edge of his seat. Hope had jumped over his stable door, cross at having missed out, so Lottie was holding him, whilst watching Max on one of the large screens. At home Beth, Nick, and the boys huddled around the television to watch.

Feeling his wonderful horse practically exploding with energy, Max started to enjoy himself. As they soared over the first fence, Max grinned with pleasure. Indifferent to the fancy fence fillers, Zhivago's long stride ate up the ground. The water fence felt like a small puddle, and then he collected himself up for the large upright fence with the Olympic rings which so far had been the boggy fence on the course. With only the final line to go, Max was a second up on the time needed. The BBC commentator was going nuts as Zhivago gave his all, powering over the last two fences.

The crowds were going wild, and the British were screaming as Max cleared the final fence. As the local commentator started announcing that Britain had won, he was stopped. The Olympic ring fence had fallen. Simon rushed forward to complain that Zhivago had jumped cleanly, and the wind must have caught the jump. He was told that as the fence had fallen before the round was completed it would count as four faults. The British officials were then forced to put in an official objection. Meanwhile, Max dismounted, and Lee threw a rug over Zhivago's back so he didn't get a chill. The stallion was rewarded with apples and hugs, whilst Max and the other riders paced up and down in frustration.

The FEI jury went away to watch a rerun of the round on the television and talk to the arena party, before coming to a decision. The crowds were getting colder and impatient, as were the riders. For the British it meant the difference between gold and fourth place, with the Germans just behind them, followed by USA and then the Dutch. At home Beth was yelling at the television, convinced that Max had jumped clear.

'For fuck's sake, what's taking them so long.' Max snapped at no-one in particular.

After what seemed like an age, the course was cleared and the medal podium brought out. It was only then, that in broken English the stadium commentator announced that in the jury's opinion the fence had been jumped cleanly, and that wind had caused the fence to fall. The British riders yelled in delight, and the whole team rushed around giving each other celebratory hugs.

Lee whipped off Zhivago's rug, and oblivious to his saturated clothes, Max jumped on his back ready for the lap of honour. As they moved forward, Max quickly felt in his pocket for the ring. Having cantered around the arena, the riders dismounted. Lee grabbed Zhivago's reins, and Max and the others walked forward and onto the podium. Standing proudly as the National Anthem played, Max gazed out into the crowds. Trying not to cry, he focused on the thousands of people leaving the stadium. He then spotted a familiar figure heading down towards the barrier. It was his father.

Seconds later they were being rushed off the platform. Max had planned this moment to do his big proposal, but realised he'd cocked up. It was Lee that was stood behind him. Feeling cross with himself, he shoved the ring back into his pocket.

That evening, once the horses had been safely settled down for the night, Simon and the head of British Show jumping took the whole team out for a meal, including the grooms, the vet and the other support crew. With feuds and rivalries temporarily suspended, Paul and Max sat together comparing notes on the course and fellow competitors. As Paul had more to drink, he started lecturing on the importance of marriage, and insisted that Max attend his wedding. Overhearing the conversation Lottie grinned to herself, as it was clear that Paul had no idea Pippa had already sent out the invitation.

By comparison Max was quiet. Secretly fuming at his missed opportunity, he knew he now needed to get the double. He had a better than average chance, but there was a lot that could go wrong. All through the evening the riders' phones buzzed with messages of congratulation. As the most sober of the riders, Max then took a call from the editor of Horse and Hound who wanted to know how it felt having to wait for the final result.

The next day there was a rest as the modern pentathlon riders took to the stadium. Their jumps were much smaller but given that these were amateur riders having to ride strange, loaned horses from a local equestrian stables, their task was equally daunting. Meanwhile the horses due to compete in the individual medal competition the following day were just lightly exercised and given massage therapy to aid sore muscles. As Hope was feeling left out Max took him into the warm up arena and gave him a good work out over the fences.

The press had been running news stories all day. After their dramatic finish, Max and Zhivago got the most coverage. Then, as the day drew to a close, a journalist from The Sun called Max to ask him to comment on the story they were intending to run with the following day. Simon was sat with Max and read the email copy as it came through. Simon was furious, and called the journalist, yelling down the phone, threatening hell and damnation if they went ahead and published.

'We have the individual rider competition tomorrow. I'm not having the rider with best chance of a gold medal being upset hours before he rides, just so you can publish some rubbish and sell a few more papers.'

Max hung his head low, wishing he could run away where no one could find him. It was kind of Simon to leap to his defence, but Cindy's kiss and tell story was simply too juicy for a newspaper to ignore. Cindy's tale of Max was one of infidelity and cocaine binges, prima donna tantrums and excessive drinking, meanwhile Cindy came across as an innocent victim.

'How much of it is true?' Simon asked when he'd called down.

'There was some truth – well up to a couple of years ago anyway. The article describes her more than me. I just don't understand how she can be allowed to say these things.'

'We'll put out our own press release at the same time,' Simon said. 'Try not to think too much about it. Within a couple of days it will be yesterday's news. Just make sure you warn Lottie.'

Lottie immediately got to work preparing a social media rebuttal, and press releases to send to other papers and the equine media. Part apology but emphasising that the limited truth related to incidents which took place a very long time in the past, Lottie hoped to defuse the situation.

After spending a tense evening, trying to get Max to relax, Lottie was the first to arrive at the stables the following morning. Having made up the feeds, she carried the buckets to the stables. Hope had his head over the door nickering with pleasure, but Zhivago didn't come to the door. Having dropped off Hope's bucket, Lottie opened Zhivago's door, expecting him to be lying down. Taking one look at the stallion, she screamed. Standing with his foreleg in the air, a large nail, attached to a small block of wood had punctured his foot.

Within minutes the British team vet had arrived and sedated the stallion, whilst an FEI steward looked on, ready to summon the police. The nail was removed, and the foot poulticed. Zhivago was given pain killers, a tetanus booster jab and antibiotics. He would soon recover, but at present he was hopping lame, and certainly his Olympics were over.

Max was distraught. Suddenly the rubbish the tabloids were printing back home seemed unimportant. Someone had deliberately hurt his horse. There was going to be an investigation, but the chances were that the perpetrator would never be found. As the story hit social media, it went viral. Within the hour Ivan Tarasov had demanded a full investigation, furious that security failings had damaged his horse, and compromised his son's chances of getting the double gold medal. He then messaged Max. Max then had to admit to Lottie that she'd been right all the time about the ownership syndicate, which involved his father, Crispin and Nick.

As Max sat cleaning his boots, ready for the afternoon class, he was summoned for a supposedly random blood test, although he suspected the news stories of cocaine binges hadn't helped. Relieved that once again, his guardian angel had stepped in, he was able to visit the medical centre without fear.

Once Max had been released, he headed straight for the stables where Lee was plaiting Hope's mane. The chestnut gelding had realised that finally his turn had come, and had started trembling with anticipation, which made rolling up the plaits so much harder.

Although it was an individual competition, Simon wanted a good team spirit and insisted that the four British riders join together for the course walk. As Max dressed, he deliberated on whether to keep the ring in the pocket of his riding jacket. His hopes of winning were now based on a miracle rather than a possibility, but scared of misplacing the ring, he ended up keeping it in situ. Aware that the betting odds on a second win had shot up after the news of Zhivago's injury, it was obvious that those in the know had no confidence in him and Hope either. He also prepared himself for the abuse he was about to receive. Although Hope loved his job, he was still a charity shop reject, and had no place at the greatest sporting event on earth.

Trying to keep a low profile, Max headed off to meet up with his fellow team members, and mentally bracing himself for the flack. He was taken aback when instead, he got huge amounts of sympathy and support. Riders from across the competing nations came to empathise. Even the French and German riders, normally such rivals, told him how sorry they were. Of everyone, these people understood the time, money, and effort it took to train a horse like Zhivago and could appreciate the pain he felt at such a vicious sabotage.

The person responsible for placing the nail in the stable carried on working quietly, unnoticed behind the scenes. Now groom to a Saudi prince, he had no real grudge against the Tarasov's, and he'd felt bad about injuring the horse. His target had been Lee. As groom, he was ultimately responsible for the stallion's welfare, and by rights should have been fired. Lee had destroyed his career, and this was meant to be payback. As he looked across at the big chestnut horse brought in as substitute, it wasn't the girl leading it. Lee was clearly still in a job. His plan had failed.

The riders were drawn in order of rankings based on the team performance, with those riders competing as individuals going first. This meant the British riders were late on, along with the Americans and the Germans. Initially, one of the favourites, Max was last to go, so poor Hope, desperate to get into the stadium, had a long wait.

With the less experienced riders generally going first, it took ages before anyone jumped clear. The course was similar to that of the team competition, but the Olympic rings upright was now the final jump. The cathedral fence caught out some of the more novice horses, and caused stops, and shies, and a couple of riders parted company with their mounts.

Paul rode first for Team GB and managed a clear, but both Marcus and Giles got four faults in the first round. Finally, it was Max's turn to enter the arena. Hope was delighted to see the crowds, and as they went past the army of Union Jack wavers, Hope nickered, and instantly won many new fans. Standing in the entrance, Lottie was so tense she could barely breathe.

Max wished he was on Zhivago, rather than the young, inexperienced gelding. Having cantered around the arena, they headed towards the first fence. Hope's ears fixed on the jump, and as he locked on Max focused intently on guiding him around the course. The next sixty seconds went in a blur. Thinking about every stride, Max carefully manoeuvred around the course. Hope's jumping ability was incredible. He was powerful, and passionate, and by listening to his rider, he managed to get around clear, albeit only just within the optimum time.

As Max left the stadium, Lottie rushed forward with treats for the expectant Hope. Max dismounted, and she gently kissed him on the cheek. 'Well done,' she said. Wrapping his arms around her, he gave her a hug. 'Thank you for everything,' he replied.

The course was changed, and some of the fences removed in preparation for the second round. Sneakily, the course builder left a huge gap between the penultimate, and the last fence which remained the upright Olympic Rings jump. The gap would tempt the riders into pushing on into a gallop, only to catch them out when their horses had lengthened and flattened too much to easily clear the last fence.

As Max was again last to go, he and Hope had the longest wait. As he'd suspected, the final fence started taking its victims, especially amongst the less experienced partnerships. Those riders who were going for double clears were generally more careful and were noticeably slower. As the competition came down to the final ten riders' things started to hot up.

First to go was Paul who clocked up a good, fast second clear. He was followed by one of the French team, and then a USA rider, both of whom got trapped by the bogey fence at the end. The next three riders then played it safe, which kept Paul in the lead. The top USA rider, Brad Burlinger then entered the arena and clocked up a fast clear. It was then the turn of Jacq, who pushed a little bit more, and paid the price on the final fence.

The world champion, Frederick Seipp then rode into the arena on his magnificent horse Wolfgang and was greeted by the cheering crowds. Brad's time was easily beatable, and with only the inexperienced Hope to go, Frederick was in confident mood. As the buzzer sounded he set off, riding a faultless, masterclass round. Not taking a chance, he slowed down for the final fence, which Wolfgang sailed over, making it look easy. The roar of the crowds was incredible. They'd seen a master at work and showed their appreciation.

'Good luck,' Lottie and Lee called out as Max rode into the arena on a very excited Hope. Once again the British supporters went wild, but after his tentative first round, most of the spectators had few expectations.

'Here comes the final rider, Max Tarasov, riding his substitute horse Hope,' the BBC commentator said. 'Just to let viewers know. There is to be an official enquiry into the deliberate injuring of Max's horse, the amazing black stallion Zhivago. The horse he is riding instead is the one found abandoned at the back of a charity shop two years ago. As one of the youngest, and least experienced horses in the competition today, Max is unlikely to beat the winning times. Meanwhile Paul Denton is currently in bronze medal position.'

The buzzer sounded, and Max directed Hope towards the first fence. Having had an easier season than most of the top horses, he was still full of energy. Taking a chance, Max pushed the pace up a notch. Hope powered over the first fence, and his ears flitted back, waiting for the next command. Giving the horse a bit more freedom, Max upped the pace, with Hope happy to respond.

'Max and Hope are starting to push on now and are only a second behind the leaders as they reach the half way mark,' the announcer said.

At home Beth and Nick were standing in front of the TV, glued to the screen, and exhausted by the tension. 'Please keep them safe,' Beth prayed.

Still clear, Max got to the penultimate fence. Safely over he decided to push on. Hope, delighted with the freedom, surged forward into an explosive gallop.

'No not so fast,' Max shouted at Hope. He pulled on the reins but nothing happened. Helplessly they careered towards the final fence.

Max reckoned that he was going to die. As a minimum he was going to crash land into the fence and be garrotted by one of the Olympic rings in front of an audience of millions.

515

'Slow down you bugger,' he called. Hope flicked back an ear, but carried on, focusing on the fence. Having spent half his life bolting away from people and places, and jumping to escape, he knew he was in control. As he hit the last stride before the fence, Max was deathly pale, but Hope contracted his body, and dropped back on his hocks. Hope saw no fear, as his body positioned itself to launch over the fence.

A second later and it was all over. Max still couldn't stop as Hope charged through the timing barrier and did another circuit of the stadium.

'They've won,' the BBC commentator screamed. 'There's something broken on the bridle and the horse is out of control but Hope the Charity Shop Horse has done his job, and won Gold for Britain.'

Max came to a halt in the entrance to the collecting ring. Pale and shaking, he dismounted, and was immediately sick. Having recovered, he turned to look at Lottie who had been cuddling Hope and feeding him apple treats.

'Are you OK?' she asked.

'Your horse is a fucking lunatic.'

'Do you mind – this is an Olympic gold medal winning lunatic, whose curb chain had snapped.'

The metal chain which should have been under Hope's chin, supporting the pressure on the bit was dangling loose. 'Not sure if this is bad luck or sabotage,' Lee said grimly. Still, if it was sabotage, it failed. That was a bloody amazing round.'

Still shaking, Max patted Hope. 'Why would

you gallop flat out at a 1 metre 60 jump? You insane bugger, still I'll let you off because you did it.'

The other riders started coming up to congratulate him. The mutterings of disapproval from people thinking he'd ridden recklessly quickly changed as they learnt the truth. Even those riders who were no fan of Max had begrudging respect for him now. Simon Palmer rushed up excitedly and patted him on the back. Paul, who'd now missed out on the individual bronze, handed Max the curb chain off his bridle so Max could re-enter the stadium under control.

'Thanks mate,' Max warmly appreciated the gesture. As he rode back into the arena, he called back to Lottie. 'Make sure you come in to hold Hope.'

The stadium erupted in a wall of cheers and calls as Max and his rather mad horse re-entered the arena, followed by Frederick Seipp and Brad Burlinger from the US who waved to all the attractive ladies in the crowd.

As they stood waiting to be presented with their medals, Max turned to his German friend. 'By rights this medal should be yours. You rode the perfect round. I won through sheer luck.'

'Bravery and determination won the day,' the world champion replied.

As the national anthem played, Max fiddled nervously with the little gold ring, now in his hand. As soon as the music stopped, with all the worlds press in view, Max jumped down off the podium and rushed back to where Lottie was stood holding Hope. Bending down on one knee, and in front of an audience of millions he said, 'I realise that I've been an idiot, but I love and adore you. You've made my dream reality. Will you do me the honour of marrying me?'

'Yes of course I will.' She paused. 'It's about bloody time.'

Having slipped the ring on her finger, he removed his gold medal and placed it around her neck. 'You deserve this as much as me. Without you none of this would have been possible.' He lent forward and kissed her. As the crowds erupted into cheering, they were nearly blinded by hundreds of flashing lights from photographers and TV crews sending the images around the world. The next day the front page of every paper ran with the headline, *Land of Hope and Glory.*

Epilogue

Max and Lottie married at Christmas, following Max winning the BBC Sports Personality of the Year. With the large commission pay out Lottie received, she funded the building of an indoor school. TM Associates purchased two more international level horses for Max to ride. The additional prize money, and revenues from the liveries, sponsorship and training meant that Max and Lottie were able to draw an income from the business, so Lottie didn't need to find another job. Two years later, Zhivago retired to stud, but only after partnering Max to winning the World Championship.

The End